PENGUIN BOOKS

JERUSALEM'S HOPE

Bodie and Brock Thoene are the authors of *Jerusalem Vigil*, *Thunder from Jerusalem*, *Jerusalem's Heart*, *The Jerusalem Scrolls*, and *Stones of Jerusalem*—the first five volumes of the Zion Legacy Series. Their thirty-two other novels include the bestselling series The Zion Legacy Chronicles and The Zion Covenant. Together they have won eight Evangelical Christian Publishers Gold Medallion awards. They live in Nevada and London, England.

BODIE AND BROCK THOENE

*J*ERUSALEM'S HOPE

THE ZION LEGACY

Book VI

PENGUIN BOOKS

PENGUIN BOOKS

Published by the Penguin Group

Penguin Group (USA) Inc., 375 Hudson Street, New York, New York 10014, U.S.A.
Penguin Books Ltd, 80 Strand, London WC2R 0RL, England
Penguin Books Australia Ltd, 250 Camberwell Road, Camberwell, Victoria 3124, Australia
Penguin Books Canada Ltd, 10 Alcorn Avenue, Toronto, Ontario, Canada M4V 3B2
Penguin Books India (P) Ltd, 11 Community Centre,
Panchsheel Park, New Delhi – 110 017, India
Penguin Books (N.Z.) Ltd, Cnr Rosedale and Airborne Roads,
Albany, Auckland, New Zealand
Penguin Books (South Africa) (Pty) Ltd, 24 Sturdee Avenue,
Rosebank, Johannesburg 2196, South Africa

Penguin Books Ltd, Registered Offices:
80 Strand, London WC2R 0RL, England

First published in the United States of America by Viking Penguin,
a member of Penguin Putnam Inc., 2002
Published in Penguin Books 2003

9 10 8

Map illustration by James Sinclair

PUBLISHER'S NOTE
This is a work of fiction. Names, characters, places, and incidents either are the product
of the author's imagination or are used fictitiously, and any resemblance to actual persons,
living or dead, business establishments, events, or locales is entirely coincidental.

THE LIBRARY OF CONGRESS HAS CATALOGED THE HARDCOVER EDITION AS FOLLOWS:
Thoene, Bodie, 1951–
Jerusalem's hope / Bodie and Brock Thoene.
p. cm.—(The Zion legacy ; bk. 6)
ISBN 0-670-03084-8 (hc.)
ISBN 0 14 20.0357 3 (pbk.)
1. Israel—History—1948–1967—Fiction.   2. Jews—History—20th century—Fiction.
3. Israel-Arab War, 1948–1949—Fiction.   4. Jerusalem—Fiction.
I. Thoene, Brock, 1952–   II. Title.
PS3570.H46 J496 2002
813'.54—dc21   2002022959

Printed in the United States of America
Set in Minion

With love to our brother,
Rick Christian,
who has the heart of a shepherd

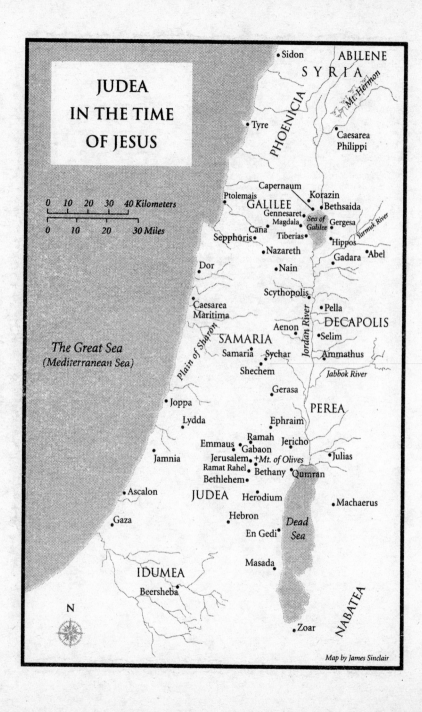

JUDEA
IN THE TIME
OF JESUS

0   10   20   30   40 Kilometers

0   10   20   30 Miles

The Great Sea
(Mediterranean Sea)

• Sidon   ABILENE
              SYRIA
                                Mt. Hermon
• Tyre   PHOENICIA
                        • Caesarea
                          Philippi

                    Capernaum
Ptolemais •   GALILEE • Korazin
                            • Bethsaida
              Gennesaret
              Magdala Sea of Gergesa
        Cana   Galilee   Yarmuk River
Sepphoris •   Tiberias •   • Hippos
        • Nazareth   Gadara • Abel
              • Nain

Dor •

              Scythopolis •

• Caesarea   • Pella
  Maritima   DECAPOLIS
              Aenon   • Selim
        SAMARIA
      Samaria • Sychar   • Ammathus
        • Shechem   Jabbok River

              • Gerasa

• Joppa   PEREA
  Lydda •   • Ephraim
        Emmaus Ramah Jericho
        • • Gabaon
• Jamnia Jerusalem • +Mt. of Olives • Julias
        Ramat Rahel • Bethany • Qumran
        Bethlehem •
• Ascalon JUDEA Herodium   • Machaerus
        • Hebron
• Gaza   En Gedi • Dead
                        Sea

                  • Masada

        IDUMEA
      Beersheba •
                        NABATEA
N
                  • Zoar

Map by James Sinclair

PROLOGUE

Friday, May 28, 1948

The plume of smoke rising from the Jewish Quarter of the Old City of Jerusalem obscured the stars and moon as Rachel Sachar and her younger brother, Yacov, returned to Grandfather's grave. There were no tears left to cry. In silence the mourners stood in the garden of the Russian compound outside the ancient walls.

Rachel slid her arm around Yacov's frail shoulders. Together they recited *kaddish*. Rachel raised her eyes as the bloodred moon broke through the fumes for an instant and then vanished. It was, she thought, like Warsaw had been during the last days in the Ghetto. Burials had been conducted clandestinely at night because it was against Nazi edicts for anyone to gather together openly.

The Third Reich had surrendered less than three years earlier, and yet Jews in the newly reborn nation of Israel were still burying their dead under cover of darkness.

Savage armies still surrounded the Jewish people, and Arab leaders vowed openly to the world, "We will finish what Hitler began. . . . We will drive the Jews into the sea!"

Would the hatred against the children of Israel never end?

Tonight the red-haired British major, Luke Thomas, warned Jewish civilian refugees in the compound, "Funerals after dark, please. No use risking more killed."

From across the blacked-out buildings of No Man's Land came the strident cry of a fighter for the Islamic Jihad, *"Allah Ahkbar! There is no god but Allah, and Mohammed is his prophet!"*

It was a strange irony, Rachel thought as she heard it, that this declaration, the foundation of Islam, mocked and taunted the ears of Jewish survivors. In the Arabic language *Allah* was the name of the god of Islam. But when spoken in Hebrew it meant something entirely different. In the writings of Torah the Hebrew word spelled, *alef, lamed, heh* was also pronounced *allah*, but it meant, "to curse, to lie, to lament!"

Indeed a terrible lament followed the rabbis, Yeshiva students, women, and children as they fled from their ancestral home in the shadow of the Western Wall.

Arab snipers bloomed thick and fierce on the Old City parapets now that the Jewish population had been driven out. There were no Haganah defenders left to prevent the Jihad Moquades from firing down at will upon civilians in Jewish-held West Jerusalem.

Though mere hours had passed since that tragic defeat, it had dawned upon the people that perhaps they would never again walk the streets of Jerusalem as their ancestors had done. The newest conquerors—men from Iraq, Syria, Egypt, and Jordan—declared to their people that Jewish exile from the holy place of El Kuds was permanent and irrevocable.

The grief at this realization was as tangible as death.

Ten-year-old Yacov shuddered and reached up to clasp Rachel's hand.

Rachel's blue eyes clouded as she thought of her father and mother in Poland. She remembered her father standing before his congregation on that last Passover before the fall of Warsaw. What words had he offered to give them courage and hope?

She cleared her throat and began haltingly. "I know what Grandfather would want me to say. Not *about* him only but *for* him . . . So many now . . . dying all around us for the sake of HaShem. For Eretz-Israel. For the promise and the hope our people have clung to for generations." She bit her lip and thought of her husband, Moshe, far beneath the mount where the Great Temple of the Lord had once stood. When would she see Moshe again? When would the people of Israel once more stand before the Western Wall and offer their praise to the Almighty? "I won't use my own words. But my father and grandfather—indeed, every Jew I knew as a child growing up—had a saying that gave us hope, even in the darkest time. They died with this hope on their lips." She proclaimed in Hebrew, "'*Ha lahma anya.* . . . This year we are slaves! Next year we will be free! This year we are here . . . next year, in Jerusalem!'"

■ ■ ■ ■

What day was it? Moshe Sachar wondered as he replaced the scroll in its alabaster container. How long had he and Alfie Halder been beneath the Temple Mount, hidden away in the sacred archives of Israel?

Moshe's watch had long since stopped. He and his companion slept and awakened, ate from the vast storehouse, bathed in the *mikveh*, sang, prayed, and remembered the world they had left behind at Grandfather Lebowitz's urging. They studied beneath the arch of the glowing universe painted on the stones of the chamber.

All that and yet they could not tell if it was daylight or dark. And now Moshe was no longer sure of the day or the hour. Was Rachel well? Was Israel still in existence? Who ruled in Jerusalem?

When Rabbi Lebowitz had first showed Moshe the secret tunnels beneath the Temple Mount, he had commanded that Moshe, a former professor turned Haganah defender, must learn to tell the time if he was to survive as guardian of the precious archives. Moshe had failed as a timekeeper.

Alfie, childlike in his acceptance and contentment with the present, declared there was no time here.

Did he mean there was no time left?

Or that time was running out for mankind?

Or had they stepped into the eternal now, which had neither past nor future?

None of that was made clear in the sheaf of instructions the old rabbi had left for Moshe about this cavern.

Inscribed beside the next scroll listed in the order of Moshe's reading was this comment from Grandfather Lebowitz:

Moshe, though you think you know Torah and Tanakh *well enough, keep the sacred writings by you as reference so you will better comprehend what is to follow. From before the foundations of the world the order of all things was established. Stay on the path to wisdom. Remember, as you read, that everything means something. In all Scripture not one letter or number is without great significance. Take nothing for granted. Every phrase is a link between heaven and earth. Not one word is misplaced by the* Ruach HaKodesh. *Every secret is revealed within. Keep the five books of Moses and the writings of the prophets close at hand as you continue your study. Then pray you have years in which to read and delight in the wonder of revelation!*

Years?

Moshe longed to see Rachel, to hold her once again. He vowed he would not think about life without her or their children growing up without him.

There was much to accomplish. The reference material was retrieved from the shelves and laid out as the old man suggested.

Alfie carried the large jug that contained the third scroll to Moshe at the long reading table. It was a simple clay jar, of the sort used to draw water from a well.

"I'm ready." Alfie sat on the bench and clasped his hands eagerly like a schoolboy.

As was his custom, Moshe examined it carefully before opening the seal. On the neck were the Hebrew words THE LAMB OF MIGDAL EDER. Impressed in the clay was a symbol like a shepherd's crook.

"All right, then," Moshe said, making notes about the age of the jug and details of its label. "Scroll three. That will leave us with sixty-seven yet to read in the first course of study. And seven thousand more, give or take, after that."

"Then hurry," Alfie urged him.

"Well, well," Moshe teased him. "Do I detect impatience in the man who says there is no time in this place?"

"That's right. No time." Alfie reached out to touch the container. "Read. There's things I never knew. And I want to know . . . everything!"

"Well, then. Maybe so." Moshe felt a rush of excitement as he carefully cut away the wax seal and removed the plug. Laying the jug on its side, he reached in and touched something soft wrapped around the tightly rolled scroll. He pulled it out. "Sheep fleece. Just a scrap."

"Like a baby's cap almost," Alfie whispered. "Look here. Tied with leather laces."

"An odd memento."

Moshe passed it to Alfie, who rubbed it against his cheek. The big man closed his eyes and inhaled deeply. "No time at all. We better get it right." And then, "Look there! Stars!"

Moshe involuntarily raised his eyes to the ceiling . . . to the sky painted on the dome. For an instant he thought he saw the glint of a shooting star. *Imagination,* he inwardly chided. *And yet . . .*

"Yes. *Yes!* We'd better get it right." Moshe carefully unrolled the first leaf of the document and began to read. . . .

KI

The Sea of Galilee spread out beneath them that spring night late in the reign of the Roman emperor Tiberius.

The night was deep, the moon not yet risen. Yet the darkness had no power to frighten the three boys. At least not while they were in the presence of Yeshua of Nazareth.

It was a time of rapidly multiplying wonders, those moments just after Avel's broken heart was mended, Ha-or Tov's eyes were opened, and Emet's ears unblocked.

Yeshua's smile was quick and approving. The Master's care had even extended to the creature who had been the boys' mascot and boon companion. Yeshua had restored to life the feathered carcass of Yediyd . . . their Beloved Friend . . . though Yediyd was merely a common brown sparrow. The tiny bird, lifted on the warm wind of affection, had soared away into the freedom of his new life.

And Emet *heard* the beat of Yediyd's wings!

The nearly five-year-old orphan had been deaf since birth, yet he heard the crackle of the thorny acacia branch Yeshua tossed into the campfire.

More . . .

Emet noted the rustle of a bat's leathery wings and heard its high-pitched squeak, sounds so tenuous they weren't even remarked by Avel or Ha-or Tov. Yet *Emet* heard them!

Yeshua caught his eye. The Rabbi nodded, understanding and commending Emet's admiration of the whole startling world of *sounds*.

The Rabbi fed them broiled fish and fresh loaves of barley bread slathered thick with butter. It was a friendly gesture for which they, each cocooned in a different form of wonder, did not properly thank him.

Emet listened to the imperceptibly sighing wind as it stirred into rustling melody the recently budded leaves of a hilltop terebinth tree.

And he observed that Yeshua, finished with his meal, studied his students by the light of the campfire.

Most particularly, Yeshua seemed to notice the matching clothes they wore. The material was cut from one cloak, striped red and green and tan. This was the uniform of the Company of the Sparrows. Eight-year-old Avel had lately been a link boy bearing torches in Jerusalem. Ten-year-old Ha-or Tov had lived as a blind beggar at a rich man's gate in Bethany. Emet had been of no use to anyone. He had left Jerusalem with Avel because there was no place else to go.

The cloak they had divided among themselves was formerly the property of the martyred prophet Yochanan the Baptizer.

Yeshua's cousin.

Though uttered on a sigh no louder than the faint breeze, Emet thought he heard Yeshua murmur, "Yochanan. Friend. You were the voice crying in the wilderness. Make straight the way of the Lord. You knew well the kingdom will be made up of little ones such as these. Hearts that trust completely. Yes." The Master touched the corner of the fabric on the hem of Emet's robe.

Yeshua's eyes were so kind, and yet so sad. Had he spoken aloud or had Emet simply overheard his thoughts?

After a time of silence, Avel licked his fingers and finally spoke.

Emet knew Avel's question wasn't meant to challenge Yeshua. No. It was asked only out of curiosity.

Avel had been listening to what went on in the Galil before that night. The confrontations, the anger of learned men against Yeshua, Yeshua's calm and deliberate replies.

And so Avel asked Yeshua: "You told the rabbis if they believed what Moses wrote, they would believe you because Moses wrote about you. Did you mean you, yourself, are written about in Torah? But how can that be? Since Moses lived very long ago? How could Moses have written about you?"

Yeshua smiled kindly at Avel. It was the sort of smile that told him he must be patient; the answer would take much unraveling. Then Yeshua turned his face upward, as if to find a place to begin the explanation.

One night would not be long enough.

"It will take a lifetime to learn all that Moses and the prophets wrote about what was, what is, and what will be. The teachers of Israel were shepherds. The secret meaning of their words are hidden among the lambs of Israel's flocks. But tonight we'll let the heavens teach the first lesson. There . . . above our heads . . . is the first book." He gestured toward the sky where streaks of gossamer clouds streamed to the east.

So Yeshua began at the Beginning. The right place for young boys who had never been taught anything.

That night the three were smooth wax tablets, which not even a childish alef-bet had yet marred.

The stylus of Yeshua's words impressed itself on their souls. They became his talmidim, students at the academy of Creation of which he was Headmaster.

Emet, who had never before heard a human voice, nor a single word of speech, experienced the Living Word.

Avel, who had never felt joy or known tenderness, was embraced by he who is Love Incarnate.

Yet Avel and Emet were mere observers compared to the wonder that swept over Ha-or Tov, drawing him upward and out of himself. For Ha-or Tov, who was born sightless and had never known the stars, was given a guided tour of the heavens. The scroll of the universe was unrolled for him, its text of miracles read aloud to him by its Author.

The embers burned low on the campfire. The smoke cleared.

"What are those things?" Ha-or Tov inquired. "There and there and . . . look there!" He gestured toward each of the thousand pinpoints of light garlanding the Galilean sky, at first singly, and then in broad swathes as he tried to take it all in at once. His mop of curly red hair bobbed from vista to vista. "Where did they come from? Who made them?"

Stretching out his hand, Yeshua reached upward. The brightest star in the constellation called *Aryeh*, the Lion, appeared to balance on the very tip of his index finger.

As Emet observed, Yeshua drew his hand downward and the star seemed to follow, as if obediently coming closer at his summons. Or perhaps it simply brightened at his touch. Emet was unsure which.

"These are the stars," Yeshua explained. "Witnesses to everything that has happened since the dawn of time." When he lowered his hand, the star swung promptly back to its proper place and size. But Yeshua wasn't finished. "And see this," he said, creating a circle with his thumb and forefinger and offering it to Ha-or Tov to peer through. Yeshua indicated a patch of sky due south.

The lights in the heavens became distinct, glimmering with unimagined color through this focus. Emet recognized Ha-or Tov's protracted exhale as the sound of reverent amazement, though he'd never heard it before. "See the spirals! Like curling loops of . . . what? Jewels?"

The constellation Yeshua designated portrayed a reclining woman. Between her imagined outstretched arms Emet could see faint smudges, like what resulted when he brushed a brass lamp with his thumb. For an instant Emet couldn't make out what caused Ha-or Tov to exult so.

Then Yeshua cupped his hand, and Emet rested his chin in the Master's palm. Suddenly those smudges transformed into shimmering webs, decked with glistening drops of dew! Perhaps Ha-or Tov was right! Jewels! Before Emet's eyes ropes of gems tightly coiled on the ebony fabric of the night! The touch of the wind made the lights dance and sparkle.

"Each spiral contains more stars than you can imagine." Yeshua's voice brushed Emet's face like a gentle breeze. "Each is so great that this world would be lost inside it. Each is so far away that just to see its light is to peer back in time . . . some for years, some for ages, and some . . . back toward the very Beginning. There . . ." He pointed to a bright blue star and said to Ha-or Tov, "The gleam you're seeing now left the star a long time ago. At the hour you were born that flash was conceived. Its light has been traveling through space to fill your eyes tonight. Before you were born that star was named for you. Ha-or Tov. 'The Good Light.' It's shining for you."

Avel and Emet drew nearer, each of them eager to know if they also had a birthday star. Yeshua nodded, then pointed to a jewel named Haver, which means "Friend." This was Avel's star. It was as golden as topaz. Constant in light and color, unwavering and true.

And the star named for Emet? Truth. It was a beacon, flashing blue to white and back to blue, calling Emet's glance to its light again and again.

"And which is your star, Reb Yeshua?" Avel queried.

At that Yeshua strummed the fingers of his right hand across the panorama of the universe. Emet's eyes widened in amazement as he heard a vast harmony, music emanating from the lights. It was the first song Emet ever heard. Countless voices sang these words:

> "*You are worthy, O Lord,*
> *to receive glory and honor and power,*
> *for You created all things,*
> *and by Your will they exist and were created!*"

Avel and Ha-or Tov chewed their bread noisily. They seemed not to notice the music.

Evidently the ears of his companions could not hear as well as his, Emet reasoned. After all, Emet's ears were new, created by Yeshua on the spot. Perhaps Ha-or Tov's recently sighted eyes were also sharper than those of anyone. And maybe Avel experienced joy more keenly because his broken heart had just been healed.

"When *was* the beginning?" Emet blurted, wanting to know everything!

Yeshua replied, "It is written in the first line of Torah: 'In the Beginning *Elohim* created the heavens and the earth.' Everything was created by his will from nothing: *bara*, in the Hebrew language. Worlds were framed by the Word of God. Things you see were not made from things that are visible. The Beginning is across a gulf so wide you could never cross it, and yet it's but a blink to the Father."

And he told them how the heavens were hung thick with brilliances beyond imagining. The sun, known as *Chammah,* was really only one insignificant star among the host of innumerable stars. And the earth was merely one of several worlds that circled the sun.

Yeshua explained that the seven lights of the menorah were meant to teach men many things. Among the lessons, the order of its branches showed a picture of this tiny corner of creation: the sun, the moon, and the wandering stars, also called *planets* . . . the Greater and Lesser Lights that illuminated day and night.

Yeshua explained that there was much more beyond what the human eye could detect, even the keen eyes of Ha-or Tov!

Deftly Yeshua's hands skimmed the sky, as if to gather swirls of stars in his palms and planets on his fingertips, like the balls of a juggler in the souk.

Above the increased noise of the breeze in the terebinth, once again Emet heard distant voices:

"*When I consider Your heavens, the work of Your fingers,*
The moon and the stars, which You have ordained,
What is man that You are mindful of him,
And the son of man that You visit him?
For You have made him a little lower than the angels,
And You have crowned him with glory and honor.
You have made him to have dominion over the works of
Your hands . . ."

One by one Yeshua displayed a sample of heavenly miracles to the young talmidim in his care. There were pillars of glowing blue and pink vapors, moons that orbited striped planets, stars innumerable that spun around one another in a dance begun at Creation.

Avel whispered in dismay, "But how can we explain to anyone about this? Men believe the earth is flat! That heaven is a bowl turned upside down! That the stars are living beings, not orbs of fire warming worlds and lighting the night!"

Yeshua laughed, as if acknowledging what mankind thought it knew. He declared to the boys that anyone could see the glory of God, visible and tangible in creation. If only a person would take the time to look.

Thus Yeshua entrusted the trio of young humans with a vision of vastness and a glimpse of eternity in his teaching. Because they had never learned the puny ideas of man about the universe they did not doubt Yeshua's word.

Every answer led to another question. "But where does God, the Almighty, dwell?" Ha-or Tov squinted deeply into space, as if hoping to spot the palace.

"And where do souls go when they leave?" Avel added with a quiet urgency.

Yeshua replied, "Your friend Hayyim is somewhere else, Avel."

Avel was no longer surprised that Yeshua knew about him—or his past. "But where? And what is it like?" Avel insisted.

Yeshua seemed to search for the right words to explain. "No eye has seen; no ear has heard; no mind has imagined what the merciful Father has prepared for those who love him." Yeshua touched Ha-or Tov's brow. "When you were blind, did you imagine that all these stars lit up the sky above you?"

"No, Lord." Ha-or Tov shook his head. "Some people tried to explain it to me, but I couldn't understand what they meant. Light. The true beauty of it. Sight. It's a new kind of music flooding into my soul."

Yeshua smiled and turned to Emet. "And you, Emet. Before you heard music, before you heard human speech, or crickets in the brush, bullfrogs in the rushes, wind rustling the branches of a tree . . . could you imagine any of these things?"

For a minute Emet listened in wonder to the sounds emanating from the night. "No, Lord. They are like a new kind of color filling my ears. There were times . . . before . . . when I felt sound. It trembled beneath my hand, but I never knew what it meant!"

Yeshua touched Emet's cheek. Finally he asked Avel, "When you were a mourner, burdened by sadness as real and heavy as a sack of stones on your back, did you ever imagine you could feel joy again?"

Avel laughed and replied, "No, Lord! I didn't know what joy was! I saw others smile, but I didn't understand what a smile felt like inside! But now I know!" Avel leaned against Yeshua, who patted him on the shoulder.

"That's right. Yes." Yeshua had made his point. "Heaven is like that. You can't see it. Yet it exists. It's a real place! As tangible as . . . the stones of Jerusalem. As solid as the hills of the Galil. Things are happening there right now, while you and I sit tonight by the fire. There are moments when you hear a song or see a rainbow or grasp a word of comfort that lifts your soul, and you get a hint of heaven. But that's merely a drop of water in the great wide ocean! And sadly, here on earth, you can't have the total freedom of heaven's joy because you are bound to the sorrows of what happens in this world. But have faith!"

"What is faith?" Emet asked.

"Faith is being sure of what you hope for and certain of what you do not yet see."

"I hope I will see my friend Hayyim again," Avel said.

Yeshua took the boy's hand. "I promise you, he's waiting to welcome you. After that you'll recognize others. You'll embrace the loved ones you ached to hold! You'll gaze into their eyes and laugh again! Then there'll be no more sorrow or suffering."

Heaven. Stars and color revealed to the blind!

Heaven. Harmony and instruments heard for the first time by the deaf!

Heaven. Jubilation and peace overflowing the heart of a mourner reunited with his loved ones!

This was Hope, indeed!

On that night, however, the enormity of it, the color and music and joy of it, was beyond what one short lesson could convey.

But it was a beginning. A starting place. An explanation of a reality far larger than this world. A definition of faith. A reason to hope.

The moon peeked over a shoulder of the mountain, casting a streak of silver on the lake.

At the same moment the wind from the west increased its force, as if trying to hold back the light.

Yeshua raised his head, as if scenting the air. He stood, dusting off his hands and smoothing out his robe. "The wind is up," he said.

"They'll be needing me." Staring out at the water he added, "There: you see?"

Ha-or Tov nodded vigorously. "The boat . . . your talmidim? They're rowing, but fighting the gale."

By squinting his eyes and scrunching his face, Emet at last made out the object of their concern: a distant black speck disappearing and reappearing against the ripples of shimmering waves.

Breezes on the Galil blew up without warning into dangerous gales; harmless swells turned into life-threatening billows. Open fishing boats caught far out on the Sea of Galilee in such a storm had but two choices, neither of them good. They could struggle forward by rowing into the teeth of the gusts, shipping water over the bow and struggling for inches of progress. Or they could attempt to turn and run before the wind, risking being capsized or swamped.

Lives were lost every year on the lake in storms like this.

Yet Yeshua didn't act anxious for his friends. Matter-of-factly he said to the boys, "I must go to them. Walk with me toward the shore."

How could Yeshua provide any assistance to the endangered talmidim? Emet wondered. Was there another stronger vessel available somewhere?

As they approached the highway that skirted the eastern shore, Yeshua gave a rucksack of barley loaves to Avel, Emet, and Ha-or Tov. "Avel, you are the shepherd of your brothers on this journey. Travel by the light of the moon. Go south. Along the way you'll meet a man you've met before. He'll lead you on a donkey over Jordan. After you cross the river, travel no farther with him. Go straight to Beth-lehem, to Migdal Eder, the Tower of the Flock. There find the shepherd Zadok. The lamb is the key to understanding Torah. Stay with Zadok till I arrive."

"Why?" Emet asked.

"Kings, priests, and prophets have longed to know the secret this old shepherd keeps hidden in his heart."

"But when will we see you again?" Emet's heart began to pound; panic rose in his throat.

"Look for the lamb."

What could Yeshua mean? Emet wondered. The fields were full of lambs this season of the year.

"But how can we prove you sent us?" Avel asked.

Gathering the three boys once more in his embrace, Yeshua said, "Tell Zadok that Immanu'el sent you to him. Tell him Immanu'el is coming. Tell him that mourners are blessed, for they will be comforted.

Don't share this message with anyone else. It's meant for Zadok alone. Be on your guard. There's danger ahead. Wolves dressed in sheep's clothing are traveling the same road you travel. . . . Now I must go." Yeshua set his chin resolutely into the gale.

Go? Emet wondered as he and his friends reluctantly parted from their Rabbi. *We have this paved road to follow, but what about him? No boat can sail into this wind.*

Beams of moonlight carved an argent path across the water, creating a highway of burnished silver on the surface of the lake. Onto this thoroughfare of light Yeshua confidently stepped, striding out toward the center of the sea as if walking the broad avenue that connected Jerusalem's Temple Mount with the western hill of the Holy City.

Could it be? Avel stooped and dipped his fingers in the water. Cupping his hands he lifted the liquid to show Emet and Ha-or Tov.

They watched Yeshua until he was out of sight. Ha-or Tov continued to report Yeshua's steady progress long after he disappeared from Emet's view. Then the three set out for Beth-lehem.

■ ■ ■ ■

The wind howled across the Sea of Galilee from west to east. The moon, like a sail unfurled, set its course into the teeth of the storm. It was still more than a week until Passover and already the hills of the Galil were dotted with campfires of pilgrims moving south to Jerusalem.

Nakdimon ben Gurion, wrapped in his cloak, sheltered in the lee of a boulder. There was a voice in this cloudless tempest. It howled a warning in Nakdimon's ears.

Metatron! Metatron! Metatron!

Was Yeshua of Nazareth the manifestation of *Elohim*'s Presence? The Being who moved in and out of the Cloud of Unknowing that surrounded the omnipotent God's throne? Disguised for His visit to earth, the one called *the Angel of the Lord* promised Abraham a son in his old age and made a blood covenant conveying a blessing on all the earth through Abraham.

He had wrestled Jacob on the riverbank and named him *Isra'el.*

He had spoken to Moses from the burning bush and led the children of Israel out of bondage through the sea and into the Promised Land.

If Yeshua was that One, someday He would drop his mortal disguise. And then men, seeing the truth of who and what He was in reality, would melt in terror.

Nakdimon himself had felt a sort of terror and awe when he witnessed the miracles and again when he heard Yeshua speak. Here was molten gold confined in the common cauldron of humanity: beautiful, glowing, consuming fire. All that and more in the disguise of a carpenter from Nazareth. Could it be? Could it? A carpenter from Nazareth?

Nakdimon would take the report back to his uncle, the great rabbi Gamaliel bar Simeon. Gamaliel was one of the few who might be capable of unraveling the perilous enigma of Yeshua without getting burned. He might separate the Glory from the kettle and say, *Here is truth!*

One must not be wrong about a matter of such magnitude. If it was true that Yeshua had stepped out from behind a star and descended from the Cloud of Unknowing to bring a gift from Elohim to mankind, then mankind had better not stumble over the gift! And yet that was exactly what the rulers of Israel seemed to be doing. Their plots to discredit Yeshua were legion. False witnesses. Spies. Talk of murder.

Nakdimon shuddered. He was hopeful and yet also terrified at the potential missteps.

The wailing of the wind died suddenly like a whining child commanded to be still. Only the sparking embers illuminated the small band of sleepers. A lull descended, as if no cricket or nightbird dared reply.

Nakdimon sat up and stared at the stars. So many. The air scrubbed clean by the wind. He imagined thrones and corridors, stairways rising up from the darkness into points of exquisite light. Had Yeshua come from some place beyond the edge of all that?

Pervasive peace. Calm.

"We had better get it right!"

"Peace! Be still! I Am! Be still and know! I Am!"

Nakdimon's traveling companions did not suspect that the enormous man was a member of the council of seventy elders who ruled Israel. He appeared common enough, more like a drover with ordinary clothes, black beard, broad shoulders, and a bullneck.

It was best they not know his rank, he reasoned. After all, beneath the skin he was no different than they. He had also come far to see and hear Yeshua of Nazareth firsthand.

He had arrived in Galilee a skeptic.

Now he believed.

But what boundaries defined his belief? That Yeshua was a man of extraordinary powers and wisdom couldn't be denied. But Israel's history and writings told many stories of such men. None of them was the Anointed One, the Prophet, Priest, and King, the awaited Messiah.

Was Yeshua that one? Or should they look for another? Yeshua had refused the crown offered to him by an exultant mob.

Why?

He had a ready-made army he might have commanded to overpower the currently ruling tyrants of Rome and Herod Antipas. He chose not to.

Why?

Instead he had slipped away into the hills. None had seen him since.

Nakdimon, along with his fellow travelers, had witnessed the feeding of thousands of men, women, and children who had paused on their journey long enough to listen to the Master's teaching. And yet the loaves and fishes merely temporarily assuaged a physical hunger. Nakdimon's heart hungered to know more, to hear more!

And what had Nakdimon taken away from his encounter with Yeshua? Besides the facts of what he had seen with his own eyes? Perhaps it was not what he had taken, but what he had left behind.

He no longer grieved for his wife, his dear Hadassah. He had let her go, heard her bless his life one last time. It was enough. She was somehow born again. Somewhere else. Living. Smiling. Talking. But no longer here! Yeshua had let Nakdimon glimpse that. And in the certainty that Hadassah was happy and safe, Nakdimon had finally become free to live again.

Nakdimon stretched his hands out to the embers. How would he tell Gamaliel these things? How could he put this into words?

No. There are no words!

All the books in all the world couldn't hold what Yeshua had done. How could Nakdimon attempt to explain? If only he could offer a glimpse. So much! So many touched, moved, changed!

We had better get it right. . . .

LO

The wind died as morning approached. Stars dimmed. The surface of the lake became placid, a mirror of reflected pastels.

This was the first dawn in Emet's new life. It was teeming with unfamiliar murmurings and the clamor of awakenings.

At the southern tip of the Sea of Galilee, the trio of boys stopped to watch the golden blade of morning slice through the darkness.

"Is that heaven, then?" Ha-or Tov cried, turning away from the painful brightness.

Avel replied, "Just the sun. Coming up like it always does."

"Don't look at it," Emet warned. "It will burn your eyes, and you'll be blind again."

For hours they had traveled through a monochrome world awash in moonlight. Their shadows had fallen on the road that skirted the eastern shore of the lake. Campfires of other pilgrims on the way to Jerusalem for Passover had dotted the countryside and caused Ha-or Tov to swivel his head at each manifestation of light. Yet only now, as colors intensified, did Ha-or Tov stop in the middle of the road and refuse to continue until he could absorb it.

"This may take a while. We might as well eat." Avel offered the bag of loaves to Emet.

Emet didn't reply. He was too busy trying to sort out the resonant hum in the air as the world opened its eyes. Far away a rooster crowed. A dog barked and was answered with the whistle of its master. The bleating of sheep mingled with the sounds of human conversation. And how many different birds called from tree, or vineyard, or brush? Emet couldn't keep it all in his head. He covered his ears with his hands.

"You'll get used to it," Avel consoled him. "After a while you won't notice it anymore."

"But I want to hear it!" Emet protested. "All of it! I have to figure out what each thing means!"

"Suit yourself." Avel retrieved a piece of bread. "It was easier going when you were deaf and Ha-or Tov was blind."

Emet dipped into the bag. He observed Avel, the mourner. His friend was changed, as if he were not the same boy. Before, Avel's eyes had been perpetually downcast. It had made it difficult for Emet to read his lips. But now! Avel gazed peacefully at a hawk circling above them. Sun shone on his golden hair. His lips curved in a slight smile.

Then Emet turned his attention to Ha-or Tov. Before last night, Ha-or Tov had shuffled when he walked. When Ha-or Tov was blind, his face had been perpetually turned skyward, wagging back and forth, as if he were sniffing the air for a hint of what might be around him. And before, when Ha-or Tov had sat on the ground, he'd swayed like a sapling in the wind. This morning, Ha-or Tov was focused, perfectly motionless as he drank in visual wonders.

Emet was likewise absorbed by a mystic harmony drifting over the countryside. It occurred to Emet that somewhere among the bird conversation was the voice of Yediyd the sparrow. Surely the bird was twittering to friends and relatives about how Yeshua of Nazareth made him alive after Kittim, once the leader of the link boys, had crushed him. This was a comforting thought for Emet. That a creature as insignificant as Yediyd had beat the cruelty of the sparrow killer!

"Is the air always like this?" Emet asked.

Avel scratched his chin, as if not comprehending the question. "I like the smell of the country air. Better than Yerushalayim, I think."

"No. I mean always singing? So . . . full?" Emet asked.

Avel munched the bread. "The noise you mean? Louder in some places. Yerushalayim is much worse. Every smell has a sound." Avel nudged Ha-or Tov, including him in this discussion. "And every sound has a color. The people! Everyone talking at the same time."

Then, without explanation, Ha-or Tov gasped and groped for a boulder to steady himself. He began to quiver. "The rebels of bar Abba! All of them with eyes that see! I didn't know what that meant before! When everything was blank I was safe . . . invisible. But if I can see them, they can see me! From far away . . . they'll recognize us!"

So the sense of peace they had all felt in the presence of Yeshua came abruptly to an end. Emet was afraid. Ha-or Tov was absolutely correct! Emet eyed Avel, the one who always knew where they were going and what they should do. Yet Avel had no answer to such a problem.

Avel contemplated the southward flight of the hawk. "We've got to be careful. If only we had wings!"

Emet asked, "Should we hide? Travel in the dark?"

Avel drew a breath and stuck out his lower lip. "Yeshua said we should go south. Straight to Beth-lehem. Find the man Zadok, he said. The Tower of Migdal Eder. I'm for going ahead. Getting to Beth-lehem quick as we can."

Ha-or Tov added hopefully, "Maybe Zadok will protect us from bar Abba and the rebels."

Emet pictured Kittim, the cruel young rebel who had crushed the tiny Yediyd under his foot! Kittim was searching for the three fugitives from the rebel band. And he would kill the boys if he found them. "Can Zadok save us from the sparrow killer?"

Avel said, "Kittim enjoys hurting people. He'll do what he can to hurt us. So . . . pass the bread."

They divided the barley loaf in thoughtful silence.

Since Yeshua left them they had traveled several miles along the broad eastern highway and far into the hill country of the ten Greek cities of the Decapolis.

"Even if we hide until sundown we're not safe anywhere," Ha-or Tov worried aloud. "Especially not here."

"But why?" Emet asked.

"The people who live here aren't Jews," Avel explained to Emet. "Or if they are Jews, they're rotten Jews who speak Greek and don't mind pagan temples and the like."

Ha-or Tov added gloomily, "The rabbis in Judea say this place . . . the very dust of a heathen country . . . is unclean! Demons live here. People worship gods which aren't the Lord. They burn babies in the arms of Molech here. Touching the ground defiles you. Like a grave with a putrefied body in it. Pus and oozing guts and the like." He accidentally dropped a chunk of bread, snapped it up, blew off the dust, and passed it to Emet.

Emet winced at his friend's unconcern. He considered this information with alarm. It had been better not knowing such facts. Yesterday a walk along the highway east of the Jordan River had merely been a tramp along a dusty road. If he had dropped his bread yesterday, he wouldn't have worried about it. "Then why do we stay on this side of the river?"

"Because we have to go south to the ford. We can cross into Eretz-Israel there. Then we'll be in Judea." Avel gestured toward the blue ribbon of the Jordan flowing through the valley below.

"Can't we cross now?" Emet pleaded.

Avel expounded. "Not until we go along farther. Crossing over here would be as bad as the Decapolis. That's Samaria on the other side of the river."

Ha-or Tov contributed, "Every Samaritan is like Kittim. They hate Jews as much as Romans hate Jews. Maybe more. Samaria really stinks. Defilement and death, the rabbis say."

"How do you know this?" Emet sniffed.

"Because I begged at the gate of a rich man. I heard the rabbis talking when they came in." Ha-or Tov mocked them, "'Quick! Get me water to wash the dust off my feet! I walked through a Samaritan village! The dust from a Roman horse is on my sandal!'" Ha-or Tov shrugged and resumed the lesson. "You pick up a lot of details when you're blind and nobody thinks you're listening. What I didn't understand I asked the gatekeeper and he told me. There's one single country where a good Jew can walk without worrying. That's Eretz-Israel, The Land God gave to Israel! And when a good Jew goes outside The Land he can't even bring heathen dust back to mingle with the dust inside The Land. And when he makes pilgrimage to Yerushalayim, he'd better not carry any dirt from outside the land back into Eretz-Israel on him! The Land of Israel is holy, see? Yerushalayim is more holy. The Temple is the holiest. Understand?"

"No." Emet wondered if such rules existed or if Ha-or Tov was making them up.

But Avel confirmed these astonishing facts. "He's right. One speck of dust from outside." He gave a low whistle. "Really bad. And this place? The Decapolis. Greek. Ten cities built by the followers of Alexander, the Greek general. Crammed with shrines to pagan idols. The worst. It's polluted." Avel corroborated the tale in its entirety.

"What will happen?" Emet's eyes stared. "If we catch pagan dust on us, I mean?"

"*Poof!* Fire and brimstone!" Ha-or Tov indicated the incineration of the unlucky traveler who carried particles of soil from outside The Land into the Holy City. "That's why the rabbis are always washing."

"Then why are we traveling this way?" Emet wailed in horror as he gawked at his dirt-caked feet. Defilement and contamination! Surely he would end up a pile of ashes!

Avel replied, "Because if you're on the east side of the Sea of Galilee, like us, you can't go south to Beth-lehem and Yerushalayim any other way. You go through Samaria, you'll get your throat cut. So you go through this part of the Decapolis and cross over Jordan into Judea farther south."

Since existing borders required travel outside The Land to get from Galil, in the north, to Judea, in the south, this condition of righteousness didn't seem particularly fair to Emet. His brow furrowed.

Was this why bar Abba's rebels hated Romans so much? Dust touching Roman toes was changed into evil! And was this why the Jewish religious sorts stamped the dirt from their sandals when a Samaritan or a tax collector in the pay of Rome passed by? This explained the reason no respectable Jew ever entered a building where a Gentile resided!

The world had become a lot more complicated. How many more regulations would he have to learn to be a good talmidim? Emet wondered.

Emet picked at the barley bread and stared at the contaminated brown earth of the Decapolis and a budding almond orchard in a swale nearby. It was a pretty plot of ground, even if it was heathen. He was sorry Yeshua had not taken them with him across the waters. Why hadn't Yeshua picked them up and carried them back to Galilee on his shoulders? Away from this polluted land! Safe from bar Abba's rebels and from the reach of Kittim, the sparrow killer! They would have been safe with Yeshua, wouldn't they? Instead the Master had sent them off on this dangerous journey to Beth-lehem.

What if someone from bar Abba's band spotted them on the way? Surely even the rebels would be traveling on this road south to Jerusalem for Passover! Kittim, the sparrow killer, had ears! He would hear the boys talking and hunt them down even in a crowd! He would slit their throats with the razor-sharp blade of his knife!

Emet felt alone and scared.

Then Ha-or Tov presented an equally disturbing thought. "Kittim is on this side of the river! I'm sure of it. He'll see us and kill us."

"He'll have to catch us first," Avel vowed. "And we can run fast now that you can see where you're going."

Then, an octave beneath the chatter of fowls and a braying donkey, Emet sensed something frightening. His head snapped erect as the voices of men in angry conversation approached. "Listen," he hissed.

"I don't hear anything." Avel frowned.

"Travelers! Coming this way! I want to go now," Emet warned, pocketing his breakfast. His heart quickened with terror. "I want to go to Zadok in Beth-lehem, where maybe we'll be safe! The place Yeshua told us to go! We shouldn't wait! I don't want to be outside The Land anymore. It's not safe!"

Ha-or Tov shushed Avel's protest that they needn't be in such a hurry. "Emet's right. I hear them. Men coming down the highway. Arguing about . . . something. They'll be upon us soon!"

Avel listened a second longer, clearly straining to catch what his companions recognized so plainly. Then Avel's face blanched. "Is it bar Abba? Or Kittim?"

They wouldn't wait for the answer. Emet leapt to his feet, and the three boys sprinted down the highway.

■ ■ ■ ■

Nakdimon ben Gurion shifted his muscled bulk on the hard, unyielding ground and wished he were at home in Jerusalem. Even rest on this journey wasn't restful.

He had completed his mission to the Galil. He had seen the miracles, questioned the Teacher one-on-one, and witnessed that marvelous feeding of an army with a handful of bread and fish.

What summary would he give to the leaders of Israel about Yeshua of Nazareth?

Every detail about the Master would doubtless reach Jerusalem ahead of Nakdimon. The pilgrims traveling to the city to celebrate Passover would spread the news.

What would they say?

Praise was the thing Nakdimon ben Gurion heard from the thousands of pilgrims along the highway that led from Galilee south to Jerusalem.

Praise for teaching! Praise for healing! Praise for bread! Praise for what would be!

Doubtless they would add ecstatic speculation to their report: *Praise for the coming rout of Romans and half-breed Samaritans! Praise for the slaughter of the profane and the cheaters and the oppressors of the poor! Praise for the restoration of fortunes, land, and freedom! Praise for Yeshua of Nazareth, who could raise a dead little girl in Capernaum. He must now raise an army to march on Yerushalayim!*

The Kingdom of God had come. Did Yeshua not say so?

Nakdimon considered again what he had witnessed and heard. What truth could he carry back to Jerusalem for his uncle, the renowned Gamaliel, who sat with Nakdimon in the chamber of the Sanhedrin, the council of seventy elders of the Jews? How would the re-

ligious leaders take the news that the people flocked to hear a lowly carpenter from Nazareth who was manifestly more than that description
encompassed?

Nakdimon surmised that whatever their reaction, it would not be
favorable to Yeshua. The holy man, like his cousin Yochanan the Baptizer, would be in danger if he came to Jerusalem.

Yesterday at the beach Nakdimon had warned Yeshua's talmidim
to keep their Master far from the crowds, far from the Temple, far from
Jerusalem and Judea until Passover was over and the mobs returned
home. Thousands of lambs would be slaughtered for the *seder*. Nakdimon didn't want the blood of Yeshua mingled with the blood of the
flock! There would come a time in the future when the gentle Rabbi
could enter the city, but emotions were too hot and high for him to
come now!

There was, of course, the unresolved conflict brewing over the use
of Temple funds to pay for Governor Pilate's aqueduct. The issue of
Korban money supplying Roman stones to rise across the fields of
Beth-lehem would surely lead to riots in Jerusalem this year. People had
bled and died for the sake of much less significant religious violations
than Roman canals built with sacred coins.

Nakdimon stood slowly. His back ached. He cleared his throat and
scanned the hundreds of travelers near smoldering campfires all
around him. There were rebels among the pilgrims, he knew. There
were possibly hundreds of swords waiting for the cry to battle. And
the Romans would swoop down. Jewish heads would fall like unripe
melons on the stones of the Temple Court unless the crowds could be
kept calm.

This much he was certain of: Yeshua would not be the one to call
down judgment and slaughter. But his presence would certainly be used
to rally the foolishly eager.

Nakdimon hoped Yeshua's talmidim had the brains to convince the
Rabbi that his attendance would simply add fuel to the embers of resentment already smoldering against the high priest and the Roman authorities!

And what had Nakdimon personally taken away from his encounter
with Yeshua?

How long had he been knocking at Hadassah's grave? Wishing she
would come back to him and the children? Angry at her for leaving him
alone with six young girls and one infant son to raise alone? Mourning
her death a hundred times a day?

Yeshua had given him hope that he would see her again, hold her again. One hundred years would pass, and all of them would be reunited in tangible form. They would smile and talk and touch one another's hands and say, "So this is what it means. . . ."

For Nakdimon that hope of a life to come was more important than the bread or the healing or the possibility of Yeshua as King over Israel.

The future. Yes. Someday, perhaps, that would be reality.

But for now there was life to live. Insurrections to quell. Government to preserve. Peace to cling to. For the sake of his children Nakdimon accepted that Gamaliel and the rulers of Israel must consider Yeshua in the context of what was expedient. The Sanhedrin and the high priest might be unsavory and corrupt, but they were also responsible for the survival of Israel in an uncertain political reality. Yeshua could tip the balance toward revolution against Rome. If the people proclaimed him king it could mean the ultimate destruction of Israel and Jerusalem.

For this reason Nakdimon hoped Yeshua would stay far away from Jerusalem during Passover.

■ ■ ■ ■

Roman centurion Marcus Longinus and his commandant, Tribune Dio Felix, had ridden all night. By so doing they had managed to reach Caesarea Maritima on the Mediterranean coast just as dawn was breaking. Long before the salt tang in the air alerted Marcus that their journey was nearly finished, Felix had already issued orders: "No ceremony this time! No stopping to bathe or for dress uniforms! Governor Pilate must hear the report on Yeshua of Nazareth without delay!"

As travel-worn as Felix was, the enforced haste was worse for Marcus. The centurion had not changed clothes since his previous appearance before Pilate. His beard itched, the rough cloth of his homespun tunic stuck to him, and his eyes and ears were plastered with the chalky dust of the wind-whipped Galil. In every respect Marcus looked more like one of the rebels he'd been assigned to pursue than a Roman officer; more like a Jewish brigand than one of the masters of the universe.

But considerations about his appearance and reputation were of secondary importance. His thoughts remained back in Galilee, concentrated on Miryam of Magdala, once Marcus' lover. Now she was in the inner circle of Rabbi Yeshua's talmidim.

Marcus also devoted much of the hurried travel to thinking about the mysterious Reb Yeshua. He was confused about the Galilean Teacher.

Marcus had personally seen the man perform unaccountable acts of healing, not the least of which involved Marcus' young servant, Carta. The centurion had likewise witnessed an amazing transformation wrought by Yeshua in the once-tormented soul of Miryam.

Thousands, including Marcus, heard Yeshua's teaching; they knew of a certainty that the Rabbi was a good man, a kind man, a wise man, a worthy man, and something beyond an ordinary mortal man.

Not long before this, Rome had little reason to take official notice of a country preacher, even if he *was* reportedly able to work miracles. Yeshua preached peace, not confrontation. Rome did not acknowledge that devotion to the Hebrew deity had any special virtue, or that love and mercy possessed any power.

Power, insofar as Rome was concerned, existed at the point of a javelin or short sword. Such power increased with the disciplined ruthlessness of a century of legionaries, then multiplied many times over till it dominated the world at the command of a Caesar to his legions.

And so it had. From the Pillars of Hercules to the great river Euphrates, from Gaul to the Nile, Rome held sway over the nations. It was a time of enforced peace, punctuated by border skirmishes and brief, brutally crushed revolts. As long as Yeshua spoke no treason, organized no armies, encouraged no rebellion, he could go about his business.

But all that had changed on a wild-flower-strewn hillside the afternoon before. There, in front of Marcus' eyes, something extraordinary had occurred. Yeshua had fed his entire famished audience of thousands from a handful of bread and dried fish. Unaccountable? Yes. Unbelievable? Indeed.

Ordinarily, rational, practical, pragmatic Rome winked at magic. The emperor Tiberius himself practiced divination, reading into the signs the messages he already expected to receive. It was a political tool to blame policy on the gods, to excuse failures and justify excesses.

Where was the harm in free bread, even if produced by something unexplained? The problem was this: Yeshua had fed an army of followers. Five thousand men. An army! As many soldiers as owed allegiance to Rome in the whole Jewish province, and four times that many women and children too!

Compounding this novelty into a crime against the state had been the response of those legions of listeners. *Yeshua for king!* they cried. *Yeshua should be king of the Jews.* Since that acclaim was offered without Rome's approval, it was not an acceptable sentiment.

And the proof of how objectionable it was to official Rome? Tribune Felix's insistence on the strenuous all-night gallop to deliver his account to the governor.

Could anyone seriously believe that a Jewish rabble on a Galilean hillside was of any political or military consequence? When compared to the might symbolized by the city that lay just ahead, it didn't appear likely.

If the lands bordering the Great Sea of Middle Earth were the tiara encircling the brow of the Roman empire, then Caesarea Maritima was the jewel on its eastern rim. Constructed as a wholly fresh, purpose-built showplace by Rome's friend King Herod the Great, Caesarea was a marvel. From the hilltop approach to the city its acres of snowy limestone made a gleaming display. Monumental structures, from a colossal amphitheater for gladiatorial combat to an ostentatious temple dedicated to Emperor Augustus, dotted the seaside. There was perhaps no place in the empire that better combined grandeur with natural beauty.

It was thoroughly Roman in its conveniences: wide, regular streets, perfect right-angle intersections, ample public promenades, and an efficient sewer system.

Nor did temples or sewers exhaust the architectural wonders of the metropolis. Caesarea possessed one of the best artificial harbors in the world: reputedly the safest mooring between Piraeus in Greece and Alexandria in Egypt. Constructed of massive stone blocks sunk in two hundred feet of water, the entire Roman war fleet could have sheltered within the embrace of its outstretched limbs. From the seaward-most point on the breakwater a gigantic lighthouse beckoned navigators. It was said that a cargo galley leaving Alexandria two hundred fifty miles away could pick up the beacon of Caesarea before half the journey was completed.

Perhaps Tribune Felix would be struck by the same comparison as Marcus. Perhaps Marcus' friend and superior officer would have cooled down when he compared the Roman superiority on display in Caesarea with the rural scenes of Galilee.

Felix and Marcus reined up in front of the marble palace that had once belonged to Herod, but was now the official residence of the prefect of the Roman province of Judea.

Currently title and mansion belonged to Governor Pontius Pilate.

A squad of eager legionaries recently recruited from Cyprus confronted the two arriving officers with crossed spearpoints to bar their entry. The decurion, captain of the ten men on sentry duty, recognized Felix but remained doubtful when the disreputable-looking Marcus was introduced.

"But in any case, you can't see the governor," the young captain said when Felix demanded admission.

"We're under orders from the governor himself and the matter is urgent," Felix retorted. "Let us pass!"

"I'm sorry, Tribune," returned the other, "but you misunderstood me. You can't see Governor Pilate because he isn't here."

"Where then?" Felix insisted. "Out of the city?"

The decurion shook his head.

It was a little past the second hour of the morning. Very early for a lover-of-ease like Pilate to be abroad.

Marcus saw a flush of angry frustration overcome Felix.

"Then where is he?" Felix bellowed at the flustered captain.

"Sir, he went to the temple of the divine Augustus for the morning sacrifice. The new coins honoring Emperor Tiberius have been minted and the governor . . ."

Felix didn't stay to hear the rest of the explanation. Flinging back a pledge to flog young officers in order to make their tongues move faster, Felix remounted his horse. He applied his riding crop with vigor, administering a lashing to the mount as a substitute for the decurion.

Marcus had hoped Felix might have calmed down since the Galil, lost the urgency to denounce Yeshua.

Now that illusion was gone.

YA'ASEH

Before Emet, Avel, and Ha-or Tov had even left the confines of the Galil the trickle of Passover pilgrims flowing south toward Jerusalem had become a river. A stream of Jewish worshippers from Nazareth and Cana poured across the pass from the Valley of Jezreel. Descending toward the river valley, they met up with more wayfarers coming from Magdala and Genneseret.

Spitting piously in the direction of the Gentile town of Scythopolis as they passed it, the pilgrims crossed over the Jordan, thus avoiding the defiling dust of Samaria.

Once east of the river they encountered more believers coming from the region of Caesarea Philippi.

And the streams coalesced into a torrent.

The mood along the route was upbeat. It was a time of family reunions, when clans gathered to catch up on gossip and merrymaking. The cold of winter was past, the latter rains ending, and the barley harvest comfortably far enough off to allow a holiday.

Everywhere the travelers were cheerful and optimistic . . . except for three small boys.

Ha-or Tov hissed for the third time in a half mile of walking, "Look at us! I never saw these striped robes before yesterday, and even *I* can tell how much we stand out! People stare at us."

It was true. The identical uniforms made from thirds of the Baptizer's cloak did attract attention.

Avel saw a young girl watching them from an oxcart packed with sisters and brothers. Soon eight siblings, together with father, mother, uncles, aunts, and cousins, commented on the three children traveling unaccompanied and dressed in identical garb.

It was not, Avel realized, solely because they matched. Many families shared cloth from the same loom, dyed from the same lot, cut according to the same pattern. Sometimes whole villages preferred material stained walnut brown, while other regions were distinctive in their sunflower yellow.

It was the stripes, Avel decided. Red, green, and tan were unique, and the quality of the workmanship remained apparent even when cut down to fit children.

As soon as the uniforms were noticed, other questions followed: what family were these boys with? Where were their parents? Why were they traveling alone?

Avel tried to make light of the problem. "What are the chances of us running into Kittim or bar Abba?"

Ha-or Tov argued, "Do we know how many rebels are around us? Do we? Some rebel is bound to recognize us before we do him. He'll tell Kittim and bar Abba! Then good-bye throats!"

Avel considered taking off the robes, stashing them in a ditch somewhere. Then he quickly dismissed the thought. He had possessed an uncanny sense of importance since donning the Baptizer's mantle. Hadn't Yeshua touched the fabric fondly as he remembered the man for whom it had been woven? Surely it was significant to wear the cloak of a prophet.

Emet, age five, was not very strong. There had been a lot of travel in the past weeks with little time for recovery, and they were on the road again. It was especially hard for one with feet and legs so small.

The warm, sheltering robes had to remain. "I've got an idea," Avel asserted reluctantly. "We split up. If Kittim's hunting for us at all—which I doubt, but if he is—he'll be looking for the three of us to be together." Avel noticed that Emet's eyes turned downward and his chin drooped at this, but he was so certain he was correct that he kept on. "Anyone by himself will be just another servant traipsing along after one family or another."

Ha-or Tov ventured bravely, "You're right. Anyone alone won't stand out so much."

Avel noticed Emet's protruding lower lip. The little boy clearly didn't want to be left unaccompanied. So Avel finally added, "Ha-or Tov, keep Emet with you."

Emet brightened a bit at this compromise. Avel reasoned that the biggest danger to them was from Kittim. Avel, who had been well known to Kittim as a Sparrow in the Jerusalem quarry, was the one Kittim most easily recognized and certainly most thoroughly hated. This was a difficult decision, but Avel remembered the charge Yeshua had given him to care for Emet. Traveling separately seemed the best way to protect his friends.

"It's settled then," Avel said. "I'll keep away from you, but where I can see you. That way if you run into trouble I can help." As he said this, Avel realized there wasn't much he could actually do. How could he oppose rebels with knives? How could he run to total strangers and ask for their assistance against bar Abba's men? "Go on," he said. "We'll meet up again after sunset."

Avel stepped away from his friends into the shade of an overhanging willow branch and immediately regretted his decision to part from them. Had he let Ha-or Tov fret him into breaking up the group? He was just getting used to the idea of the new name given him by Reb Yeshua: Haver, "Friend to the brokenhearted."

Alone again he could sense Avel . . . the mourner . . . creeping back into his heart, stealing his courage.

Peeping out of the branches, Avel watched Ha-or Tov and Emet attach themselves to the rear of a family group. When they were a hundred yards ahead Avel could still recognize them by the robes, but he judged the distance between them was enough. So Avel merged with the throng once again.

■ ■ ■ ■

Prominently displayed on a man-made knoll in the center of Caesarea was the Temple of Caesar Augustus. It had been commissioned by Herod the Great as the centerpiece of his new city. From the front terrace of the rotunda there was a splendid view over the harbor, which meant the structure was the first thing noticed by a seafaring visitor upon his arrival in port.

The sanctuary was also placed so the main avenues of town crossed immediately before its base. Thus foot travelers couldn't avoid noting its significance either. It had suited Herod the Great to make certain the whole empire recognized his devotion to Augustus.

Though Augustus had been dead and gone this decade and a half, his adopted heir, Tiberius, found it suited the Imperial dignity to be the son of god. It was not Roman policy to interfere in matters of local religion if the local populace understood clearly that in the scope of things, all gods were not created equal.

It was one of the ironies of life in the Jewish province, Marcus reflected. Herod, the former king of the Jews, had not been a Jew by either birth or piety. Had he not been a brutal murderer he might have gained a reputation as a famous compromiser. He spent lavish sums to promote Augustus to godhood, then poured out money like water, renovating and expanding the Jerusalem temple to the unnamable Hebrew deity.

This sort of duality was perfectly acceptable in a world that saw the heavens as crowded with godlings. Being recently promoted, like Augustus, or of longer standing, like Zeus, made little difference . . . anywhere except Judea. Alone in the empire, only the Jews insisted there was *one* true God. They also taught that He could only be properly worshipped in Jerusalem, and that one of His cherished commandments involved repudiating every other god.

Despite the early morning hour, a crowd of dignitaries gathered on the slope below the temple. There were visitors from every other province of the empire . . . and no Jews. At least there were no Jews recognizable as such, and certainly no Pharisees, Levites, or priests.

The time was near for the Jewish Festival of Passover, and no religious Jew wanted to risk ceremonial uncleanness at such a time. It was impossible to enter Caesarea without being defiled. To a pious son of Abraham the entire city was an abomination.

As Marcus and Felix arrived below the temple, Governor Pilate appeared in the center of the crowd on the terrace. Pilate stepped upon a raised dais so he could be seen by all. In his hand he held a *simpulum*, the saucer-like clay container used for pouring out libations to the gods. A minute later he spoke to the assembly while wine that flashed red in the sunlight drizzled from the *simpulum* over a marble altar. The stone was emblazoned with the carvings of bulls garlanded with flowers and the name of Augustus.

Though Marcus was too far away to hear Pilate's words, he could guess at the meaning: invoking the blessing of Augustus on Emperor Tiberius, on the province of Judea, and on Pilate himself as the humble servant of the empire.

Beside the tall, thin-lipped governor stood another notable dressed like him. Both wore the *toga praetexta*, the long, substantial, multi-pleated robe of state. Their official clothes were bordered with the dark crimson stripe referred to as "purple," denoting the emperor's representatives.

Marcus recognized the second man. He was shorter and squatter than Pilate, more tanned from more years in the region, with a permanent squint from campaigning against the Parthians in the desert. This chief guest was Prefect Vitellius, governor of Syria and Pilate's superior officer in the diplomatic corps of Rome. Marcus understood Vitellius had wintered in Rome. His recent return from there had to account for the timing of this ceremony: Pilate wanted Vitellius to see how well he was performing as a junior governor.

Felix visibly fidgeted, wanting to approach Pilate with his news, but forced by propriety to delay until the ceremony ended. Marcus observed the two Roman dignitaries receiving the congratulations of the leading citizens of Caesarea. Pilate's smile looked fixed, even forced, to Marcus' way of thinking. As each participant passed in the receiving line, Pilate dipped his hand into a leather pouch and handed something over.

It had to be a commemorative distribution of the newly minted coins. Pilate's motive was clear: he wanted to cement his close connection to the emperor in the minds of the populace. At the same time it didn't hurt Pilate's standing to display a respectful crowd of well-wishers, eager for a fleeting touch of the gubernatorial palm.

It was all so calm and organized. A century of legionaries kept the common people away. No rabble, no potential rebels would be allowed to disturb the dignity of the service.

Marcus recognized the sharp contrast to the Purim disturbance a month earlier. On that occasion Jerusalem had nearly been plunged into full-scale rioting. The tetrarch of the Galil, Herod Antipas, had decided to celebrate his birthday by flinging bread and money to the masses. People had been killed, and further insurrection had been prevented only by the timely arrival of Marcus and his men.

Pilate was taking no such chances today. Rome had no qualms about breaking whatever heads needed to be broken, but political unrest was bad for commerce. Keeping taxes and trade flowing in an orderly manner was a governor's highest priority.

The rite concluded, the crowd began to drift away. Pilate and Vitellius retreated into the cool interior of the temple, followed by a squadron of troopers.

Felix identified himself to the captain of the guard but was told he would have to wait yet again for the two officials to complete their private devotions.

As Marcus' eyes grew accustomed to the dim interior, he made out the thrice-life-sized statues. Augustus, portrayed as Olympian Zeus, sat enthroned, complete with an upraised arm holding an eagle-headed staff. The unmoving icon of Corinthian bronze extended its burnished left foot for mere mortals to kiss. Seated beside Augustus was the less threatening but still colossal figure of Roma, or Mother Rome, dressed as the goddess Hera.

Kneeling before Augustus was Pilate. Vitellius was down on one knee in front of Roma.

The two men, supposedly locked in their prayers, were instead enmeshed in discussion. From the particulars it was no doubt supposed to be confidential. But Vitellius had probably lost part of his hearing to the desert winds, and his voice, combined with the acoustics of the domed building, conveyed every word to Marcus.

"The coin's a good gesture," Vitellius said to Pilate, "but simply a start. You have a lot of ground to make up with Tiberius."

"Really?" Pilate's jocular reply was meant to sound confident, but a higher-than-normal pitch betrayed his anxiety. "Then I'd better send him more of those white Judean dates with the juice like honey. That should soothe him." Tiberius' sweet tooth was well known. Such trifles truly did please the man who commanded the wealth of the empire.

Vitellius mocked, "Dates! You saw the letter. If ink were brimstone, his comments to you would have scorched the fingers of the scribe! Did you think he forgot what happened two years ago? Putting up the standards was stupid enough, but then capitulating to a mob . . . and a Jewish mob at that! Tiberius was unable to control his fury when news came of what happened in Jerusalem at Herod Antipas' birthday last month."

Pilate murmured a protest that the Purim riot had not been his fault, but Vitellius cut his words short. "You're the governor! *Anything* that goes wrong here *is* your fault! Believe it! If you can't control the province any better than that, Tiberius will replace you with someone who can!"

No wonder Pilate's smile had resembled the rictus of a corpse. Word of the disturbances had reached Rome before Vitellius' departure, in time for the emperor to vent his displeasure.

"It took all of Sejanus' wheedling to placate the emperor. Otherwise it would have been a notice of recall!" Vitellius concluded.

To Marcus' eye, Pilate's back was as stiff as a pilum shaft. Sejanus was the prefect of the Imperial Praetorian guard and chief advisor to Tiberius. Pilate was his protégé and owed his appointment to Sejanus.

"And don't try to honey-coat your reply," Vitellius warned. "Tiberius wants the truth."

Pilate's uneasy chuckle crossed the dome more in betrayal of nervousness than lightness of spirit. "What is truth?" he queried mockingly. "Isn't it in the ear of the beholder?"

Vitellius, evidently not amused by Pilate's attempts to improve the mood, snorted. "I know what Sejanus whispered to you who cling to the hem of his robes. He said Tiberius is feeble, losing his grip; that every day Tiberius relinquishes more of the government to his favorite, Sejanus. Remember: Sejanus is not as secure as all that!"

Felix cleared his throat loudly.

Vitellius and Pilate jerked their heads around while Marcus ducked his in amusement. Felix, as the senior military officer present, had decided the material being overheard was too sensitive and elected to warn the politicians.

Religious duty instantly forgotten, Pilate and Vitellius rose and turned their backs on Augustus and Roma.

"Tribune," Pilate acknowledged Felix. "You have a message?" The governor peered disdainfully down his long, pinched nose at Marcus, offering him no greeting. "Prefect Vitellius, you know Dio Felix, my young commander of the Galil?"

"Yes," Vitellius agreed, "and his family. Your father is well, Tribune. He sends his greetings."

This bit of politeness was more than it appeared. Felix's clan possessed influence in Rome and he was better-born socially than Pilate. It was a reminder to Pilate that Sejanus was not the sole power broker in the empire. The allusion was meant to further remind Pilate how precarious his position was.

"Thank you, sir," Felix said. "I apologize for my appearance—"

Perhaps fearful that Felix would blurt out more bad news in front of Vitellius, Pilate hastily interrupted. "The tribune is just back from a routine inspection. We won't bore you with the details."

"Routine, of course," Vitellius echoed skeptically, eyeing Marcus. "And Centurion Marcus Longinus often masquerades as an Idumean horse thief . . . but never mind. I'll leave you to it. I must get on the road." Drawing Pilate aside, but still able to be overheard, he continued, "No more mistakes, understand?"

"The new aqueduct will please all Jerusalem," Pilate promised. "There will be good reports going to Rome very soon."

"Control!" Vitellius emphasized. "Tiberius doesn't care if you use bribes or daggers, so long as you stay in control. Keep that in mind." Then, with a flourish, the governor of Syria swept up his entourage and exited the temple to begin the overland part of his journey back to his capital in Damascus.

Pilate directed Felix and Marcus into an antechamber of the shrine where they could continue their discussion without other witnesses.

"Yeshua of Nazareth," Pilate snapped when the three were secluded. "Is he leading a revolt? Yes or no?"

Marcus struggled against crying out a protest. A simple affirmative by Felix would cause Yeshua's arrest and crucifixion. Men had already been executed for much lesser offenses.

Slowly, carefully, Felix framed his response. "He . . . is not."

Marcus' shoulders sagged with the release of tension.

"During our return from the Galil I pondered what I saw," Felix continued. "He fed a hungry crowd."

"Fed?" Pilate demanded.

"I don't know exactly what I witnessed," Felix admitted. "He seemed to take a handful of bread and turn it into enough for everyone. Then the crowd wanted to make him king."

Marcus' eyes took in the frown frozen on Pilate's brow. The danger to Yeshua was not yet over.

"And did this magician agree?" Pilate asked.

Marcus couldn't control himself any longer. "Your pardon, excellency, but the answer is no," he reported. "I stayed long enough to see. In fact, Yeshua was anxious to avoid the issue. He did not acknowledge the cheers of the mob."

Pilate folded the thin, perfumed fingers of his right hand and rested his chin on them in thought. Rousing himself at last, he said, "Left when it sounded treasonous. That must have disappointed the rabble! He's afraid . . . and rightly so!"

"But the crowd," Felix added. "That's the worry. They'll be searching for another leader. Someone who won't draw back. Many of them, fresh from shouting for a king, will be in Jerusalem for Passover."

Now that the focus had shifted away from Yeshua, Marcus could admit Felix was correct. "Jerusalem is the key," he concurred.

"I'm going up to Jerusalem for Passover myself," Pilate noted. "I'm going to receive a delegation of Jews who want to thank me for building the aqueduct. And I've already prepared a little surprise for any rebels who might appear. Tribune Felix, you will remain here and accompany me to Jerusalem."

"And what orders for me?" Marcus inquired.

Pilate sniffed. "In Capernaum you supervised a religious building?

Made the Jews happy, didn't you? Clean yourself up and go to Bethlehem tomorrow. Review the connections between Herod's old water system and my new one. I want no slipups."

So Marcus was still not regarded as reliable since he had fallen out of favor. His decline had begun when he had placed honor above personal advancement by spurning the patronage of Praetorian Prefect Lucius Sejanus. He had crossed words and swords with another Sejanus protégé, Praetorian Centurion Vara, a man of brute strength and brutal appetites. Marcus' love for Miryam, a Jewess, had contributed to the decline. Certainly his sympathy for the Jewish populace had speeded it along. And finally his tacit admiration of Yeshua of Nazareth and the God of the Hebrews had made him a pariah in Roman thought.

As a result, instead of being placed back in command of his men, he was to be an engineer in a tiny village away from the action. "By your command," Marcus said, clapping his arm across his chest.

With a dismissive wave Pilate turned to Felix. "Join me in making a sacrifice to Augustus before we conclude," he suggested. The overt friendliness to the tribune was transparently political.

"And Centurion Longinus as well?" Felix asked.

Unaccountably Marcus was reluctant. Slit the throat of a pigeon below the unwavering stare of the emperor's statue? He had never hesitated before. If the god had any real power, then it was a sensible gesture. If not, what harm did it do? Why was he unwilling now? Sacrificing to the emperor had never bothered him. What had changed? Why did he now sense that worshipping bronze images of men was wrong?

He hoped his lack of enthusiasm didn't show. "The governor will please excuse me," he said, gesturing at his mud-stiffened, dusty clothes. "I am not in a fit condition."

"Quite right," Governor Pilate stated. "Centurion, you are dismissed."

■ ■ ■ ■

Hours passed quickly as Avel traveled on the road to Jerusalem. The boy was cognizant that among the legitimate pilgrims were spies variously in the pay of Pilate, Herod Antipas, and the religious factions of the high priest and the Sanhedrin.

It had always been so since the days of Herod the Great. Large gatherings had been forbidden. Any hint if disloyalty had been dealt with swiftly and viciously. The hesitation to speak openly about important issues was ingrained among the populace of Judea and Jerusalem.

The Galileans, however, were less circumspect.

Conversation between strangers was cautious, avoiding the topics of politics, possible revolt, and especially the distribution of the Korban funds for the new aqueduct. These were matters to be discussed only over the table with close friends and family. There was safety among those who could be trusted.

Still, here and there, between fathers and sons, brothers and members of a clan, such discussions took place in guarded tones.

The one topic discussed candidly by everyone was Yeshua of Nazareth. Who was he? Would he come to Jerusalem for the holy week? What did it mean that he fed the thousands but refused to be proclaimed their king? Yeshua might have been riding south at the head of an army of thousands willing to fight for him.

Instead he had vanished into the hills.

Avel kept himself from telling about the amazing encounter he, Ha-or Tov, and Emet had experienced. How foolish would he be if he drew attention to himself in such a charged atmosphere?

The journey continued like this for a time. Occasionally Avel strained his eyes ahead to pick out Ha-or Tov and Emet, but they were always where they were supposed to be.

His plan was working perfectly.

When the sun stood directly overhead, groups gathered by the roadside for a noon meal. Avel, who plucked at his bread in solitary contemplation, was asked to join a family group. This was a way to honor the Jewish command for hospitality to strangers. In inviting Avel perhaps the family hoped they were entertaining one of the many angels who traveled each year with the pilgrims to Jerusalem.

But Avel was no angel. He was frightened and hungry. He had a twinge about losing sight of his friends as they continued down the slope in front of him. Then he decided they would have to stop sometime, and he would overtake them again.

After bread and fruit had been passed out and shared, a woman asked Avel his name. Where was his family, she continued, and would they be worried about him?

He assured her, "They're ahead." It was true as far as it went; Emet and Ha-or Tov *were* ahead.

This was accepted without further details as Avel split an orange with a younger boy. Dividing the ripe globe, he bit into a plump slice, savored the sweet juice, and tossed the peel toward a squirrel perched on a rock pile.

Like Avel, a passing pilgrim turned his head to watch the rodent dart toward the prize.

Avel gasped and froze as he recognized the familiar face. Dull and haggard, with a grizzled fringe of dirty hair framing his sunburned features . . . it was one of the rebels Avel had met in bar Abba's camp!

It was Asher! Asher! Slow of speech but quick with his dagger! The only one who had been kind to the boys when they had been captives.

But the one who walked with Asher struck fear in Avel's heart! Stalking angrily alongside, with a scowl on his face, was Kittim! At once Avel took in the thin beard, the cruel dark eyes, the hands that once beat Avel, and the feet that joyfully crushed the bones of a tiny bird. Avel's worst nightmare had come true: Kittim swaggered defiantly among the throngs!

And he would happily slit Avel's throat for nothing.

Avel's heart skipped a beat, then began a terrified racing.

Asher seemed more interested in the squirrel than in his fellow pilgrims. Kittim, however, scrutinized everyone, as if sizing them up as either potential enemies or targets for robbery.

Or, in Avel's case, as a lamb for slaughter.

The orange turned sour in Avel's mouth and he couldn't swallow.

"Are you listening, Avel? More bread?" the boy beside Avel inquired loudly.

Avel cringed. Had Kittim heard Avel's name? Was he caught?

No. Kittim glared down the trail. There was no sign that he recognized Avel.

But Asher's head swiveled toward the family. Avel tucked his chin and rubbed his forehead in an attempt to conceal himself among the children. He prepared to flee! But where? West of the road was a marsh, impossible for running.

Into the rock piles?

The men's longer, stronger legs would surely overtake him.

Avel saw and sensed Asher's eyes sweep over him, past him, back to him. They lingered just an instant . . . and then Asher passed on without stopping. The brigand's face snapped forward at a command from Kittim.

Exhaling a sigh of relief, Avel found that the boy was staring at him curiously. The woman also regarded Avel with a puzzled expression.

"Are you unwell?" she asked kindly.

"No. I'm . . . I've never had an orange before." Avel struggled to respond, his attention focused on the retreating backs of the two rebels. It had been so close, too close! If Kittim had not been distracted by something up ahead . . .

What was Kittim focused on? The sparrow killer raised his head, as if sniffing the air for prey!

Avel jumped to his feet when Kittim nudged Asher in the ribs. The two hesitated an instant, then resumed, picking up their pace!

The sparrow killer had spotted Emet and Ha-or Tov!

"Sorry," Avel said, thrusting the rest of the orange and the bread back into his companion's lap. "I'm late. Have to catch up!"

He bolted.

Darting onto the first switchback, Avel caught sight of Kittim racing down the trail, cutting across corners in his haste to overtake Emet and Ha-or Tov.

And what could Avel, commanded by Yeshua to care for Emet and Ha-or Tov, do to stop their capture?

Kittim was almost upon Avel's unsuspecting friends. Asher was only a few paces behind.

If Avel called out the warning that there were rebels on the road, would anyone believe him? And how many would be hurt when Kittim and Asher drew their knives?

Too late!

In his second of indecision Avel saw Kittim reach out and grasp Ha-or Tov's collar. Ha-or Tov's curly red hair flung wide from his head as Kittim spun the boy around to face him.

Emet's mouth was open. He was shouting something. Shouting to be left alone! Shouting that they were being attacked by robbers! It was an unlikely scenario: two young boys being robbed. But it was effective nonetheless.

A broad-shouldered, bull-like man reared up from his lunch in the grass and boomed into the dispute with a roar of indignation.

Avel recognized Nakdimon ben Gurion! Dressed in a commoner's clothes, the black-bearded member of the Sanhedrin was taking the part of the two boys!

Asher turned from his path and slunk off, evidently not wanting to encounter a foe as formidable as Nakdimon. Kittim blinked down into the eyes of Ha-or Tov, released his grip, raised his hands in a sort of apology, and backed away.

As abruptly as it began, the encounter was over.

To Avel's surprise Kittim thrust Ha-or Tov aside and yelled back at the big man. Asher, hood over his head, jogged past. Kittim joined him, and the two rebels disappeared in the distance.

What had happened? How had tragedy been averted?

Realizing that rejoining his two companions wouldn't be sensible at the moment, Avel forced himself to calm his heart, his breath, and his pace.

Ha-or Tov and Emet trailed close at the heels of Nakdimon the rest of the journey to the next caravansary.

Avel kept his distance and considered the danger that lay ahead on the road to Beth-lehem.

ADONAI

Bathed, dressed in the red tunic of a soldier, his hair washed and lightly oiled, and his feet in clean sandals, Centurion Marcus Longinus felt more relaxed than at any time in weeks. Ever since Felix had suggested Marcus discard his uniform and pass as a civilian in order to investigate Yeshua of Nazareth, the centurion had been uneasy.

Marcus had gained a reputation for heroism at the battle of Idistaviso, where he had saved the left flank of the Roman army from disintegrating. He was a man of honor who kept his vows and spoke the plain facts as he saw them. Spying had not come naturally to him, nor had the assignment been to his liking.

He was grateful to be getting back into uniform. He was not ashamed to be a Roman centurion, so let his appearance announce the truth. All that was left of his disguise was his beard and untrimmed hair, and both those items would be attended to presently.

Felix joined him an hour before sunset on the curving promenade connecting the officers' quarters to the harbor. The breeze from the sea was bracing.

Extending a cup of wine, Felix indicated a stone bench. "Marcus," he said, "I value you as a veteran and loyal officer with fifteen more years' experience than me. I have learned a great deal from you. Unlike some political appointees, I don't think instant wisdom comes with my lineage, or that the ability to lead is automatically conferred with a purchased insignia of rank. I also think of you as a friend."

Marcus sipped the wine. It tasted of dark cherries and summer hay fields and warmed his throat and stomach. He waited to see where this speech led.

"You're riding south tomorrow," Felix continued. "But before that happens, I know you have a few questions for me . . . and I have things to say to you as well."

"Why did you spare Yeshua?" Marcus asked, taking the invitation at face value. "You had the power to condemn him with a single word, yet you didn't. Why not?"

"Because I'm not Vara," Felix said. "Killing people doesn't amuse me. Don't misunderstand . . . I think the Rabbi may be a danger to Rome, and if I'm right, he'll have to be crushed." Felix stared across the rim of his silver goblet into Marcus' eyes. "And if it comes to that, you'll have a tough choice to make. Why do you want to save him?"

Why indeed?

Marcus had experienced respect for brave enemies before and yet remained remorseless when battling them. Yeshua was a Jew . . . a race despised and ridiculed throughout the empire. It was Marcus' sworn duty to uphold the authority of Rome, the prestige of Rome, the superiority of Rome.

Why should he risk his career and his life to shield a Jewish preacher?

"Because he is more than a mere man," Marcus said at last. "Felix, I once heard him pose this question: 'Which is harder to heal, a broken body or a broken soul?'"

"So?" Felix scoffed, tossing back half a cupful of wine. "Greek philosophers say such things all the time to their admiring lackeys. Isn't this just a Jewish version?"

"No," Marcus replied slowly. "The difference is . . . he can do both. It's not simply word games."

"You mean you think the business with the bread was real? On the journey from the Galil I thought about trying to explain that to Pilate and knew I couldn't. It's part of the reason I drew back from denouncing Yeshua. Why should he suffer for something I can't understand?"

"Nakdimon ben Gurion, the Jew you met who is on their supreme council . . ."

Felix acknowledged that he remembered Nakdimon's credentials.

Marcus continued. "Nakdimon is also studying Yeshua's claims. I'd like to speak to him more about it."

Shrugging, Felix said, "You don't need my permission for that. Our job is to see that Governor Pilate's aqueduct gets built and that bar Abba's rebels are either captured or driven into their caves. As long as Yeshua speaks no treason he can be whatever kind of miracle worker he fancies. But he should stay away from Jerusalem."

"Pilate still doesn't understand the Jews," Marcus said at last, unwilling to unveil any further his thoughts about the Rabbi of Nazareth.

"What makes you say that? Their own Council voted him the money from their Temple treasury to complete the aqueduct. Everyone knows how badly Jerusalem needs it. He'll be a hero."

Shaking his head, Marcus disagreed. "Nakdimon told me the money was Korban, sacred to their God. Hear me, Felix. It will cause more turmoil than hanging the face of the emperor over their Temple Mount."

"But they need the water . . . and their own leaders agreed to the arrangement. Surely the rabble will see reason!"

"I hope you're right," Marcus conceded. Then as an afterthought he asked, "Did you get one of the new coins?"

Felix nodded.

"May I see it?"

Felix fished in a leather pouch hanging from his belt. He retrieved a circular, stamped bit of bronze, no bigger than his thumbnail. On the far horizon the sun, which had plunged into a thin layer of cloud, emerged just above the sea. A beam of light reflected off the shiny copper surface of the penny as Felix handed it over.

Marcus studied one face of the coin and then the other. "Three years," he said. "Three years as governor, and he's learned nothing."

"What do you mean?"

Tracing the engraving with his finger, Marcus described what he found there. "A sheaf of barley. Around the rim the words *Tiberius Caesar.*"

"What's wrong with—"

Waving his friend to silence, Marcus reversed the image and continued. "And on the other side . . . a *simpulum* beneath a *lituus.* A cup for pouring wine onto an altar and the spiral-topped rod of a diviner when he reads the entrails of a goat!"

"So? They aren't images of men or beasts. Just things!"

Marcus shrugged. "Then you don't understand either. Since before the time of Alexander the Great, through all the wars with Antiochus and the Maccabees, the quickest way to rouse a Jewish mob was to threaten their beliefs. Pious, *peace-loving* Jews will regard these coins as rude, an affront to their faith. The more rebellious will use them as one more proof that Rome wants to destroy their faith altogether."

"All that from a penny?" Felix said incredulously. "It takes two of them just to buy a man entry to a public bath. Why would anyone take offense at something so minor?" The sun slipped beneath the sea, announcing its departure with a final greenish flash. "Anyway, it doesn't matter. Pilate is ready for trouble, be it aqueduct or coin. He's given Vara the special assignment of riot control. The governor is determined not to lose either control or dignity ever again."

"A bloodbath in the making?"

"Vara has strict orders about how much force..." Felix's words trailed away. Both men knew Vara was a raging wild animal. Certainly not noble, like a lion. More like a hyena, pulling down the weakest prey, and insatiable. "You stay away from him," he said in warning. "He's planning to destroy you."

"Just as well that I'll be heading off to the wilds of Beth-lehem then," Marcus joked. "Or would be if that barber ever showed up!"

"Ah," Felix said with a guilty start. "I forgot. I sent him away. I want you to keep the beard so you can go back into disguise if needed."

■ ■ ■ ■

The caravansary outside the town of Salim had sleeping accommodations and prepared food for those who could pay, as well as heaps of straw and access to common cook fires for those who could not. The inn was really only an open courtyard surrounded by a porticoed terrace. Families who arrived early in the day sheltered in the alcoves in a semblance of privacy; latecomers shared the central square with hundreds of strangers, donkeys, and oxen.

There had been no more alarms or close calls during the rest of the day's journey. Avel hadn't seen Kittim or Asher, or any other rebels, but that fact had not allowed him to relax. Being taken so completely off-guard earlier made him anxious. Avel was afraid to enter into any more conversations for fear of being distracted. Only by keeping his nerves balanced on a knife's edge could he stay alive. He had spent the entire afternoon glancing behind him and ducking around rocks to see if anyone was following or even staring at him.

Given the oddity of his behavior, it wasn't surprising that everyone *did* seem to be staring.

Avel was doubly desirous of nightfall, and unhappy that Ha-or Tov and Emet turned into the caravansary's entrance. He would have preferred finding a secluded spot away from the other pilgrims, perhaps up the nearby streambed, but in any case away from prying eyes. Besides, the inn's entry was also its only exit; it was too easy to be trapped there.

In the end, Avel had no choice but to follow. After lurking opposite the gate for a time, like a recently beaten dog skulking beyond the fire's light, Avel finally darted across the open space and into the thickest shadow he could find.

Expecting his friends also to be tucked back in a sheltered corner, Avel was surprised to hear his name called from one of the brightly lit recesses. There, beside a fire, reclining on straw, were Emet and Ha-or Tov. Emet was unwrapping a length of bloody rag from his left foot; Ha-or Tov was drinking from a jug of water.

"Where've you been?" Ha-or Tov greeted him. "We were worried about you."

"What are you doing?" Avel hissed. "Get out of sight!"

Ha-or Tov shook his head. "We have a protector," he said, gesturing with the clay container. "Nakdimon ben Gurion. He's over there talking to the fellow with the donkey."

Because of the crowd it took Avel several tries to locate the man. Eventually he spotted Nakdimon. His back was to Avel, but he appeared to be bargaining with the owner of a dun-colored swaybacked animal.

"It's the man we saw at Deborah's house in Capernaum," Ha-or Tov added unnecessarily. "He said for us to stay with him and he'd look out for us."

■ ■ ■ ■

Emet's blistered feet.

Nakdimon approached the problem brimming with good intentions after his long conversation with Yeshua of Nazareth. But in spite of his original plan, execution of the deed had taken on an extremely unpleasant aspect. The simple act of hiring a donkey to carry beggar boys to Jerusalem had become an arduous process.

"I won't take a penny less." The traveling hawker ponderously wagged his massive head atop narrow shoulders. Tugging the drooping ear of his half-starved donkey, he added, "I took him in as payment of a debt. He's been useful. Gentle. Dependable. You wish to hire him, you say. To carry the boys to Yerushalayim, you say. Well, then. All right, I say. But what if he dies on the way? What if you are not truly Nakdimon ben Gurion, the nephew of Gamaliel? And when I go to the address you give me in Yerushalayim to get my donkey back you have absconded with my beast and I am left with nothing but what you paid to hire him?"

"For that price, he *should* be mine. Three times over!"

The hawker reddened. Clearly he was losing patience. "Not during Passover week! Two silver shekels for the hire of him! Two more in deposit, or your boys can walk on bloody stumps."

"If you were a righteous man, you'd *offer* me the use of your beast for no pay whatsoever." Nakdimon's ire was roused. "This is Passover. Such a deed is a *mitzvah,* is it not?"

"I'm a hawker, not a priest. With a donkey for hire!"

"Two shekels for the hire? And two shekels more for deposit! On a normal day I could buy three donkeys for that much. And in better condition!"

"In Yerushalayim he'll fetch twice what I'm asking."

Nakdimon peered into the animal's mouth. "If he lives that long."

A shrug. The hawker whined, "He's practically a colt. Five. Maybe six."

Nakdimon knew the long yellow teeth indicated the animal had been carrying burdens for at least twenty years. "He's old enough to pay taxes."

The hawker feigned injury. He sucked his blackened teeth petulantly. "Suit yourself. No one else in the khan is hiring out livestock. No one is selling. I happen to have taken a liking to your boys. That's why I make you this offer. The little lad with the bloody feet. How else will you carry him to Yerushalayim? He is your son. You must think of such things."

"He's not my son," Nakdimon started to explain but caught himself.

"Not your son? Then who . . ."

Nakdimon snapped a reply he had learned in Torah school. "Haven't you heard that to care for travelers is as great a matter as the reception of the Shekinah?"

The peddler fleetingly considered this wisdom and then shook his head. "No."

"Or whenever a poor one stands at your door, the Holy One, blessed be his Name, stands at the right hand?"

"A lovely sentiment." The fellow applauded weakly. "So. These boys are nothing to you. Just beggars, are they? A ticket to get in good standing with the Almighty?"

"What does it matter to you who they are? We are speaking of the price of your animal's hire. Here to Yerushalayim. You retrieve it at the end at my house. Nakdimon ben Gurion. You know my name. And everyone is satisfied, eh?"

"Pay me what I ask."

"This will not stand well in the eyes of the Lord."

"I'll take my chances."

"The hooves are split."

"If you are who you claim to be, you are a rich man. You can afford to hire ten donkeys. I'm a poor man. I offer you this deal and you insult my animal. As a matter of fact, according to your own proverb you insult the Almighty. You don't know. I may be an angel sent to travel to this khan to meet you! To test your generosity."

Nakdimon knew well that the khan was packed to the brim with angels, prophets, holy men, pilgrims, rabbis, peddlers, spies, rebels, bandits, and thieves—all on their way to Passover. Whatever this fellow might be, he was not an angel.

But there was the donkey. A much more attractive creature than its master. Better teeth anyway. It was probably the lone beast of burden for sale or hire between Galilee and the Temple Mount.

"Last chance," the thief bargained.

Nakdimon dipped into his purse and removed the coins. "You leave me no choice. For the sake of the boy's feet. But it's robbery."

Decayed teeth flashed a solicitous grin. Grimy palm extended to collect the cash. "May the Eternal bless your honor! May you enjoy prosperity all your days for your generosity toward a poor man! You won't regret this! I will come to your door and collect my little beast."

"And refund my two-shekel deposit."

"Yes. Yes. Until then may he serve you well." Thrusting the lead rope into Nakdimon's hand, the fellow scurried away to bilk another traveler out of hard cash.

"Religious holidays bring out the best in people," Nakdimon grumbled. His uncle Gamaliel often said it was the duty of a righteous man to consider all men as if they were robbers but treat them as if they were the Messiah himself. Well, there was no doubt about this hawker. He was not the Messiah. But his donkey might well save some battered soles.

Nakdimon absently stroked the pitiful creature's thin neck as he gazed around the khan for the two boys for whom he had become protector and traveling companion. Then Nakdimon would go home to his children in Jerusalem. It really was not a bother. Probably not worth an honorable mention in the record book of the Almighty.

Never mind.

And there they were. Huddled beside a pillar. Striped robes as obvious as the clothes of a jester in the court of Herod Antipas. The Good Light and Truth. How could a man with any religious training turn away from performing a good deed on behalf of children with such names as these?

Hadassah would have taken them for angels. Human and grubby though they might have been, they would have been swooped up and bundled home for supper. She would have made certain they were apprenticed to an artisan in the market of Jerusalem before she let them go!

Two boys. Yes. Not angels. Yet the two had become three. Three dressed alike. Nakdimon clearly recognized the newcomer as one of the Jerusalem link boys! He was a Sparrow! A bit cleaner than when Nakdimon had last seen him. Yes. Better dressed too. But there was no doubt it was The Mourner. The boy who had refused to light his torch on the night of Purim after his friend Hayyim had been killed. How had he come to be in a khan filled with thieves and rebels this far north of Jerusalem?

Never mind. Avel was here. Avel was there. He shared the bread of Ha-or Tov and Emet. The trio were boon companions; that was plain enough.

With a practiced swipe along the sagging spine of the donkey, Nakdimon judged that the pathetic creature could carry three.

■ ■ ■ ■

At least the straw for sale as bedding in the khan was fresh. New bundles had been brought in, in anticipation of the thousands who would pass through on the way to Jerusalem. Torches burned brightly, as if in welcome, but latecomers were turned away. There was no room left in the inn tonight.

Nakdimon would have received preferential treatment had he let it be known that he was one of the rulers of Israel. Instead he chose obscurity. Clothed in the garb of a commoner, he was able to listen in on the conversations of those around him. So far all popular sentiment focused on the hope that the Carpenter from Nazareth would wrest control from the high priest, the Sanhedrin, and Rome.

Nakdimon purchased a bushel of clean straw and sat down to share bread with Ha-or Tov and Emet. Avel was introduced as a brother who had been separated on the road.

Nakdimon warned them that tomorrow would be a long day if they were to make it all the way to the ford of the Jordan. The donkey would speed them along somewhat, but they would have to be on the road before first light. Emet and Ha-or Tov seemed content with this. They spread the additional bedding and were out cold the minute they lay down.

Avel stared at Nakdimon with suspicion and did not go to sleep with the others. At last the boy challenged Nakdimon. "I was a quarry Sparrow."

"Yes," Nakdimon acknowledged. "I remember. The Mourner. Avel. You carried a light for me on Purim."

"Along with the other Sparrows."

"So. You remember me as well." Nakdimon was caught.

"I couldn't forget. You paid us all a penny each. Even me."

"It was Purim." Nakdimon leaned back against the wall. "What did you do with your penny?"

"Kittim, chief of the Sparrows, beat me and took it from me. So I left the quarry." The boy's tone was one of unconcern. "I'm glad I left."

"But you're going back to Yerushalayim?"

"No." Avel considered him frankly. "Why are you dressed like a laborer?"

"It's safer." Nakdimon pulled the hood of his cloak over his head against the chill.

"Safer than what?" Avel challenged.

"There are bandits on the road."

"Why travel alone?"

"My companions left the Galil ahead of me. I stayed behind awhile."

"You were in Capernaum. You were in the Galil. I saw you with Ya'ir, the father of Deborah. You were at the house when Deborah . . . fell asleep. You were there when Yeshua came and woke her."

"How do you know this, boy?"

"We were in the barn . . . hiding. Deborah fed us. Hid us."

"Hid you? From whom?"

"Bar Abba's men."

"The rebel?"

"Deborah hid us from Kittim, Asher, and the others. Then she got sick. I climbed a tree and saw it. Saw you. The others. I saw what happened."

"You were with the rebels?" Nakdimon studied this young witness in the flickering firelight. Perhaps it would be wise to keep tabs on him, in case testimony was needed before the council.

"Kittim was the one you drove away from Emet and Ha-or Tov today."

"Bar Abba's men? Heading south?"

"What did you think?"

"Why did you leave bar Abba's gang?"

"We found Yeshua."

"Yes. Everyone in the Galil has found him. And what did you see?" Nakdimon inquired.

"Deborah got sick. Yeshua came with his talmidim. He put everyone out of the house except her mother and father. A handful of others. And then she woke up."

"She was . . . very ill."

"Dead, I'd say." The boy was matter-of-fact in his report.

"Yes. So it seemed."

"You doubt it now that you're a few days down the road. But I saw what I saw. And you saw it too." Avel covered his legs with the fresh straw. "What will you tell them?"

"Who?"

"The important men who give charity straw to the quarry Sparrows? The men who sit in the marble halls of the council chamber? The ones who sent you to bring a report?"

"You know a lot for a young boy."

"I carried the torches through the streets of Yerushalayim for the likes of your honor. Such important men often talk in front of Sparrows as if we're deaf. Or very dumb. But we're not. And so ask a little bird what secrets there are in Yerushalayim. We can tell more than you think."

"You're a clever lad. Would you like to come back to the city with me? Tell what you saw and heard to the learned rabbi Gamaliel?"

Avel shook his head firmly. "We're going to Beth-lehem."

"Why Beth-lehem?" It was a curious choice for a destination. Beth-lehem was an inconsequential village, mostly inhabited by shepherds. It was near the place where Rachel, wife of the patriarch Jacob, died giving birth to the youngest of Jacob's children. Her tomb was there still.

"To Migdal Eder."

"The Tower of the Flock? But why?" Nakdimon's interest was further aroused. There had always been a watchtower for the shepherds called *Migdal Eder,* ever since Jacob's day. Jacob, renamed *Isra'el* by the Lord God, had pitched his tents there, raised his flocks there, and reared his brood of twelve sons there.

"I have a message to carry to someone."

"The message being?"

Avel shook his head. "I'm only to mention it to the one it's for."

Nakdimon raised his eyebrows. "Well, then. Take your message to Beth-lehem and then come back to Yerushalayim. You give your report, and I promise I'll find an apprenticeship for you. What occupation would you like to learn?"

"I wanted to kill Romans. But I changed my mind." Avel glanced down at Emet's bloody feet. "Maybe a shoemaker. I'd make Emet a pair of shoes to fit his feet."

"Come along with me to the Holy City. Testify to what you saw in regard to your rebel friends and Yeshua, and I'll find you a position."

The child studied the crust of barley bread in his hand. "You saw what I saw. And you're a ruler of Israel. They'll take your word for it over mine."

"I'd like them to hear you."

"No, your honor, thank you. Now I'm a messenger."

Nakdimon probed. "What message? Who at Migdal Eder are you to see?" Was this a hint at rebellion? Clever. Who would suspect a child to carry word of Galilean revolt to the shepherds of the flock? It was a possibility.

Avel's mouth clamped tight. Had he read Nakdimon's curiosity as a threat? Yes. Perhaps it was a threat. What if these three children were part of the rebel band from the north? Did they bring some plan for revolution? The shepherds of Migdal Eder had easy access to the Temple when they brought their flocks in from Beth-lehem.

Nakdimon had pushed too hard. Avel was not talking. The boy slipped down into the bedding and squeezed his eyes shut. Avel was not asleep, Nakdimon knew, but he was finished with this conversation.

A wave of weariness washed over Nakdimon. He tucked his chin against his chest and finally drifted off.

ELOHIM

The next day it was not much out of the way to detour through Bethany on the way from Caesarea to Jerusalem. Marcus Longinus, acutely aware that Miryam lived nearby with her brother and spinster sister, slowed Pavor's pace as he approached the town.

The market square was bustling with activity. Mistresses of households, with children and servants following behind, moved from stall to stall.

Was she among them?

The aroma of baking bread surrounded him. It was a tangible thing, awakening his senses and making him hungry.

In the same way, he sensed her nearness. This was the street where she walked as a child. There, beyond the well, was the synagogue where her family had doubtless prayed. Behind the withered faces of merchants lurked memories of her girlhood, of her father, her mother, the scandal of a life taken by madness at the edge of the water.

What if he stepped from Pavor, his fiery black horse, and bought a bunch of figs to eat from that old woman under the striped awning? What if he asked her as he held out the coins, "Do you know Miryam? Sister of El'azar? What sort of young girl was she before her mother killed herself?"

Just to hear someone else describe her as she was, as she had been known! That would be like fresh hot bread to Marcus' famished soul.

Her soul was a flower before the stone fell on her.

And somehow, in an instant, Yeshua had made her bloom again. Then suddenly, without grief or guilt or bitterness to weigh her down, she had drifted away from Marcus forever. He stood tottering between the reality of his occupation and the hope that someone like Yeshua could change the world for the better.

Marcus, afflicted by duty and doubt, gladly afflicted others. He would not be good for Miryam since she had let go of her past. He wanted everything, wanted her as he had known her, though he loved her better now that she was someone else. After she met Yeshua, she wanted what she had only so she could give it away. Marcus would drag her down, weigh her down like stones, if she were to love him still.

He knew she didn't cling to even one shred of anger.

But he carried anger like a sword in its scabbard, waiting to be drawn and used.

If only he could see her . . .

He scanned the faces of the market crowd in search of her. He would know her walk, the way she held her head and reached out her hand to examine an orange.

She was not there.

He listened for the familiar laughter. He would follow the sound of it the way a weary man follows the path to a cool spring.

She was not there.

On impulse he stopped at the baker's stall and purchased a warm loaf. Holding it up to inhale the aroma he asked the baker, "The house of Master El'azar of Bethany? You know where it is?" Marcus felt clever that he hadn't let on he was really asking where Miryam the notorious sister lived.

The fellow eyed him with suspicion. Why would a centurion want to know such a thing? He raised a flour-dusted hand and pointed beyond the boundaries of the town toward a fig orchard and the red tiled roof of an enormous villa. "There." He might have added, *And what makes you think you'd be welcome?*

Marcus paid him a penny and bought a jug of cider to wash down his breakfast. He stood in the street for a while and stared at the red roof floating like an island on the green sea of the orchard.

As he rode past the lane that led to Miryam's home he imagined what she would be doing at this hour of the morning. Perhaps she would walk out? Stroll with her sister into the village, see him riding by on Pavor, greet him and gaze at him the way she used to?

But the lane remained empty.

Still, he wondered if she was somehow aware of his passing by so near her this morning.

■ ■ ■ ■

The journey south from Galilee had been long and dusty. Nakdimon's three youthful companions on the back of the donkey had finally lapsed into the silence of exhaustion. Forward progress along the highway slowed as they approached the eastern bank of the river.

The waters of the Jordan were swollen with heavy Spring rains. The ford beyond Jericho was usually no higher than mid-calf. Today the current was swift and waist deep, making the crossing difficult.

On this eastern bank Jacob had wrestled with the Angel of *Adonai's* Presence. At the end of the struggle Jacob was renamed *Isra'el*, meaning "Prince of God."

It was also near this place that the Lord had parted the waters of the river for Jacob's descendants. Led by the Ark of the Covenant and carrying the bones of Jacob's son Joseph, the Israelites had returned from Egypt's slavery to the land promised to their fathers.

Evidence of the Lord's power had not been visible in Israel for centuries, Nakdimon mused, as he took his place in the line waiting to cross. No parting of waters. No pillar of fire. No Shekinah glory suffusing the sanctuary. What was the Temple if the Shekinah was not within? Glorious stones rising like a mountain on Zion. Songs of praise. Endless prayers for forgiveness. The collecting of tithes. The bleating of tens of thousands of sheep. The blood of sacrifices.

But no miracles.

Nakdimon considered again that this crowd of farmers and peasants, a microcosm of the nation, was thickly larded with thieves, tax collectors, and rebels. Saint and sinners, they were the children of Israel. They crossed over Jordan into the land as one nation.

In recent days the cry of Yochanan the Baptizer could be heard on this riverbank: *"Teshuvah! Return! Turn your heart to the Lord! The Kingdom of God is near! Behold the Lamb of God who takes away the sin of the world!"*

Until Yeshua of Nazareth arrived on the scene, miracles over the centuries had been few and far between.

Hope among the *am ha aretz*, the people of the land, had grown cold over generations.

Until now.

Perhaps the waters of the Jordan did not magically part today. Yet the tangible sense of expectation passed from one person to another. The throng inched forward to cross over Jordan in memory of the first Exodus, the first coming home to the land of Israel.

Yeshua of Nazareth! Worker of miracles! Prophet! Deliverer! Messiah? Lamb of God? Surely he will come to claim David's throne in Yerushalayim and free us from tyranny!

A rope stretched from shore to shore across the expanse to steady those who waded into the water. A long unbroken line of pilgrims, children on shoulders, belongings on heads, passed beneath the outstretched arms of a priest.

He and they sang in antiphonal chorus as they stepped into the stream: "*I will lift up my eyes to the hills—where does my help come from?*"

And from the waters the people responded with the chorus, "*My help comes from the Lord, the Maker of heaven and earth.*"

From the west bank a second priest blessed them yet again as they entered Eretz-Israel, *The Land!* "*He will not let your foot slip—He who watches over you will not slumber; indeed He who watches over Israel will neither slumber nor sleep.*"

And so continued the songs of ascent throughout the thousands who crossed.

"*The Lord will watch over your coming and going both now and forevermore . . .*"

Ancient words took on fresh meaning as the river washed away dust from outside the land. Was this to be a new day for Israel?

Nakdimon, donkey and boys in tow, approached the water's edge. Of all those generations that had crossed this river to find the promise, was he finally living in the age that would see God's promises fulfilled on earth?

The priests and people sang the words of Psalm 132:

> "*For the sake of David your servant,*
> *do not reject your anointed one.*
> *The Lord swore an oath to David,*
> *a sure oath that he will not revoke:*
> *One of your descendants*
> *I will place on your throne.*"

Was the name of that son of David Yeshua? God Saves? Immanu'el? God-with-us?

A sense of awe and hope mingled inextricably with terror as Nakdimon led the boys across the wide Jordan. What if this was not the hour of Israel's deliverance? What if Yochanan the Baptizer had been wrong in his declaration that Yeshua was the Lamb of God who would take away Israel's sin? What if Yeshua wasn't the one Israel had been waiting for? Longing for? A lifetime had been spent hoping the promised King would come and rule in justice and mercy in Jerusalem!

What if Yeshua was not the fulfillment of the prophecies? Could Nakdimon carry a good report back to his uncle Gamaliel and not also express his doubts?

Nakdimon thought of his children waiting for him back in Jerusalem. If he judged this affair wrongly in favor of a false messiah, they would be in danger.

It was this last concern that caused Nakdimon to weigh carefully what words he would offer to Gamaliel about Yeshua. How could anyone be sure?

Nakdimon sang with the others in the stream as the torrent rose above his waist:

> *"For the Lord has chosen Zion,*
> *He has desired it for his dwelling:*
> * 'This is my resting place*
> *forever and ever;*
> *here I will sit enthroned,*
> *for I have desired it—*
> *I will bless her with abundant provisions;*
> *her poor will I satisfy with food*
> *I will clothe her priests with salvation,*
> *and her saints will ever sing for joy.*
> *Here I will raise up a king for David*
> *and set a lamp for my Anointed One!*
> *I will clothe His enemies with shame,*
> *but the crown on His head will be resplendent.'"*

Washed clean from the waters of the Jordan, they entered the territory of Judah. Bethany and Jerusalem lay ahead in one direction. The most direct route to Beth-lehem and Migdal Eder, the Tower of the Flock, was another.

Nakdimon offered, "Come back with me to Yerushalayim and I'll see to it you have apprenticeships."

Avel, as leader and spokesman for the trio, declined the invitation. "Our path leads only to Beth-lehem! Only to Zadok of Migdal Eder. We are messengers. Yeshua said we shouldn't go anywhere but to Zadok."

And so it was settled. *Yeshua* had given the command and these three orphans would not deviate from his word even for their own good.

At the fork in the road, Nakdimon and the donkey parted company with the boys. Nakdimon paused and watched them until they disappeared from sight over a low hill.

Somehow, he had the feeling he would see them again.

■ ■ ■ ■

Marcus leaned over the parapet of the Antonia fortress. His view in the deepening twilight first took in the Temple Mount, where the evening sacrifice was just concluding. The Roman-held tower on which he stood was the highest point in the city. At his feet lay the whole expanse of Jerusalem, from the cross-shaped form of the Temple sanctuary, to the magnificent palace built by Herod the Great on the western hill.

The courtyards and terraces of the Temple were packed with worshippers and sightseers, as were the streets of Jerusalem. The approaching Passover celebration was one of the pilgrim feasts, gathering whole families of Jews from all over Judea and the Galil. Indeed from other parts of the empire many had started on their journeys weeks earlier. The number of people crammed into the Holy City doubled at this time of year, with every house swarming with friends, relatives, and even total strangers who could by Jewish religious laws of hospitality claim lodging.

Guard Sergeant Quintus, old enough to be Marcus' father, was at his side. "Sorry you're not back in command here, sir," he offered sympathetically. "Just a month ago you stopped a riot, that's certain, where Praetorian Vara would have killed thousands to accomplish the same thing."

Quintus had been with Marcus through many years of their service to Rome. He didn't understand Marcus' sympathy for the Jews, but he respected Marcus as an officer and a warrior. Clearly, Quintus argued, it was misguided politics to send Marcus off to supervise a building project when the larger need was here.

As tesserarius of First Cohort, Quintus had risen as far as his ambition, education, and intellect could take him. But Marcus found his insights invaluable. Marcus was anxious to hear everything Quintus suspected but had no wish to openly encourage disloyalty. "Praetorian Vara has the confidence of the governor," he said simply.

Quintus spat a date seed over the battlements, but in deference to Marcus, aimed it to fall outside the Temple Mount platform. "He must," Quintus agreed. "Two full legions posted here in the last month. Half the whole force in the province, and they say another legion is coming with the governor and Tribune Felix. Scarcely enough left elsewhere to guard caravan routes and such, and them the dregs. All the best cohorts are here."

"Expecting trouble, then?"

Quintus gestured toward the city, where the first lighted torches of the Jerusalem Sparrows were appearing. "A million Jews. Those from foreign parts just now hearing about the execution of their holy man, the Baptizer. Others up in arms about some sacrilege to do with Temple money. The place is ripe for rebels and assassination and riots. You can feel the tension everywhere."

The bustle echoing up from below faded as the crowds drifted away from the Temple. Previously masked noises replaced it: the bawling complaints of legions of lambs. The holy mountain was always partly a stockyard because of the ongoing sacrifices, but this time of year the pens were full to bursting.

Jewish law required that one sacrificial lamb must be provided for every ten to twenty worshippers for the Passover supper. That obligation meant that in addition to the usual flocks of animals the number of lambs for this one ceremony would increase by thousands and thousands. Twice as many as Marcus could see would . . . every one . . . have their blood spilled before the week was out.

Marcus hoped the Jewish God would confine the bloodshed only to lambs, but he doubted it. He too had noted the strain in the atmosphere.

"Two whole legions?" Marcus queried. "I haven't noticed anything like that number of troopers. Where are they?"

"That's just it," Quintus explained, pointing toward his own red tunic. "First Cohort is in uniform . . . some others too. But fully a legion and a half are wearing cloaks over their swords and going about in disguise. Vara says he's got a surprise ready for any rebels who show up; that he's ready for anything that might go wrong."

"Vara is *hoping* for something to go wrong," Marcus declared in an unguarded moment. "Watch yourself, Quintus," he added. "Something bad is coming. I can feel it."

"Needn't worry about me, sir," Quintus returned stoutly. "The back of my neck has been prickling this week, same as it was before the Cherusci came howling out of that German forest. But you're right. Let any Jewish prophet or rebel leader speak a single word of revolt, and he'll find a Roman boot on his throat double-quick."

Marcus did not feel reassured. Quintus was a good man who did not go about looking for trouble, but all the Roman troopers in Judea and many of their commanders were Syrian, Samaritan, Idumean, or of other nationalities equally hostile to Jews. Given Vara's ruthless leadership, such men might quickly decide that *all* Jewish throats needed to be stepped on. Marcus hoped again that Yeshua of Nazareth would stay far away from Jerusalem for at least the next week.

"Tomorrow I'm taking a detail to Jericho," Quintus noted. "Would you care to accompany us?"

Since Marcus had no authority over any of the soldiers in Jerusalem, it was a courteous gesture meant to show Quintus' respect for him.

"No, thank you, Quintus," Marcus replied. "My orders are to inspect the aqueduct project. Tomorrow I'm riding to the far end of the construction. I'll work my way back from there . . . in time to return to Jerusalem by Passover," he added significantly.

This warranted a tightened jaw and a quick gesture of approval. "I'm glad of that, sir," Quintus said.

■ ■ ■ ■

Nakdimon came to the house of El'azar of Bethany after sundown. *Better not to travel on to Yerushalayim in the dark,* he reasoned, and besides, there were important matters to discuss.

He was welcomed and offered quarters for the night. It was as if the siblings wanted to reconnect with someone who had also experienced the wonder of events in Galilee.

He sat down to supper with El'azar, Marta, and Miryam. They had not been on the hillside when Yeshua fed the multitudes, so Nakdimon repeated the story. Details were being passed on from person to person and village to village throughout the land. No doubt the tale would reach the ears of the Sanhedrin and High Priest Caiaphas before Nakdimon arrived in Jerusalem.

Nakdimon shared with the siblings what had unfolded before his eyes: the feeding of thousands on what had been five barley loaves and two fish. There followed a cry from the people that Yeshua should be King! But he denied the offer and disappeared into the hills at dusk.

Miryam, her deep brown eyes shining when she spoke, recounted, "It's been half a year since he changed my life and I first followed him. And there isn't ink enough to record what Yeshua has done and said."

Short, plump Marta and lean El'azar exchanged looks. It was clear the most amazing miracle in their lives had been the beautiful Miryam's

change of heart. And perhaps, Nakdimon thought, the radical difference in their own attitudes.

"I was a cynic." El'azar dipped his bread into the sauce. "But no
more."

His openness brought Nakdimon to the point. "Would you be willing, if called upon, to share what you witnessed before the council?
Even if it cost your standing among the elders?"

"I'll tell what I saw! What really happened," El'azar declared, scratch-
ing his wiry, reddish beard. "Anywhere. To anyone. It doesn't matter
what it costs."

At this Marta's thin lips pressed together in a tight line of disagreement, but she said nothing. Instead she rose from the table and cleared
the dishes. It was plain that the dowdy, middle-aged spinster was not
quite willing to throw everything out the window and follow the Master.

Miryam, on the other hand, smiled and placed her hand on her
brother's sleeve. "So, El'azar! You're willing to give everything you have
to follow him. To speak the truth bravely, even if it means losing all?
Reputation? Position? Respect of others?"

"A small price compared to what this may mean to Israel, isn't it?
The restoration of our people to freedom." El'azar's clear green eyes
blazed with determination. "The return of righteous rule in Yerushalayim? Sending Herod Antipas and the Roman governor packing once
and for all? Yes! I'll risk everything for that!"

"Treason, brother," Miryam said. But she was smiling, evidently
pleased at her brother's change of heart.

"Here's to treason then," he said, gulping his wine.

"Then you've come to it at last," Miryam added softly. "As I did."

"Yes," El'azar replied, seeming surprised by his sister's assessment.
"It's too important, isn't it? We'd better get it right the first time."

Nakdimon informed them, "The Sanhedrin has hired fellows to
move with Yeshua's followers. Spies. Unsavory sorts. All of them. Twisting what they've seen and heard into something false. Accusing Yeshua
of wanting to overthrow Rome and the rulers of Israel. Ominous
threats. I've heard their testimony. We need men of standing to speak
the truth."

"There'll be many who stand with us," El'azar declared. "There are
men of intelligence and honesty on the council. Your uncle, Gamaliel?
What's he think about this?"

Nakdimon hesitated before answering. "He's wise to be cautious. I'll give him my report tomorrow when I get home. The *cohen hagadol*'s party is in opposition to Gamaliel. Looking for a way to discredit him. Yes. My uncle will require proof. He'll need to see a sign for himself. And Yeshua doesn't give signs for the sake of proving something to someone. Only to touch on a need, I think. Gamaliel may want to meet with you ahead. That is, if your testimony is accepted before the council."

Miryam beamed. This cause of proclaiming the unarguable power of Yeshua of Nazareth had clearly united two parts of the estranged family.

Nakdimon observed Miryam. She was so utterly changed inside that even her physical appearance seemed altered. What had been hard and seductive before now had softened into a quiet beauty. Desirable in a different way, and yet . . .

Nakdimon guarded his thoughts. No. Miryam's history remained a subject of gossip. Changed though she might be, she could never again be considered respectable among polite society. No acts of charity in faraway Magdala could restore what people knew about her past.

His hand touched hers as they dipped their bread. Warm color climbed into his face.

She averted her eyes. There was an awkward pause. Did she know what he was thinking?

Marta returned, her heavy face puckered in disapproval. Had she seen the way Nakdimon looked at Miryam?

As if to put an end to speculation, Miryam excused herself and retreated to her room.

Marta followed shortly after.

Discussion of politics and Israel's future continued into the late hours between El'azar and Nakdimon.

Nakdimon was keenly aware when the light shining from Miryam's slatted door finally went out. Only then did he excuse himself and wearily trudge upstairs to bed.

DAVAR

The rattle of dishes and the smell of food roused Nakdimon from his dreams. He washed and changed into clothing more suitable to his rank than the traveling clothes he had been wearing. Covering his head with his prayer shawl he began morning devotions.

He heard the light tread of a woman's footsteps on the balcony outside his room. Moments later the scent of perfume drifted in through the slatted door and lingered like a feminine presence in the chamber, clouding his focus. "Blessed are You . . ."

That would be Miryam, he thought. The notorious. The beautiful. And now the follower of the Rabbi of Nazareth. "O King of the Universe . . ."

Her voice answered the call to breakfast from her sister, Marta. "I'm coming! No. I don't know if he's up yet." Then a tentative rapping at his door. "Reb Nakdimon?"

He inhaled her fragrance, then cleared his throat gruffly. "A moment please . . . morning prayers," he informed her.

"Pardon," she whispered, and he did not hear her retreat.

He attempted to resume, but his thoughts were far from prayers. There were many things to think about: the certain conflict in Jerusalem, Yeshua of Nazareth, the response of the Sanhedrin and his uncle Gamaliel when he brought his report from Galilee.

And yet despite these weighty matters, Nakdimon was thinking about finding a mother for his children. Thinking about a wife. Remembering what it had been like to wake up beside Hadassah. And now imagining he might be able to wake up next to another woman and find the same measure of contentment.

He was, in spite of his recitation of the words of praise and blessing, thinking about the woman exuding the aroma of a garden as she walked past his door, enticing in her newfound innocence.

Except that her past put her beyond reach.

But not beyond dreaming.

Certainly Marta might make a more suitable mother for his seven offspring. But then he had servants to help with the children. And there was always his mother.

This morning his prayers were a jumble of once-again-awakened longings. Not for Hadassah, who was beyond his reach, but for someone very much alive.

He folded his tallith and left the bedchamber. Miryam was in the atrium, gazing into a pool of water. Long dark tresses cascaded over her shoulder.

At the closing of his door she glanced up and smiled at him. "Good morning, Reb Nakdimon. Did you sleep well?"

"Yes," he lied, not telling her that his sleep had been filled with visions of her.

■ ■ ■ ■

It was near evening on the third day of their journey when Emet, Avel, and Ha-or Tov reached the outskirts of Beth-lehem. The boys were tired from the long hike up from the ford of the Jordan near Jericho. Emet's feet were again raw and bloody.

Avel had set the rapid pace. Since their destination was in sight he now seemed willing to rest. "Ready to eat?"

Emet put a grubby hand to his empty stomach in reply. Hunger tore fiercely at his insides. "Please."

Ha-or Tov grumbled. "About time, I'd say."

Avel made for a large flat boulder where they could scan the horizon for the tower and finish the last of their barley loaves.

It was, Emet thought as they divided their supper, a kind of celebration. They had made their pilgrimage safely, and they would find the man they sought at Migdal Eder. They would give him Yeshua's message. Zadok would be their protector until Yeshua came for them.

"What does a tower look like?" Ha-or Tov queried.

"Tall and round like the trunk of a giant hollow tree. Made of stone."

Emet breathed a sigh of relief as he ate his meager supper and studied the landscape below them.

Beth-lehem, "the House of Bread," was appropriately named. The town was made of neat, whitewashed little dwellings with domed roofs that resembled loaves of unbaked dough on a baker's slab. The village had once been the home of Ruth, Boaz, Obed, Jesse, and David. It was surrounded by rich fields of winter wheat and threshing floors, like the one where Ruth had first spoken to Boaz, her kinsman redeemer.

Along the more precipitous slopes were terraced vineyards and almond orchards. Vast flocks of sheep grazed on the stubble of recent grain harvested in the valley nearby.

It was Avel who first spotted the Tower of the Flock. "There. Look there! Migdal Eder."

At the center of the pasture was the round stone structure. It was from this watchtower that Temple shepherds tended thousands of sheep purchased with sacred Korban money. These were the animals destined for sacrifice at the high altar in Jerusalem. All firstborn male lambs born in Beth-lehem within the vicinity of the Tower of Migdal Eder were set apart as offerings to the Most High.

The earth undulated like the surface of the Sea of Galilee.

"Sheep?" Ha-or Tov asked.

Emet nodded. He had never seen this many creatures in one place. "Thousands."

"Almost Passover," Avel explained. "Every day they'll take some of them from here to Yerushalayim for sacrifice."

Ha-or Tov gestured past the herd toward an enormous castle high on a hill beyond Beth-lehem. "But what's that?"

Avel explained, "Herodium. The fortress of the old dead king. The butcher king. They say it has ghosts. Haunted by the spirits of people he murdered. Demons dance on the walls, they say. Also, there are gardens and ponds where you can sail a boat. Marble and ivory on the floors, they say. A Roman garrison stays there. And the men who work on Pilate's aqueduct."

"I wouldn't sleep in such a place." Ha-or Tov's eyes grew wide, as if he was contemplating a night with devils dancing on the walls. "And I wouldn't want to be one of the traitors building Rome's aqueduct, either! It's cursed. I heard the rebels say it! It's cursed of God."

Emet could see the elevated arches of the aqueduct, which would carry water northward to Jerusalem when it was completed.

Compared to Roman building projects and the glowering palace of Herodium, Migdal Eder appeared insignificant.

Emet stared at the heights of Herodium. A chill coursed through him. It was an evil place, casting a long shadow over the peaceful valley of the sheepfold.

Avel wiped his mouth nervously on the back of his hand. Had he also sensed the darkness? He leapt to his feet. "Finish your bread," he ordered Emet and Ha-or Tov. "It'll be night soon. There's more than a mile to go. We stayed too long."

■ ■ ■ ■

Twilight pursued the boys down the slopes and into the Valley of the Sheepfold. From high atop the tower a shofar blared a signal that resounded across the swale.

Rousing, as if it recognized the meaning, the flock began to stir. The smell of dung grew strong as the animals were brought in from their pastures for the night. The racket of bleating drowned out other sounds. Dust choked the air.

As Emet, Avel, and Ha-or Tov approached Migdal Eder on a path between two pastures, Emet could see that vast acres extended out of sight. The near fields were divided by stone walls the height of a man's hip.

Pregnant ewes, sides bulging with imminent birthing, were nearest the Tower of Migdal Eder. Fat, woolly mothers with tiny, newborn lambs inhabited the next ring of pastures.

There were lambing stables built into caves along the limestone cliffs, stocks for shearing and castrating, and sheds for bales of wool. Beyond these was pasture for recently weaned lambs and fields where the ewes grazed freely with a ram picked for qualities to breed the finest offspring.

On the other side of the tower were holding pens to fatten the unblemished male lambs. There they awaited the journey up the road to Jerusalem.

Overseeing the sheep-rearing operation was an army of weather-hardened herdsmen. Crooked staffs in hand, they were accompanied by fierce-looking, sharp-fanged dogs. To Emet, the canine assistants looked as if they were merely one step removed from wolves, yet they trotted attentively at the sides of their masters. Commands were issued to them in the language of whistles, which instantly sent dogs to circle the herds and nip at the heels of reluctant sheep.

"Get up! Up! Up, I say! Return! Return! Return!" came the call from the tower, echoed throughout the valley by the throats of scores of shepherds.

Why had the Master sent the boys here? Emet wondered. And how, in this bustle, would they find the man named *Zadok*?

Avel, more confident than the other two, led the way. He had a strange smile on his lips, Emet noted. Avel marched toward Migdal Eder like someone coming home after a long journey.

Migdal Eder loomed five stories high. It had one door, and above the second story windows were set around at regular intervals.

Emet raised his face as a figure moved on the rooftop and leaned slightly over the parapet. A white-haired shepherd raised a shofar to his lips and issued one short, sharp note. This was followed by a series of calls, like a warning, and concluded with another clipped, emphatic blast. The signal reverberated in the hills as the gates of each sheepfold slid into place for the night.

■ ■ ■ ■

After spending the day in further discussions with El'azar, Nakdimon finally arrived at the gates of Jerusalem that night. He hired a pair of link boys to lead him home with their blazing torches.

Business was good, they told him when he asked. The country bumpkins in town for *pesach* needed guides to take them from one place to another. Yes, the Jerusalem Sparrows were enjoying a boom in business.

Nakdimon ventured, "Do you know a Sparrow named Avel?"

The two exchanged wary looks. "He's long gone."

"What happened to him?"

"Went to find the Messiah and kill Romans, last we heard."

"Who is the Messiah?" Nakdimon tested.

"Does it matter? As long as he sets Yerushalayim free. Kills our enemies! Everyone's looking for him to come this Holy Day. We'll join him and fight with Avel."

"A daunting task for one so young."

"He'll grow up. We'll grow up. Messiah will lead us, and then they'd better watch out!"

This was the sentiment on the streets. Remembering Avel and the poverty of the Sparrows, Nakdimon paid them twice the set fee for a link and sent them away.

At the sound of Nakdimon's voice, Zacharias, the elderly Ethiopian servant, threw back the gate and cried like a baby as Nakdimon entered.

"Oh, Master Nakdimon! We heard you'd been hurt! I told herself it was a rumor, but just the same we were worried! The children looked for you to come each day! Your uncle Gamaliel sent your servant Eli to the Galil yesterday to seek you. I suppose since you're here, he'll come back without you. The whole world is boiling like a stew. Not a time for a man to be away from his family. Your dear mother has been . . ."

"Nakdimon!" Nakdimon's mother, wrapped in bedclothes, scurried into the courtyard. She scolded, "Where have you been?"

He embraced her, kissed her cheek. "How are the girls?"

"All six of them . . . in need of a mother."

"And little Samuel?"

"In need of a mother."

"Well, Em, I've come home empty-handed this time. Nothing in my satchel could remotely pass for a female. A grandmother will have to do for a while longer, I suppose." An image of Miryam flitted through his mind. But no. Not Miryam either. Not unless they closed the Yerushalayim house and moved to Gaul.

Em patted his cheek. "You need a bath, son." She flicked her fingers, sending Zacharias off to deposit the donkey in the stable and heat water for Nakdimon. "Are you hungry?"

"I ate today at the house of El'azar in Bethany."

Her eyebrows went up. "Stopped at that house, did you? Poor tragedy."

"They traveled with me to the Galil to hear the Rabbi of Nazareth. They're not the same since."

She was dismissive. "You can't easily erase such misfortune and shame. It lingers like the smell of . . ." She paused, sniffed, and frowned. "Nakdimon! You'll wake the dead. Go wash and change your clothes. I'll fetch a bite of supper. A little wine. You can tell me all about it. Good?"

■ ■ ■ ■

At Migdal Eder men converged on the tower from all directions. Their charges temporarily stowed away for the night, it was time for a quick meal.

Hesitating outside the massive wooden door, Emet smelled a delicious aroma: a pot of simmering stew. Whereas moments earlier he had been happy with a bit of bread the fresh assault on his senses made him hope that Zadok was both easily located and generous.

The arriving shepherds were tired men, burned dark brown by the sun. Coarse-featured, greasy, and smelly, they were also men of short sentences, as if spending much time amid the constant noise of their animals had reduced their ability to speak other than in clipped phrases.

Avel was in front. "Come on!" he urged, dragging Emet by the arm.

At the unexpected approach of three boys in matching robes, several of the herdsmen nudged their comrades in their ribs.

One burly fellow planted himself squarely across the boys' path before they could enter. "What d'ya want here?" he inquired. "Clear off. No beggars allowed."

"Please, sir," Avel said in a respectful manner he learned as a Jerusalem Sparrow, "we've come to see Zadok. We've brung a message for Zadok."

"I'm Jehu, chief shepherd of milk goats. I'll take the message to himself," he declared importantly.

"We were told to find Zadok," Avel persisted.

"Zadok is it?" challenged their interrogator. "Tax collector sent you? Afraid to come himself?"

This sally brought a gale of rough laughter from the shepherds. "Look 'ere! They're in uniform too!"

Emet, ready to turn and run, was proud of Avel for standing his ground. "No, sir," Avel persisted. "No tax collector. We've come all the way from Galilee with a message for Zadok."

Jehu bent down eye level with Avel. He sneered through blackened teeth. "And did the sender tell you Zadok bites the heads off little boys? Answer me that!"

Another herdsman, slimmer than Jehu, cautioned, "Enough, Jehu! If they know Zadok's name their message must be real. Else why would they come clear out here?"

From inside the ground-floor hall of the tower came the sound of dice rattling in a cup. This was followed by a clatter as the lots were cast on the paving stones.

"Jehu!" bellowed a voice from within. "You've drawn first watch! Get back up to the high field. There's been a jackal hanging about the draw. Stay sharp!"

"But I haven't et yet," bawled Jehu in protest.

The noise of rattling spoons stopped, and the murmur of voices within was replaced by the menacing stomp of heavy feet coming toward the door.

Emet backed up into Ha-or Tov, and even Avel shrank away.

So did Jehu's companions.

The figure that appeared in the lighted doorway was massive, almost filling the full height of the entry. He was square except for a slight slope to his left shoulder. His white beard, parted in the middle, was braided into two cords tucked into the front of his robe. Likewise, his long white hair was plaited into a single thick cable.

But it was his face that drew Emet's attention. In place of his left eye was a patch that emphasized, rather than disguised, the cause of his loss. The cleft of a scar began at his hairline, passed beneath the scrap of black leather, and reemerged to continue down to his jaw. Someone had tried to cleave his head in two and nearly succeeded.

"Were y' arguing with me?" growled the one-eyed apparition.

"No, Zadok," Jehu responded. "I . . . these boys . . . a message."

"Get!" Zadok roared. The unfortunate Jehu disappeared toward the fields. Zadok turned his good eye toward the trio. "Triplets, is it? Same ewe? Or is your coat stole off the same drying line?"

Emet was disappointed. The kind Yeshua had sent them all this way to encounter such an ogre as this Zadok! They had not stolen their clothes! Why would he insult them in such a way? Emet considered saying this, but the appearance of Zadok made him forget that he had a voice.

Zadok growled, "What's this about a message?"

Visibly plucking up his courage, Avel advanced again. "Yeshua of Nazareth sent us to you."

"Who?" Zadok demanded. "I don't know anyone in Nazareth. And I'm not taking on any more apprentices this season! Ten thousand lambs a day to move to Yerushalayim; ten thousand more being born! What was the Almighty thinking of when he put Passover in lambing time?" That this complaint was as old as Passover itself did not reduce the agreeing mutters from the herdsmen. "Hardly time enough for the lambing! None for suckling children."

Emet was ready to agree and run away. If this was the one Yeshua had sent them to, he'd rather take his chances with bar Abba!

Avel was tongue-tied till Ha-or Tov poked him in the back. "Give him the message!"

"Sir," Avel ventured quickly, before Zadok could roar again, "he said . . . Yeshua that is . . . he said to tell you . . . Immanu'el is coming."

Zadok stopped and straightened his back so that he rose even taller. From Emet's point of view the man reared as high as the tower itself.

"Immanu'el?" he repeated, giving a thoughtful tug at his beard. His eye narrowed. "So. He said that, did he?"

"Yes, sir," Avel replied. "He said it was the proof we needed."

"Did he, now?"

"Yes, sir."

"And three scrawny yearlings are messengers, are they?"

"He sent us. If that's what you mean." Avel puffed out his chest defiantly.

"Have y' names and rank then, to come here with such a bold word?" Zadok's mouth twitched slightly in amusement.

"I've been called Avel. I was lately of the Company of Sparrows who carry torches through the streets of Yerushalayim."

"Aye? A link boy, are y'? A beggar just the same." Then Zadok inclined his head and glared at Ha-or Tov. "And what about yourself? Red hair like a torch. A link boy too, then?"

"No sir." Ha-or Tov stepped forward bravely. "I'm Ha-or Tov. Lately blind beggar at the gates of El'azar of Bethany."

"Blind, eh? An imposter, eh?"

"No, sir!" Ha-or Tov challenged.

"Well, then, Good Light. And have y' also got a message for me?" Zadok demanded.

Ha-or Tov considered the question. He stuck out his chin and stared openly at the patch and the scar. "When he comes, you'll see."

Zadok raised the patch, revealing the sagging eyelid and empty socket. "Not likely." The patch snapped back. His large face swiveled to take in Emet. "What about you, boy? Must I find a ewe to suckle y'? Or are y' weaned?"

Emet nodded, uncertain how to answer. "My sister left me with Avel so she could be a slave. But I'm too little to be a Sparrow. I'm Emet."

"Well, then!" Zadok bellowed. "The Truth at last blown in with the wind. And what am I supposed to do with it?"

Emet's chin quivered. "The stew smells good."

"So it does. Come with me, then," Zadok said, scattering the listening shepherds with a sudden turn on his heel. There was a flurry of activity within the tower as Zadok shouted for a clay pot of stew and a jug of milk to be brought to him. Tucking the containers into a leather pouch slung round his neck, he strode out into the darkness without further comment. He walked up the path but did not look back to see if the boys were following.

At a single snap of Zadok's fingers, two dogs appeared out of nowhere. With pricked ears and pointed muzzles, they flanked the man one step behind him. As if the shepherd were not menacing enough, his wolf-like companions added another layer of apprehension to Emet's pounding heart.

Zadok's stride was so long and the pace he set so vigorous that Emet, Ha-or Tov, and Avel jogged to keep up. Nor did the flock master believe in wasting time with paths or gates. When a stone wall loomed across his chosen course, Zadok stepped over with scarcely any effort and no discernible loss of speed.

Boys and dogs were left to scramble after him as best they could. All the while the night was full of the rustle of sheep. Even their soft plaintive sounds struck Emet's ears as powerful when multiplied by tens of thousands.

Emet wanted to ask what this was about, where they were going, where this giant was leading them. But he had no extra breath for inconsequentials. And, anyway, Zadok's manner didn't encourage conversation.

As the evening deepened, so too did the slope become steeper and the earth underfoot more uneven. Leaving the pastures and pens behind, the group climbed toward the sheds and caves tucked under a limestone ridge.

By glancing over his shoulder, Emet glimpsed the Tower of Migdal Eder, like a candle flame glowing in the distance. How had they come this far already? How much farther were they going? His feet, already blistered and bloody from their trek, ached miserably. Every step made him grit his teeth. The boys were no longer in an arc close behind the dogs but were strung out in a line, with Avel in the lead, Ha-or Tov next, and Emet falling more and more to the rear.

Finally Emet slipped on a patch of gravel and fell. Although he jumped up as fast as he could, Zadok was nearly out of sight. When Emet tried to run to catch up, he limped with the burning pain in his right foot and cried out, "Wait!"

Zadok's form swung around. It seemed to Emet that the shepherd recrossed the intervening space in no more than three strides. Without speaking or warning, Zadok bent down and scooped Emet up. He tossed the boy over one shoulder like a wayward lamb.

Suddenly Emet was flying. It was like he'd been seized by an eagle and swung upward into the sky. With his head bobbing beside Zadok's braid of hair, the ground appeared very far away, and his two friends very short indeed.

As the climb stiffened, Emet heard Avel's breath come in gasps; Ha-or Tov made puffing sounds. Even the dogs lunged into each step to keep up with their master. But Zadok seemed unaffected by the climb.

Then, as abruptly as it began, Emet's flight was over. Lifted off Zadok's shoulder, he was deposited beneath an overhanging cliff halfway up the hillside. A horizontal strip of light streaked the bluff's face, identifying a low crevice that opened into a cavern.

"Lambing barn," Zadok said as Avel and Ha-or Tov struggled up the last bit of incline to reach the level landing. He put Emet down. "Stay," Zadok said, pointing a bony index finger downward.

The two dogs, revealed by the glow of lamplight to be alike in form but differing in color, sat immediately. The one with the reddish coat studied the hillside for potential threats, but the darkly mottled one never took his blue eyes off Zadok.

Emet wasn't sure if the command applied to boys as well as dogs. But when the shepherd ducked his head and entered the cramped fissure, Avel did also, followed an instant later by the others.

Once past the entry the ceiling height opened enough for Zadok to walk upright, but the space retained a hushed, almost reverent air. The grotto stretched quite far along the face of the cliff, but didn't extend too far back into it. Emet saw that most of the space was taken up with cramped pens, some containing ewes about ready to deliver and others with mothers and tiny, newly born offspring.

"Is this where you were taking us?" Avel asked. "Or are we going on somewhere else? I've never seen this many sheep. Are they yours? This is nicer than the quarry where the Sparrows live."

The bubbling queries produced a ripple effect on the flock. Throughout the cavern ewes lifted their heads from munching hay or turned from nuzzling lambs to seek the source of the unknown voice.

Zadok raised his index finger again. But instead of pointing he held it in front of Avel's lips, silencing him.

The flickering oil lamps played tricks with shadows, exaggerating the cleft of the scar on Zadok's face, making him *more* frightening. Who would argue with him?

Zadok led them along the third row of pens. Unlike the dusty pastures and open paddocks where hundreds of sheep milled about, the air in this enclosure was sweet. The aisles between the stalls were swept, the straw in every enclosure freshly changed.

The flock master stopped about fifteen yards down the rank. In this particular stall was a single ewe, bulging so much at the sides that she appeared as broad from side-to-side as she was long from head-to-tail. Near her, kneeling in the straw, was a young man Emet guessed to be twenty years old from his size. Of the shepherds Emet had seen, this was the cleanest. His clothes were not dusty. Though he wore an apron from neck to knees, it was unspotted.

In a whisper so low that Emet had not imagined Zadok capable of it, the shepherd said, "How is she, Lev?"

Lev shook his head. "Nothing yet. More'n one in there, sure. Going to bust if she don't go soon."

Lev's manner and speech convinced Emet he had been wrong about the man's age. He sounded much younger than he appeared.

"She'll go tonight," Zadok said, peering at the ewe's flanks and belly for signs apparently discernible only to him. "Come get me if there's trouble. What about thirty-one?"

"I worked her good, like you showed me. Going back there next."

"Stop and eat first," Zadok said, setting down the clay pot of stew outside the pen.

Emet eyed the stew hungrily. So Zadok intended for Lev to eat it.

Zadok instructed Lev, "Keep using that goose grease on her bag and keep stripping the milk from the blocked teat."

"Yes, sir," Lev replied. "I won't forget."

Emet saw Avel exchange a glance with Ha-or Tov and mouth the word "Half-wit."

"Anything else?" Zadok queried.

"Old Girl looks to go tonight too," Lev ventured.

Zadok agreed. "She's been down that road often enough to give lessons . . . be no trouble there, I warrant." Then a thought appeared to strike Zadok and he fingered the corner of his eyepatch. "What about the black who was rejected by his mother?"

Lev's head dropped. "Doing what I can for him. He'll take milk off my fingers but no ways else, and I can't be there all the time, can I?"

"He won't make it then," Zadok declared. "All right."

Emet was unaccountably saddened. A motherless lamb would die for want of care. He shivered, though the air in the lambing cavern was not chill.

"Are y' gonna sleep, sir?" Lev asked.

Zadok nodded. "After finishing my rounds."

Lev persisted. "You've not slept in three days, sir. Things was different when herself was with us. She'd not allowed it."

To Emet's surprise there was no explosion of ill temper. Instead Zadok answered quietly, "You're right. It *was* different then. But I'm going to the house. I'll be there if you need me."

Outside the lambing caves Zadok again scooped up Emet, snapped his fingers for Red Dog and Blue Eye, and the procession was off on another cross-country trek. Though the night was deep and the path poorly marked, the hike was neither long nor strenuous.

The yellow moon rose like a fire on the hills.

As the limestone outcropping slid northward toward Jerusalem, the height of the cliff diminished. In no more than five minutes' walk, at Zadok's pace, the ridge had shrunk to a rolling hill. On the brow of the last knoll, before the crest subsided completely, stood Zadok's home.

Though it overlooked Beth-lehem, it could not be called part of the town. It was still closer to the sheepfolds than to the village.

From Emet's bouncing perch he could see that the squat, square building was freshly whitewashed. A set of exterior stairs scaling the west wall gave access to the roof, while behind the structure was a bit of garden.

As they neared the house Emet noticed that the air swirled with a kaleidoscope of scents: sweet and tangy, pungent and cloying. He couldn't understand where it was coming from. He saw no orchards nearby, certainly no flowers blooming. There was the garden plot, and it was mostly barren because of the time of year.

Upended again, Emet was deposited on the doorstep and told to wait with the others. Zadok retrieved a live coal from his cook fire, blew it into flame against a bit of lint, then lit a pair of lamps.

The dwelling had two rooms. The room in which Emet stood contained a table and benches, a cook pot and shelves. A doorless opening beside the fireplace gave access to the one room beyond. That was all.

All, except that the aromas of spice and flowers were still more intense inside the house than they were outside.

"Sit," Zadok instructed. Apparently this time he did mean boys and dogs both, for while Emet, Ha-or Tov, and Avel sat on one bench facing the fire, Red Dog and Blue Eye guarded the ends of the table. "Take off your shoes," Zadok commanded.

Over the smoldering coals hung a pair of large kettles. From one vessel Zadok ladled warm water into a wooden bowl. Stretching upward he retrieved two bundles of dried plants hanging from the rafters.

That was when Emet discovered that the rafters were blooming thick with dried flowers and herbs. The ceiling was a garden of preserved plants. Some, like sage, he recognized; others were unfamiliar. But they combined to produce a sense of wholesome purity.

Crushing pale blue flowers together with dark green leaves, Zadok kneaded the mass into the bowl as if making bread.

"Lavender and mint," Zadok said. "You first, I think," he added, indicating Emet.

With surprising gentleness in one so gruff and apparently harsh, Zadok massaged and soothed Emet's scraped and blistered feet. Though the warm water and the scent of the herbs combined to make him sleepy, with Zadok kneeling close in front of him Emet was able to study the black eyepatch and horrific old wound close up.

Who was this man who was such a mix of contradictions? What was his story? And why had Yeshua sent them to him?

Emet looked away quickly when Zadok raised up, before the old man caught him staring at the eyepatch.

When Zadok finished patting Emet's feet dry, he rubbed goose grease into the worst sores and bound them loosely with linen strips. "That should serve for now," he said. "There's broth in the other kettle. Help yourself. Bowls on the shelf."

As Zadok proceeded to minister next to Ha-or Tov, Emet selected a bowl from the stack on a shelf. The walls of Zadok's home were bare except for the shelves that ran around three sides of the room. Clay pots, drinking cups, and utensils were neatly arranged in a precise, orderly fashion.

Emet couldn't explain exactly, but the home displayed a feminine touch. It had no finery about it, but something spoke of a now-absent woman's loving care.

Ha-or Tov wasn't shy about Zadok's injury. "You know," he said, "you should go to Reb Yeshua. He'd fix your eye for you. I know."

Emet tensed. Was that too much of a challenge to the man? Would he turn surly again, or get angry?

Zadok grunted. "Is that so? Well . . ." Then he refreshed the medicinal soak and began to work on Avel.

Emet breathed a sigh of relief.

When Avel's feet had likewise been doctored and all three boys had eaten their fill of broth, Zadok directed them into the room at the rear. "Straw-filled pallets in the corner," he said. "The sheep fleece is to lay on. Go to sleep. We'll talk tomorrow. I've got my accounts to cast up."

The soft white wool beneath him was unlike anything Emet had ever felt against his skin. Both Ha-or Tov in the middle and Avel against the far wall lapsed into sleep seconds after lying down. Emet, on the outer edge of the bed, closed his eyes. He inhaled the aromas and breathed a sigh of contentment. Such luxury! Was he dreaming? If he had lain down in a palace, could he have experienced such comfort? He forced himself to stay awake, to relish this sense of well-being and to observe the old shepherd as he moved about the other room.

Zadok produced a wax tablet from inside the fold of his robes. With a sharpened goose quill dipped in ink, he transferred the tally of lambs born to a more permanent record on a parchment scroll.

All the while the dogs blinked up from where they lay by the fire. They followed their master's every move.

Emet struggled against sleep. He watched as Zadok finished his work, then took down a tall clay jar from a shelf. From it the old man removed another scroll covered with columns of Hebrew script. Zadok spread the document out on his table and began to study, line by line, in the lamplight. What was he searching for?

The old man glanced up at Emet. A flicker of amusement crossed his face. "Still awake?"

Emet pressed his lips together. "Yes, sir."

"Do y' know what day it is?"

"No, sir."

"*Shabbat.* The day of rest."

"I'm not tired, sir."

"The only ones excused from rest on *Shabbat* are shepherds of Migdal Eder at lambing time. The Almighty makes exception for those who tend his sheep."

"I like it here," Emet ventured.

"So y' must have a shepherd's heart then, eh boy? Else you'd be resting."

"I hear the sheep. Far off. Like music."

Zadok scanned the text before him. "The one who sent you to me?"

"Yeshua?"

"How old a man is he, now?"

"Couldn't say, sir." Emet could merely judge faces as young, middle, and old. He did not know what "how old" meant. "Not as old as you. Older than Lev. I don't know."

"Did he tell y' why you're to come here? To Migdal Eder? To me?"

"He said you needed us."

The corner of Zadok's mouth turned up. "Did he, now? I need you? To tend the flocks? To herd the sheep?"

"To remind you, he said. I don't know what he meant. He said . . . since she was gone . . . you needed us. We didn't know who she is. But he said what he said . . . and then he left. We came to Beth-lehem to find you and give you the message."

"To tell me Immanu'el was coming?"

"Yes, sir."

The old shepherd's face clouded with unexpressed emotion. He leaned forward with interest. "Do y' know the meaning of *Immanu'el,* boy?"

"I don't know much of anything, sir."

"Well, then. It's enough you've come." Zadok lapsed into silence and returned to his study.

For a long time Emet watched the old man search column after column of text. The fleece beneath the boy was soft and warm. Emet struggled to keep his lids from closing. But in the end . . . no use. No use.

The shepherd, buried in concentration, was hunched over the writings when Emet finally gave in to sleep.

■ ■ ■ ■

That same night, over cold chicken, apples, cheese, and wine, Nakdimon told the story of Yeshua and the events in the Galil to his mother.

Skeptical and wary, she received the message coolly. "I'm an old woman, Nakdimon. I've seen enough of this sort of thing come and go to know that hope for a Messiah always ends in someone's death. Stand back from it awhile before you carry such tales to Gamaliel and the Sanhedrin."

"I have to tell what I've seen. What I know."

"There's a frenzy in the streets already. People whisper in the souks that the hour has arrived. I'm sure I don't know what hour they're talking about, but it's making the *cohanim* nervous I can tell you!"

"If he comes . . ."

"If he comes it won't end well. I didn't raise a fool for a son. You know what could happen."

"Em, I don't believe he's preaching the overthrow of any government. Only the tearing down of what's false in us . . . in our hearts . . . and building something pure and clean again."

She exhaled in disapproval. "Fanatic."

"Righteous man."

"Fanatics usually are righteous until you peel away the message and find pure lust for power underneath."

"Em . . . Mother . . . his is a different sort of power . . . mercy and love . . . I wish you could hear him."

"If he comes to Yerushalayim, the whole world will hear him! In chains he'll give testimony about his kingdom, and Rome will nail him to the nearest cross. Mark my words! Could he be such a fool as to come here now?"

"When the time is right . . ."

"So much for another Messiah. They're as common as sparrows these days. A Messiah in every family tree and on the branch of Jesse . . . or whatever it was Isaiah wrote about him. It's a fable. Not meant to be taken literally. It costs too much to believe such things! There's always a slaughter of little lambs at the end of the story. Or have you forgotten?"

Nakdimon fell silent for several minutes. Then he finally said, "Well then. We have come to a disagreement about him. He may be the one who could restore our nation to the glory of King David's throne."

"Those are words of revolution, Nakdimon! Treason. Dangerous. King David is dead. His tomb is a half mile from here. I'm saying that your Rabbi from Nazareth would join David within the week if he comes into the city. What good is a dead Messiah to anyone? Or a dead member of the Sanhedrin with seven orphan children? You speak openly in favor of this fellow and you're a dead man too. Think of your children. Your position."

Nakdimon nodded, deferring to her opinion. "I'll give my report to Gamaliel in the morning. And then we'll see."

■ ■ ■ ■

A short time later Nakdimon made his way up the stairs to the dormitory room where his seven children slept.

Strange how coming home again had instantly reemphasized his loneliness. Since Hadassah had died there had not been a waking hour in which she was not somehow vivid in his mind. It was the absence of her that bored a hole in his heart. The continuity of grief had connected the moment of her leaving to the present. A bleak future had stretched out before him . . . existence without Hadassah!

And then, in the eyes of Yeshua, he had glimpsed hope again, a tangible awareness that time and this earthly existence were an aberration in eternity.

You will see her again. Yeshua promised.

How could Yeshua have known that this was the one question for which Nakdimon required an answer in order to go on! Death was not the final chapter. It was a beginning of something else. Beyond this life was life eternal, and somehow Yeshua held the key to that door. He alone had stepped out of eternity and demonstrated the power to call back the soul and breathe life into clay once again.

I am the resurrection and the life! No man comes to the Father except through me!

What could he mean by that? Was Yeshua's claim arrogance? Madness? Or truth?

Before the foundation of the world you were given to me!

Before? How could that be?

Nakdimon's visit to the Galil had burdened him with more questions than answers. And yet he was certain of this one thing: Yeshua of Nazareth was no mere mortal man. He held a power of life and death, and more so than the temporal authority of an earthly king who could condemn or spare a man from execution. Every human, including kings and princes, was on a journey toward the grave. Man's destiny led him irrevocably to physical death. But Yeshua proved that death had no power over those who trusted him and called on his mercy!

What a wonder was in this revelation!

What joy and illumination would come to the hearts of all mankind if every knee would bow to such a one as this! If only it was true! If Messiah's kingdom was established now, could he not call forth the righteous dead from the dust and make them live again?

All these things were in Nakdimon's thoughts as he stood over the beds of his sleeping children. He whispered their names with renewed hope for their future. "*Shalom.* Peace. Hannah. Susanna. Ruth. Sara and Dinah. Leah. Little Samuel." What would their world be like if Yeshua came to Jerusalem as Messiah and King?

"*Shalom,*" he said again.

KI IM

In the midst of a dream Emet heard the click of a dog's nails on pavement and the tramp of footsteps approaching the door of Zadok's home. A muted whine was hushed by a low command.

Were these things parts of his dream?

A rapping intruded on Emet's vision. He felt the vibration of the knocking come through the air, then noticed the scrape of the bench legs on the stone floor as Zadok pushed away from the table.

"What?" the shepherd demanded.

Red Dog and Blue Eye stood beside the entry, their tailless hindquarters showing a slight quiver of unalarmed anticipation.

Not an enemy, then, or a threat, Emet thought.

"Sir, she's having an awful time," Emet heard Lev's voice explain. "I couldn't do nothing, so I come for you."

Zadok coughed, cleared his throat, and opened the door, nodding Lev into his front room where a lone lamp flickered above a length of scroll.

Everything outside remained pitch black. Which watch of the night was it? How long had Emet been asleep?

"Did I do right, sir?" Lev queried with downcast gaze. Evidently disturbing the chief herdsman at his dwelling was not undertaken lightly.

"Yes, yes," Zadok assured him. "Go back. Keep her quiet. I'll be there soon."

Emet sat up and watched as Zadok took the time to carefully roll up the scroll he'd been studying and replace it in the urn. Avel and Ha-or Tov, wakened by the disturbance, stirred as well.

Avel queried, "What's . . ."

"The matter?" Ha-or Tov concluded when a yawn interrupted his friend's question.

Beside the shelf Zadok studied the three staring children, then made a decision. With a peremptory gesture he said, "Come on, then. Time to find out what we're about here. Hurry it up."

Merely seconds passed before the trio were ready to follow the old shepherd.

With a rattle of the door on its leather hinges, Zadok, two dogs, and three sleepy and curious boys exited into the Judean night, heading again for the lambing barn.

■ ■ ■ ■

The pregnant ewe remained stock-still and shivering. As Emet neared the pen, a convulsion passed through her body and she strained without visible result.

Zadok took down a lamp in his giant callused hands and passed it to Lev, saying softly, "Not any too soon. You were right to get me. She's in a bad state." Then to the boys he added, "Keep out of the way and out of the light. Pay attention and y' might learn something."

Lev patted the ewe, assuring her in soothing tones that the master was here and everything would be all right, that they would help her.

Despite the breadth of the load she bore, it was clear to Emet that the ewe was rather narrow and delicate compared to other sheep. Zadok's hands were too big to assist easily in the birthing.

"I tried all I know'd," Lev offered apologetically. "Nothing worked."

"You've grown since last lambing," Zadok observed. "Your hands are big as mine. Watch me: I'll try to hook a foreleg with one finger." Zadok expended the utmost care as he worked to extract the lamb. Beads of perspiration appeared above the strap of his eyepatch and trickled down the crease of his scar.

Emet saw Avel and Ha-or Tov staring with the same wide-eyed wonder that he experienced himself.

"Got it!" Zadok announced with terse excitement, then, "No. No. That foot doesn't belong to the same body. I'll have another go."

Once more the scene in the lamplight was a frozen tableau of Lev's anxious grimace, the silently intense onlookers, and Zadok's minute, almost imperceptible movements. Zadok remarked to his young audience, "Sheep are tough in one way: they can live rough, crop poor grass, and make do with little water. But delicate in another: can't be rough in birthing lambs."

A measured groan came from a nearby pen, but no one paid it any heed. All were focused on the present drama.

Just when Emet wondered how much longer they could remain

motionless, Zadok declared, "Got the right one. Tangled, though. Have to maneuver around more."

Lev studied the panting ewe. Her head drooped and her mouth hung open in silent agony. He pointed out these signals to the concentrating flock master.

"No time, then," Zadok concluded, "we're losing her." And he exerted pressure with two fingers of one hand.

At this crucial instant Avel leaned forward, blocking Emet's view. Ha-or Tov put his hands over his face.

But Emet wanted to see! Careful not to interfere with the light, Emet worked his way around the pen for a better view.

Zadok's thumb and forefinger gripped something. The muscles in the shepherd's neck tightened as he tugged.

A tiny hoof appeared, followed by a foreleg, then a shoulder and then another foreleg.

So that was what Zadok meant: twin babies, entangled in the womb. And the mother was too diminutive to allow easy correction of the snarl.

The scruffy head of a lamb appeared, then the shiny nose of another followed, then another tiny hoof. "That's it," Zadok muttered to himself. "One foreleg bent back and caught in the hind of the other. Have to bring them both together."

Emet was entranced and horrified at the same time. How could this be so urgent and move so slowly? What would happen to the lambs if the mother didn't survive?

Hands around the heads and shoulders of the half-birthed lambs, Zadok braced himself and tugged.

From immobility everything came with a rush.

The lambs came free together in a gush of blood. Zadok sat back in the straw, cradling both babies in his arms.

The ewe gave a single feeble bleat, then toppled over on her side. She was dead.

A bulge in her flank caught Zadok's attention. "There's the cause," he said. "Third lamb in there." Turning toward a startled Avel and Ha-or Tov, he commanded gruffly, "Take these two. Rub them with straw, but keep out of the way." He thrust the two infant lambs at the boys.

Emet tried to climb into the pen with the others but was roughly ordered back by Lev. "Not you, stump!" the shepherd said. "Too little."

Zadok first checked the ewe's glazed eyes and protruding tongue, and then drew a short, curved knife, like a small claw, from somewhere in his robes.

Almost before Emet could comprehend what was happening, Zadok had sliced open the sheep's belly and produced a third lamb, identical to the others. Lev took it without being told and plumped down in the pen, showing Ha-or Tov and Avel how to rub the babies briskly with knots of straw. The chafing dried the damp fleeces and encouraged the infants to breathe and move, just as their mother's tongue would have done had she lived.

Emet cried without realizing it. Three lambs, all born alive and all orphaned at the same time, and he was too little to even help them!

Straightening up, Zadok surveyed the scene. "Well," he said, as if considering what was to be done next. Stretching cramped muscles, he peered into an adjacent pen and remarked, "Seems Old Girl got along without us."

Since he was of no use to anyone, Emet clambered around the rails to where he could also see into the other enclosure. There a ragged, patchy-fleeced, knock-kneed elderly ewe nudged an oversized lamb lying on the straw. Bumping it with her nose, she pushed her baby to stand, but there was no response.

Another death! Birth was hard and cruel and dangerous.

"That's the answer," Zadok mused aloud. Then to Lev he explained, "Old Girl's had a stillborn. We'll put these three onto her to foster. She's always let down milk enough for three."

Soon the three white orphans—"All ewe-lambs," Lev remarked—were in the same pen with Old Girl. But the aged ewe would have none of them. As they plaintively circled her flanks, Old Girl dodged and sidestepped, wanting nothing to do with babies that were not her own.

Would this tragedy never end? Was there no remedy that would save the lives of the babies?

Zadok and Lev conferred over the limp body of Old Girl's stillborn offspring. "She's mostly blind," Lev put in. "It's possible."

What were they speaking of?

Once again Zadok's blade glittered in the lamplight. With practiced skill he skinned the dead lamb, then divided its bloody fleece into three parts.

As Emet shuddered and wondered at the callousness of it, Lev tied a strip of fleece to each of the three white lambs.

Zadok knelt beside Ha-or Tov and Avel. "It'll be all right," he said to the boys. "Now where are we at? Here, Old Girl," he crooned to the distraught and pacing mother. "Here's your flock."

Emet held his breath as Zadok placed a lamb under Old Girl's nose.

Cautiously at first she sniffed the fleece, which held the scent of her dead baby. She withdrew a pace.

The lamb, clearly frightened of Old Girl, struggled in Zadok's grip, casting around imploring looks that Emet believed were aimed straight at him.

Old Girl advanced and sniffed again.

Then she nuzzled the lamb's head and neck, swiped her tongue over the baby, and made low crooning sounds of her own. When Zadok released the baby she tottered uncertainly at first . . . and Old Girl nudged her firmly toward her udder. When she pushed the baby again from behind, the lamb's head butted Old Girl's bag . . . and everything fell into place.

The three white orphan lambs in their borrowed coats were accepted by Old Girl with barely a struggle. Soon they were nursing as the aged ewe made happy, chuckling noises from deep in her throat.

■ ■ ■ ■

Avel had remained silent as they watched the gruesome operation of skinning the dead lamb and transferring its hide in pieces to the backs of the three orphans. Ha-or Tov was among the trio, guiding each to Old Girl's milk-swollen udder.

Zadok and Lev stood up stiffly and exchanged glances. They seemed content that there would be three survivors at least.

Emet huddled over the pen of the languishing charcoal-colored lamb at the back of the stable. The rejected baby lay limp and near death in the straw. His mouth was slightly open, breath coming in shallow gasps.

"What about this one?" Emet asked.

Lev responded gruffly, "He's a goner, that one. Dead by morning. Mother won't have him. He doesn't want to eat from my hand anymore. I've tried. Sorrow's killed him, and there's an end to it."

This pricked Avel's emotion. He knew what it was to want to die. And he knew how wonderful it was to have lived. He joined Emet, peering through the rails at the pitiful sight. Yes. The black lamb was dying.

"Can't we put fleece on him too?" Avel asked.

"Not enough to go round." Lev began to clean up.

"There's a scrap left over. From the head," Emet argued.

Zadok stared at the carcass of the stillborn. He chewed his lip in consideration. "Well, then, bring the thing here to me."

Little as he was, Emet scrambled over the fence and managed to gather the rejected black lamb in his arms. It would not, or could not, walk, so the boy passed it to Avel, and the two of them carried it forward to where Zadok and Lev were working.

Zadok took one look inside the mouth of the baby and warned Emet, "Not much color in his gums. I can't say this one'll make it even if Old Girl accepts him."

But Emet's expression pleaded with the old shepherd that they should at least try to save him. "I'll care for him," Emet promised.

Avel knew Emet was good for his word. After all, Emet had hauled around the dead carcass of a sparrow until Yeshua had breathed life into it. At least the black lamb was still breathing.

Zadok replied, "We can only do what we can do. The rest isn't up to us."

And so the remaining scrap of fleece from the skull of the stillborn body was stripped away. Zadok fitted it securely to the head of the fragile creature in Emet's arms. Dark ears poked through two holes, and strips of hide were tied under the baby's chin. But the cap had no evident restorative powers. The black lamb lay weak and unresponsive against Emet's chest. The boy stroked the cheek and crooned to it.

Lev muttered that this was a waste of time and energy. But Zadok silenced his assistant with a stern expression.

"What next?" Avel asked on behalf of Emet, who was uncertain what he should do next.

Zadok instructed, "Help Emet carry the baby into Old Girl. She'll need to get a sniff at his head. That will tell the tale. She'll trample him if she knows he's not her own. If she accepts him, we might have a chance, but then he's got to have a will to eat. To live."

The black appeared to have no fight left in him, Avel thought as they brought him toward the muzzle of the ewe. Old Girl blinked at them, lowered her nose, snorted, and turned away.

Zadok coached Avel and Emet. "Give her a minute. That's right. Stand away while the others nurse. All right, then. Bring him under her chin. Slowly. Present the top of his head. Let her get a good whiff. Yes. Yes. She's interested."

The black lamb, fearful of the ewe, struggled weakly to escape.

Avel noted the intensity of Emet's expression. He was a good lad, even if he was too small to be of use and too headstrong to be practical about things.

Emet's voice chirped, "See, Old Girl? You've had a lovely baby here? Give him a kiss? Eh, Old Girl?"

The ewe lowered her broad, smiling face to inspect the package once again. Nostrils flared as she probed the bloody fleece bonnet. Her enormous tongue shot out and tipped the fringe for a quick taste. And then she gave a resonant bleat of possible acceptance.

Again the baby struggled to escape. After all, his own mother had nearly killed him with a kick when she saw he was not correctly colored.

Avel caressed the baby's head. Emet imitated the language of baby sheep with surprising accuracy.

"Come on. Come on." From Old Girl's flanks Ha-or Tov urged them to bring the baby back to where the milk flowed like the proverbial Jordan.

Avel and Emet, with Old Girl's conditional approval, waded into the thick of twirling tails and contented slurping. With difficulty they parted the triplets and managed to work the black lamb's face close to the teats.

Zadok directed them, "Emet, hold his mouth open. There. Yes. That's the way. Now Avel, you take hold of a teat. Direct it toward his mouth. Give a squeeze."

Avel obeyed the instructions. The first stream hit Emet on the cheek. He scowled and lifted the lamb's face until it intercepted the milk.

"Again! Get his interest! He's gotten used to being hungry! Wake him up!"

Amazingly Old Girl didn't seem to mind the crowd of baby lambs and boys pushing in at her flanks. Avel grasped the soft finger-like teat and gave it yet another pump. Again milk spurted out in an astonishingly strong stream!

This time he was right on target. The baby black's tongue darted out for a taste. He wriggled in Emet's grasp.

Zadok encouraged them, "Put his mouth right over it. Yes. There y' are. Yes. He's got it! Hold him there! He's not strong enough to compete. You'll have to hold him up, or the sisters will drive him off!"

Avel held the teat within reach as Emet pushed the baby's face right against the source of nourishment. Time passed as Avel milked directly onto the baby's tongue. Milk dripped down onto Avel's clothes, soaking his feet. Emet was splashed with misdirected spray. Once or twice Old Girl turned her woolly head around to see what was going on back there.

Would the baby never catch on?

And then, suddenly, the eyes of the black lamb sparked with interest. As though waking from a trance, he kicked his delicate forelegs and struggled to stand. The three sisters crowded in. The scene was a tangle of baby lambs' behinds and milk-soaked boys—all aimed at the same target.

"All right, boys," Zadok cheered. "Give him a bit of room. Let him have it on his own, Avel. Come out from there. Emet, stay with him. Put your hands under his belly. Prop him up! That's it!"

Avel scrambled back as the baby lunged and latched on fiercely to Old Girl's spare faucet. Trembling with excitement, the baby began to suck on his own. His tail swung to and fro, finally erupting into a swirl of delight.

At the final linkup Old Girl bobbed her head approvingly. Avel imagined he saw the old ewe's wide mouth turn up in a sheep smile. Of course it couldn't really be true.

But it looked like it all the same.

GALAH

When Emet next woke, he was pleased to find that he knew immediately where he was, and that he was grateful to be there. It was a pleasant, secure, content awakening, unlike any he could remember.

To the mingled scents of thyme and sage, mint and lavender, another pleasant smell was added: the aroma of flat bread toasting beside the fire. Emet yawned and stretched. His two companions roused at the same time.

In the other room Zadok moved a kettle off the fire.

When had they come back? Or had the nighttime excursion truly happened at all?

The shepherd rattled the tongs when he lifted the pot. The noise was louder than was strictly necessary, Emet thought.

Neither dog was in sight, but through the open front door glorious yellow sun streamed in. A thin mist hung over the green slopes. The fragment of a rainbow flickered on a beam of light against the vapor, set to dancing by a bit of breeze.

Zadok abruptly appeared to notice the boys, as if he had forgotten their presence. "Still abed? You princes of Judah, that y' sleep so late? You'll get no breakfast!"

That brought the boys tumbling out in a tangle of arms, legs, and Ha-or Tov's wiry curls.

"Put up your bedding," Zadok growled.

Fleeces and pallets were folded and stowed, and the three companions waited expectantly beside the table.

Zadok raised his nose to the herb-laden ceiling. "Did three boys follow me home, or three goats? You stink! Out and wash, out and wash!"

"Where, sir?" Avel asked.

"Follow me," Zadok said, toting the kettle of hot water along.

Behind the house, around the side away from the garden, were the necessary and another structure enclosing a natural stone hollow.

Though merely a depression in the rock, the cavity resembled a *mikveh,* the bath used for ritual cleansing before religious ceremonies. Zadok emptied the steaming kettle into the tub, then added three buckets of cold water from a barrel.

"Dump your clothes on the ground," Zadok commanded gruffly. Then, muttering to himself, he added, "Washing won't do . . . need boiling! What're y' waiting for? Jump!"

The three complied.

Zadok indicated clumps of hyssop and soapwort bound together with twine. "Scrub," he said. "Ears and neck. Hair too. Clean clothes on the bench. Make it quick!"

Emet was almost afraid to exchange any words with Avel and Ha-or Tov in case a scrap of conversation would cause a delay. Bathed, he stood up to climb out when Avel said, "Lemme see your nails."

When Emet displayed his fingers, Avel shook his head. "He's sure to check," Avel noted.

Ha-or Tov nodded solemnly.

Finally, scoured thoroughly, Emet went to the piles of clothes. Simple tunics with cords to tie around the waist were folded and waiting, but another gift was underneath: each boy received a pair of boots. Made of sheepskin with hardened leather soles, the hides were stitched with the fleece inside.

Emet could scarcely believe how much better his feet were since yesterday . . . or how different Zadok's manner seemed over the same elapsed time. "What changed?" he hissed to Ha-or Tov.

Emet's red-haired friend shrugged. "Maybe he's grumpy at night," Ha-or Tov ventured.

Once back inside the house, each boy received a platter of toasted bread, goat cheese, and sliced apples.

Emet ate everything, and when he shyly lifted his head, Zadok refilled his plate. "You three are so skinny if you were lambs I'd not give a penny for the lot," the shepherd said.

When half an apple and a wedge of cheese lay untouched on Emet's plate, Zadok ventured a question. "What education have you had?"

Emet ducked his head, but not before he saw Avel and Ha-or Tov exchange embarrassed glances.

No one spoke for a painfully long pause, then Avel offered, "I know my *alef-bet,* sir."

Harrumphing, Zadok asserted, "All right, then. Days for work and nights for study. And no complaints, or out you go."

Emet's heart soared. Had he heard correctly? Had they just been offered a chance to stay?

Avel, ever the doubter, asked, "I thought you weren't taking any more apprentices this season."

Emet wanted to strangle him.

Grabbing one braided cable of beard with each hand, Zadok tugged thoughtfully. "Why else would y' be sent here? Of course you're apprentices. Didn't I say so?" Zadok snatched up his staff. "You've had enough to eat? Rested. Clean. Belly full. A good beginning. From now on you'll not eat till your ewes are fed. You'll have to learn the way of it."

"Our ewes?" Avel asked excitedly.

Zadok pinned him with a steady gaze. "Y' don't think you'll stay here without earning your keep, do y'? It's lambing. Lev could use a hand. There's work to be done. The flock comes before all. Before your own comfort."

The words sounded harsh, but Emet sensed that here was the day's lesson: feed the sheep before yourself. Hadn't that been what Zadok had done with the boys last night? Washed them. Bandaged their wounds. Fed them. Put them to bed before he thought of himself.

Thus began their instruction in shepherding.

Zadok set off to the lambing pens.

Avel ran after him at a jog, almost matching the enormous strides of the shepherd. Ha-or Tov was next in line, his gangly legs and long spindly arms gyrating clumsily in all directions. Emet, being smallest, brought up the rear. A dozen paces behind, he was heeled by Blue Eye, who nosed the back of Emet's leg as though he were a straggler in the flock who must be urged forward.

Red Dog, tongue lolling in an openmouthed canine grin, sprinted joyful circles around them.

Breathless as he ran to catch up, Emet glanced down at the Tower of the Flock. There was enough of everything in this magical place for him to live here content for the rest of his life! Enough *was* everything! Had he ever imagined there could be enough? Stomach full. Washed from head to foot. Dressed in clean clothes. With a prospect that he would be fed again, have clean water in which to bathe and a bed upon which he could sleep! Migdal Eder was a boy's paradise! Now he understood why Yeshua had sent them into the care of this curious old man.

Bright sunlight flooded the hillsides. The first of a Jerusalem-bound flock was being herded up the road. The din of two thousand departing sheep was countered by the insistent racket of bawling lambs and bleating ewes in the stables.

And then Zadok paused mid-stride to glare at the castle of Herodium high on the hill beyond Beth-lehem. A Roman standard was raised on the parapet as a flurry of trumpet blasts announced that Imperial Rome was awake and watching the people of the sheepfold.

Emet, Avel, and Ha-or Tov followed the old man's gaze.

Zadok's face hardened with resentment. His lips tightened as though he were holding back a curse against the soldiers who occupied the fortress. "Stay away from there," he menaced. "They're devils. All of them."

"The dead king's palace," Ha-or Tov murmured somberly. And then to Zadok, "Who was he?"

The shepherd raised his finger absently to the scar beneath his eyepatch. It was a long moment before he replied. "The man who built that banqueting house was supper for worms long ago, boy. Those who occupy it now will also be food for maggots. We're comforted by that. What was can't be changed, can it?"

"What would they do? Soldiers and such," Ha-or Tov persisted. "I mean if someone was to go up there."

"We tend the sheep here and mind our own business." Zadok raised a warning finger. "Stay clear of that place is what I'm saying." He dismissed Ha-or Tov's question, turned from the blatant display of Roman authority, and moved on, this time more slowly.

Emet glanced over his shoulder at the mountain where evil presided. He shuddered. Ghosts and devils danced on the walls. Avel had told him so. But whose ghosts? And how many devils? And did they ever swoop down upon Beth-lehem and take boys as prisoners? Emet wondered.

■ ■ ■ ■

Nakdimon hurried to Gamaliel's Jerusalem home, located not far from his own in the southwest corner of the city. As always, the forecourt was crowded with people. Some sought Gamaliel's patronage in obtaining positions. Others were there because the learned man was also a magistrate who acted to settle civil disputes. One such case was in progress even as Nakdimon arrived. The clash appeared to concern a shipment of broken pottery.

Gamaliel acknowledged his nephew's entrance with a raised eyebrow and nod, but continued listening to the presentation of the defendant. At his elbow a young man Nakdimon recognized as one of Gamaliel's talmidim took notes.

While Nakdimon settled against one of the plastered wall panels painted to imitate green marble, Gamaliel delivered his verdict. The decision went in favor of the plaintiff, but stopped short of giving him all the relief he sought. The two men left grumbling and shaking their heads.

"Difficult judgment?" Nakdimon inquired.

"Not at all!" was the reply. "Both sides are unhappy. That means I handled it properly. Anytime either of the parties leaves entirely satisfied, then I'm the one who's been wronged. Completely one-sided guilt is a rarity in lawsuits, or have you forgotten everything I taught you?" Turning to his secretary, Gamaliel said, "Saul, dismiss the others. That's enough for today."

Drawing up a wicker chair close to Gamaliel's own seat, Nakdimon didn't delay his recitation for any small talk. As soon as the secretary was out of the room Nakdimon said, "I've seen such amazing things! Do you remember how we sensed the divine fire from Yochanan the Baptizer? Well, Yeshua is the wind! He's a healer, a magnificent teacher, he sees into men's hearts and . . ." Nakdimon leaned forward. "He can raise the dead! I saw it myself. There are others I have asked to testify. El'azar of Bethany. His sisters. Marta and . . . Miryam, who has become a follower of Yeshua."

"The harlot sister of El'azar? That *is* news."

"But she's different. Changed and . . ."

"The council would as soon have her openly condemned. She will never do as a witness. Never."

"What I can say is this: she's not the same. They are not the same family. Yeshua has made some . . . difference in them. How can I explain? He simply changes everything he comes near."

Gamaliel gave no sign of astonishment, did not demand details from Nakdimon. Instead, with his elbows on the arms of his chair, he propped his chin on steepled fingers. "So you believe he's the Messiah?" he asked softly.

"I . . . ," Nakdimon began, then stopped. "He does things no one else can do and knows things no one else can know. I won't ask you to believe unless you see for yourself, but . . ."

"But is it enough?" Gamaliel demanded. "There are rigorous tests that must be met before I will acknowledge a Messiah. Fail one and fail them all, agreed?"

"Agreed. But tell me quickly . . . there are rumors even in the Galil about the coming Passover. What's happening?"

"The Sanhedrin presses ahead with the aqueduct scheme, despite my efforts to caution them. Caiaphas and his faction attempt to justify the Korban use at every turn, but they know there'll be protests. When the population of Yerushalayim doubles for the festival, there'll be trouble. Caiaphas knows it, the Romans know it, and I know it. The question remaining is: 'What form will it take?' Listen!" Gamaliel touched an index finger to his forehead. "The two matters are linked. If this Yeshua declares himself at the feast and takes up the Korban issue as his own cause, there will be rioting . . . and many will die."

"But what if he really is the Holy One of Israel?" Nakdimon queried. "Then he would be right to take up sacrilege as his cause!"

"So you also have been reviewing the words of Dani'el," Gamaliel noted. "Of course that's the whole point: could he truly be the Awaited One?"

"You said yourself the years allotted in Dani'el's prophecy have nearly ended," Nakdimon pointed out.

"But what does 'cut off' mean? Caiaphas grows more frightened every day that the doom applies to him." The learned Pharisee laughed. "He's taken to having his father-in-law attend council meetings and deferring to his opinion . . . as if the Almighty might be fooled into picking on the wrong *cohen hagadol!*"

Nakdimon chuckled too. Annas, Caiaphas' father-in-law, had been high priest years before and still insisted on being addressed by the title.

"Start at the beginning," Gamaliel challenged. "List the requirements a Messiah must fill and tell me how the Nazarene fares."

"He is of the tribe of Judah and the family line of David," Nakdimon reported. "I'm satisfied of that. The prophet Isaiah says he'll be preceded by another voice . . . and Yochanan himself baptized Yeshua and acknowledged him as the Master. Isaiah also records that he'll perform miracles . . . which he clearly does, and be anointed by the *Ruach HaKodesh,* which Yeshua clearly is!"

Saul, Gamaliel's student, reentered the chamber and stood behind his chair. "But he violates Sabbath!" the young man protested. "He heals on the Sabbath, in direct contradiction of the Law! He eats with sinners and women! Notorious women!" By this, Nakdimon surmised the student referred to Miryam. "This Yeshua doesn't keep the laws of cleanliness! Such a one can never be the Anointed One! Never!"

"Nephew, meet my shy and tongue-tied student, Saul of Tarsus," Gamaliel said dryly.

Unabashed, Saul continued, "What about this? Doesn't the prophet Micah say that Messiah will be born in Beth-lehem?"

Gamaliel quoted the reference, "*But you, Beth-lehem Ephrathah, though you are small among the clans of Judah, out of you will come for me one who will be ruler over Israel, whose origins are from of old, from ancient times.*"

Saul interjected, "How could the Messiah be called a Galilean?"

Nakdimon was stumped. "I don't know," he said. "His father was a carpenter in Nazareth until his death. His mother has recently moved from there."

"There, you see?" Saul said triumphantly. "He's a fraud. A drunkard and a man who goes with whores."

To the surprise of the younger men it was Gamaliel who held up a cautioning hand. "Not so fast," he warned. "This Yeshua is about thirty years of age?"

"Thirty-two, I believe," Nakdimon reported.

"And how old was he when he first began to teach publicly?"

"About thirty."

"The same age as David when he became king."

"He refused the crown that people tried to force on him."

Gamaliel nodded. "It came to me in the night. The age is right. He *could* be the one. Simeon, my father, used to tell of a child brought into the Temple for dedication thirty-two years ago. My father believed he was the Deliverer. He spoke of it often. After that three foreign astronomers came to old Herod's palace here in Jerusalem. They told Herod they had seen a sign in the heavens announcing the birth of a king in Israel. Herod called the scholars to him. Father was among them. I remember what happened when Father showed him the prophecy of Micah." Gamaliel reflected on that dim memory. "A slaughter. You can read it for yourself. All of it. It's recorded in the archives as one more fit of Herod's madness. But," Gamaliel emphasized, "since that time those of us who know the prophecies and calculate the exact times haven't spoken openly about them to secular rulers. As in the days of Moses, the innocent are made to suffer when kings and princes of this world seek to stop the words of *Adonai-Elohim* from coming to pass. Make no assumptions! Learn all you can. This isn't a time to be on the wrong side! Let's speak more tomorrow!"

■ ■ ■ ■

It was on the slope below Herodium, almost in the shadow of that fortress, that Marcus Longinus located the camp of the engineers. There he found Gaius Robb, chief of the surveying crew, examining a map of the region and matching charted features to their real counterparts.

The line of hills on which Herodium perched extended southward toward Hebron. These westward-facing heights intercepted the last of the Mediterranean moisture from wind-borne clouds. The escarpment divided the fertile plains of Judah from the Judean desert. Here rainfall effectively ended.

From the caravan routes crisscrossing Idumea to the south, to the town of Arimathea on the edge of Samaritan land to the north, Judea possessed no more than a dozen creeks. Water, though plentiful in the Jordan River Valley, could not escape the confines of that gorge to be useful for people living above it to the west.

Water was never abundant. Where it bubbled up and pooled, orchards prospered and stock fattened on the grazing; when it failed, so did the villages its life-giving properties had nourished.

Between Hebron and Herodium the convergence of two canyons formed a natural catch-basin to use as the headwaters for Pilate's planned aqueduct. From several springs in the area, as well as seasonal precipitation, water would be made to flow to Jerusalem. In order to have sufficient height for the precious fluid to reach the capital of the Jews, almost the entire length of the watercourse would have to be raised significantly above ground level. This elevated construction had to begin as soon as the channel emerged from the hilltop reservoir.

The intended route as laid out by Pilate's predecessor passed beneath Herodium and crossed the pastures of Beth-lehem. Beside Bethlehem it joined Herod the Great's existing aqueduct at a place called *Solomon's Pools,* only a couple miles away.

"Hail, Centurion," Robb greeted Marcus formally, then extended his hand in friendship. "What brings you to such an out-of-the-way place? Did the governor send you here to check up on me?"

Marcus smiled. Robb was a promising young officer previously attached to the Tenth Legion in Syria. Marcus had met him once in Damascus. Pilate must have bribed Vitellius to part with him. "Just the opposite," Marcus declared. "Pilate sent me here to keep me out of trouble. How is the work progressing?"

"Well, I think," Robb offered with a noncommittal flick of his fingers toward the chart. His green eyes sought Marcus' steady gaze. "Actually, I'm glad you're here. I . . . I do have concerns."

Marcus knew Robb to be an intuitive mathematician with a practical bent. He was highly regarded by Vitellius for certain improvements in siege weapons, and he was equally at home designing defensive fortifications. Slightly built and scarcely more than five feet tall, the inventive engineer had boyish features that made him look even younger than his twenty-four years.

Right now those boyish features were troubled. Marcus waited for him to continue.

Sighing heavily, Robb folded a pair of dividers, stabbed the prongs into the wooden arm of his drafting chair, and resumed. "It seemed so straightforward. The aqueduct, I mean. Water is precious here, and no people on earth crave it more than the Jews. Wash before eating, wash after eating, bathe before worship, bathe before making a vow, before signing a contract, before going to a wedding. In all the world, no people appreciate fresh water more than we Romans do, unless it's the Jews! And not merely for the simple pleasure and relaxation like us, oh no! With them it's sacred, religious, a sign of piety."

Undoing his chin strap and doffing his helmet, Marcus tossed it onto a camp chair. None of this analysis was news to him. "So?" he queried, though he already knew the answer. "What's the problem?"

"Everything!" was the retort. "There's a dispute about the funds to build the aqueduct . . . and I don't understand since the high council of the Jews voted the money."

Marcus explained what he understood about the Korban dispute. "The high priest Caiaphas slipped the measure past the council with a rigged vote," he said, "knowing that many consider it sacrilegious. Once named as Korban, the Temple money can't be used for anything other than religious purposes."

"But much of this water is for their Temple," Robb protested.

Marcus spread his hands. "That's the same argument Caiaphas tried, but some still aren't convinced. And that's beside the point. A knottier problem is a rebel band like bar Abba's, who might seize on this issue and use it to rally an uprising. Has there been any rebel activity in your area?"

Robb scratched his sandy-colored hair. "Yes and no. There was one slash-and-burn raid . . . no more since. But the Jewish stonemasons, quarrymen, and laborers I employed are afraid to stay in their work camps at night . . . say they'll be targeted as collaborators."

"Don't you have legionaries assigned to guard the works?"

Bobbing his head, Robb added, "But only one cohort. They can't be everywhere at once."

"So what's the situation?"

Robb pointed out toward the arches and spans looming over the sheepfolds. "Instead of camping near each construction site, the workers go back to Herodium every night, where they'll be safe! That's the problem! It takes too long to get them back to work every morning."

Humming to himself, Marcus said, "I'll look into the guard details so you can concentrate on the engineering. Who's your captain of legionaries?"

"Centurion Shomron, sent out from Jerusalem. Praetorian Vara said he was the right man to keep the Jews in line."

Inwardly Marcus groaned. Vara, with his innate cruelty, was bad enough, but Shomron too! Shomron was a Samaritan who made no secret of how he detested all Jews and especially the more religious ones. The combination appeared as likely to remain peaceful as applying a torch to a pile of sulfur. "I'll see what I can do," Marcus vowed. He gazed across the horizon toward the Tower of Migdal Eder. "Go back to your plans."

■ ■ ■ ■

The smell of sweet, fresh hay filled Emet's senses as they entered the lambing stable. He closed his eyes and inhaled.

At the end of the long corridor of stalls, Lev was turning the straw.

Such luxury! When Emet and Sister had wandered the streets of Jerusalem, they had slept in doorways, begged on street corners. A bed of clean straw was a dream in those days. Sister had sold herself into servitude for the sake of food and shelter. At the stone quarry entrance she had left Emet, who was no use to anyone, in the reluctant care of Avel.

And what about Avel? The Sparrow boys who lived in the Jerusalem quarries received new bedding six times a year from the Temple charity. And how Emet had envied that charity. How he had longed to be a Sparrow! To sleep beside a fire among the other boys! To carry a torch and earn a halfpenny for each link! Enough daily bread to fill his belly! That had been his ambition. But here he wanted to be a shepherd! In the whole world could there be an occupation as fine as this?

Emet watched as Avel leaned on the rail and stared wistfully down into the pen. He reached out to touch the soft wool of two recently arrived babies.

Emet and Ha-or Tov joined him to gawk.

Zadok studied Avel's face. "Well? I see words in your eyes. What is it? What? Speak up, boy." The old man cupped his hand around his ear.

Avel replied solemnly, "We've fallen in a tub of butter."

Zadok guffawed a hearty belly laugh. "So you have!" And then he asked Ha-or Tov, "And what is your opinion on the lambing stable?"

"Very fine butter at that."

"Y' like the place, I take it," Zadok replied. He placed a hand on Emet's head. "And what's running through your mind, little one?"

Emet was ashamed to mention his thought that it was far better to live in a sheep pen in Beth-lehem than as a human beggar in Yerushalayim. He fixed his gaze on the pair of newborns tugging at the udder of their mother. Tails flicked with delight as they nursed. "Pretty things."

Zadok raised his chin slightly and winked as he whispered, "Lambs, boy. They're everywhere hereabouts. You'll soon get used to the sight. Twin ewes, these."

Last night that stall had been home to one fat, miserable ewe. This morning she was flanked by tiny white creatures bumping and tugging merrily at the feed bag! Their arrival had been accomplished as Emet and the others slept. The lambing stable of Beth-lehem was a veritable palace of miracles!

Lev tossed the pitchfork into a mound of fodder and hailed Zadok. "They're up and at it, sir," drawled the big youth. "That one there? She's been eating all morning. Making up for lost time. Like y' said."

"I've brought y' the three strays as day workers, Lev." Zadok nodded continually as he spoke. "You'll be in charge. They're ignorant of the ways of the fold. It'll take a load of teaching. Are y' up to it?"

Lev blinked down at Emet. "Sure. Sure. Sure. I could use a hand. But . . . scrawny things, aren't they?"

"Need to put muscle on them, I know."

"These two'll fatten right up," Lev said about Ha-or Tov and Avel, as though they were sheep instead of boys.

"That's right. Good big bones on this one." Zadok patted Avel's back. "He'll be strong enough for pasture work. Herding. Big feet. Always charging off in front of the others. A mover. A header. We'll teach him to work with Red Dog."

Lev sucked his teeth thoughtfully and scowled at Ha-or Tov. He picked up the boy's arm at the wrist and gave it a shake. "Delicate boned."

"As y' know from last night, we can use a pair of small hands and a good imagination. This one has both. We'll teach him lambing," Zadok said.

Lev pointed at Emet. "What will I do with this? Until it grows, the ewes will knock it over and trample it!"

Emet flushed with worry. Would Lev make him leave? Would old Zadok consider him too puny and unworthy to work with the flock?

Zadok glowered at Emet. Then he said, "We'll find something useful. He's eager enough."

"It's barely got its eyes open, sir. Can't we sent it off to the village? Let a woman watch it till it grows? Let it dig turnips in a garden?"

"I'll grow!" Emet protested. "I promise!"

Avel stepped up. "I'll watch over him. I've been looking out for him awhile now. He's no bother. Quiet. No trouble."

Zadok tugged his beard in contemplation. "Then it's settled. Emet's to stay here. Avel, you'll see to it he doesn't get into trouble, eh?" And then Zadok brightened, as if a solution came to mind, and instructed Lev, "Emet can tend to Old Girl and the orphans. Never was a ewe more gentle than Old Girl. She'll teach him which end of a sheep is which." He nodded toward the pen where the elderly ewe resided with her four adopted offspring.

"Well, then," Lev said, accepting this arrangement. "Old Girl won't trample it at least." Lev cocked an eye sternly at Emet. "You fancy tending the sweetest old ewe in Judea?"

Emet agreed promptly. Anything! As long as he was not to be sent off to Beth-lehem to work in a turnip garden!

Zadok called Red Dog and Blue Eye, then took Avel and Ha-or Tov out into the sunlight where a group of twenty-four lambs and ewes awaited transfer back into the pasture.

Lev grasped Emet's shoulder and directed him farther into the stable, to the cubicle where Old Girl lay in the straw among three white lambs and one black.

There was nothing attractive about Old Girl. She blinked drowsily at Emet when he repeated her name. "*Shalom*, Old Girl. I'm Emet." Her fleece was ragged and patchy, yellowed from sun, weather, and age. She seemed a huge and formidable creature. Amber eyes with clouded corneas considered his hazy form with vague interest, as if he were another ewe's lamb. She chewed hay languidly.

Lev explained, "This is your flock then, runt. Herself and the four little ones. Old Girl does most of the work. She tends them four as need tending."

Each of the four lambs still had the extra strip of fleece secured to it. Lev pointed at the black lamb with knock-knees who wobbled toward Old Girl and stuck his nose in her ear. On his head was the cap of white fleece tied with a leather cord under his chin. Black ears poked out through the patch. "I give her a bit of grain so Old Girl's got enough milk to nourish the four about three quarters of what they need every day. I've been feeding them milk from the goats. I'll show you how it's done." Lev hoisted Emet over the barrier.

Emet hung back, uncertain what he should do. The black lamb approached him with stiff-legged curiosity. Emet stuck out his hands, and the black probed his palms.

"Pet him!" Lev said impatiently. Then Lev nudged Emet aside and entered the nursery. "See here. Give me your thumb." Lev formed Emet's fingers into a fist, leaving the thumb up. This he poked into the lamb's mouth. "Here's the way to get him to follow."

Emet smiled as the baby latched on. Smooth, toothless gums, a rough tongue, and a corrugated pallet formed a fiercely sucking vacuum. "It doesn't hurt." Emet giggled.

"That's the trick. A little goat's milk on your fingers, and they'll follow y' to Damascus and back for the promise of it." Lev straightened. "So. I'll teach y' to milk the goats out back. How to feed the babies. But most important, your job is to keep those scraps of fleece tied onto the four. See here! If the coats come off too soon, Old Girl'll reject the lambs. Maybe hurt them. You understand?"

Emet nodded vigorously. "Sure." But he didn't really understand. Questions rattled around in his brain. Would Old Girl still reject the orphans if they didn't wear the extra coat of wool? Emet decided he would ask Zadok later. He didn't want Lev to think he was too ignorant to accomplish this task.

Lev pulled Emet's thumb free from the black. It was red. Lev shrugged. "You're not much bigger than a lamb. A bit smarter maybe. But it doesn't take a clever fellow to tend sheep."

Zadok returned to the barn with Avel and Ha-or Tov in tow. "Is he managing, then?" Zadok inquired after Emet.

"It'll do," Lev replied. "A bit timid at first. But it'll come along."

Then beyond the stable Emet spotted Jehu, the gruff shepherd from Migdal Eder. Jehu, warlike in demeanor, devoured the path with long strides. His grizzled face was set in consternation.

Lev saw him too. "Here comes Jehu."

Zadok turned and sighed. "His face says trouble. I put him on guard against a jackal last night."

"Two-legged jackal." Lev wagged his head and lifted Emet out of Old Girl's domain. "Jackal in a Roman cloak, more like."

Jehu called from a distance. "Sir! Zadok! Bad news! Six from the Korban flock stolen last night! The best of them! Yerushalayim bound today they were! Gone! Slaughtered!"

Zadok set his chiseled features against Herodium's outline. "Come along," he said to the boys. "We'll deal with this right now."

SODO

On horseback, skirting the cone of Herodium, Marcus Longinus studied the construction project spreading out across the valley in front of him. The purely Roman part of Marcus admired the audacity of the undertaking. Bringing water from two hundred leagues off in a man-made river of stone and lime mortar represented an achievement of Roman will and ingenuity: taking an unruly, unproductive land and subduing it into fruitfulness and civility.

But the portion of his nature drawn from his Britannic princess mother, born in freedom but destined to live in slavery, recoiled at the same view, or at least sympathized with Jewish objections.

Pylons and half-completed aqueduct supports stalked across the pasturelands, like figures from Jewish tales of Goliath and his Philistine brothers returning to do battle with the puny Jews. And this time where would they find a David to deliver them?

While Judea would benefit from the water, the sheer size and permanence of the watercourse would proclaim to the entire world . . . and most pointedly to the Jews . . . the superiority of all things Roman.

Aqueducts and bridges were distinctively Roman. In fact, one of the divine titles claimed by former emperor Augustus was *Pontifex Maximus, highest bridge-builder;* the god-man who spanned the gap between heaven and earth. The emperor was the embodiment of Rome, and Rome alone could assess the needs of her subordinate peoples, command the resources to address those needs, produce a Rome-approved solution, and enforce gratitude for the conclusion.

Marcus patted Pavor's neck absentmindedly while he pondered this. He had not thought of his mother in some time. Not long ago he had believed himself so wholly Roman in his worldview that no doubts could possibly have intruded. From where did such questions arise, and why now? His doubts about the empire had certainly increased since meeting Yeshua of Nazareth. Was he the source of this uncertainty?

Yes.

To cross the valley between Herodium and Beth-lehem the aqueduct's arches would be some of the highest of its entire route. This part of the waterway had been begun by Pilate's predecessor, then abandoned because of a lack of funds. Now that Governor Pilate had access to the Korban money, the scheme was once again under way.

Suddenly Marcus' attention was drawn to a gang of thirty or so men grouped at the base of the nearest arch. As a thin rivulet of gray smoke trickled into the pale blue sky, an altercation developed. Even from this distance it took no eagle-eyed awareness to recognize that shaking fists and waving arms didn't represent peaceful discussion. Sun glinting on blades proved that bloodshed was imminent.

Clapping his heels to Pavor's flanks and clamping his knees tightly, Marcus plunged off the roadway and down a steep gorge on the most direct route toward the trouble. On a plateau above the argument scene Pavor drove right through the middle of a flock of sheep, parting them like a ship pushes aside the sea.

As Marcus drew nearer, it became apparent that not two but three distinct groups of men were involved in what was nearly a brawl.

The easiest of them to recognize were the legionaries in their red tunics and flashing armor. Though not numerous, the soldiers, with their javelins at the ready, were prepared to attack. Marcus counted a decade of troopers and recognized a centurion with his distinctive transverse-mounted plume.

Beside these were fifteen or twenty laborers clad in leather. From the style of their dress and their brawny arms Marcus took them to be Jewish aqueduct workmen.

Opposite these and doing most of the arm waving were men whose hooked staffs announced them to be shepherds. Five herdsmen accompanied by three boys were angrily shouting at the others.

Hammers, javelins, and wooden staffs squared off.

Serious injury and death hovered close at hand.

At the drumming of Pavor's hooves the group sprang apart. All turned to gauge what sort of threat was thundering down on them. Spears, mallets, and shepherds' crooks formed a temporarily united phalanx of weapons confronting Marcus.

He rode directly toward the centurion and shouted for an explanation.

The Roman officer faced him, waving not a short sword or javelin but a roast leg of lamb. "Greetings, Marcus," the centurion boomed. "Heard you'd be along."

It was Shomron. Worn out in the service of Rome, the mostly bald centurion was usually on duty in the Antonia in Jerusalem and seldom left there.

"What's all this about?" Marcus demanded of the squat, leathery-faced Samaritan officer.

Shomron pointed with the sheep shank toward the shepherds. "Those fellows accused us of stealing. I explained that this lamb . . . and five or six others . . . wandered into the aqueduct right-of-way and were fair game."

"It's a dirty lie!" pronounced the biggest shepherd, a giant, white-haired man missing his left eye. "Jehu here saw those men driving off part of a flock bound for the Temple, and we tracked them here!" He leveled his staff at a dark-skinned, heavy-browed, thick-necked laborer who acted like the leader of the working men.

Marcus turned toward the stonemason, who deferentially tugged his forelock. "Oren is my name, sir. The army is supposed to supply us with midday rations, but for the last three days we've had nothing but weevilly meal mixed in cold water. A man can't bust rocks and haul mortar on that, can he, sir? What were we supposed to do?"

A babble of voices, like the unintelligible muttering of thousands of sheep, overwhelmed Marcus' hearing. Everyone blamed everyone else, everyone had a complaint, and all voiced them at once.

"Silence!" Marcus bellowed. "Shomron, set the laborers back to work. Then you, Oren, and—" Marcus looked at the scar-faced shepherd.

"Zadok," the man volunteered. "Chief of shepherds for Migdal Eder."

Marcus nodded. "Shomron, Oren, Zadok, and I will sort this out. The rest of you, back about your business!"

Over the vociferous objections of the shepherd named Jehu, Zadok sent his companions back to Migdal Eder.

"You, boy," Marcus added to a slender, blond-haired youth. "Hold my horse."

With surprise Marcus identified Avel, the beggar boy from Jerusalem whom he had last seen in Galilee. The light of recognition was in the boy's blue eyes too, but neither spoke.

Then Marcus noted that another diminutive figure was Emet, the deaf-mute. But the boy appeared healthier than when Marcus had seen him last. Happier too. Perhaps he had met Yeshua, as Marcus had suggested.

"Follow me," Marcus gruffly said to the three men, and he led them to a nearby tent.

Sunlight filtered through the fabric of the tent and moved in dappled patterns across the carpeted floor.

Marcus sat opposite the centurion, the stonemason, and the shepherd.

Of the three Zadok remained aloof, refusing to sit when offered a chair. Nor would he accept refreshment. He stood tall in spite of his advancing years. Instead of leaning on his staff, he gripped it as a soldier might carry a javelin. Marcus guessed from Zadok's scar that the shepherd had been a warrior at an earlier time in his life. The gash that marred his face carried the pattern of a Roman blade. Marcus had seen enemy skulls split open in exactly the same place by a legionary's blow. From the crown of the head through the eye, cheek, and into the jaw. It was invariably a fatal strike. An ordinary man would not recover from such a wound.

But Zadok seemed anything but ordinary. Proud and dignified, he was no simple shepherd. One fact was evident in his demeanor: he hated Rome and hated Marcus. He hated Shomron, the Samaritan centurion, even more. And he held the Jewish stonemason in utter contempt.

Zadok was, Marcus thought, perhaps the best man in the room.

Marcus began, "I arrived this morning. Sent here by Governor Pilate to oversee a project jointly undertaken by the Jewish Sanhedrin and Rome to bring water to Jerusalem. A benefit to all."

Zadok calmly cut to the heart of the issue. "The Paschal lambs you stole are Korban. Set apart from birth for sacrifice at the Temple."

"Stole!" Shomron reddened. "By law we are entitled to take what we need from the flocks to feed our men."

Zadok did not look at him. "I see you are Samaritan. You have no understanding." Then the shepherd's face turned ever so slightly toward the stonemason. "But you. A Jew. You know what it means to kill a Paschal lamb that is Korban and use it in an unworthy way."

The mason defended himself: "I worked on the Temple in Yerushalayim for sixteen years! We ate the meat from sacrificed lambs the same as any priest."

"A Roman aqueduct is not the Temple. That is the dispute which rages in Yerushalayim even now, is it not? And these lambs were not sac-

rificed," Zadok countered. "They were simply butchered." He leveled a stern gaze at the mason. "You know what you've done? You know what curse you've laid on yourself and your men by eating unworthily something which is the Lord's alone?"

The mason blanched. He opened his mouth and then closed it again, as if he couldn't think how to respond.

Marcus spread his hands on the desk in front of him. "What's done can't be undone. How can we . . . Rome . . . settle the loss?"

Zadok's brow furrowed as he considered Marcus' question. "You're a Briton?"

The question caught Marcus by surprise. "My mother."

Zadok's thin lips curled in an enigmatic smile. "Well, then. That island has yet to be conquered by Roman legions. Why do you wear the armor of Rome? Why are you here?"

A strange, probing question. One Marcus had lately asked himself. "We were speaking of lambs."

Zadok disagreed fiercely. "We speak of that which is holy. Sacred. Freedom. The Paschal lamb. Set apart for a single purpose. To die at Passover for our deliverance. To die in memory of the first Passover. In that hour the blood of the lamb marked the doorposts of Hebrew slaves in Egypt. The angel of death saw the blood as a sign of belief and passed over the Jewish households. But death came to the firstborn of Egypt who hadn't marked their doors with blood of the lamb!"

Marcus rebutted, "A worthy tradition. But hardly worth coming to blows over."

Zadok held up his finger, commanding silence. "That's not all. The sacrifice of a Paschal lamb recalls how Moses delivered the children of Israel from slavery in Egypt! Led them to freedom in a new land. This land. Our land. Eretz-Israel. Not Rome's. God's promise to Abraham is remembered every Passover by the sacrifice of a firstborn male lamb delivered in Beth-lehem in the stable of Migdal Eder." Zadok pointed the crook of his staff at the stonemason. "Son of Abraham! Dig and find wisdom. The death of the lamb symbolizes God's deliverance from the slavery of sin for the human soul! Deliverance for the seed of Abraham, Isaac, and Jacob! And through them Torah teaches that the whole world will be blessed! This is what the Eternal One promised to Abraham on the mount in Jerusalem where our Temple stands now.!"

The stonecutter covered his eyes with his hand and shifted uncomfortably in his seat.

Thus ended the lesson. The old man had made his point clearly. The stolen animals were much more than just a meal. Grave desecration had been committed by Roman legionaries and by Jewish stoneworkers.

Marcus said in a businesslike way, "Your philosophy has no place in this dispute."

"The lambs your mercenaries stole and butchered were the first-born males of the block. Unblemished. Perfect. Beloved by the shepherds who watched them grow. Each had a name. They were raised by hand in the Lord's lambing pens. Born within the circle of Migdal Eder's pastures. Reserved for sacrifice on one exact day of the year in Yerushalayim . . . Passover . . . to be offered to the Eternal One alone."

Shomron snorted at this. "They're sheep like any other!"

Zadok ignored the Samaritan centurion and addressed the Jewish stonemason. "Is that true, mason? Is an unblemished male lamb born in the stable of Migdal Eder in Beth-lehem and reserved for Passover just like any other lamb?"

The mason flushed and glanced down at his feet. "Get on with it!" he blurted.

The shepherd had managed to shame the stonecutter. Whatever Zadok was getting at went right over the Samaritan centurion's head. As for Marcus, he wished merely to prevent human bloodshed. There would be a vicious confrontation if the controversy wasn't resolved. And Marcus knew that in the end it would be the shepherds of Beth-lehem who would get the worst of any fight.

"You'll admit the workers have to be fed," Marcus protested.

"You have missed my point." Zadok was confident. "I intend to take word of this desecration to the Sanhedrin. Explain to them what goes on here! How Rome's soldiers and Jewish apostates mock our beliefs! Then the council will take the matter to the *cohen hagadol,* who will carry the matter to Pilate. And Pilate will certainly call you before him to explain why you allow our holy flock to be profaned."

Effective. The old shepherd had a persuasive way about him. The world was about to explode over a handful of sheep in Beth-lehem, and everyone would be blaming Marcus.

Marcus inquired, "What's the price of the Korban lambs? How many were butchered? Six? What's the price? Rome pays its debts."

"They can't be bought to feed the appetite of heathens."

"Understood. But what's done can't be undone. Your Passover lambs can't rise from the dead. Rome will make restitution. What we have wrongfully killed by . . . mistake . . . we will pay for. How much?"

Zadok considered the offer. "During Passover an unblemished lamb is purchased at the Temple for two and a half pieces of silver."

Shomron blurted, "Six lambs! That's fifteen shekels! Outrageous!"

Zadok ignored Shomron and explained to Marcus, "During Passover a lamb taken from the flock of Beth-lehem is sacrificed on behalf of a company of Israelites who share its flesh in a holy meal of remembrance. Tens of thousands of lambs. Hundreds of thousands of Jews. Each man pays a share of the price. That's the way of it." Zadok did not retreat from his demand. "We will be satisfied if Rome will pay for what it took. Six lambs. And . . . make restitution by purchasing six more to be sacrificed to feed the poor in Yerushalayim!"

Marcus was being herded into a corner by the clever shepherd. "A fair sum . . . for pardon of a religious error. A misunderstanding." Marcus leveled an angry gaze at the stonemason, who had surely known better. "In Rome a man who commits sacrilege can be crucified for it. So you see, Imperial Rome requires a man's life for his religious mistakes." Marcus then glared at Shomron as the centurion opened his mouth to protest. If this blew up into a religious riot, Marcus would make sure Shomron would be the officer Rome would execute. The intense look warned Shomron to say no more.

Marcus continued, "You Jews substitute the life of a lamb to pay for a man's transgressions. Civilized. Admirable. So . . . for the sin of our workmen we'll dock the pay of the stonemasons and the legionaries. And . . . six more lambs for the poor. Twelve lambs in all. Will thirty pieces of silver purchase atonement?"

The mason and the Samaritan scowled down at the floor. Zadok seemed satisfied, but he was not finished. "I also require your promise that your men will not steal Korban lambs again."

"Agreed. Those who do so will be punished." Then Marcus asked Zadok, "But my men have to be fed. There are other sheep in the flock. Those unworthy to be sacrificed to your God?"

Zadok turned the full force of his gaze on Marcus. Confusion flickered in the old man's eye an instant, as though he heard someone else speaking to him. He put a hand to his forehead and whispered, "You . . . Why are you here? The stonecutter has forgotten who he is. This Samaritan centurion sold his soul long ago. But you? Why defend them?"

"We're all Romans," Marcus snapped irritably. Why did Zadok put him on the spot in front of Shomron and the stonemason? "The whole world is Rome, in case you hadn't noticed! The chief priests at your own

Temple understand the realities of life. The Sanhedrin voted money for this aqueduct. Like it or not, it's a Jewish aqueduct. It will carry Jewish water to your Temple. I've made you a fair offer. We have to eat. What do you say?"

Zadok raised his face to gaze intently into Marcus' eyes. Fingers curled around the staff. "The settlement is fair. I'll go back now. We'll discuss which sheep we might sell off to you legally. In the morning bring the price. Temple coin. No Roman silver in the treasury of the Tower of the Flock. Come to Migdal Eder."

EL

Emet, Ha-or Tov, and Avel filled waterskins in the trough beside the well. They had been cleaning stalls all day, and toting water into the stable for two hours. The work was far from finished. The sun of late afternoon was hot on Emet's back. He splashed cool liquid on his face, sighed, and gazed across the valley of the fold. Blocks of stone rose up and men, like ants, climbed the scaffolding.

The boy viewed the graceful stone arches of the watercourse with new understanding. It meant Rome was encroaching on the sacred pastures, the herdsmen said. One tower at a time Caesar was stamping his image on the face of Israel. A bad thing. A change in the way things had been since the time King David had herded sheep in this very place.

The sheep didn't seem to notice the intrusion, Emet thought. They peacefully cropped grass among the pylons, oblivious to the *tink, tink, tink* of stonecutters' hammers or bored soldiers in scarlet tunics.

Closer in, near the Tower of Migdal Eder, Emet could see the tall, powerful figure of Zadok among the lambs who were bound for Jerusalem at first light tomorrow. The old man passed slowly through the flock. One last time he checked the condition of the Paschal sacrifices. Any imperfect animal was cut from the herd by Red Dog and driven to the gate, where Jehu separated it from its brothers.

Avel said, "Look at the lambs. These are best of the lot, Lev told me. Reserved for the *cohanim* and Levites."

Ha-or Tov added, "And when Zadok speaks, the sheep know his voice. Lev says in pitch-black night Zadok can call out and they'll come to him. There!" He pointed. "They lift their faces when he passes."

Yes. That was true. Emet agreed. The old man touched heads, scratched ears, caressed muzzles one at a time. "He's saying good-bye. He raised them from babies, and now he's saying good-bye."

"I suppose." Avel frowned and turned away. It was clear he didn't like to think about good-byes. "He's a odd old bird," he muttered.

"What about his scar?" Ha-or Tov wondered aloud.

Avel replied authoritatively, "Probably got it fighting bandits. Defending the herd."

Ha-or Tov twirled his red locks thoughtfully. "Maybe. Ask Lev."

Avel shook his head. "Not me. You do it."

Ha-or Tov declined. "Not me. I'm half-scared of him. He's not as stupid as he looks. And he doesn't like questions."

Both boys rounded on Emet. Avel remarked, "Lev's taken a liking to you, Emet. You're little. He thinks you're too young to have a brain. He wouldn't mind someone small asking him how Zadok's face got split open and his eye gouged out."

"Not me," Emet protested.

Avel threatened, "One word from me that you can't haul water without help, and it's the turnip patch."

And thus it was decided that Emet would ask the questions the others were afraid to ask.

The trio hauled the watering skins back to the stable. While Ha-or Tov and Avel emptied the contents into individual troughs, Emet approached Lev, who was doctoring the umbilical stump of a tiny newborn with a mixture of wine and oil.

Emet, his expression somber, waited patiently as Lev crooned to his patient.

Avel and Ha-or Tov cast furtive glances his way, encouraging him to get on with it.

At last Lev glanced up and scowled. "Well? Does it want something? Or is it dumbfounded by the chore of fetching water?"

Emet shook his head from side to side. His heart was pounding. Avel motioned to him to speak. Emet couldn't form words around his curiosity.

"Speak up, stump!" ordered Lev impatiently.

"Zadok." Emet managed.

"Yes. Yes. Yes. Zadok. What?"

Emet placed his hand over his eye, indicating the old man's eye-patch. "That."

Lev set the baby down and drew himself up. In a surprisingly calm voice he replied, "Oh. That. Y' think I know, do y'?" he confided. "Every day since I was a wee boy like yourself wandering around this place I've wondered the same. My father, who was a lambing shepherd here before me, knew about it. But he wasn't telling. Then he died. There were times when I thought herself . . . Zadok's wife . . . might speak of it. But she flew away with her eyes full of sorrow. She touched his scar like it was a memory sometimes when she didn't know I saw. And they shared the sadness. So, I don't know. I wish I did. And the old ones who are still around won't talk about it." Lev cupped his hands around his mouth and shouted to Avel and Ha-or Tov, "We're in the same boat, y' might say!" Lev snorted and laughed. "If y' find out, tell me. Else I'll grow old and die and go to the grave wondering what creature would dare be brave enough to strike a blow against Zadok, shepherd of the flock."

■ ■ ■ ■

Emet sat on the low barrier of his flock's stall and contemplated the little ones in his care. Three white and one black. The black male had made up for lost time. He was clearly larger, stronger, and more daring than his sisters . . . and all this in less than a day!

The hitherto unknown emotion of pride swelled in Emet's chest. These were his. What would he name them? The white triplets were identical in almost every respect. Sweet-faced and easy of disposition, they crowded around their surrogate mother like woolly sprouts on a bunch of cauliflower. How would he tell them apart?

Emet plucked at the threads of the handwoven robe supplied by Zadok until he managed to work loose the end of three strands of yarn. One yellow. One red. The last, blue. He tied a different color strand to each of the sisters.

He declared to the first, "Yellow is like the heart of a lily. You'll be Lily." And to the second, "Red is the color of the roses on the trellis outside the rich man's house on the Street of the Cobblers. Sister always liked the roses. So you're Rose." He attached the blue thread to the last of the three girls. "Blue." He stuck his lip out in consideration of such an important decision. Emet gazed thoughtfully out at the patch of sky beyond the mouth of the lambing cave. It came to him, plain as anything. "Cornflower."

And what should he name the curly black male who trotted boldly among his adoptive sisters? Emet wondered. He was the first at supper, the last to lie down to sleep. It was clear from the way he nibbled at Emet's shoe and tugged playfully at his cloak that this intrepid creature liked Emet.

Emet dubbed him the Bear.

For the fourth time in an hour Emet retied the fastenings of the white fleece cap beneath the black lamb's chin.

The most important task assigned to Emet was to keep the lambskin coats secured to the four babies in his care. Emet's fingers were clumsy. Not having had proper shoes, he had never learned to tie laces. He was afraid to admit this shortcoming since this was the one thing old Zadok assumed he was capable of. It was, he soon discovered, not as easy as it seemed at first.

Lambs, being like children, gamboled in the stall, nipped at one another, and jostled for position at Old Girl's udder. In these activities the strips of fleece on Lily, Rose, and Cornflower would slip sideways, become tangled, and be torn away. As for Bear, every time he butted against Old Girl for a squirt of milk, the cap would work loose and be trampled by tiny cloven hoofs before Emet could retrieve it.

Lev was no help when asked how the coverings might be better attached. "There's not enough of it to do it any other way!" he growled. "One hide! Four lambs! Old Girl's the only ewe who'd accept a shared fleece like this! See to it!"

And when Ha-or Tov, watching Emet's struggle, inquired why the things were still necessary Lev replied, "What! Are y' a total idiot?"

Lev clearly didn't like being questioned. Nor did he wholly approve of the intrusion of the three boys into his domain.

Emet remained silent the rest of the day. He turned the straw and fetched the required amount of grain, which he hand-fed to Old Girl as the babies nosed her flanks to find their meal.

As Emet, Avel, and Ha-or Tov were gulping down a morsel of flat bread, milk, and cheese, their break was interrupted. There was a ruckus in the pens. Old Girl began to bark and stamp her feet.

Lev sighed, stuffed his cheeks with the remaining bread, and in clear disgust rounded on Emet. "Now you've done it. Something's come loose. Don't y' know how to tie a proper knot?"

Avel and Ha-or Tov watched sympathetically as Lev clasped Emet by the arm and dragged him to Old Girl's pen. An altercation was in process between Old Girl and the black lamb, who was once again capless. Bear frantically attempted to dash in between his sisters as Old Girl whirled to face him, charging, threatening, and stamping a warning. Lily, Rose, and Cornflower huddled together, trembling, behind Old Girl's broad rear end.

Had Old Girl gone off? Emet wondered in astonishment at the rage in the aged ewe! She acted as though she had never seen Bear before! As if he were an interloper!

Lev snapped up the fallen scrap of fleece and scooped the terrified lamb into his arms. He bellowed at Emet, "You'll have to do better than this, stump!"

Tears of shame pushed at Emet's lids. His throat constricted. He had failed. Losing the covering of fleece had nearly resulted in injury to Bear.

Lev tugged the lamb's ears through the holes in the cap and secured the leather strap in a double knot. He held his handiwork out to Emet. "See here! That's the way you tie a knot!"

Emet's hands shook. He nodded in silent acknowledgment of his failure. And then, worse than anything, the shadow of Zadok fell across them.

The old shepherd glowered down like a thundercloud. He reached out to touch Bear, who was panting in terror and confusion. "What's this, Lev?"

"The runt let the fleece come off the black one," Lev complained. "And, sir! Look at herself, will y'! Old Girl's in a fright. Her udder will shrivel. She'll go dry, and then we'll have a time keeping these alive. This boy's not old enough for the lambing barn. Can't even tie a knot."

Zadok stooped till his face was level with Emet's. "Is that true, boy? About the tying?"

A tear escaped. Emet nodded. No, he did not know how to tie.

Zadok scooped up Emet's tear on his index finger and studied it. He held it to his lips as if to drink it. Then he almost smiled. Not quite, but nearly. "Then you shall learn."

■ ■ ■ ■

Leaving the aqueduct behind, Marcus rode toward Herodium. In addition to the castle on the summit Herod the Great had created a palace for his guests at the foot of the hill. An enormous artificial lake stood amid an orchard of date palms and transplanted balsam trees. In the midst of the otherwise barren surroundings and perched on the edge of a wilderness, it was a place where members of the monarch's entourage took their ease.

Marcus wondered how much ease was possibly experienced by a visitor to Herod's brooding tower. The suspicious monarch was apt to see hidden meanings and secret plots behind innocent observations . . . and a stay at Herodium could easily move from palace to dungeon in short order.

A trio of legionaries were bathing naked in the pool. They did not stop their diving and spouting when Marcus rode up. Since Marcus was not their officer, they apparently recognized no need to show respect for his rank.

Idumeans, Marcus guessed from their swarthiness; bazaar toughs hired to make up the complement of a legion. Certainly not soldiers Marcus would have permitted to remain part of First Cohort when he commanded.

The low wall enclosing the pool was marred with chalked graffiti. *Lucius likes goats*, read one scrawl. *Pythias used to be hot-blooded*, ran another, *but now there's only hot wine in his veins.*

None of it was very clever or original. Marcus had heard the witticism about Pythias applied to the aging Emperor Tiberius.

There was an air of seediness and decay about the place. Two of the palm trees had been sawn down, their ragged stumps left to rot. The trunks of the balsam trees were scarred with the slashes of those who stole the valuable sap. Lawns and shrubs were dead. Dust was heaped in the corners of the sunken garden paths, and a thin green slime floating atop the pool was ignored by the bathers.

Since Judea had been made a province ruled directly by Rome rather than a client state, Herod's palace belonged to the emperor for the use of his representatives. But Governor Pilate seldom left Caesarea on the clean seacoast. He rarely forced himself to visit Jerusalem; Herodium, never.

Leaving the crumbling guest facilities behind, Marcus urged Pavor toward the hill's north side. Here Marcus found a legionary who at least was in uniform and knew how to salute. Entrusting Pavor to the legionary's care, Marcus entered the underground tunnel that pierced the cone and was the sole entry to the fortress. A walk of several minutes took him through a black tube poorly lit at irregular intervals by smoldering torches.

Emerging from the tunnel, Marcus found himself beside another pool likewise surrounded by trees and garden, but located inside the basin of the hollow cone. Five stories of fortifications stretched upward above him. It was rumored that additional, secret levels existed below him in labyrinthine tangles.

Cities, monuments, temples, and towers had all been constructed by Herod and named to venerate the emperor, deceased relatives, or powerful friends.

But this lonely mountain, this malevolent symbol of arrogant authority poised on the skyline like the broken fang of a monstrous beast, Herod had chosen to name in honor of himself.

Herod had built the place to last for the ages, as an outpost against marauders coming out of the desert, a palace, and a retreat of last resort from revolution. It was also the royal mausoleum.

On the far side of the colonnade encircling the garden was a marble dome as large as a small house. It was placed so beams of sunlight would penetrate even the two-hundred-foot depth of the hill, illuminating Herod's crypt.

On the carved sides of the tomb were representations of everything Herod believed worthy of remembrance from his reign: leading military campaigns, receiving a coronet from the hand of Augustus, designing the harbor of Caesarea, laying out an aqueduct. All the scenes offered chiseled depictions of the king of the Jews as a heroic figure. Given a particular pride of place was a profile of Herod beside a view of the front of Jerusalem's renowned temple.

Clearly Herod wanted his memory linked both with what he had done to honor the man-god of the Romans and the favors he'd performed for the unnameable God of the Hebrews.

Sometime in the thirty-odd years since his death and burial here, someone had hacked off Herod's nose. Vengeful relative, vicious rebel, or idle soldier?

A voice spoke from behind Marcus. "My grandfather worked on this place a half century ago." It was Oren, the Jewish stonemason. He was covered in lime dust, and there was a bloody scrape down one shin. The man appeared to be exhausted. "My father labored on Herod's tomb there, and the two of us on the Temple." He gestured toward the detailed outline of the sanctuary.

"The workmanship is very fine," Marcus praised.

"Now I wonder if I'll ever worship there again."

"Why?" Marcus inquired. "There's no shame in building an aqueduct."

"May have to take my family and move away" came the reply. "Alexandria, maybe. There is work to be had there for stonecutters. You heard what the shepherd said: I'm apostate, defiled, cursed."

"That's paid for," Marcus corrected him. "Soon forgotten."

Oren shook his head. "As long as the aqueduct stands, it will divide Jews like me who worked on it from those like Zadok who hate it. Temple money or Beth-lehem sheep, it doesn't matter. Once declared Korban, they belong to the Almighty alone. I knew it but took the job anyway . . . my family has to eat, don't they? Don't they?"

Uncomfortable in the presence of so much unmanly emotion, the stoic Roman changed the subject. "You're hurt," Marcus said, indicating the leg wound.

"It's nothing," Oren replied. "Bad piece of stone. It cracked as we lowered it into place in the arch and tumbled down. I jumped clear just in time . . . almost," he concluded ruefully. "My own fault really. I inspected the blocks for soundness, but I must have missed that one."

"Will you be going up to the City for your Passover?" Marcus asked, knowing that the Jewish laborers could be excused for the religious holiday.

"Not me," Oren argued. "I'm defiled, remember? It's already too late to get cleansed in time for the ceremony."

"Because of a Roman waterworks and a Jewish lamb?"

Oren disagreed. "We're all defiled anyway. All of us stoneworkers." He pointed over Marcus' shoulder. "We're sleeping in a tomb."

There was an indecipherable air of evil and decomposition about the place. Marcus sensed it, though he wasn't given to superstition. Could it be a remnant of the malevolent executions Herod had carried out? Or was the smell of death really coming from Herod's tomb?

"Where's the harm in a grave?" Marcus maintained stoutly. "He's only food for worms."

Oren looked grim. "They say he was eaten up by worms *before* he died. If there is any lingering wickedness connected with any tomb, surely it must be this one."

And this was the place where the aqueduct laborers were housed and where the Roman soldiers guarding the construction were bivouacked. Rebel attacks and simmering revolt outside, evil spirits inside, and Marcus caught in the middle.

■ ■ ■ ■

It was the grizzled Samaritan centurion Shomron who led Marcus to his luxurious quarters in the lower palace of Herodium. Shomron was drunk and uncharacteristically jolly. The grease from the stolen roast lamb clung to his beard. A single louse paraded boldly across his bald dome from the eastern thicket of fringe to the west.

There were many marble baths in Herodium, Marcus noted, yet Shomron had not found a use for them.

The two centurions, old and young, ascended a staircase to a dark, wide corridor paved in marble.

Shomron puffed, "You having the *corona obsidionalis* as your crown of honor and being the hero of Idistaviso and all. I suppose you won't mind sleeping where the mighty have slept, eh?"

"I'll sleep mightily, no matter where I lay my head tonight," Marcus replied.

"There's not much for a man of action as yourself to do here. But it's a fine, easy duty. Quiet. No trouble."

"I've been chasing rebels in the wilderness most of the last months."

"Well. Yes, not much for us to do. But it's cream of the quarters for officers." He threw back a bronze door and thrust the torch forward to reveal an elaborate suite adorned with cobwebs and marble pillars surrounding a round canopied bed. Polished bronze mirrors on every wall caught Marcus' dim reflection in the light. The floor was an intricate geometric mosaic. The entire room was overly feminine and rivaled the most elegant brothels in Rome.

"Not decorated for a soldier." Marcus hung back.

Shomron guffawed. "I was garrisoned in this fortress as a lad forty-one years ago. While the old butcher king was on the throne slaughtering everyone he took a suspicion to. Fifty of us stinking up the barracks while he's up here in luxury conjuring demons and murdering his relatives. I'm glad to have moved up in the world, I can tell you!" He winked. "I'm sleeping in the old butcher's bed myself now!"

"And what is this?" Marcus sensed an eerie chill as he scanned the chamber.

"Mariamme's room. The Hasmonaean queen. A true descendant of the Maccabee clan. Herod poisoned her in a fit of rage, and as long as I was around he regretted her dying. Wandered these corridors crying for her. Wailing her name in fits till he died."

Marcus ached between his shoulder blades. He hadn't slept in a proper bed in weeks. But this was not the place he wanted to start.

"Not for me." Marcus could clearly picture the dying queen convulsing on the floor at his feet. "Officer's quarters will do."

Shomron's face puckered in disappointment. "Suit yourself."

He retreated back into surly silence as he led Marcus down the winding staircase to the dreary row of cells that served as bedrooms for servants and soldiers. He slapped the door with the flat of his hand, indicating this was the place.

Handing off the torch, Shomron padded away toward the wine cellar without another word.

Marcus entered the musty chamber. Four unadorned stone walls. A narrow bed. A rack of dowels for hanging spare gear. It had the safe, familiar feel of a barracks. He could have been in the military quarters of any fortress between Rome and Alexandria. Here he could close his eyes without thoughts of butcher kings, murder, and madmen roaming the halls of Herodium.

Carefully he untied his bedroll and took out a bronzed leafy crown. The *corona obsidionalis* was the highest award for bravery in the Roman army. It was all Marcus had left to prove he had once been a rising star in Rome. But when Marcus had impulsively offered this crown, along with his sword, to Yeshua of Nazareth, the Master had declined both. Instead he had promised Marcus that one day he would wear a crown in Jerusalem, and that Marcus would be at his feet in that hour.

Did Yeshua mean to claim the throne in Jerusalem next week? When the city was packed with citizens from all over the Roman empire? Not now, Marcus hoped. Not when every sword of Rome in Jerusalem would be ready to strike.

Marcus hung the *corona* on the wooden peg beside his sword. He groaned audibly as he threw himself across the sagging rope bed and closed his eyes.

One day perhaps he would again offer Yeshua the crown, as well as his sword and his loyalty. For the present there was an aqueduct to be built for Pilate and the Jewish Sanhedrin. There were also angry shepherds to placate. Not a difficult duty. No glory to be gained in the Valley of the Sheepfold. It was a well-known maxim that Rome continued to thrive by the execution of ordinary tasks, not in dreams of glory.

Tonight Marcus slept the dreamless sleep of exhaustion.

ADADAV

Emet's mind was as cluttered with weary thoughts as his muscles were full of aches. A day spent tending Old Girl and her flock involved mucking out, sweeping up, hauling water and feed, and innumerable occasions of tying and retying the disguising fleece shawls and bonnets.

And Emet was in misery because he couldn't tie properly

Avel and Ha-or Tov gabbed nonstop over their barley soup about what they had seen and done in the fields around Migdal Eder. Their talk was full of commentary in regard to the Roman water project and the Jewish workmen.

Emet was too downcast to take part in the discussion.

He replayed what he had seen in the stable. In particular, he thought about the black lamb named Bear. One day earlier the lamb was clearly in trouble: skinny, weak, and headed for death. Now he had energy enough to try to butt Emet, and to annoy his sisters and his adoptive mother with his antics. Bear ate almost nonstop too, indulged by Old Girl as he pushed in ahead of Lily, Rose, and Cornflower . . .

. . . as long as the cap stayed firmly secured, Emet reminded himself ruefully.

And those changes happened as a result of a scrap of bloody hide?

In the busy life of the sheepfold there had been no opportunity to talk to Zadok about the mystery. Lev was the other possible source of explanation, and he was too scornful for Emet to want to inquire of him about anything.

If only Emet were just as good at being an apprentice shepherd as Bear was at being a baby sheep. Emet dreaded the idea that he might yet be sent away. The vision of being forced from this place to tending someone's turnips renewed the boy's gloom.

Emet heard the tromp of Zadok's feet as he approached and entered the house.

"So dinner is done? Clean up, then. Don't wait to be told."

After dishes and boys were both washed up, Emet gazed at the soft pile of bedding and decided his questions for Zadok could wait till the morning.

But in this he was wrong.

After a critical inspection of the supper utensils, Zadok lighted two more lamps. Taking down another clay jar from the shelf, he said, "Days for work and nights for study, eh? Gather around and pay attention."

Emet saw Avel and Ha-or Tov exchange a weary look, but no one ventured to protest.

Unrolling a length of parchment scroll, Zadok staked the corners firmly in place with smooth white stones. Calling their attention to the title that headed the entry he challenged Avel to read it.

"*Bet, resh, alef, sheen . . . ,*" Avel recited, continuing to note the individual letters until he had spelled out the word. "*B'resheet . . .* beginnings . . ."

"It means," Zadok explained, "that this is the book of the beginnings of all things."

Ha-or Tov brightened. He pointed out the open door, which framed stars like a picture. "In the beginning *Elohim* created the heavens and the earth!"

"You know this then?" Zadok seemed impressed with Ha-or Tov's response.

"In Galilee. Yeshua taught us. He gave us birthday stars, and taught us about the heavens," Avel asserted quickly, as if not wanting Zadok to have a higher opinion of Ha-or Tov. "He said you'd teach us about the earth. What was. What is. And that then we would understand what will be."

Zadok appeared struck by these words. Then doubt flickered across his face. "This rabbi of yours? Things of the earth he left to a shepherd to teach? Too much to learn in so short a span as one lifetime." A long silence followed. The boys didn't dare speak as the old man searched the writings before him. At last he asked in a whisper that sounded as if it were directed to someone other than the boys, "Who are they that they should know the secret? And I, that I should teach them?"

After a full minute Ha-or Tov cleared his throat and added, "He said the chief shepherd of Migdal Eder would unravel the mystery of the lamb . . . whatever that means."

"He said that, did he?" Zadok asked.

Avel spoke up. "Yes. He told us Zadok and the flock would teach us."

Emet's face drooped further. He had nothing to add to this discussion.

"And did he say where," Zadok pressed, "we would begin?" Rising from his chair he loomed above Emet. Was the boy about to be punished for knowing nothing of beginnings?

Emet stared at his clumsy fingers. He wished he could learn something practical tonight, like how to tie. He blurted the question that had been plaguing him all day: "What does it mean that my lambs wear the fleece of a dead lamb?"

Zadok tugged his beard. "So. A logical beginning, I suppose." Scooping Emet up with one hand, Zadok held the boy aloft while he sat again and drew himself up to the scroll. Then he plopped Emet down on his lap. "Closer," he insisted to Avel and Ha-or Tov. "Torah is a book about the sheep of *Elohim*'s pasture. In it is the WHY of all things. Listen, then, to what it means when Emet's lambs wear the fleece of a lamb who died."

For several minutes Zadok read aloud from the scroll of beginnings. This was a story none of the boys had heard before. It was a good story. Interesting. Yet it did not explain the skullcap on the head of the black lamb.

And then Zadok began to elaborate.

"After the Almighty created the heavens and the lights, in the time before time there was a terrible war in heaven. A rebellion of angels. The earth, beautiful and pristine, was engulfed in chaos. It became without form. Without life. And the spirit of *Adonai Elohim* brooded over it like a hen broods over the eggs in her nest. And he created the earth anew. The waters and the grass and trees and fishes and the birds and creatures of earth, and a special garden." Zadok said, "Last of all, he made the man, Adam, from the dust of the earth, and he breathed into him life, making him a living soul. And the Lord told Adam that he was in charge of the garden and all the creatures. In fact, he brought the animals to Adam to name."

"Just like I named the lambs?" Emet inquired with a start. "Lily and Cornflower, Rose and Bear?"

"Just like that," Zadok agreed. "So, y' see, the first man was by profession a herdsman, a shepherd, because he had the care of the sheep and the goats and the cattle."

"And lions and wolves?" Avel interjected.

Nodding without pausing for the interruption, Zadok continued, "And he tended a bit of garden too, as I do. Adam was happy with his duties and not ashamed that he had much to learn."

Emet grew warmer inside at that thought.

"And everything there was good to eat," Zadok continued, "except one tree that bore fruit Adam was commanded not to eat."

"Why not?" Emet wondered aloud. "Was it poison?"

"You might say so," Zadok said. "It was in the center of the garden, and it was called *the tree of the knowledge of good and evil.* The Almighty warned Adam that the very day he ate fruit from that tree, he would die."

"Why didn't the Almighty uproot such a dangerous tree?" Ha-or Tov inquired. "Adam might have eaten the bad fruit by mistake."

The braids of Zadok's beard moved from side to side as he disagreed. "No. Adam was smart. He knew where that one tree was and he knew not to eat its fruit. You see, in all the world there was just *one* thing Adam was not allowed to do. The Almighty had to leave that tree there to see if Adam would obey his instructions."

"How tough could it be to not eat poison fruit?" Avel challenged.

"Watch and see," Zadok replied. "Things went well for a time, but Adam was lonely because he had no mate."

Zadok paused unaccountably. His eye searched the small room, as if he were looking for something. When his gaze turned back to them, there was a sadness in it. "Rams had their ewes," he said as he resumed, "roosters their hens, but Adam had no mate. *Adonai* saw this and decided to do something about it. He made a woman for Adam from Adam's rib."

"From his rib?" Emet repeated incredulously.

"And from this flesh and bone and blood that was Adam's very own the Almighty fashioned his bride, our first mother. Her name was Ishah. She was beautiful. And Adam and Ishah were happy together. They and the Lord God walked and talked together in the garden every day."

"Did they have children?" Avel asked.

"You're getting ahead of the story," Zadok scolded, but he didn't sound angry. "One morning Mother Ishah was walking through the center of the garden, near the tree of the knowledge of good and evil. When she stopped to look at it, she noticed that the fruit appeared especially ripe and juicy, plump and enticing."

"Uh-oh," Emet breathed.

"Mother Ishah heard a voice calling her name. But it wasn't her husband, and it wasn't the Lord God either. It was the Adversary, the Accuser. . . . Do y' know who I mean?"

The boys bobbed their heads in rapt attention. So ominous was Zadok's tone about what was coming in the story that none of them wanted to speak Satan's name.

"He who had been the Angel of Light had become the Prince of Darkness. The Father of all lies and liars! I speak of Lucifer, created by the Almighty. Much beloved by *Adonai*, Lucifer was the first being ever to rebel against the Lord. He said, '*I will ascend to heaven, I will raise my throne above the stars of God!*' And that was why the Lord God cast Lucifer down to earth from heaven. So Lucifer appeared to Mother Ishah as a serpent."

The flickering lamplight threw shadows into the corners of the little room. Emet's eyes searched them for crawling snakes, and his ears investigated the air for hisses and slithers. Zadok caught the boy's uneasiness. "In those days," he explained, "the serpent was a beautiful, attractive creature, and very clever. Not like snakes nowadays."

"Oh," Emet said.

"Listen carefully to what the serpent said to the woman," Zadok instructed with a warning finger tracing the letters on the expanse of scroll. He began to read aloud:

"'*Did God really say,* You must not eat from any tree in the garden?'

"*The woman replied to the serpent,* 'We may eat fruit from the trees in the garden, but God did say, You must not eat fruit from the tree that is in the middle of the garden, and you must not touch it, or you will die.'"

"Wait a minute," Ha-or Tov interrupted indignantly. "God didn't say anything about not *touching* the tree, did he?"

"No," Zadok said, smiling. "Well done, boy. Y' see, the woman was changing God's commands to suit herself. A little here. A little there. Speaking as if she had God's own authority. And this opened her soul to what came next."

The old man resumed reading from the text, "'*You will not surely die.* . . . *For God knows that when you eat of it your eyes will be opened, and you will be like God, knowing good and evil.*'

"Y' see," Zadok continued, "the Adversary presented Mother Ishah with the same sin he himself fell into . . . wanting to be like God."

Ha-or Tov covered his eyes, as if he didn't want to see what followed, but Zadok nudged him with his elbow and pointed toward the writing again. "So Mother Ishah plucked a piece of fruit from the tree and ate some."

"Oh, no!" Emet mourned.

"And she took some to her husband and Adam ate too. Suddenly they were ashamed! They knew they'd done wrong. They realized they were naked. They tried to cover themselves by making fig leaf aprons."

"Then what happened?" Avel asked.

"The sun was setting! Adam remembered what the Lord God said about how if they ate the fruit they'd die that very day! And they heard *Adonai Elohim* walking in the garden, calling for his friends, '*Where are you?*' And even though Adam wanted God's help so they wouldn't die, Adam told the Lord he was hiding, because he was naked. Well, of course God knew what happened, but he asked anyway, '*Have you eaten from the tree that I commanded you not to eat from?*'"

Red Dog rose from beside the fire and padded toward the door, stopping on the threshold to stare out at the night.

Emet shivered.

Resuming his tale, Zadok said, "God asked Adam what happened, and Adam blamed Ishah. This woman that he loved more than life itself . . . he blamed her for what he did! And Ishah? She blamed the serpent. And people have been blaming others for their own sins ever since! But every person is responsible for his own soul. Everyone is given a free will to do right or wrong."

"But did they die? What happened?" Emet worried aloud.

Zadok reached around Emet to unroll a bit more of the scroll. "Now we come to why I chose this lesson to begin our studies," he said, picking up the story as it was written, "*The Lord God made coats of skin for Adam and his wife, and he clothed them.*"

"Where did the Lord get their coats?" Avel asked.

"From the flock. Lambs died instead of the man and his woman," Zadok said. "Innocent lambs who had never done anything wrong. And the Lord wrapped the first man and the first woman in the bloody skins."

Emet's head snapped up. "Just like we did with the orphan lambs? Just like the little cap on Bear's head?"

"Exactly," Zadok said. The chief shepherd's scarred and weathered face was gravely approving. "Emet, tell me what you saw in the lambing barn."

The boy twirled his earlocks on his finger as he replied, "Old Girl took the orphans . . . because they wore the coat of her own lamb who died."

Zadok snapped his fingers. "When she looks at the orphans she doesn't see strangers, but her own beloved baby. The ways of the flock help us understand how God saves us from our sin. The Lord God himself made the first sacrifice of a lamb as atonement for man's sin. It was that innocent lamb which died instead of Adam and Ishah. And we who raise the lambs of Migdal Eder for the Temple are part of God's picture of redemption for mankind. Our sheep are sacrificed at the Temple as a substitute for men's transgressions against the laws of God."

Avel remarked, "Very unfair to the lambs!"

"This is what was," Zadok stated. "And what is. And it shows us what will happen here on earth in the future."

To know the future seemed like a good thing to Emet. Suddenly he was not so tired anymore.

Zadok's face was animated, as if he enjoyed teaching what he knew. "After the fall of man the garden ceased to bloom by itself. Now the earth is rank with thorns and the pastures grow weeds, causing our constant labor. On the day Adam and Ishah were banished from the garden, the Lord declared to Lucifer, '*I will put enmity between you and the woman, and between your offspring and hers; he will crush your head, and you will strike his heel.*'"

"What does that mean?" Ha-or Tov asked, bewildered.

Zadok replied, "This was Torah's first prophecy about the coming Savior, our Messiah. It was the beginning of war between the Lord and Lucifer over the souls of mankind. It is the promise of God that someday a woman will give birth to a righteous son who will fight against the Evil One and win the battle over death."

"Will there be armies?" Emet clasped his knees and pictured thousands of armed soldiers facing one another in the valley.

Zadok explained, "No. There will, in the end, be only Messiah standing alone against all the forces of evil and darkness. Our Savior will be a man of sorrows. The whole world, even his friends, will turn against him. He will meet death despised and betrayed by all."

"But why?" Emet felt a pang of grief.

Avel's expression was full of anguish. "It's not fair!"

Zadok calmly traced the words of the scroll for the answer. "It must be. It will be. Scripture teaches that the Lord God will send Messiah like a lamb. With his own life he will pay the penalty for man's sin once and for all. His blood will redeem our souls from Satan's power. Satan demands our deaths because we have broken God's commands. But God's mercy provides the Messiah to die in our place. By his blood we are offered eternal life if we believe. The prophet Isaiah tells it clearly. See here?"

The old shepherd unrolled another document and scanned the contents until he found what he was looking for. "Here it is. Plain as can be. By Messiah's wounds we are healed. He'll live among us within the humanfold as God's perfect lamb. There will be no sin in him. He'll teach us about God's love. He'll give sight to the blind. The deaf will hear. He'll mend the hearts of the lonely. In the end he'll lay down his life as the final sacrifice for all men, everywhere. Then the Lord of heaven will look down on us . . . like Old Girl looks at her orphans. They are adopted and loved, because they are clothed in the coat of one she loved. Old Girl sees only the image of her own beloved offspring. One lamb died so that many would live . . . In this same way every man, woman, and child who asks for God's mercy will be clothed in the pure white fleece of Messiah's righteousness. He is our Savior and Redeemer. And we who were lost and without hope will be adopted into God's family as his own beloved children."

Emet considered the story of the lambs. It contained a harsh and horrifying lesson.

Avel's eyes brimmed with sorrow. "Must he die? Will they kill him so we can live?"

The old man nodded. "I have studied a lifetime. The plan . . . It's all written in the law of Moses and in the prophets. And it's the only way."

Avel cried out, "But we only just found him!"

Ha-or Tov whispered, "I was blind, and he made me see."

Emet added, "And my ears are open now!"

Zadok considered this revelation. "So. He sent you ahead as messengers. Three small boys. To this house. Yes. This empty house. Well. Yes. He would do that after all. . . . And so? *Immanu'el.* God-with-us. Thirty-two years have passed since I first heard that name." He closed the scroll. "I had almost given up hope."

HA-NEVI'IM

Come morning Zadok presented each of the boys with the gift of a shepherd's staff cut to size. Perfect for Avel, Emet, and Ha-or Tov. Where had they come from? The old man simply produced them from a corner of the room, as if he had been waiting to give them away to three boys. Better than swords, they were. It came to Emet that the staffs of shepherds were carried by lion slayers, wolf tamers, defenders of the innocent, poets, scholars, kings, and saviors!

"You'll carry these with you into Yerushalayim," the old man announced. "At Passover. Together we'll bring in the last of the flock to the Temple. You'll enter Sheep Gate as shepherds of the flock."

It was a great honor.

This morning, after all the lambs at the lambing barn were cared for, the trio of apprentices followed Zadok into the pastures. Red Dog followed close at the heels of Emet as he trailed after Zadok and the other two boys.

Blue Eye ran ahead, skirting the perimeter of yearling ewes pastured beyond the tower. At Zadok's command Blue Eye cut the least desirable sheep from the herd.

With the swipe of hyssop dipped in scarlet dye, Zadok marked the backs of those culled for sale and slaughter. For the sake of his apprentices the old man listed the conditions of rejection. "Unsuitable for breeding. Too small. See here? Hindquarters too close. That one? Narrow shoulders. Feel the fleece. And now this one. Inferior grade of wool. You'll learn. In time, you'll learn. There. That one! Stringy muscles. Tough meat. And that? Swaybacked. Lame . . ." The list of reasons grew as the flock master worked. Only perfection would do in breeding stock. Those who did not measure up would pass bad qualities on to offspring and ultimately diminish the standards of the future herd. Therefore the yearling ewes reserved for breeding had to measure up in every way.

Those not good enough would be sold off to the Roman garrison at Herodium at fair market price, stringy meat notwithstanding.

The officer was coming this very morning, Zadok explained. There would be bargaining and counteroffers for the inferior sheep, but the end was inevitable. Rome would buy.

It was Avel who first spotted the approach of the tall black horse and his Roman rider. The proud creature pranced nervously past the fields of bleating livestock. The eyes of the warhorse rolled in suspicion and terror at acres of woolly backs.

Zadok observed the skittish progress of man and mount as they neared the Tower of Migdal Eder. "He should have come on foot."

There was something familiar about the horse, Emet thought, as the centurion came closer. They had seen him yesterday, but the recollection of familiarity had not become clear until now. What was it?

Avel remarked, "His horse." Avel nudged Emet. "I think . . . look! It's the same horse who threw Kittim on his head at the rebel camp!"

And so it was. Only in full-blown wildness did the identity of the animal become certain. Black, proud, nostrils flared, eyes wild and rolled to one side, the creature progressed at a sideways skip across the field. Emet grinned at the recollection of the wild men of bar Abba's band trying to ride the creature into submission. One by one the rebels had been thrown off like rag dolls into the mud. Emet, Ha-or Tov, and Avel had cheered for the horse as it reared and tore itself free from its tormentors. Kittim, a devil in the skin of a man, had been determined to butcher the animal for meat. But Kittim had been defeated in the end. The beast had fled into the wilderness beyond Jericho. Apparently it had been found and semi-tamed.

"So," Avel remarked with satisfaction. "He's fetched up under a Roman saddle. If a Roman can ride something that terrible, bar Abba should be worried."

Ha-or Tov laughed. "For the moment. Looks like the Roman won't be on board long."

But the centurion remained solidly on the back of his mount, as if such equine antics were normal.

Zadok strode toward the tower where they would meet. There was business to transact.

The soldier did not glance to the right or the left at hostile glares from the shepherds as he rode up the slope. And when stock dogs charged unchecked by their masters to snarl at the hooves of the stallion, the rider sat calmly atop his frantic mount. His demeanor seemed to say this was all in a day's work.

The Roman was a fellow who, in retrospect, made the bandits of bar Abba's camp appear to be clumsy fools, Emet thought. He said, "When we saw him first in Yerushalayim he didn't seem a bad sort."

Zadok's brow furrowed. "Where do you know this Roman from?"

Avel explained, "He's the centurion who gave Emet alms the morning we left to find the rebels!"

Zadok considered this information with interest as they watched from the knoll. "He knows you then?" Zadok's tone indicated the Roman wasn't fully human and certainly couldn't be trusted.

"Yes, sir. We were running away from Yerushalayim because Kittim, who was the leader of the quarry Sparrows, beat me and said he would kill me. The Roman was waiting in the street across from the old palace of Herod. It was raining, and we didn't see his armor under his cloak. I told him we were going to find the rebel bar Abba and learn to kill Romans."

"And what did he say to that?" Zadok inquired.

"He gave me two silver denarii," Emet explained. "Not a bad man, sir."

"A Roman. They don't give unless it's to gain something by it," Zadok remarked with passion. "Remember this, boy."

"Yes, sir." Emet ducked his chin. Was old Zadok angry with him?

The centurion was upon them. He saluted Zadok in Roman fashion, his fist over his heart.

Red Dog crouched and snarled. Zadok did not call him off instantly, but waited as the Roman horse spun in a tight circle.

"You should have come on foot," Zadok admonished. "Warhorses don't like sheep."

The soldier patted the lather-flecked neck of his horse and replied, "Now you know the secret of defeating a Roman cavalry in battle: send out a flock of sheep . . . before your infantry." He flashed a smile. "And your sheep dogs. Don't forget the dogs."

Zadok snapped his fingers, commanding Red Dog and Blue Eye to his side. They sank back, panting, on their haunches. The horse calmed a bit.

The Roman said, "There's nothing a Roman cohort fears more than a flock of sheep. Especially those sheep that pasture near Migdal Eder in Beth-lehem." He stepped down from the stallion. "I promise you, my men will not go near them again!"

Zadok, resolute and stern, replied stiffly, "Then they have learned a well-taught lesson, Centurion Marcus Longinus."

"Zadok, chief shepherd of the flock . . . My men tremble at the sound of a single bleat." Marcus raised his hand as if taking an oath.

A glint of humor passed across the old shepherd's face. "We have a less fierce flock to sell you. No warrior lambs. Your men need not tremble over their stew any longer."

"Well, then." The centurion sounded pleased.

Emet thought that the Roman was not so bad as Zadok imagined. But the boy looked down quickly, lest anyone see in his eyes he did not hate the fellow.

The Roman took notice of Avel and Emet. "And you're here. I saw you yesterday but was unsure. . . . Emet . . . Truth . . . that's your name, isn't it? I remember. And Avel! The Jerusalem Sparrows who were away to the wilderness to find the rebel camp! To fight at bar Abba's side!" He eyed the crooked staffs. "A better sort of weapon than a sword. So how many enemies have you slain?"

Avel's chin jutted out. "Not so many as your horse, I'd say."

The Roman laughed and gave the muzzle of his horse an affectionate stroke. "Pavor only shakes at the sight of sheep, as I said."

Emet ventured, "But we found Yeshua . . . the one you told us to find."

Amazement passed over Marcus' rock-hard features. "I can hear that fact with my own ears, boy. You speak well enough. I'm glad for it."

"He sent us here," Ha-or Tov volunteered.

But the boys had said too much to the Roman. Zadok stepped between them and Marcus.

Zadok intoned, "You will excuse my lads' forwardness in speaking to an officer of Rome. There's work in the stable for them and bargaining for us. I have a number of sheep I can sell you."

"And I've brought the price of redemption." Marcus withdrew a leather pouch from his armor. "Thirty pieces of Temple coin as agreed."

"A fresh beginning," said Zadok, accepting the payment. "So. We start on level ground."

With that Zadok sent the boys back to chores in the barn. He did not invite the Gentile into the Tower of Migdal Eder. Their business would be settled outside, in the sheep pens.

■ ■ ■ ■

Avel and Ha-or Tov had been assigned to help with shearing.

Emet, much to Lev's displeasure, was left at the stable to perform menial chores.

Old Girl had fed her troops. She munched contentedly on the grain Emet provided for her. By night a fresh supply of milk would replenish the sagging, deflated udder.

For the moment her four lambs were gorged, bellies fat and round. They watched drowsily as Emet cleaned the enclosure.

Such a tiny pen, Emet thought as he removed the trampled straw.

"All right then," Lev instructed, wanting to be rid of him. "After y' fetch water, go to the tower."

Emet did not reply. There was one more thing he wanted to do before the day was gone.

The black lamb waited at the gate for Emet and Blue Eye. Emet dropped a loop of twine around Bear's throat, cracked the gate to let him out, then led him toward the sunlight.

Lev, sharpening his knife on a whetstone, grumbled, "Where do y' think you're going then?"

"Zadok says lambs need exercise. Need to get acquainted with grass, he says."

Blue Eye danced along behind, eager to protect this diminutive shepherd and flock of one sheep.

Without looking up, Lev remarked, "Taking it out for a stroll? Sheep's sheep. You've made it into a dog. It won't end well. That's all I've got to say."

Out of Lev's hearing Emet scrubbed Bear's cheek and leaned close to his ear. "Never mind Lev. He's never much out of the stable."

Other lambs gamboled in the open at the sides of their mothers, didn't they? Only those who required special care remained cloistered in the cave. Zadok had told Emet boys and lambs needed to walk and run a bit to grow strong.

So? Once in the open Bear tried his legs, scampering sideways and kicking up his heels.

Yes. This was good.

Emet squinted at the brilliant sunlight. Who could imagine that there could be this many shades of green? Clouds sailed across the azure sky, casting shadows on the ground.

A flock of sparrows flew above Emet's head. He watched their course. Was Yediyd among them? Would the little bird recognize Emet and fly onto his hand? The birds circled in one unified movement and settled near the top of a craggy hill.

Emet had a waterskin. A bit of bread to share with the dog.

The boy set his sights on the heights beyond Beth-lehem, where the sparrows had gone. A patch of pasture streaked its slope with green. Farther up was a copse of pine trees along the ridge. There was a path leading to a granite terrace at the top. Zadok had told them that King David had walked that path. He had carried his harp and sat on a flat stone where he composed his music. Perhaps, Emet thought, some of the shepherd king's music lingered there like a bird that had not yet flown away. And surely Emet could see the whole world from there. He imagined the distant Tower of Siloam and beyond, all the way to Jerusalem on a clear day.

Bear was still too small for such an arduous hike. Once out of Lev's domain Emet carefully tied his keffiyeh into a sling around Bear's middle, then carried the lamb over his shoulder to the top of the peak.

■ ■ ■ ■

On his second visit to Gamaliel, Nakdimon sat silently, unwilling to say more until Gamaliel dismissed Saul. The student left the room reluctantly. Only then in a hushed voice did Nakdimon repeat what Yeshua had said about Moses. "I've been searching my memory for everything. Every detail. There's more."

"His exact wording, please. If he is the One, then every word from his mouth will have incredible significance, layers of meaning we must seek in the Scriptures."

Nakdimon nodded. "He said, just as Moses lifted up the serpent in the wilderness, so the Son of man must be lifted up."

Gamaliel frowned. "You're sure of it? Son of man?"

"Yes. The prophecy in Dani'el."

"Lifted up?" The sage hurried to a cabinet containing myriad scrolls. He selected the scroll of the prophet Isaiah and carried it to a broad study table. Unrolling the document, he scanned the writing and then exclaimed, "Here it is! In the section we know foretells the coming of Messiah!" He beckoned Nakdimon to his side and moved the lamp so they might read the words.

Nakdimon followed along as Gamaliel read the passage aloud: "*He will be raised and lifted up.*" Gamaliel paused. "It's here in Isaiah 52 that we should begin our study."

"Will he declare himself king then?"

Gamaliel replied, "You haven't read far enough, nephew. Perhaps lifted up and raised do not mean what we think. Suffering follows. It's also known that this passage is linked to the one in Dani'el that speaks of the Holy One being cut off. Read it to me."

Nakdimon considered the word choices of the prophet. The verses that followed were a startling picture of suffering, sorrow, and even death.

"The Messiah's appearance was so disfigured beyond that of any man and his form was marred beyond human likeness. He was despised and rejected by men, a man of sorrows and familiar with suffering. . . . Surely he took our infirmities and carried our sorrows. . . . But he was pierced for our transgressions, he was crushed for our iniquities; the punishment that brought us peace was upon him, and by his wounds we are healed."

Gamaliel put a hand on Nakdimon's arm. "This is, of course, a picture of temple sacrifice. On the Day of Atonement one goat, the scapegoat, is chosen by drawn lots and then set free. The other animal is sacrificed for atonement of the sins of Israel. Its blood is sprinkled on the altar. It has always puzzled me that Isaiah writes as though the atonement will be made by the blood of Messiah himself. See here, at the beginning of this passage . . . *'so will he sprinkle many nations.'"*

Nakdimon considered the passage. "Yeshua said that Moses wrote about him. That if we believe Moses, then we'll believe him. I've been thinking . . . The picture of sacrifice is also seen in Passover. The salvation of those Israelites who obeyed the command God gave to Moses in Egypt. When the blood of the lamb was sprinkled on the doorposts of the house the Angel of Death passed over."

Gamaliel hummed thoughtfully. "Yes. Passover." He carefully rolled up the scroll and set it to one side. "What was it Yochanan the Baptizer called Yeshua?"

"He said, 'Behold the lamb.'" Nakdimon swallowed hard. "'The lamb of God . . . who takes away the sins of the world.'" Nakdimon's brows knit together as the significance of the messianic prophecies and their possible meanings tumbled through his brain.

Gamaliel closed his eyes in thought for several minutes. When he opened them again he was pale and subdued. He warned Nakdimon, "Say nothing about this to anyone. If Yeshua of Nazareth *is* the Messiah, then the meaning of every prophecy will become clear. There's no changing what is written even though we can't understand it completely before its fulfillment." The meeting was finished. "Go home. Pray. Study. Write down every word you heard. I think perhaps . . . everything he says means much more than it may suggest at first hearing. Search it out. Question everything. Ask yourself what he might have meant. Check his teaching against the words of Torah and the prophets."

Almost as an afterthought, Nakdimon mentioned the journey from the Galil. "I met three children on the road south. One boy worked as a link boy. A Sparrow. His name is Avel. He claims he was sent to Bethlehem to deliver a message from Yeshua to Zadok of Migdal Eder."

Gamaliel sat forward with interest at this information. "Zadok, you say?"

"He wouldn't tell me what the message was."

Gamaliel considered the news. "We should have a word with this boy. And with Zadok." The rabbi called out for Saul to bring quill, ink, papyrus, and sealing wax. "Zadok will bring him if I send for him. Your house? Two days?"

■ ■ ■ ■

On the crest of the hill Emet put Bear down and let him sniff the grass. Then, in a sudden burst of energy, the baby tore across the green expanse toward the forest.

Blue Eye jogged behind, blocking his escape and herding him back toward Emet.

Emet sank to the cool earth, clasped his knees, and surveyed the Valley of the Flock. Beth-lehem, City of David, looked much as it must have in David's day. White brick houses clung to the hillside like sheep.

Emet shuddered at the sight of women tending gardens on the terraced slopes. He was glad to have escaped women's work. Now and then the shrill voices of young children rose on the wind.

In the distance was Migdal Eder and beyond was the hated Roman aqueduct. Farther south, the menacing parapets of Herodium loomed over all.

As Emet watched, the gate on the lowest level yawned open. A new shift of stonecutters marched from the gloomy palace of the dead butcher king.

Emet ate his lunch and strained to hear the music of David. Instead he heard the rush of wind through the dark green branches of the trees.

And then . . . there was something more. A murmur, barely audible beneath the sighing breeze. A voice? Voices? Emet recognized the urgent whisper of men's voices from the thick copse of trees.

How many? Emet counted three distinctly different tenors.

"*We'll stay here awhile. The boy will be on his way and we can finish.*"

"*What if he sees us?*"

"*What of it? Judea is packed with travelers. We've stopped to shelter in the woods before traveling to Yerushalayim. That's all.*"

"*And if he tells someone?*"

"*Tells someone there are men in the woods?*"

"*Shut up. Doesn't matter. Who will care?*"

"*He could report it. . . .*"

"*There's rancor enough in the valley between shepherds and masons. They'll be blaming each other when it comes down on them.*"

At this Emet turned his head to search the woods for some sign of who was within. Tree trunks provided a united front, shielding the watchers from view.

A sudden hissing called for silence as Emet scanned the trees.

Had he imagined it? Or had he overheard a fragment of ancient conversation that had snagged on a branch to echo old words when the wind was up?

More.

"*Have you seen enough?*"

"*I've got the lay of the land all right. The tower . . .*"

"*The tower . . .*"

"*Before the moon is up . . .*"

"*The boy is facing this way. I think he's heard us.*"

Emet's head snapped forward. A chill coursed through him. This was no antique scrap of syllables but a present-day exchange.

Someone was up to no good.

Emet's voice shook as he called to the dog. "Blue Eye! Home!"

"*There. See? He's leaving. . . .*"

"*Leaving . . . back down the hill . . .*"

The tricolored dog nosed Bear toward Emet at the head of the path. Resisting the urge to peer over his shoulder at the menace, Emet slipped the noose around the black lamb's throat and headed down to the stable.

■ ■ ■ ■

Lev was not pleased to see Emet return to the stable so soon. Nor was he impressed with Emet's report.

"There's a jackal living in those woods!" Lev scolded. "You're lucky it didn't sneak out and eat that little black creature you're so fond of!"

"It was men I heard."

"One jackal's the same as another."

"But there's someone up there!" Emet pleaded.

"It's near Passover week. What do y' think? They camp up there every year. Nuisance! Two years ago some dolt set fire to the woods. If it hadn't rained a torrent . . ."

"But they're up to something." Emet was certain he was correct.

"So's everybody up to something," Lev spat in irritation. "*I'm* up to something!" He raised his hand as if to smack Emet across the mouth.

Blue Eye growled a warning and stood stiff-legged to protest the hostile gesture.

Lev lowered his hand. "So. Et tu, Blue Eye? Always taking the side of scrawny worthless things, aren't y'? Well, just remember who feeds y', dog! All right then. Tell this stump of a boy you're so fond of to shut up or I'll take a switch to him when the dogs are away!"

Blue Eye sat down on his haunches, content to have Lev back off. Emet gave up. Why should he expect Lev to be impressed with anything he said?

Lev didn't care one whit that there were men lurking in the woods beyond Beth-lehem. Maybe Emet shouldn't care either.

ZEH DEVAR

The synagogue at the fortress of Herodium had been declared unclean so long ago that Roman soldiers freely used it for dice and the practice of fighting techniques when the weather was bad.

At the request of Oren, Marcus banned the games. The nearly forgotten Torah scrolls and copies of the writings of the prophets were removed from storage and once again made available for the stonemasons to study on *Shabbat* and during their off hours. It was good for morale among the guilt-ridden and much-maligned workmen. The synagogue became a house of worship where the outcasts of Israel could meet, study, and pray once more.

Marcus was invited by Oren into the sanctuary. It had been scrubbed clean, Latin graffiti removed from the pillars. The place was, in fact, a beautiful structure.

"I remember the stories of this palace from when I was young," Oren remarked. "My father told me that the future tomb of old Herod was more glorious than the tombs of Israel's true kings. But it didn't make Herod the true King of Israel."

Silence. Then Marcus asked, "Who *is* the true King of Israel?"

"All that's behind us," Oren said. "Our King was meant to be from the line of David. Herod clearly was not. He had the genealogy records destroyed at the Temple the same year the star appeared in the heavens."

In a flash of memory Marcus recalled one of the anecdotes he had heard about the madness of Herod the Great. "Thirty-some years ago. In Beth-lehem. A rival king being born and . . ."

"I was a boy. A great star appeared. We used to sit up on the roof to watch its progress. I remember it! I was five or six that summer. Everyone said it meant something wonderful. A king born in Israel to save us all. But nothing came of it . . . except it pushed Herod further into madness and cruelty."

A sign in the heavens? A star? A king from heaven born to redeem the suffering world? Marcus knew that in the lore and legends of Rome such visions had been seen and written down. Always, however, they related to Rome's pantheon of gods, and often to human rulers. Could myth be truth in this case? He waited to hear more.

"I can show you in Scripture. Everyone learned it well." The stonemason shyly opened the first scroll of Isaiah. Scanning the page he found a place and began to read:

"Behold, a virgin shall conceive and bear a son and shall call his name, Immanu'el. That is, God-with-us. *The people that walked in darkness have seen a great light . . . For unto us a child is born, unto us a son is given: and the government shall be upon his shoulder: and his name shall be called Wonderful, Counselor, Mighty God, Everlasting Father, Prince of Peace. . . ."*

Oren scanned the rest silently for a moment. At last he raised his face to Marcus. "This was supposed to be our promised Messiah." He shrugged. "Some have said he's alive. In the north. The Galil. Yeshua of Nazareth. Have you heard of him? Many are saying he'll come to Jerusalem this year."

Marcus didn't admit he had seen Yeshua or that he believed if any man could be the king and savior of a hurting world it was Yeshua of Nazareth. To speak such a thing aloud would be tantamount to treason against Rome.

Some phrase of Roman poetry stirred in Marcus' mind. "I've heard this prophecy before . . . something like it. An oracle recorded by our poet Virgil." He closed his eyes and remembered the stern face of his tutor during recitation. Then he spoke the words aloud to Oren:

> *"Now comes the time sung by Cumae's Sibyl,*
> *When the wheel of ages starts afresh.*
> *Now is the virgin made herself known*
> *And the reign of Saturn on earth;*
> *Now is a child engendered by heaven.*
> *Smile, chaste Lucina, at the birth of this boy*
> *Who will put an end to our wretched age,*
> *From whom golden people shall spring.*
> *Now does your own Apollo reign!"*

Oren stared at him in amazement.

Marcus had heard those stanzas applied to the Emperor Augustus, the god-man who had brought the golden age to earth.

There were other supposedly miraculous occurrences connected with Augustus, but everyone rational understood them to be political propaganda.

Nobody had ever seen Augustus raise the dead.

Besides, Marcus thought, it was possible the verse of Virgil had been lifted from the Isaiah scroll and adapted to fit Roman religious belief. Yet it was clear that there were those in Rome who expected a god to be born of a virgin and to reign on earth. To a certain degree they, like Marcus, would comprehend the meaning of the son of God taking human form and coming as a king.

"Messiah. King," Marcus said. "The Caesars of Rome claim they are sons of gods. Though I've yet to see one heal a cripple or raise a little girl from the dead. Rome won't appreciate anyone who is capable of these things."

"Then you've heard of him?" Oren stared at him intently.

"Who hasn't heard of him?"

"I'd like to hear him teach. For myself, I mean. See the miracles. I'd given up hope until I heard ... all the stories. Do you think it's possible?"

Marcus considered his words carefully. "If he is what people say he is, God help him. There's not a more stiff-necked nation in the empire than your people! And if the sons of Herod the Great are half as jealous as their father was, they won't take kindly to competition. Herod Antipas made his position clear when he executed Yochanan the Baptizer, didn't he? And as for Rome's pantheon of sons of the gods, they'll resent him, surely."

"But if he is the Messiah, they won't be able to harm him," Oren stated.

"Well, there's a test for you then. But I don't suppose it will keep them from trying."

■ ■ ■ ■

Emet watched the glowing orange ball of the sun sink rapidly toward the west. The late-afternoon sky was a pale blue, daubed with translucent white smears of clouds.

The boy was anxious to get his next chore completed and wished it would start soon. He, Ha-or Tov, and Avel were to take an evening meal to the shepherds on the far side of the valley. The longer their departure was postponed, the darker the return journey would be.

Despite Lev's derision, since hearing the voices on the wind, Emet was afraid of what ... or who ... lurked on the hillside. Fear of ridicule made him draw back from sharing his concerns with anyone else, but in Emet's heart a shadowy dread grew.

Ha-or Tov sat on the edge of the stone wall, dangling his feet as they waited for the baskets of provisions. He appeared totally unconcerned with the approach of darkness. As he said, after living in its totality for so long, night was a mere inconvenience and nothing more.

Avel teased Emet about his nervousness. "We're surrounded by thousands of sheep and a hundred shepherds. The stonecutters go back to Herodium at night and the Romans go out on patrol. What's scary in any of that?"

Rejecting the notion of taking Avel and Ha-or Tov into his confidence, Emet substituted, "It's the jackal. There's still a jackal out there."

Ha-or Tov considered this. "It's plenty light right now," he said, gauging the angle between the sun and the horizon.

"But it won't be on the way back," Emet argued. "What if it grabs us?"

Zadok approached with three wickerwork containers of food. After handing the larger ones to Ha-or Tov and Avel and a smaller one to Emet, he extracted something else from the folds of his robe: three leather slings, their straps cut down in size to fit young boys.

"If you're to be shepherds," the white-haired man said as he offered the weapons, "y' must practice with these. An accomplished slinger can hit a mark at a hundred paces. Good protection from jackals . . . or other creatures."

Emet was confused. Did the old man somehow know about the voices on the wind? If so, he said nothing further.

"No hitting sheep with these," Zadok instructed sternly. "Practice against trees and rocks and remember: a slingstone can kill a man if it hits him in the head."

The three apprentices agreed to be careful, indicating their understanding of the gravity of the new tools.

"It was from near this very spot," Zadok continued, "that the youngest son of Jesse of Beth-lehem . . . it was David, who was later our king . . . set out to watch his father's flocks." Zadok's words stopped as his face turned toward the setting sun. Emet wondered what extraneous thought about a shepherd's son had disturbed the old man's concentration.

Shaking his head, Zadok returned to his lesson. "In his day David killed lions and bears with one of these."

"At my age?" Avel asked.

"Only a little older," Zadok returned. "And then he struck down the giant Philistine warrior, Goliath of Gath. One stone to the forehead was all it took."

Avel and Ha-or Tov immediately searched the ground for suitable rocks for their slings.

Emet continued to watch Zadok. How was it possible that such a battle-scarred, gruff elder could at times display a side of such understanding of boys?

"Off y' go, then," Zadok said sternly. "No dawdling! I don't want you falling into a pit because y' got lost in the dark. And the night watch won't like it if you spill their suppers either!"

■ ■ ■ ■

The night was the thickest Emet had ever experienced.

That was the only word he could think of to describe the sensation of the darkness. He could almost touch it.

Or, more correctly, he could sense its touch on him.

A surreptitious caress on his cheek, the barely felt lifting of the hair on the back of his neck. And sounds! So many sounds! Too many! The air moaning with the wind. The breath of sheep kneeling in sleep on the slope. The hum and tick of insects. Things creeping in the brush. And the murmur of men's voices carried in dark octaves of sound.

The journey was full of broom brush that mimicked bears and boulders that appeared as lions. But none of these was as terrifying as the writhing, groaning blackness itself.

Patting the fold of his robe where the sling was lodged didn't comfort Emet. The one thing that would help would be to get this duty completed, rejoin Avel and Ha-or Tov, and, as quickly as possible, return to the safety of Zadok's house.

They came to the hilltop above the Valley of the Sheepfold. Standing beside a chalky boulder as big as Jerusalem's Dung Gate, Avel said: "Here's where we split up. Emet, you go down there, to the watchmen in that canyon. Then we meet back here."

It sounded like a reasonable plan. That is, until the darkness closed in around him without any watch fire being seen, without any hungry shepherds eager for their supper.

When Emet looked back, he could no longer see the boulder that was the sentinel of safety. He thought then about retreating, about running up the slope all the way to the meeting place.

But how could he explain his failure to deliver the basket?

Avel would be ashamed of him. When the story got out, Lev would make his life miserable.

He pressed ahead.

The walking got easier, but Emet's sense of terror didn't abate when the canyon opened out into a flat. Ahead of him, looming over the distant slopes, was the broken fang of Herodium. Its turreted windows smoldered with orange lights, but there was no comfort in gazing at the brooding castle of the butcher king.

Even worse, reaching toward him like an outstretched tentacle, was the sinuous line of the aqueduct, ending in the claw-shaped Tower of Siloam.

Was he hopelessly lost? How could he go so far astray when all he had to do was walk down a hill and find men gathered around a fire?

Then he spotted a momentary gleam at the base of Siloam Tower. A blue spark appeared, flickered, then disappeared almost before Emet was certain he'd seen it.

It came again. Someone striking a flint, trying to light a flame.

He'd found the camp after all, Emet thought, flooded with relief. Perhaps the shepherds had followed a lost lamb, or perhaps Avel hadn't really known where the night watch was located. But no matter, Emet had succeeded.

Marching toward the structure, Emet observed the shadowy forms of dark-clad men against the lighter expanses of stone. A half-score or more he saw when their lumpish forms marred the clean, straight lines of the scaffolding.

What were they doing?

A groaning sound reached his ears. It came from the timbering near the top of Siloam Tower. It sounded as if the structure itself moaned and screeched.

He froze.

A hand grabbed him by the hair. The prick of a knifepoint gouged his throat. "What're you doing here?" a guttural voice demanded.

Asher!

Would he be recognized? Was Kittim nearby?

"Speak up!" Asher ordered. "Who sent you?"

"I . . . I'm lost," Emet said. "Nobody sent me. I'm lost."

There was an instant when his head was tugged backward. Emet expected the sweep of the blade across his neck. He cried out, but instead of his throat being cut, a palm clapped across his mouth.

"Quiet!" Asher commanded.

Emet had not been recognized. He blessed the Almighty for the darkness! Nor could his words give him away; he'd had none when he and Asher had last met.

Asher hissed horrifying visions into Emet's ear.

"Don't tell anyone!" Asher warned, snarling hot breath against Emet's cheek. "If you tell, I'll come for you. You won't see me, but I'll see you. I'll come in the night and . . ." Asher made a gurgling sound, then shoved Emet away. "Go!"

Dropping the basket, Emet escaped.

The orange eyes of Herodium watched him flee. Every time he stumbled into a thornbush and scrambled upright again, its gaze followed him. He didn't stop running until he reached the rendezvous where Avel and Ha-or Tov awaited him.

They teased him for running, teased him for being frightened, then stopped teasing when they saw his hands and face streaked with the blood of puncture wounds and heard his breath coming in painful gasps.

Emet, so grateful for his newfound voice, did not speak all the way back to Migdal Eder.

ADONAY

The note from Zadok arrived at Herodium by the hand of a sullen messenger just after dawn.

Marcus studied its contents with concern:

To Centurion Marcus Longinus; Gaius Robb, engineer of the Roman aqueduct; and Oren of Jerusalem, foreman of the masons;

from Zadok of Migdal Eder, chief shepherd of the flock:

Gentlemen, contrary to our original agreements regarding the sanctity of Beth-lehem pastures, your stonemasons continue to destroy our grazing land with callous disregard. I myself have visited the most fertile land of our valley and found it trampled and destroyed by those who carry stones onto our field. These grazing grounds have been considered holy to the flock since the days of our ancient shepherd King David once watched over his father's sheep. The land you defile is more than simply a pasture, just as the sheep your men have stolen were more than sheep. The Tower of the Flock was in place long before this new Roman tower that destroys our valley. The sanctity of our purpose on this land supercedes the outrage you inflict on sacred ground. Please see to it before further damage takes place.

I look forward to a speedy resolution to this matter. I have sent a copy of this letter, as well as further elaboration of the violations by your workmen, to the Sanhedrin for their consideration.

Signed, Zadok, chief shepherd of Migdal Eder

So. The old man had found something to complain to the elders in Jerusalem about in spite of Marcus' meeting and payment for the stolen sheep?

So be it.

Now the focus had shifted to trampled grass, had it? Well, then.

Angry at the charge, Marcus skipped breakfast and unrolled the plans for the aqueduct.

In reviewing the schematic representation Marcus quickly spotted its most important feature: the junction between the existing water supply route and the new one. This would also be the edifice most crucial to engineer properly.

The surrounding land was at the heart of Zadok's grumbling.

Marcus mounted Pavor and rode out again from Herodium.

On the way he passed a line of drovers goading their oxen toward the same place. Their carts were loaded with building materials for the work.

It was these carts that had become the focus of controversy between the shepherds and the stoneworkers. Marcus was in a foul temper. Most likely there would be a fresh complaint every day. When Marcus had accepted the assignment, he hadn't expected a constant stream of unpleasantness. He had thought perhaps he could, on occasion, find a reason to ride to Bethany.

After all, Miryam of Magdala was at Bethany with her brother.

Miryam had been uppermost in his mind as he rode south.

He knew well that he had been picked by Pilate for this assignment in Beth-lehem for two reasons. First, he had managed to get along with the Jewish leaders of Capernaum. He had helped them build their synagogue, hadn't he? But could he also tame the ire of the wild shepherds of Beth-lehem? They were a different breed than the Galileans he had come to know and respect. Second was the belief that perhaps Marcus was too sympathetic toward the Jews. After all, Marcus had taken a Jewess as his lover, had he not? And was he not supportive of Yeshua of Nazareth in his reports? Did the record not show that Centurion Marcus Longinus had a certain compassion toward the Jews?

Compassion in a centurion wasn't a quality valued by his superiors.

Well, today whatever sympathy Marcus had arrived with vanished! This obscure assignment was bound to be a position rife with trouble and complaint every moment! Chasing bar Abba and the bandits in the wilderness of Jericho seemed like a peaceful stroll through the Lyceum compared to controlling the simmering hatred in this stinking, woolly stockyard!

The problem stretched across the valley below him.

East of Beth-lehem, not far from the trade route connecting Jerusalem and the Dead Sea fort of En-gedi, was the reservoir feeding the aqueduct built by Herod the Great. It was at this point that Pilate's project and the existing water supply route would unite.

Herod's aqueduct, ponderous and ungainly by Roman standards, carried the precious fluid simultaneously on two levels. The higher channel had enough elevation to supply the Temple Mount. Once it reached the Holy City, conduits of fire-hardened clay conveyed the water into the cavernous cisterns beneath the platform of the sanctuary. There the liquid was in constant use, both for the ritual bathing required of the priests and, more prosaically, for cleaning up after the countless sacrifices and sluicing thousands of gallons of blood into the Kidron Valley.

The lower channel answered the secular purposes of Jerusalem's population. When it arrived at the city, it delivered its water into the Pool of Siloam at the city's southern extremity.

Because of this ultimate destination, the structure built to unite the new aqueduct with the old was to be called the *Tower of Siloam.*

Seeps and springs spilling into Herod's reservoir made the land around the tower site extremely fertile, some of the best pastureland for the flocks of Migdal Eder. Even in the dry season, and indeed during dry years, the natural bowl provided feed in plenty.

In the wet season, like the one just ended, it was lush with green grass higher than a lamb's back. By judicious rotation of pasturage, the shepherds were able to preserve the bountiful nature of the area, using it specifically to fatten lambs destined for priority transport to the Temple.

The first thing Marcus noticed when he arrived on-site was the new tower rising adjacent to the existing aqueduct. There was as yet no connection between the two structures, but three courses of mammoth foundation stones were in place. Above these a timber scaffolding outlined the location of the graceful arches that would eventually stand there.

The second thing he noticed was hundreds of sheep contentedly munching their fodder, seemingly oblivious to the construction.

These were both positive notes automatically filed by Marcus for his report to Pilate and defense against any further accusation.

But the situation was not all good news.

Ringing the inner and outer slopes of the lake basin were wagon tracks . . . lots of them. Heavily laden with blocks from quarries miles away, the wheels of the oxcarts and the hooves of the beasts themselves had ground the precious pasture into the mud. Even worse were the marks left by the passage of wheel-less sledges. Dragged along the ground, they had planed the hillside like a carpenter smoothes the edge of a beam. Loads of cut stones, heaps of timber, and mounds of sand and lime for mortar indiscriminately littered the landscape.

The scene resembled a city fallen to a siege and knocked to pieces by its conqueror.

All right then. The old one-eyed shepherd had validity to his complaint.

The unnecessary destruction of much valuable grass would not go unchallenged. Perhaps, Marcus thought, this was fodder for insurrection. This possibility was evident from the sour looks Marcus received from the shepherds he passed.

On-site Marcus spotted Gaius Robb, chief of the surveying crew. He was discussing a feature of the construction with the Jewish stonecutter Oren and Oren's apprentice son, Benjamin. "You see where we had to remove the wings buttressing the existing primary arch," Robb said, "in order for the tower to form a proper connection. I cannot stress strongly enough how crucial the scaffolding is at that point and how fast your men must work. Until the new structure is properly braced, the weight of the old will be pushing outward . . . a dangerous situation."

Oren's reply was confident. "I understand. The way the work is arranged there will be no more than one day's danger . . . two at most. Thereafter the tower will be more solid than Herod's builders ever imagined."

Marcus observed, not wishing to interrupt such a pivotal discussion. After a moment Gaius Robb saw him.

"Centurion," Robb said, inviting him to join them. "An interesting problem, this." He flipped over several charcoal-on-parchment sketches, giving details of props, bracing, and reinforcement. "Meshing two different styles of building is always a challenge, eh?"

"We have another problem," Marcus said bluntly, passing Zadok's message to Robb. "Is there a reason the material is scattered all over? And why wasn't a proper road staked out?"

Robb scanned the note but seemed baffled by the criticism. "Does it matter?" he asked. "There's nobody here but sheep. What's the value of a bit of grass more or less?"

Marcus studied Oren. It was clear the stonecutter knew instantly what was at issue. Even his son, Benjamin, shifted his weight from one leg to the other and stared uneasily at the rubble heaps in the field.

Finally Oren claimed, "I asked about making a road and laying out a supply depot, but was told those would cause unnecessary delays."

Marcus said sternly, "Even though you knew anything less would destroy the pasture? Who prevented you?"

"Praetorian Vara," Oren admitted.

Vara again! At best the man had a callous disregard for the concerns of others. But Marcus believed the man made most decisions affecting the Jews out of deliberate spite.

Many Roman officers and their mercenary troopers felt the same.

"Robb," Marcus said, "we need to consolidate the blocks and timbers and mark a road that the wagons must keep to."

"Over a bit of grass?" Robb repeated obtusely. "Aren't you making—"

Robb's statement was interrupted by the sounds of shouting from outside the tent. More ominous still was the whiz of stones flying, followed by exclamations of pain.

Drawing his sword, Marcus rushed outside. The caravan of blocks had arrived. Not only did the convoy of oxcarts cut another swath through unspoiled pasture, but at the construction site each had turned aside to park, crushing fifteen separate spokes of fan-shaped desolation.

The herdsmen had had enough! Over thirty shepherds, slings in hand, advanced on the wagons!

The drovers were clearly getting the worst of the confrontation. Several shepherds used their slings to good advantage. While the stone-haulers cowered behind their loads, oxen bellowed as missiles aimed at their masters hit the animals instead. One beast, startled into sudden motion, attempted a tight circle to escape, and the heaped-up load of timbers overturned. Eight-inch beams scattered like straws.

Clambering down from the scaffolding, laborers wielding hammers leapt to the defense of the drovers.

It was a near riot.

"Stop this!" Marcus bellowed. A stone whizzed past his helmet, striking Benjamin in the head.

From behind him Oren gave a cry of alarm and rushed forward.

Marcus tripped him, making the mason sprawl on his face.

Recognizing Jehu among the herdsmen, Marcus shouted, "Jehu, stop your men!"

A stonecutter charged toward the shepherds, wooden maul in one hand and the spike of a chisel in the other. Marcus leapt in front of him! The man raised his club to strike down Marcus.

Unwilling to kill if it could be avoided, Marcus reversed his blade and drove the hilt of his sword into the man's nose, felling him.

He then confronted three more aqueduct workmen with a flashing sweep of naked steel. "Back off!" he snarled.

From the other side Jehu barked, "Stop! Ephraim, drop that sling! Meshach, put down that rock!"

From his knees on the ground Oren called out, "Enough! Benjamin, Amos, stop!"

Bleeding from a cut over his eye, Benjamin struggled angrily to rise and continue in the fray. "But they started it, Father! The shepherds attacked us!"

"They've no cause to ruin the pasture!" retorted the shepherd Jehu. "This abomination is bad enough without deliberately spoiling the rest! We asked you to stop, to listen to reason."

"And when they didn't, you attacked them with slings?" Marcus demanded.

Jehu and his men stared defiantly.

"Now listen, all of you!" Marcus roared. "I've given orders to organize the building material into a single location and to stake out one single road. Jehu, will this solve the problem?"

The shepherd grudgingly admitted that it would.

"Then you are bound to keep the peace. Oren," Marcus said, turning toward the stonecutter, "see to it. There will be penalties for any willful destruction of pasture."

"But my son!" Oren challenged, pointing to Benjamin's blood-smeared face.

"Enough!" Marcus concluded. "What's done is done. But whoever disturbs the peace again . . . or interferes with the building . . . will have me to answer to!"

■ ■ ■ ■

The arrival of the hawker to reclaim his spavined donkey surprised Nakdimon. He had expected the fellow to vanish with his two-shekels deposit, which was far more than the worth of the beast.

Nakdimon was lost in study in his second-story library when he heard Zacharias arguing in the courtyard.

"No need to disturb my master. I'll fetch your donkey, sir, and receive from you the two-shekels deposit."

The hawker was insistent. "No. I must speak to Reb Nakdimon myself. In person. Face-to-face, as it were. I've got intelligence he must hear from my mouth to his ears."

"I'm acting steward of his household," declared the Ethiopian. "I myself am most trusted to carry messages to my master. Tell me your business, and I will convey it to him."

"What I have to say I'll not say to any but your master." The hawker was adamant. "It's a matter of life and death what I have to say, and I'll not repeat it to anyone but himself. And here I'll stay until I see Nakdimon ben Gurion."

Nakdimon laid down his stylus and went to the balcony. The hawker had stubbornly seated himself on the rim of the fountain. Crossing his arms, he acted immovable.

"You can't stay here." Zacharias scowled. "You seem a dangerous sort. Get up, sir. Or I'll fetch the cook to help me remove you."

"And what will he do if I won't go? Roast me for supper?"

"Stand and kindly wait outside the gate while I fetch your donkey!"

Nakdimon interrupted the confrontation. "Zacharias, I'll see to this. Retrieve this fellow's animal. I'll have a word with him myself."

The hawker smirked.

Zacharias, with dignity, bowed and shuffled off to find the animal as Nakdimon descended the stairs.

"What is this?" Nakdimon demanded.

The hawker, more filthy than before, grinned obsequiously. "Ah, your honor! So it was truly you yourself who hired my little beast! And all this time I thought perhaps some villain had used your name and rank to get a better price from me."

Nakdimon, frustrated at the disruption of his studies, frowned. "And I thought you would run off with my deposit and leave me with a creature who is on its last legs."

"Who? I? Never!"

"Since we have proved ourselves to be honest men in a world of thieves and gougers, let's get on with the business at hand. You owe me two shekels, and I owe you one spavined donkey." Nakdimon extended his hand to receive payment.

"But no, your honor!" The hawker evidently remembered the true reason he had taken a seat at the great man's fountain. "Truly the Almighty was guiding you to me as we bargained in the caravansary! You are most fortunate that it was I, myself, who loaned you my beast! Never was a man as blessed as you, sir!"

"No doubt you're the most honest of peddlers," Nakdimon conceded. "But I have work to attend to, if you don't mind. . . ."

"But no! I've brought news to you, sir! News that may save your life and the lives of your wife and children. Perhaps news that will save the lives of the rulers of Israel if I am allowed to speak boldly."

"Speak. Please," Nakdimon said impatiently.

"It's this way, sir. You may wish to go before the council to tell what I tell you."

"Tell me."

"Sure. You're as good as any man on the council. And big enough you'll be harder to kill than the others too."

"What do you mean?" Was this fellow simply prating on in hopes of reward? Nakdimon wondered. "Be short."

"I'm not a tall man, so I will be short. But the news I have is big."

"Then speak briefly or I'll call the cook, who is enormous, and together we'll throw you out as an intruder."

"The cook again?"

"She's bigger than I am. Now. Out with it. Or out with you."

The hawker sucked his blackened teeth and nodded, as if sobered by the thought of a woman bigger than Nakdimon ben Gurion.

"Well, sir, here it is. They mean to murder you."

"Who?" Nakdimon eyed him with renewed interest.

"You. Yourself. Everyone of the Sanhedrin they can lay hold of. And wives and children as well."

"I mean, who are these assassins?"

"Rebels."

"Have they names?"

"Bar Abba, for one. This news is worth a coin or two, I'd say."

Nakdimon grasped the hawker by his throat. "So you're an informer. You must be one of them, or how would you know such a thing?"

The hawker squealed. "No, sir! I swear it! I'm just what I seem to be!"

"A liar?"

"An honest hawker, sir!"

"You admit to being a cheat, then?"

"A man intent on doing a good deed."

"Then do it. Quickly. Before I lose patience. Tell what you know and how you came to know it!" Nakdimon released his grip.

The man, gasping for breath, sat back and rubbed his throat. "Being a man in the trade I'm in, sir, I am here and there. There and here. In inns and among travelers in need. This is high season for my business, sir. I've been among the people as you would expect. And I came upon three members of bar Abba's army: Asher, Kittim, and bar Abba's captain, Dan the well-known murderer."

"Where?"

"In the shade of an oak outside Sepphoris."

"And?"

"They were talking politics with a Galilean fellow. Recruiting him to join them. And they tried to recruit me too."

"It's a long way from politics to murder."

"Shorter than you think. But the knives I sold them were long bladed. Knives from Persia. They thanked me and said such weapons were perfect for carving up the corrupt men who sat on the Council of the Sanhedrin. The curve of the blade would hook a fellow's intestines, they said, and pull them out a very small wound." He frowned and rubbed his round belly. "I think they're serious."

"Half the men in Galilee hate the rulers in Yerushalayim," Nakdimon remarked. "Why would you think they'll carry through?"

"They say they'll be among you and you'll never see them until you stumble on your own guts. It gave me a start, I can tell you. I couldn't eat my noonday meal for thinking about it."

"And how many are there?"

"From the sound of it, half of Galilee, like you said. I saw the three. And then the young fellow clapped hands with them in a bargain and also bought a knife. That makes four. But word on the street is that every fourth man may be one of them."

"You made out well on the deal," Nakdimon glowered.

"I'm a hawker, sir."

"When will this plot be hatched, hawker?"

"They didn't say what moment. Only that they'll be watching the council chambers for the right time."

"You know enough you might be one of them."

"I'm no rebel."

"You smell of death."

The hawker sniffed his armpits. "Well, bathing costs money, sir. There's hardly a place to bathe between here and Sepphoris."

This fellow was too dense to be dangerous, Nakdimon conceded. "What do you hope to get from me for this information?"

"To be honest, sir, two shekels. It seems fair enough."

"Two shekels? High price for words. For that you'll have to repeat your story."

"I'll tell it again."

Zacharias entered the portico and bowed slightly. "The beast is ready to be taken away, sir."

Nakdimon glared at the wretched man sitting by the fountain. "You'll come with me then. Three days from now. To the chambers of the Sanhedrin and tell them what you know."

"Oh no, sir!" The hawker drew back in terror. "Didn't you hear what I've said to you? They'll be watching the council chambers. Waiting for you! They'll see me! They'll know I've come to tell you what I heard!" He dropped to his knees and groveled before Nakdimon.

"And then they'll pull your bowels out with the knives you've sold them, is that it?"

The man began to blubber. "Yes! Yes, sir! They'll kill me like one of those lambs. And me, just trying to do a good deed!"

This was no act. The hawker was genuinely terrified. His terror was the confirmation of the truth in his tale.

"All right, then."

"Oh thank you! Thank you, sir!" The hawker began to kiss Nakdimon's feet.

Nakdimon pushed him away. "Enough. The high priest will want to hear what you have to say. Where are you staying?"

"Here and there. There and here. Among the people."

"There's an inn beside Sheep's Gate. You'll stay there until I send for you." Nakdimon snapped his fingers. "Zacharias, accompany our friend to Sheep's Gate Inn. Pay the proprietor to make him comfortable. To feed him three meals a day. To keep him locked safely in the room on the second story and tell no one he is there."

Again the hawker fawned in gratitude, seemingly uncaring that he was being made a prisoner.

■ ■ ■ ■

After the previous night's encounter with Asher, Emet stayed close to Migdal Eder. Though he told no one about the rebels, he was still frightened. It kept him inside the lambing barn, where he felt safer.

While sheltered inside the grotto Emet practiced tying. It wasn't perfected yet, but Bear's bonnet remained in place longer each time.

It was while renewing this exercise near evening that Emet overheard a conversation he wasn't intended to hear. In a vacant pen three rows back from the lamplit passage, the boy was shorter than the railing and almost invisible.

Evidently, Jehu smarted from criticism leveled at him by Zadok over the incident at Siloam Tower. When he stormed into the caverns with Ephraim and Meshach trailing after, it was clear he was boiling mad. After a cursory examination convinced him no one other than Lev was present, he launched into his complaints.

"What's happened to Zadok?" he fumed to his followers. "Has he lost his courage? Taking the side of Romans and apostates against his own people?"

"It's bad enough the aqueduct defiles the land, but destroying the pasture as well?" put in Ephraim. "That centurion may say he'll correct the problem, but you can't trust him! Nothing will really change. You'll see."

"I know it," Jehu growled. "Nor will it stop there! Watch: in less than a year Migdal Eder's best grassland will all be trampled! That cursed aqueduct!"

Ephraim added, "And lambs continue to disappear! It hasn't stopped because Zadok made a deal with the Romans."

"You know," Meshach said with a lowered voice and a glance around that suggested he had an ominous secret to share, "the water in the Roman canal will pollute the sacrifices."

"What?" Jehu demanded. "What do you mean?"

Nodding vigorously, Meshach explained. "I heard it from my cousin Rehoboam, who got it from his best friend, Amaziah: part of the aqueduct crosses a cemetery!"

Emet peered between the slats of the pen to watch the response.

"Are you certain?" Jehu inquired.

Meshach thumped himself on the ear. "May my brains be turned to steam if it isn't so! Across a graveyard! Not only is the water in the channel polluted, but it will defile every drop in the Temple cisterns! All our care to provide spotless lambs will be worthless!"

"Someone needs to do something!" Ephraim insisted. "We should tell Zadok about this."

"That's right," agreed Lev, speaking for the first time. "Zadok will tell the high priest. And he'll make the Romans stop."

"You will *not* tell Zadok," Jehu insisted, rounding sharply on the lambing barn attendant. "He'll find a way to compromise again. He's getting too old! And too soft to be chief shepherd."

Lev looked dubious. "But the appointment is for life," he objected dully. "Zadok will always be chief shepherd . . . till he dies."

Was there a hint of hopefulness in that? Emet wondered. He squeezed his eyes shut and wished he were somewhere else. Bear nuzzled beneath Emet's arm. Emet buried his face against the lamb's soft fleece. Perhaps being able to hear was not such a fine thing at moments like these. The word *betrayal* popped into Emet's mind.

"Look," Jehu argued in a softer tone. "Lev, you're a clever fellow. That's why we took you into our confidence, eh? Zadok talks to you about his plans when he doesn't speak to the rest of us. And you'll tell us what he says, won't you? It's for his own good, you know."

"I don't know," Lev countered. "Isn't that like spying?"

"Lev," Ephraim offered in a wheedling tone, "if that centurion hadn't interfered, we'd have driven the stoneworkers away and stopped the ruin of the pasture . . . isn't that right?"

"I guess so," Lev responded.

"Of course it's so," Meshach seconded. "You should have seen them ducking from our slingstones! Cracked that son of Oren the stonecutter right on the head." He smacked his hands together.

The noise made Emet jump. Bear bleated and backed away, scampering across the pen to Old Girl. Emet was glad that the rustle of straw his movement caused couldn't be distinguished from the other crunching sounds made by the ewes and their lambs.

"If that Roman hadn't interfered . . . ," Meshach continued.

"But Zadok has taken sides with the centurion . . . which means, with the defilers, right?" Ephraim noted. "We have to help him. But how can we if we don't know what he's thinking . . . what he's planning?"

"But don't say anything to Zadok . . . just listen and tell us," Jehu put in sharply. "Got it?"

Lev agreed.

"We need," said Lev slowly, "a big earthquake to knock that tower down. Then everyone would see how offended the Almighty is. And the whole thing would stop."

Jehu and the others exchanged tolerant looks. The Almighty didn't often express His displeasure in such ways. But let Lev think what he wanted. Lev would be of use to their purposes. "Knock the whole thing down," Jehu concurred. "Let the Gentiles and the apostates pack up and get off our land for good!"

Even though Jehu and his two friends left right away, Emet didn't emerge from his corner until he heard Lev working at the far end of the stalls. Then he slipped out unseen and went home.

■ ■ ■ ■

Tonight Avel sat close to Zadok at the watch fire. "And David slew the lion with his sling. A rare thing nowadays for a lion to threaten a flock. There were plenty of quiet nights when David learned to sing. Sheep like music, I think."

Emet and Ha-or Tov, with the black lamb curled up between them, dozed as the old man told stories of long-ago shepherds. Emet had dreamed terrible dreams the night before. He had quaked and started throughout the day, yet would not give the reason why. At last he had fallen into a sound sleep. It was a good thing, Avel thought.

But Avel hung on every word out of Zadok's mouth. In this way they passed the night.

Already several lambings had gone easily. Ewes and new babies were settled and safe in their pens.

And there were more stars than Avel had seen in one sky.

"So this is what David meant when he sat here on this hill and praised the glory of God's creation," Zadok said. "In all the world only one creature doesn't easily recognize God in creation: man. Our eyes turn inward to our own thoughts, backwards to a word, an insult, a gesture from another, until we can't see the *now*. In Yerushalayim, in the city, when we go there, you'll see it on their faces. They're taking on burdens not their own, like a servant stuffing his marketing bag with stones. They turn their minds toward objects and away from the God who made them. That's what was meant when the Lord commanded that we have no other gods before him. Business. Family squabbles. Gossip. Disapproval. The next big deal. Men arrange. Their plans go wrong. They rearrange. It's seldom what they hoped it would be. They are disappointed. Or they're satisfied with mediocrity when there is much more joy to be grasped by simply looking around and remembering to praise God!"

Zadok reached his gnarled hand toward the stars in a gesture that reminded Avel of Yeshua that night in the hills of Galilee. "Look at it," Zadok breathed in awe. "And yet for most of mankind not one single hour of one day is spent in the pure wonder and praise of being alive!" He gestured toward the torches on the parapets of distant Herodium. "Humans who dwell in towers of stone are fleeting shadows against the walls. They pass through corridors of power and vanish. Names and

achievements are forgotten after one generation. Only the stones remain where they used to be. A house. A room. Someone else living there. They who live a life without praising God for constellations and sunsets live without living! They miss the joy of standing in awe beneath the stars God made for their pleasure because they are thinking of yesterday and worrying about tomorrow. They can't see what is beyond themselves . . . to *now!* Do y' know what I'm saying, child?" Zadok held Avel in his gaze. "Listen!"

Avel nodded, listening to the creak of the world in the night. It was a sort of harmony. Music too deep for words. "I hear it."

"Yes! Yes! *Now* you're alive! See the miracle of your own hands. A beautiful creation, hands. Babies sit and stare in wonder for hours at little fingers. I always admired that about my own babies."

Avel studied his hands. Dirt beneath his nails. The scar on his thumb. The pattern of lines on his palms. The way his fingers moved at his unspoken desire. Yes. Miraculous. Worthy of amazement. Of praise, even.

Zadok's face glowed with pleasure at Avel's understanding. "To comprehend this is to understand the heart of a shepherd. He says to his flock: 'Now you are safe! What have you to fear at this moment? If there is danger I'll protect y'. If you're hungry, I'll feed y'. If y' thirst, I'll lead y' to water!'

"And this is what God, the Father who watches over his flock, wishes us to know.

"Now there is beauty shimmering in the night sky! It costs nothing. It cannot be bought or sold, and yet it is glory beyond measure! All around! Hear it as we shepherds have always heard it! How the air hums with the slow breathing of the sleeping flock. Remember! You're sheep in his pasture. He cares for y', child! Trust God for *now*. This moment, and this moment! One moment at a time. And that'll get y' through anything."

The aged shepherd touched his scar and smiled, as if it contained evidence of that trust.

Avel glanced up at the sky as a meteor carved a blaze of light across the black vault of heaven.

"That's the blessing of a shepherd's life," Zadok said softly. "Now the meteor streaks through the sky, and we alone in all the universe are privileged to see its passage. *Now* is all we're promised. The past can't be changed; the future may not exist for us. And yet most mankind dwells in one or the other. And so our Father in heaven whispers on the wind to us, both the shepherds and the flock, 'Be still and know that I am God!'"

They passed the next hours one moment at a time. Avel had never felt such contentment. He felt a kinship with David, the shepherd boy who became the great king over Israel.

But it had all started here, in Beth-lehem.

■ ■ ■ ■

It was nearly morning when the summons to Zadok and Avel arrived at Migdal Eder by way of a Temple courier on horseback. Zadok snapped open the dispatch and sighed as he silently read the words. Impressing his reply on the wax, he sent the rider back to the city.

"So, Avel. You and I are summoned to Yerushalayim. To the house of Nakdimon ben Gurion. He and Gamaliel of the Sanhedrin wish a word with the two of us about matters of grave importance. I have to know, boy, did y' tell him the message you were sent to give me?"

"No, sir. Only that we were sent to Migdal Eder in Beth-lehem."

"Good. It must remain locked in you."

EL ZERUBAVEL

The next day Avel and Zadok waited on the stone bench inside the atrium at Nakdimon ben Gurion's house. Zadok put a finger to his lips, indicating that Avel must not speak unless he was addressed.

An elderly Ethiopian servant brought them large cool draughts of pressed apple cider to drink, a tray of dates and almonds, and water for washing. He knelt to remove Zadok's shoes and washed the old shepherd's feet. He left Avel to tend to himself.

The slave had ebony skin and teeth like aged ivory. His white hair was a sharp contrast to his jet-black complexion.

"Master Nakdimon will be with you shortly." The servant's voice was heavily accented. His left ear bore the mark of an awl, indicating that he had chosen a lifetime of servitude in the house of his master. And why not? Avel thought, as he peered around at the luxurious surroundings. A slave in bondage to a man like Nakdimon lived better than nearly every free man in Israel. Avel remembered the generosity of the ruler with the Sparrows. It was clear from what Avel saw around him that Nakdimon could afford to be generous!

So this was what lay locked behind the gates of a rich man's palace. Avel drank it in. The air was cool and still, except for the pleasant gurgle of water in the fountain. This was a different world from the stink and press of Jerusalem's packed lanes. Massive stone walls, topped with shards of broken pottery, blocked the clamor of the rabble and kept thieves from entering.

Beneath the shelter of the portico was evidence that children lived here. Toys were neatly arranged on a shelf beside a door. From a far-off quarter in the mansion Avel heard giggling and laughter.

Avel envied the comfort of children raised in such plush surroundings. Then he proudly reminded himself that they were not privy to every meteor that flashed across the sky like he was.

The bondsman came to take away the washing bowl and towels and then sized up Avel. He smiled, showing gaps in the long yellow teeth. "Young master. Come over here to the fountain. Master keeps fish within. Frogs too."

And water lilies. Fish darted among them. It was peaceful here, and yet Avel felt uneasy.

The murmur of conversation drifted out of the house. Avel thought he recognized Nakdimon's voice. There were others with him.

Avel dipped his fingers in the courtyard fountain. A frog leapt into the water. Honeysuckle vines wound around the pillars of the portico, surrounding this sanctuary of the mighty with a sweet aroma.

In the old days Avel had often caught the scent of blossoms as he and Hayyim had passed by this house. Avel thought about his old friends at the stone quarry. He remembered how they used to strain to see inside the massive gates of the men they led from place to place by torchlight.

Ah! The stories Avel would have told Hayyim, if only Hayyim had not died!

The Ethiopian emerged from the main house and bowed slightly. "The master bids me ask Master Zadok, honored shepherd of the flock, and his young apprentice to enter into his house."

Zadok stood and shook out the folds of his cassock. He adjusted the eyepatch. With a swipe of his thumb he wiped a smudge of dirt from Avel's cheek and smoothed back a lock of hair.

"Remember your place, boy. Great teachers of Israel have summoned you here. Speak only the truth. Do not speculate on any matters beyond what you are certain of. No guessing. No maybe this or that, eh? And give them only as much information as they ask. You understand me, boy?"

Avel nodded solemnly. He remembered Yeshua facing the hostile questions of those who hated him. Always the Teacher managed to turn their mocking back on them. Avel wished he were as clever as that.

Zadok followed the servant inside. Mosaics adorned the floors with scenes of gardens and flowers. The walls were clean and plastered. Morning light streamed through the windows, which looked out on a broad lawn and fountains.

So much water for the gardens. Was this waste of water the reason many common folk were upset by the use of Korban for the aqueduct? Avel wondered. Would the lawns of the Sanhedrin and the priests benefit from Pilate's construction project?

On the patio Nakdimon ben Gurion sat on a low stone bench opposite his uncle, Gamaliel ben Simeon. Intimidated, Avel hung back. With a stern glance from his shepherd eye, Zadok demanded Avel come along.

The two rulers were sunk in conversation. They fell silent and stood when Zadok and Avel joined them.

"So! Zadok! *Shalom, shalom,* old friend!" Gamaliel clapped the herdsman on his back.

Avel was amazed at the familiarity!

Zadok clasped hands with both men, but his scarred visage remained grim, his tone curt. "*Shalom.* You have called me here with my apprentice on such a day. The day of preparation is almost at hand. This is important?"

Nakdimon extended his hand to Avel. "You found your shepherd, I see."

Avel blushed at the attention. Had his conversation with Nakdimon on the highway somehow gotten Zadok in trouble?

"Yes. I was sent to find Zadok. In Beth-lehem. Like I said."

"Well done. Clever boy to bring your two friends so far at the command of Yeshua." Nakdimon and Gamaliel exchanged a knowing glance.

Avel noted the look and figured the comment was meant to get him talking. He rubbed his eyes and considered how he might reply. But he didn't know how to answer. He thought he glimpsed the hint of a smile on Zadok's lips.

Then Nakdimon turned his attention to the old shepherd. He indicated Zadok should sit. "I know we have inconvenienced you. This is an extra journey in your busiest time."

"Lambing and Passover." Zadok scowled. "Always the same time each year. Hardly a moment to sleep or eat for anyone in Beth-lehem or Migdal Eder."

Nakdimon continued, "You're managing, Zadok? I was sorry to hear of Rachel's passing. It must be difficult."

The old man glanced down and touched the scar on his face. "I have my work."

Gamaliel spoke. "Rachel bore her loss well these many years."

Zadok sighed and nodded. "She was ready in the end. Ready to see our boys. They would be men now. I always marked the passing years and considered what age this one would be and that one. But they remained always babies . . . small boys to her. She didn't look back when she left this world."

Avel pressed his lips tightly together. So there had been a woman and sons in the life of Zadok. And they were gone. Dead. Finally Avel understood the expression of grief that was permanently etched in the old man's ravaged face.

"But enough." Zadok stroked his beard. "I am not the only man who has lived longer than he might like. Nakdimon, you're also left a widower with children to raise alone. But y' didn't call me away from my duties with the Temple flock to inquire after my grief."

"You're right." Gamaliel leaned forward. "The rumors, Zadok! There are rumors!" He seemed barely able to say the words. "You must know them! That somehow the child survived . . . And there are two men among us who are of the right age. And they claim to be for the people! For Israel! Bar Abba's name means 'Son of the Father'! And then there is the other. Yeshua. Teacher. Healer. Hardly king-like. But impressive. Rumors are growing that he's the one. Oh, yes! Nakdimon has seen him. Spoken to him. Witnessed what miracles he is doing among the people! Rumors are that he's coming here to Yerushalayim for Passover this week. But it's one year more, Zadok, according to my calculation of the prophet Dani'el. I called for you because . . . until now you have refused to speak what you know. You heard what you heard all those years ago. . . . Could either of these two men be the child? Is it time?"

Avel observed that the herdsman clearly knew more than he would admit to. His jaw was set. His brow furrowed. "That was long ago," Zadok said, resisting. "I've heard no more since that night."

Gamaliel probed, "It's been thirty-two years. Your own sons would be men, you said. How old?"

"Enoch, thirty-five. Samu'el, thirty-three. Gaddi. He was a babe in Rachel's arms. He'd be thirty-two." The old man's shoulders drooped visibly as some horrible memory played out before him. "What can they have to do with anything? Herod was mad."

Gamaliel said intensely, "It's written in the book of the prophet Jeremiah . . . a lamentation so loud it would be heard in Ramah. Six miles away from Beth-lehem. Yes? Even now the old ones remember that the wailing of Beth-lehem's mothers *was* heard in Ramah. 'The voice of Rachel weeping for her children and she would not be comforted because they were no more. . . .' Why do you refuse to speak? Why don't you tell us what you know?"

"I've sworn an oath. Until I'm released, my life is bound by a covenant of silence. Would you, a teacher of Torah, compel me to break a blood covenant?"

Gamaliel sighed, as if beaten by Zadok's reply. "But before that terrible hour there was hope! It was you who first brought the good news to my old father at the Temple when you brought in the herd of lambs for sacrifice! You were the messenger of the Almighty then, Zadok."

Zadok replied in a barely audible whisper, "I'm nothing but an old man. Waiting like your father, Simeon, waited. And if I'd known what grief that message would bring I never would've spoken a word. Nor will I speak of it again until I'm released." Zadok raised a finger to his eyepatch. "Doesn't this convince you, Reb?"

"Well, then. Well, well." Then Gamaliel turned the full power of his gaze on Avel, locking him into his seat. "On the journey to Beth-lehem you told master Nakdimon you were sent to give a message to Migdal Eder in Beth-lehem."

"Yes, sir." Avel's heart quickened. Were they trying to trap him into betraying Yeshua in some way? Or Zadok?

"What was the message?" Gamaliel demanded.

Avel glanced at Zadok for permission to speak. The old man nodded once.

"He said . . ."

"Who said?" Gamaliel asked.

"Yeshua said . . . to tell Zadok that Immanu'el was coming to Yerushalayim," Avel repeated.

"Immanu'el. The very name. God-with-us. Did Yeshua mean himself? Or another? When? This Passover? Now? This week?"

"I couldn't say, your honor."

"You couldn't say? Or you won't tell me?"

"I don't . . . know . . . when. Only that he's coming and we'll go with him."

"Where?"

"Wherever he takes us. Just with him."

Gamaliel pressed him. "Nakdimon says you were in the camp of bar Abba for a time?"

"Yes."

"Where is bar Abba?"

"They were planning to come to Yerushalayim for Passover."

"For what purpose?"

Avel searched his memory for snatches of hushed conversation between bar Abba and his officers. "They say that what's been done with the Korban . . . that the aqueduct is a wrong thing."

"And what will they do about it?"

"Fight."

"Romans?"

"And Sanhedrin."

"How do you know this?"

"They were going to use us boys as spies."

Nakdimon raised his eyebrows in surprise. "And would you go along with them?"

"We ran away."

Gamaliel sat back, as if amazed at Avel's reservoir of information. "Is there any connection between bar Abba and Yeshua of Nazareth? Are they in league with each other? One to carry a sword and the other to claim the throne of David in Yerushalayim?"

There was a connection, but indirectly. Avel remembered Yeshua's pupil Judas Iscariot coming into bar Abba's camp. Dark eyes. Brooding features. He was eager to make Yeshua king in Jerusalem, eager to change the way things were. He spoke to bar Abba about this very thing. The Kingdom was at hand, he said.

"Why do you hesitate in your answer, boy?" Gamaliel asked. "Do they mean to bring revolt here? Revolution because of the aqueduct?"

"Yeshua is nothing like bar Abba."

"Is that true? What do you mean?"

Avel challenged Nakdimon. "You saw Yeshua! You saw it all! What happened to Deborah! You saw Yeshua the same as we did. Tell Reb Gamaliel they're nothing alike! They're not the same! You know the truth. Tell him!"

Nakdimon agreed, "No. They're not the same."

Avel blurted his defense of Yeshua. "Ha-or Tov was blind and now he sees! Emet's ears are open!"

"And what happened to you, Avel?" Gamaliel queried. "The Mourner. Isn't that your name?"

"Not anymore. I . . . I'm different." Avel couldn't elaborate. There were no words to tell what had happened inside his heart. Everything had changed. The boy considered Zadok. The old man had seemed to wither at the reminder of his grief. How many years had Zadok been in mourning? Suddenly Avel knew there was another reason Yeshua had sent three boys to the shepherd in Beth-lehem. Avel added gravely, "There was more that Yeshua wanted me to say. To Zadok. Another message for Zadok."

Startled at this news, Zadok said gruffly, "Well?"

Avel knew he was right to go on. "Yeshua said I should tell Zadok this . . . he said he wants you to know: Blessed are you who mourn. You will be comforted!"

■ ■ ■ ■

The encounter with Asher two nights before seemed like a bad dream in the daylight.

Emet brooded throughout the morning, wondering if he should tell what he had seen at Siloam Tower. And who would he tell? Zadok and Avel, accompanied by Red Dog, had left before sunlight for Jerusalem and a meeting with Rabbi Gamaliel.

Perched on a boulder, Emet observed the final selection of lambs for the next shipment to the Temple. Blue Eye operated at Jehu's commands. The dog separated out those animals who had torn an ear, were lame, or exhibited any sign of sickness. Migdal Eder had a carefully guarded reputation to maintain: no imperfect creatures would be part of the Passover sacrifices.

Lev was charged with examining each suspect animal to see if its defect could be corrected. All these lambs had earlier passed muster as unblemished, but the flock was subdivided into three: those ready for Jerusalem, those to receive immediate attention, and a final third that would be permanently culled from the rest.

It was difficult work keeping the three factions from coalescing back into one. Ha-or Tov aided Lev, but the lambing barn attendant had roughly rejected Emet's offer to assist, telling him to keep out of the way.

Dejected, Emet stared in the direction of Siloam Tower and listened to the sounds of hammering coming from there.

■ ■ ■ ■

There was little that Roman ingenuity and willpower could not accomplish in short order, Marcus thought as he studied the changed landscape around the Tower of Siloam. In just a day the supply yard was visibly more ordered and a single wagon track was clearly delineated. The scarred pasture yet exhibited its wounds but would heal up after another rain.

The work on the new supporting structure for the juncture of the two aqueducts was proceeding nicely.

There was still no love lost between the shepherds and the masons, but at least today's exchanges were in words and not blows.

Oren and his son, Benjamin, brought a report to Gaius Robb as Marcus stood nearby. "We're ready to remove the last of the old buttressing and let the bracing take the load," Oren said. "Ahead of schedule."

"And no more riots," Marcus put in. "And no more stolen lambs.

Peace comes to Siloam, which they tell me means 'sent.' Do you know why it's called that?"

Robb didn't look up from the wax tablet of computations over which he muttered to himself, but Oren seemed surprised that a Roman would be interested in Jewish customs. "Everyone knows," Oren said, "how parched Yerushalayim is for water. We're especially grateful for it and regard it as divinely 'sent' to the Holy City. That's why the pool at Yerushalayim is called that. At the fall festival the *cohen hagadol* sends for a golden pitcher of water to be brought from the Pool of Siloam to the altar of sacrifice. Then the high priest gives thanks and prays for rain for the coming year."

"I've seen a man who said he was the water of life," Marcus noted. He recalled when Yeshua of Nazareth stood up at the Jewish Temple and made this puzzling announcement just as the water from Siloam was being poured out. "What do you think he meant? Was he claiming to be sent from your God?"

Oren's face clouded, and his expression grew guarded. "I can't imagine."

Ruefully Marcus interpreted the change in mood. Oren must suspect all Romans of trying to implicate Jews in rebellion. Given the machinations of Pilate, Herod Antipas, and the high priest, Caiaphas, there was ample reason for him to be suspicious.

Robb contributed, "Says he's water, eh? Probably a madman. This country has more than its share of crazy holy men."

"What kind of . . . ," sputtered Benjamin angrily. After silencing his son with a look, Oren visibly stiffened. There would be no further open discussion of Jewish beliefs.

Marcus tried to recapture the friendliness. "At least you and the shepherds have worked out your differences. Like water from the Tower of Siloam is *sent* to Jerusalem, perhaps we can *send* peace from here to the city of peace, eh?"

It was a wasted effort. When Oren spoke again, his tone was markedly cooler. "Centurion," he resumed, "you may think things are settled, but you're wrong. Just this morning my son was accosted by a pair of shepherds and accused of stealing more lambs."

Marcus glanced up sharply. "He didn't, did he?"

As Benjamin blustered Oren snapped, "Of course not! What reason would he have? The shepherds hate us because they hate the aqueduct. They're trying to start more trouble. You should hear them muttering about earthquakes and curses and the stones tumbling down on our heads."

"Do you frighten that easily?" Robb inquired dryly. "Because that's what the herdsmen want."

Oren ignored the jibe. "Don't try to play peacemaker here," he warned Marcus. "Some of them really wish we were dead. It'll be enough to do our jobs and get the water for Yerushalayim. Then I can go home and forget about the Tower of Siloam." With that he gave Marcus a cursory salute, snubbed Gaius Robb altogether, and, with Benjamin, exited the tent.

"These Jews." Robb sniffed. "Did you ever see a people more prone to argument and controversy? It's lucky for them we're here to keep order."

Robb wasn't expressing any unusual sentiments as far as Roman attitudes toward Jews, so Marcus didn't bother to reply. Instead he asked, "What about the threats? Is there any reason to take them seriously?"

"You mean sabotage?" Robb pondered. "Surely not."

The workman named Amos poked his head through the tent flap. "Pardon, Engineer," he said, "but you asked to be alerted when the final braces were moved to take the weight atop the wood scaffolding. We're ready now."

"I'll be right there," Robb returned. "Join me, Marcus? You might find this interesting."

Square-based, tapering pyramids were the architectural wonder of Egypt. Graceful marble columns were the peculiar contribution of the Greeks. But the most memorable achievement of Roman design was surely the arch. Using soaring, buttressed parabolas, Roman engineers were able to suspend spans higher over obstacles with less visible support than any civilization's previous efforts.

Though so far only outlined in timber scaffolding, it was already clear that the new project would be a swan to old Herold's ugly duckling.

"This is the time when the outward pressure of the existing structure is transferred to the temporary bracing," Robb pointed out. "There'll be a momentary shaking, and then it will come to rest."

Nodding to one of his assistants, Robb signaled for the work to proceed. By use of a flag system and shouted orders, the command was relayed to men atop the scaffolding. The workers there were poised with heavy hammers.

The resulting crash of stout clubs against wooden beams sounded like a colossal drumbeat, the call to arms of a phantom army.

There was a corresponding thump as the bracing dropped only a matter of inches into the joints and grooves prepared for it. This secondary vibration was not as loud as the first, but much more powerful. As the shock transferred to the ground, Marcus noticed it in the soles of his feet.

A cheer went up from the stoneworkers and laborers.

Shepherds in the nearby pasture turned to see the cause.

An insignificant cloud of dust at the base of the column was easily dissipated by the morning's breeze.

But not the tremor. Marcus sensed it rising up, as if the earth itself were trembling.

"Robb," he said with concern, but that was as much as he managed before the air stretched with creaking and groaning . . . the screeching of straining timbers. Massive planks corkscrewed, as if a giant unseen hand twisted them like wisps of straw.

The scaffolding shuddered.

The top of the existing tower bowed outward, visibly overhanging the workmen underneath, who scattered in alarm.

Gaius Robb, heedless of the danger to himself, ran toward the structure shouting, "Get clear! Get out, now! It's not going to hold!"

A block shattered at the top of the arch. Fragments struck a worker in the head, knocking him off the construction and propelling him sixty feet to the ground.

Another fleeing mason looked up. The far end of a ten-foot beam dropped loose, pivoted, and swung free, clouting the man as he hung from a ladder. The blow batted him away like a swatted fly.

Marcus tackled Robb. "Get back!" he yelled. "The whole thing is coming down!"

Arms flailing in a futile attempt to fly, a stonecutter jumped clear of the collapsing tower. He plummeted through the air and landed atop a heap of sand.

The arch leaned still further, lumber cracking louder than whips as eight-inch-thick planks snapped like twigs. Then, roaring like an avalanche, a rockfall of hewn stones and tree-trunk-sized planks poured across the pastureland.

Marcus sheltered the diminutive Robb as best he could, while trying to get as much of himself under his helmet as possible.

A jagged shard struck him in the back, then a blast of choking dust, roiling outward from the destruction, swept over him like a black sandstorm.

LEMOR

E met was the first to catch the shuddering. His head snapped up. There was no wind, no hint of cloud. What was that sound? He experienced the grumble in his chest, the same way he had sensed vibrations back before Yeshua gave him sound.

The rumble rolled over the pastures of Migdal Eder like thunder out of a cloudless sky.

Others noticed the sensation too and looked around with alarm.

Jehu pointed toward the line of Herod the Great's aqueduct. The three pylons within sight swayed, bits of mortar flaking off.

Emet read the man's lips: earthquake, he said.

A half-dozen lambs guarded by Ha-or Tov while awaiting Lev's inspection bolted in fright and disappeared back into the flock.

A swirl of dust rose up in the direction of the Tower of Siloam, blocked from Emet's view by an intervening knoll. "That's not just an earthquake," he heard someone shout. "The tower's collapsed!"

Emet was the last of the shepherd band to reach the top of the hill. The others from Migdal Eder already stared at the destruction.

Stones and timber lay everywhere. Where the scaffolding had been was a heap of rubble. Some blocks lay a great distance away, as if trying to return to the quarry from which they were mined. Emet recalled a time when his sister was beaten for dropping a skein of yarn and tangling it up. This disaster was that sort of snarled confusion on a colossal scale.

Wails of pain reached Emet's hearing. Around the scene men stirred, picking themselves up slowly. Some had dangling, useless arms. Others limped as they walked.

Dust-covered, many of them bleeding, workmen tore into the rubble.

Then Emet realized that the horror had not ended: there were men trapped under the ruins.

■ ■ ■ ■

Marcus jumped to his feet. His bruised back arched in a spasm that made him grit his teeth. Seizing Robb by the collar of his tunic, Marcus hauled the engineer upright. "Are you all right?" he asked.

Wiping dust from his eyes, Robb replied, "Yes . . . yes, I think so."

"Come on, then," Marcus urged. He approached the debris and immediately located a worker half-pinned underneath. When Marcus grasped the man under the arms and attempted to drag him free, the fellow screamed in pain and fainted.

"Here," Marcus ordered, grabbing Amos and another dazed laborer. He thrust a beam into their hands. Locating a hollow at the base of the heap, Marcus planted the end of his makeshift lever. If anything went awry it would be the centurion's hands crushed under the stone. "On three, push with all your weight and hold it till I get him clear. One! Two! . . ."

The quarter-ton weight raised bare inches, but enough for Marcus to draw the pinned man toward release.

The pry bar slipped and the load wobbled.

"Can't hold it!" Amos shouted.

"A couple of seconds more!"

The rock slithered sideways.

With a tremendous backwards heave, Marcus dragged the injured worker loose . . . an instant before the mass slid off the lever and dropped with a crash.

Marcus gazed down at the man he'd rescued.

"What can we do, Centurion?" Amos asked urgently.

"Nothing," Marcus said dully. "He's dead. See to the others."

Benjamin rushed up to the centurion. "Over here! Help me!" he pleaded. "It's my father."

Marcus found Oren caught between two timbers. The master mason was conscious despite a gash on his scalp that bled profusely. There appeared to be room for Oren to slip out between the imprisoning beams. "Can't you move?" Marcus asked, fearful that the man's spine was broken.

"It's my arm," Oren replied, panting. "Plank splintered when it hit. Think . . . something went through . . ."

Crawling around behind the wreckage to Oren's other side, Marcus located the truth of the stonecutter's words. A wooden shard, as sharp as a spear and as broad as a man's palm, had pierced Oren's left arm.

The point had emerged from Oren's flesh and was wedged in the debris, pinning the man to the ground.

Benjamin stood nearby, crying out that his father was killed.

"Benjamin," Marcus snapped. "He isn't dead! Get me a saw! Jump to it."

When Benjamin didn't respond, Amos brought the requested tool.

Determined not to lose another life to the tragedy, Marcus worked feverishly, bracing his back and legs against another canted fragment of scaffolding. He pressed upward to give himself some working room as he sawed at the wooden barb to cut it loose from the beam.

All the time Marcus could hear Benjamin muttering, "It's those shepherds! They've killed my father! They did this! They caused this! I'll make them pay."

As the saw chewed through the splinter, Marcus heard Jehu's voice.

"Do you need help?" the shepherd called.

With a jagged chunk of rubble, Benjamin gave an incoherent yell and rushed toward Jehu, his weapon ready to strike.

Marcus was caught. Oren's arm was almost free, but not quite. Worse, the bulk of the plank pressing on Marcus' back had to be shifted to prevent it from falling and further injuring Oren.

The centurion needed to intervene between Benjamin and Jehu, but could not.

He couldn't prevent what was about to happen.

■ ■ ■ ■

Jehu, Lev, and five other shepherds were in the front rank of those who arrived on the scene of the tower's collapse.

Ha-or Tov and Emet were ten paces back.

All looked stunned at the ferocity of Benjamin's attack.

Jehu warded off the first blow with an upraised shepherd's crook, but Benjamin's assault didn't stop. In a frenzy he slashed right and left. As he did so, he yelled for the other workmen to come help him kill the saboteurs!

"Are you crazy?" Jehu demanded.

Benjamin paid no heed. A swipe of his weapon sliced open the back of Jehu's hand. Another wallop creased Jehu's forehead, and he dropped to one knee.

Lev swung his crook at Benjamin but missed, and then the battle was truly joined.

Roaring about revenge for their comrades killed in the tower's fall, nine laborers swinging mallets and grabbing up rocks waded into the outnumbered shepherds.

Blue Eye snarled and rushed forward.

The mason named Amos struck at the dog. Blue Eye dodged, snapped at Amos' leg, and connected. Off balance, Amos tried to push the dog away.

Lev struck again, hitting Benjamin in the shoulder.

Two workers belabored Jehu, who from his kneeling posture defended himself one-handed against their blows.

Running between Jehu and his attackers, Emet yelled, "Stop! It wasn't shepherds who did this. Stop!"

A sweeping backhand clout of Amos' callused hand knocked him aside.

Blue Eye pounced on the hand, sinking his teeth into bone.

Even as Emet cried out, Amos smashed his hammer against Blue Eye, killing the dog.

With Lev assailed by three other aqueduct workmen, Benjamin returned to the assault on Jehu.

Emet saw the Roman centurion rush forward, but Marcus was too late.

Raising his clenched fists for a two-handed blow, Benjamin brought his stone spike down on Jehu's head.

Lev escaped his attackers and sprinted toward Jehu's defense, but Amos intervened. The shepherd swung his staff at Amos' neck.

Emet heard something snap, then Amos toppled to the ground, falling across the lifeless Jehu.

The boy was shocked into muteness . . . as if he'd never learned to speak a word.

■ ■ ■ ■

Marcus batted at Lev's staff, knocking the crook from the shepherd's hands. With the point of his sword at Lev's throat he bellowed, "Down weapons, all of you!"

A shepherd ignored the command, acting as if he would strike Benjamin. But the shepherd stopped when Marcus threatened to kill Lev. "If one more blow is struck, this man dies," Marcus said. "And whoever doesn't obey will be crucified! I'll take this scaffolding apart and use it for crosses!"

Cursing and jostling continued as the panting groups of bloodied men separated, but with Marcus' threat the fight had gone out of them. All knew that a Roman centurion was as good as his word when promising punishment.

All could visualize a line of crosses paralleling the aqueduct and bearing their tortured and dying selves.

Marcus looked in their eyes and saw it: naked fear had replaced the rush of anger.

He shook his head at the absurdity of this senselessly compounded disaster. His own wrath rose up, and he tasted bile in his throat. At that moment he could easily have ordered twenty crucifixions and had no remorse.

But he did not.

Even though he was but a lone man, easily overpowered, such was the authority of Rome that not one of them offered to resume the violence by challenging Marcus. These were not rebels, not assassins, and they had no desire to be martyrs.

Violence ceased as self-preservation came to the fore.

Blame, however, was another matter.

"We came to help!" a shepherd protested. "And he," the man argued, leveling his staff at Benjamin, "he killed Jehu! They started this!"

"You caused it!" Benjamin said, sweeping his hand toward the ruins of the scaffolding. "You cursed us, and then you made it happen. You killed my father."

Cries of protest from the shepherds made no impression on the angry masons, but Marcus said, "Oren's not dead. He and the other injured need help." Then he added bitterly, "Help! Not more bloodshed! I *will* investigate this, and the guilty *will* be punished." After pausing to let the full weight of the implications sink in, he resumed. "You," Marcus said to a herdsman, "take Jehu's body. Get your men out of here. Send Zadok to me. Tell him I have Lev at Herodium. He and Oren's son are being held for murder."

■ ■ ■ ■

The men of Migdal Eder bore the body of Jehu away on a broken gate.

Excluded from the tight ring of grief, Emet and Ha-or Tov followed at a distance. They were newcomers. Outsiders.

Jehu's eyes were wide, fixed in horror. Blood flowed down his left arm and dripped from his index finger. With each jarring step the dead man seemed to beckon them to follow, first pointing at Emet, and then at the sky.

Emet looked up. The soul of Jehu must still be just a little above them. If the dead suddenly gained insight, did Jehu blame Emet for this?

Emet stepped cautiously around the gruesome trail. Hands trembled. He tucked them into his sleeves. He felt sick. He was to blame for everything. Everything. The sabotage and collapse of Siloam Tower. The death of the stonecutters. The fight.

And this.

Hadn't he heard the voices of watchers in the woods? On the dark hillside hadn't Asher cowed him to silence by threatening to kill him if he told? Now Jehu was dead. Lev in prison. Certainly Lev would be condemned to be crucified. And it was Emet's fault for remaining mute.

"Blue Eye." Ha-or Tov mourned the dog.

Yes. Yes. And Blue Eye too. The dog was almost a person, wasn't he? Kinder than Lev. Braver than any man. Loyal to old Zadok when Jehu had been a secret complainer.

And yet the carcass of Blue Eye was left in the field. At the thought of their four-legged guardian Emet began to weep quietly.

He tried to say, "My fault," but his voice would not form the words.

Ha-or Tov attempted to spit. "My mouth. I've got no spit."

Emet kept his gaze on the path as they dodged red droplets. He lagged farther behind, unwilling for his friend to see that the responsibility for this rested on his shoulders.

"Come on," Ha-or Tov urged him impatiently.

A messenger was sent ahead to notify Jehu's wife that he was killed. What would Zadok say when he came back to find everything had gone wrong?

Wailing commenced in the City of David. Emet recognized the sound of keening for what it was, though he had never heard it before.

Strange: the sheep of the doomed flock grazed on, as if nothing had happened. And yet the world of Migdal Eder was shaken.

Women dashed from the houses and ran down the path to meet the procession. Emet raised his eyes long enough to see a woman supported by two others. Jehu's wife. She screamed the name of the fallen man. At the sight of Jehu's body she fell to the ground and flung dust into the air.

Ha-or Tov said, "If Yeshua was here, this wouldn't have happened."

But Yeshua was far away in the north. Death was unrestrained. Violence unhindered. Men were given over as playthings of fury and sorrow. Heads cracked like ripe melons and life spilled out in the blink of an eye. And there was no putting it right.

Only Jehu was serene.

The killing was not done. They all felt it, knew it. Death whispered in their ears that the men crushed beneath the stones of the shattered tower and this lifeless remainder of a shepherd were glimpses of each living man's destiny.

Emet thought of Lev sharpening his knife on the whetstone in the stable. Soon he too would be dead!

And the son of the stonecutter? Young Benjamin, who had slaughtered Jehu! He would die with Lev!

The makeshift bier was carried above the heads of the shepherds toward Beth-lehem and to Jehu's house.

The pair of boys remained outside as the shepherd was placed solemnly on the floor of the cottage and the sounds of mourning increased.

So many colors of green on the hillside. Flowers bloomed beside the doors of little houses. Terrace gardens, newly planted for summer, were littered with tools flung away at the instant of calamity. Shovels and hoes and sacks of seed among the half-dug furrows identified the moment when everything changed.

There the stones and timbers of the tower collapsed.

There the first blow was struck.

And there Jehu's brains spilled out.

There Lev killed a man and thus put an end to his own future.

Emet, sinking down beside a stone fence, covered his face with his hands. Frail shoulders were racked with sobs. He could not make himself think about Jehu, a man. No. His heart cracked for Blue Eye.

Ha-or Tov awkwardly put an arm around him. "Emet! Brother! Brother! Go ahead. Cry. Go ahead." Yes. There was relief in tears, but Ha-or Tov could not know the reasons Emet wept.

■ ■ ■ ■

Zadok and Avel returned to Beth-lehem with the sound of mourning ringing in their ears. Red Dog, panting alongside, scanned the scene in search of Blue Eye.

After the old man received details of the tragedy from a shepherd outside Jehu's house, he seemed to shrink within his frame. It was as if there were room for two inside his huge hide but only one remained.

He bowed his head but did not enter Jehu's house. After a time some men came out. Zadok spoke in nearly inaudible whispers to those who gathered around him to express their terror.

"Sabotage, the Romans say."

"They blame us! They'll be coming for us all. Not only Lev!"

"Lev's doomed for certain!"

"The boy of the master mason started it!"

"Self-defense is what it was!"

Zadok had no solution.

The dust of chaos choked the air of Beth-lehem. Emet could smell it—acrid and thick. The horizon of the valley had changed. The proud Tower of Siloam was missing. A rubble heap of broken bodies, stones, and shattered timbers lay where it had stood.

Nothing would be the same. Death had come secretly among them. From the cover of the familiar wood Evil had searched for weakness in the men of the valley and had found it.

Emet had remained mute. Guilt threatened to crush his soul. Hours passed. In the late afternoon Zadok found the boys huddled beside the wall.

Zadok's back was to the sun. The blinding glare hid the old man's face. Emet squinted up at him. The shepherd's shadow over them seemed young and powerful.

"Boys," Zadok commanded. "Come home."

Red Dog nosed them to their feet. Zadok, his stride slower than usual, led them to the house. Following his example they washed hands, feet, and faces before crossing the threshold. This connection with ordinary routine after a day of confusion was a relief to Emet.

With a ragged sigh, Emet inhaled the scents of lavender and thyme. He raised his eyes to focus on the bundles of herbs hanging from the ceiling.

The trio stood, unmoving, in the center of the room as their mentor busied himself around them.

Sticks on fire. Bread heating on the flat stone that rested on the coals. Hummus, olives, and dates removed from storage jugs and placed out in bowls for supper.

At last Zadok spoke. "Well? Sit."

They obeyed. He sank down opposite them and blessed the bread, distributing it to each.

"Today as you know I was called away to Yerushalayim."

Did he not want to know the details of the tragedy? Emet wondered.

"Avel and I met with certain members of the Sanhedrin." He gave Avel a hard look. "With Reb Gamaliel and his nephew Nakdimon ben Gurion. You know them?"

Ha-or Tov nodded. "We traveled south from Galilee in Nakdimon's protection."

Zadok clearly knew this already. "After today there is sure to be a trial of our shepherds before the Sanhedrin."

"Will Lev be crucified?" Ha-or Tov ventured.

The old man stared out the doorway in the direction of Herodium. At last he drew a long breath. "Jehu paid the price for rebellion. For disloyalty. Perhaps the hand of the Almighty has also punished the men killed at Siloam Tower. But every shepherd of Migdal Eder may be accused of sabotage before the week is out. And all may stand condemned before the Roman judges and the council of seventy. Nakdimon was kindly disposed toward you. Perhaps you should go to his house in Yerushalayim."

Emet sensed the blood drain from his face. "But! No!"

"The Holy City. For your own safety, boy," the old herdsman instructed.

Emet blurted, "But they aren't guilty!"

Zadok considered Emet's response curiously. "It will take a court to sort that out," Zadok countered.

"I know who broke the scaffolding!" Emet declared. "I heard voices in the woods! I told Lev, and he said I was crazy."

"You heard . . . ?" Zadok leaned forward intently. "What are you going on about?"

Emet began to weep as he confessed everything. The calamity was all his fault, he was sure of it! He alone should be punished, not the shepherds! Not Lev! He told about his encounter with Asher in the night beside the Tower of Siloam. Rebels! Men everywhere on the scaffolding! Asher's knife. Emet's terror of the darkness. The awful dream that Asher slit his throat like the throat of a lamb. Blood flowing from gaping wounds, soaking his clothes. At last Emet collapsed, sobbing.

At first Zadok contemplated all this, saying nothing. He searched the startled faces of Avel and Ha-or Tov. The two elder boys clearly had not heard it before.

Zadok inquired gently, "Emet? Did y' know what they intended? To kill men and destroy the tower?"

The boy shook his head. He knew only that they were up to something evil. "And I was too afraid to tell you. Asher said . . . I am bound by blood covenant . . . if I told . . . he'd slit my throat, cut me in two, and carry my blood in a golden bowl to the high altar!"

"Do y' understand the meaning of a blood covenant, boy?" Zadok asked.

"No, sir."

At this the shepherd's face flooded with compassion. He gathered Emet into his arms and held him close. "It's the most sacred of all covenants between the Lord and the nation of Israel. Made on the day *Adonai* declared to Abraham that one day his children would be a great nation! From the seed of Abraham and Sarah one day a Messiah would be born to save and bless all the world. By this the promise to our nation was sealed in blood between the Lord and Abraham. The covenant passed on through Isaac, Jacob, to us, and the nation of Israel forever. It does not depend on Israel's faithfulness to God, but upon God's unfailing faithfulness to Abraham and the nation of Israel!"

Avel piped, "But why would Asher use such a threat against Emet?"

Zadok explained, "There are times of significance when men still perform the blood covenant with one another. If the vow is broken, then the life of he who breaks it is required as forfeit. The Lord pledged his own glory . . . his holy honor . . . in making his covenant with Abraham. Such a promise is too sacred to ever be used lightly or as a threat against a child."

"Have I broken a vow?" Emet cried in alarm.

"No, boy. No covenant was made. False and hollow words binding you to silence through fear," Zadok soothed. Then he whispered this prayer, "So, Lord!" He lay his cheek protectively against Emet's head. "May he who falsely declared this vow to an innocent child pay the price for his words and deeds." Then to Emet, "And by my own life, Emet, he'll not harm a hair of your head. Can you believe me in this, child?"

Emet rested his cheek on the old man's chest and listened to the steady heartbeat. Relief. Exhaustion. "Yes," Emet quavered.

"All right, then. You'll have to tell the whole truth to the Roman centurion at Herodium. Perhaps you'll have to be a witness in Yerushalayim to others in authority as well. Truth is the only way."

■ ■ ■ ■

In excited anticipation of the approaching Passover holiday, Nakdimon's children built an open fire in the pit in the garden when Nakdimon came home. That evening they roasted apples on sticks and sat round it and asked a million questions about his discussions with Uncle Gamaliel and his trip to the Galil.

The true reason for his quest remained a secret. To speak openly of

Yeshua to his offspring would mean that his opinion would be known to their friends by tomorrow night. Bekah, the cook, would overhear and gossip with the servants of their neighbors. Nakdimon's mother, Em, would complain about tradesmen running off to follow a teacher in the Galil. And hours later Jerusalem would be aware that Nakdimon ben Gurion had spoken with the man who might well be Israel's Messiah.

Holding his sleeping son in his arms, Nakdimon chatted instead about the little boats scudding across the Sea of Galilee. Of children working in the fields as he passed. Of kindnesses he encountered. Meals he ate. Places he slept. And stories he had heard.

"Who then was the good neighbor? The *cohen?* The Levite? Or the Samaritan? . . ."

Only a month had passed, and yet it seemed like such a long time to be away. Nakdimon drank the vision of his children like good wine.

Hannah had blossomed. Soon enough she would be a woman ready to become betrothed. Nakdimon couldn't look at her without thinking of Deborah, the daughter of Capernaum's cantor, who had been dead but was now alive by Yeshua's hand.

Susanna, ten this month, knelt and blew the embers into flame. She had become such a responsible girl. Ashes scattered. She brushed off Nakdimon's sleeve and plopped down beside him.

Ruth was not interested in her father's tales. She had her own stories to regale him with. ". . . and the tower of Pilate's aqueduct collapsed on the workers! We were in the souk with Em, and they brought the dead men right past us on stretchers! Bloody! Blood covered with dust, but blood all the same!"

The twins, Deborah and Dinah, chimed in, "Everyone in the souk was saying it fell on them by the breath of the Almighty!"

"That these were fellows who deserved to die because their wages were paid illegally by Korban!"

Hannah tossed another log on the fire. "Still, they were men like anyone. I was talking to Bekah in the kitchen this morning. She says one of them leaves eight children!"

Leah, the youngest girl, said sweetly, "I feel sorry for them. Who will tuck them in at night?"

Who indeed? Nakdimon wondered.

Nakdimon kissed the top of Samuel's head. The sleeping boy did not stir, but lay contented in his father's arms. It was times like this which made Nakdimon wish he had nothing to think about but these few.

He caught himself staring at Hannah, and thinking then about Ya'ir, Deborah's father.

Would Nakdimon have brought Yeshua home after hearing his child had died?

Or would he have given up and gone back to mourn alone?

It was a question that had plagued him for days. The answer for Ya'ir was the right one. He had received his only child back from the grave.

The apple juice hissed as it dripped on the coals. Nakdimon guessed that if it had been Hannah laying on the bier, he might have sent Yeshua away and gotten on with the burial.

Nakdimon tested the apple with his tongue. Hot. Cooked through. He ventured a bite as Hannah asked, "So, Father, people are saying we'll have a new king in Yeshua of Nazareth. Did you see him? What do you think?"

Nakdimon shrugged and ventured a bite of his roasted apple. "What do the people think? What are they saying?" he asked, begging off the question.

Hannah answered, "Some say he's Elijah. Others say maybe even Moses. Everyone hopes he's coming here for Passover."

■ ■ ■ ■

Few within the fortress of Herodium were sleeping, it seemed. Eleven more bodies extracted from the rubble of the fallen tower lay on wood planks in a cellar morgue. They would be buried at first light tomorrow.

The stonecutters, mourning in silence, separated themselves from the off-duty Roman soldiers whose bawdy drinking songs echoed through the corridors.

Marcus leaned against the parapet of the highest tower and observed the winking fires of the shepherds. The moon had set. Starlight was a profuse web frosting the black face of heaven.

This peaceful reality had been shattered today. By tomorrow it would be utterly destroyed . . . unless Marcus found a way to convince Pilate that the destruction of Siloam Tower was not what it seemed to be.

An unwelcome voice interrupted his reverie.

"We've got a muddle on our hands, eh, Marcus?" Centurion Shomron joined him. He smelled of wine. "Not unexpected. As long as I've been in the army there's always something brewing with the Jews." Drinking made the gruff, grumpy Shomron much more loquacious than usual.

Marcus grunted his reply. Shomron, as a Samaritan, rejoiced in Jewish calamity. Marcus had never liked the old warhorse. He was too matter-of-fact about death, too ready to arrest any troublemaker and crucify him on a charge of *maiestas,* disrespect for Rome.

Shomron drawled, "In my younger days, the old King Herod would have crucified the whole lot of them. Shepherds. Their kin. Everyone. And I would've been on the detail to complete the task."

"This place has a feel of death," Marcus muttered.

"And so it should. Herod murdered his two sons by Mariamme here, they say. Poisoned her, and she being the one who gave his line proper pedigree, you might say, back to Israel's kings. Herod was no Jew. Idumean, he was. And oh how the Jews hated him!"

"Even after he built the Temple?"

"Yes, well. There's more rotten about the man than the good he might have done. He burned all the records of Jewish genealogy stored at the Temple because he feared the day when some descendant of David would be born right there in little Beth-lehem and grow up to become King of the Jews." Shomron scratched his beard. "Oh the slaughters of innocents that came about over that myth! I could tell you things! And the soldiers . . . young men we were. Just following orders. Worst duty in the empire. We rode from this very fortress and joined Herod's personal guard to put an end to baby messiahs and future kings in Beth-lehem. Ask them. There's no men there between the ages of thirty and thirty-three. A whole nest of little Jews . . ." He drew his finger slowly across his throat.

Marcus snapped, "Worthy enemies, were they?"

"Ah well. Gone and forgotten. Except the Jews have a day of remembrance to *celebrate* the day Herod died. Sure. All mourning is forbidden. A real butcher that one. But he was quite the builder, all the same."

Marcus was aware that Augustus Caesar had once remarked about Herod the Great that he would rather be Herod's pig than his son. There was much about the past Marcus didn't want to hear. Not tonight. There were present-day slaughters to avert. He couldn't contemplate the inglorious past.

"You'll have to crucify them come morning. Young and old." Shomron spit over the wall. "Teach them a lesson."

"It's nearly Passover. Executing anyone right now could tip the scales toward riot and revolt in Jerusalem."

"You'll have to kill these. Come what may. And Jerusalem? Packed with messiahs, they say. Maybe that Yeshua from Galilee. Or bar Abba, the rebel. Let them come, I say. From what I hear, Praetorian Vara and his cohorts will take care of any and all who raise their faces to defy Rome in Jerusalem this Passover. It'll be a bloody holy day indeed. Who needs lambs, eh? They'll get what they've got coming to them. One and all."

Marcus' head throbbed. How could he keep Yeshua from walking into what was poised to be a wholesale massacre? Had the Master come south, even after refusing the crown?

And what about Miryam and her family? Surely they planned to attend the ceremonies at the Temple in Jerusalem. With Vara in charge of maintaining peace, there would be no peace. Pilate, Herod Antipas, and possibly the members of the Sanhedrin were in no mood to indulge a hint of disagreement.

Yes. The collapse of Siloam Tower was merely the warning of approaching disaster.

Marcus bade Shomron pleasant dreams and retreated to the privacy of his own bedchamber. He held the light up to the *corona obsidionalis*, which hung on a dowel beside his sword. Surely it had been easier to face a howling tribe of Germans at Idistaviso than to deal with the convoluted intrigues of the stiff-necked children of Abraham.

From somewhere in the enormous cone of Herodium Marcus thought he heard the muffled sound of a man weeping.

LO VE-HAYIL

At dawn the next morning Marcus emerged from the tunnel at the base of Herodium. In pale, shimmering light he made his way to the road circumscribing the hill. He was just outside the boundaries of the fortress grounds when he stopped.

Beside him was Oren, his arm bandaged and hanging from a sling about his neck. Centurion Shomron and a decade of troopers flanked the two prisoners. Benjamin and Lev were chained hand and foot.

Marcus observed others approaching from the direction of Migdal Eder. Even in the mist of early morning that hung about the slopes Marcus had no difficulty recognizing Zadok's distinctive form. The old man was accompanied by three boys and a reddish-coated dog.

Zadok looked weary, troubled by what had happened, and grimfaced about what would be the sequel. "You're up early, Centurion," he said to Marcus.

"I knew you'd arrive at first light," Marcus returned in a matter-of-fact tone. "Does it suit you to speak here?" Stepping closer and lowering his voice he added, "I know you cannot enter Herodium's precincts without defiling yourself on almost the eve of your Passover."

Zadok's eyes widened in surprise. Perhaps he'd never met a Roman officer who even understood, let alone cared about the scruples of religious Jews.

"Yes, here, thank you," Zadok replied. "I have news. The tower was sabotaged, but not by shepherds. This boy," the flock master said, indicating Emet, "saw the perpetrators. Speak up, boy."

Marcus bent close to listen as Emet's voice was reedy and barely above the level of his breath in volume. "It's my fault. I saw them. Asher and the others."

"Asher of bar Abba's men?" Marcus noted sharply.

Emet's head bobbed. "He said he'd kill me if I told anyone . . . so it's my fault! It wasn't shepherds. Please don't kill Lev! I'm the one who should be punished."

Straightening up again, Marcus said, "Your punishment I leave to your master here." Then to Zadok he added, "Gaius Robb and I reviewed the tower's collapse. He and I agree that it was not an accident. Robb wanted me to arrest all of Migdal Eder, and without other evidence I might have had no choice. But I also believe your witness. These boys were with bar Abba's band for a time . . . I overheard them. If Truth says it was Asher, I believe him."

Zadok regarded Marcus with curiosity. "You are an unusual man, Centurion. Why is that?"

"Another time," Marcus concluded gruffly. "Twenty-one men killed and twenty-five maimed in the tower's collapse we can blame on bar Abba. But there remains the matter of two murders that came after. Your man, Jehu, and the stonecutter, Amos, were slain by these two captives. No one disputes their guilt. Shomron and Robb think I should crucify the two of them as examples."

"No!" Emet cried.

Zadok grasped the boy by the shoulder and pulled him back. "You have that right," the chief shepherd acknowledged.

Oren, who had been listening intently, surged forward. "One of the condemned is my son," he pleaded. "He was angry because of what happened to me. He did wrong. But if you must make an example, use me! Don't take my son's life!"

"You see where it stands," Marcus added. "Two dead, two to be punished. A stern warning to any who would disturb the peace. That would be the simplest course . . . unless you can think of another way to guarantee calm between the aqueduct workers and the shepherds."

Oren fell to his knees. "Please," he begged. "In the heat of anger blows were struck on both sides. Hasn't there been enough killing already?"

"Perhaps there is a way," Zadok said carefully. "A blood covenant. A life for a life is demanded, but we have a fearful vow that may serve the purpose. It will only cost the lives of two lambs and not two more men."

Marcus listened as Zadok explained. At the conclusion he said, "You understand that I only accept this proposal if two of high standing will act as guarantors. Their lives are forfeit if there is any further violence. Is that clear?"

With dignity Zadok said, "I, myself, will represent Migdal Eder. Does that suit you?"

Even before Marcus agreed Oren implored, "Use me for the stone-cutters' vow! My life for my son's if there's any more fighting."

Marcus stood for a time, stern and implacable. He knew Shomron and Robb believed that the guilt lay with the shepherds for their hostility toward the aqueduct. In their minds Jews were either totally acquiescent to Rome's authority or they were rebels. Shomron in particular would have crucified them all. Any leniency shown by Marcus would be equated with weakness. The least response required was a double execution.

Marcus made up his mind. "I'll spare them," he said. "But the ceremony must take place today, soon! I'm riding after the rebels who carried out the attack."

■ ■ ■ ■

Emet waited beside the Tower of Migdal Eder, together with Avel and Ha-or Tov. A phalanx of shepherds was drawn up around Zadok, who was dressed in white robes, almost like a priest. Wives and children, friends and neighbors from Beth-lehem, were all on hand as witnesses.

The mood was somber and angry, fearful and mournful, all mixed up together. Sorrow at the loss of Jehu mingled with apprehension that Lev would yet be executed. Indeed there was concern that Roman justice would reach out and strike others of Beth-lehem's shepherd community.

There was also a simmering undercurrent of animosity. The aqueduct was an abomination; the misuse of Korban, a sacrilege. The Jewish laborers, being paid out of stolen Temple funds, were traitors and blasphemers.

Emet overheard some say the Almighty brought down Siloam Tower on apostate heads as a fitting punishment. Besides, how could Migdal Eder be blamed? It was none of their doing, even if they approved the collapse. Nor had they started the battle that resulted in the death of the stonecutter.

But you couldn't expect a Roman to understand. Quick to condemn, quick to punish. That was the Roman vision of justice when it came to Jews.

Emet knew some of the shepherds carried skinning knives in the sleeves of their robes. If the centurion had lied . . . if he came to arrest and punish . . . then Migdal Eder would in fact join the rebel cause and fight back!

As for Emet himself, he recognized the confusion of emotions while experiencing only the sorrow. He alone possessed one sentiment not shared by anyone else: guilt.

By not telling anyone about the rebel saboteurs, Emet was responsible for Jehu's death, for the mason's death . . . for all those killed by the fall of the Tower of Siloam.

It was a crushing burden for a five-year-old to carry.

The detachment from Herodium arrived early, but Zadok was prepared. "Oren, representing the masons, and I, on behalf of the shepherds, will go alone to select the lambs for the covenant. By the sacrifice of innocent blood, we bind ourselves to keep the peace, or else our own lives are forfeit. Y' understand that they cannot be Passover lambs, because then we would be compounding bloodletting with sacrilege."

Marcus signaled his acceptance. "We'll remain here with the prisoners."

Emet observed the trudge of Zadok and Oren up the hill toward the lambing caverns. In the perfectly clear, bright daylight, it was easy to watch them all the way to the cave entrance. He imagined what Zadok was feeling. Lev was chained between a pair of Roman legionaries and under sentence of death. Zadok had one chance to get this right; one opportunity to hold at bay the malice of Rome.

And what was in Oren's heart? It was his own son who was threatened. Emet had heard him welcome the opportunity to put his own life on the line . . . to publicly announce his willingness to be crucified . . . in order to save the life of his boy.

Emet shivered, despite the warm sunshine.

Silence fell over the witnesses as Zadok entered the lambing barn first. Moments later he emerged with a lamb cradled in his arms.

Then Oren disappeared into the cave.

No one spoke. The chief mason was gone for several minutes.

When he reappeared it was difficult to see the lamb he carried, though it should have been easily identified by the contrast of its fleece with his dark brown tunic.

Where was it? Wrapped in his cloak?

Then the creature struggled in Oren's unfamiliar grasp. Ha-or Tov, evidently seeing the truth before anyone else, reached out for Emet's hand. Next, Avel gasped.

And Emet knew.

Bear bleated helplessly, the black limbs futilely resisting.

Emet cried out, an incoherent expression of grief and pain. But there was nothing to change the outcome. The choice of the beloved black lamb had been made. Bear would pay the price for transgression.

■ ■ ■ ■

The sun stood directly overhead.

There were no shadows, neither of men, nor of hills, nor even of the Tower of Migal Eder.

The earlier mist had dissipated, and no clouds marred the brilliance of the blue sky.

It was, Marcus thought, as if nothing that could obscure the coming ceremony was allowed to remain. There would be no excuses that anything had been done in secret or left questionable in any way.

And there were ample witnesses: hundreds of shepherds, aqueduct workers, townsfolk from Beth-lehem, and Roman soldiers, planted as mute, motionless onlookers to the unfolding scene.

A level space in front of the tower of the sheepfold had been swept clean to bare turf. A plot, forty paces in length and outlined with white stones, pointed directly from Migdal Eder toward the fallen structure of Siloam.

The carcasses of the slaughtered lambs had been divided and carried in procession around the rocks marking the covenant path. Portions were placed between the markers, on either side of the lane.

The blood that dribbled from the slain crisscrossed the bare ground. It was so intermingled that no one could say which drops came from which animal.

Opposite the crowd, at the head of the track, stood Zadok and Oren. Zadok's bloody hands were folded across his chest. Oren held up the weight of his injured arm. Both men's features reflected the solemnity of their task.

Marcus stood at the head of the contingent of legionaries flanking Benjamin and Lev. If all went well, blood of lambs would be all that was spilled today. If not . . .

Zadok spoke. In the unnatural silence his voice boomed. Marcus imagined it could be heard in Herodium. "The blood covenant is a sign so ancient that its origin is from a time out of remembrance. Oren, on behalf of the stonemasons, and I, on behalf of the shepherds of Migdal Eder, have each selected a lamb. We have laid our hands on the animals and then killed them, pledging that the innocent blood shed here wipes out the debt of blood between our two peoples. What we do now is to bind ourselves by this most compelling vow to keep the peace. We pledge our own lives to this promise, recognizing that our lives are forfeit if anyone . . ." Zadok's piercing eye pinned each shepherd and each stonecutter before he continued, "if anyone raises his hand against another."

Last of all, Zadok looked at Marcus, who nodded his acceptance of the proposal. "Moreover," Zadok boomed, "the centurion has agreed that Lev and Benjamin shall not die if we keep our promise." That was all the acknowledgment of the Romans that Zadok intended. Resuming his speech, he said, "We descendants of Abraham are the children of the promise made to him by the Most High. He brought Abraham from Ur of the Chaldeans to give him this land. And when Abraham asked how he was to know that he should possess it, the Almighty performed a blood covenant as proof. The animals of sacrifice were cut in two, just as we have done. A deep, terrifying darkness fell on Abraham, and then he saw a smoking brazier and a flaming torch pass between the halves of the sacrifice. *El'Elyon*, God Most High, unlike what we do here today, needed no partner to his covenant but himself. He made his promise unconditional, swearing by his holy honor and his own glory. And the Lord God said, '*To your descendants I give this land, from the River of Egypt to the great river, the Euphrates.*' "

It was a call to all Jews to remember their heritage, to recognize that the bonds connecting them were more powerful than any dividing them. It was a challenge to the stonemasons to remember that they were Jews first and employees of their Gentile masters after.

Marcus wondered if the other non-Jews present in the throng recognized the import of those words. Zadok asserted that the God of the Jews had made an eternal, unbreakable pledge. On His very honor and glory, the Almighty had promised this territory as a Jewish homeland forever. How would Pilate have responded to those words? Would Tiberius view them as a challenge to his rule, or as a historical curiosity? In the mouth of a rebel chieftain they could be interpreted as a rallying call to revolt: drive out the foreign invaders!

What did Yeshua of Nazareth think of that ancient vow?

Oren and Zadok clasped right hands. At a slow, deliberate pace, they walked together between the stones of remembrance, between the bodies of the innocent slain, treading in the path of blood.

When they reached the end of the forty paces, they stopped, but still no one spoke.

Marcus glanced down. A thin crescent shadow cast by his crested helmet lay at his feet. The sun had moved; the moment suspended in time was over. "I agree to the terms of the covenant," he said. "Lev and Benjamin are released. Unchain them."

Marcus heard Shomron grumble at how soft Marcus had gotten. Marcus was sure the events of the past day and how he'd handled them had done him no good with Governor Pilate. How much damage to his career he'd managed was still to be determined.

"Release them!" Marcus repeated.

Freed, Benjamin ran toward his father.

Lev, head down and hands clasped together, stumbled away from the scene toward the pen housing the culled, imperfect lambs.

"We march at once after the rebels who caused the collapse of Siloam's tower and brought about injury and death," Marcus concluded.

At least he'd gotten to say that in front of hundreds of witnesses . . . not that it would do any good. Marcus had met just one man who could truly change hearts and minds. And for that unique ability the Teacher, Yeshua of Nazareth, was hated by those in authority and plotted against for his very life.

■ ■ ■ ■

The search for the rebels who sabotaged the Tower of Siloam yielded nothing immediate except the fact they had left the area. In a bare, waterless canyon that was of no interest to either shepherds or aqueduct workers, Marcus found evidence of their encampment. It had been hastily vacated, which was no surprise. After tampering with the scaffolding and causing death and destruction, they never intended to remain behind and fight a pitched battle. Their weapons were night attacks and terror; they were cowards, not soldiers.

The deserted camp showed the rebels had been living well indeed. There were enough charred lamb bones for the meat to have fed an army for a month. Clearly this was where the stolen sheep had ended up. There was even a curious weapon dropped and abandoned in the hurried departure: a three-pronged instrument designed to cause wounds like the slashing attack of a wild beast.

The rebels had taken no particular pains in covering their tracks. They headed north toward Jerusalem.

This also made sense to Marcus. With the Passover crowds swelling Jerusalem to twice its normal size, bar Abba's men could disappear into the throngs without fear.

The teeming streets and the abundance of unknown pilgrims

swarming the city also suggested more attacks, assassinations, and insurrection. Since the rebels had shown themselves willing to cause the deaths of Jews as well as legionaries, anything was within their scope.

Governor Pilate and Tribune Felix were certain to be in the Holy City by now. Marcus would carry the warning of his suspicions to them there, in addition to delivering his report on what had happened at Siloam's tower. "Form half the men into patrols to guard the line of the aqueduct day and night," he told Shomron. "I don't think they'll hit it again, but we'll take no chances. Then take the other half and march to Jerusalem. I'll ride on ahead."

From Shomron's expression it was clear he didn't envy what Marcus faced when he made his report. The tower had been attacked only shortly after Marcus' arrival. Although there were not enough troopers to guard the full route all the time, Rome would not take that as an excuse.

The Roman army was not known for tolerating failure. When a tree branch once brushed against the emperor's carriage, he had ordered a halt. The centurion in charge of the road-clearing detail had been flogged to death while Tiberius applauded.

No, Shomron wouldn't envy Marcus his trip to see the governor.

On Marcus' part, he steeled himself for what lay ahead. With the certainty of an old campaigner, he knew that something was going to happen in Jerusalem. Now that he had concrete proof the rebels were headed there, he hoped his warning would be in time to thwart their plans.

But most immediately he had another warning in mind, and it was toward Bethany that he rode.

There was plenty of time on the journey to recall Miryam. Would she be at El'azar's home, or was she back at her estate in Magdala, tending young, needy mothers and children? Or was she off somewhere else quite unknown, following the Rabbi from Nazareth, possibly into the teeth of coming disaster in Jerusalem?

Marcus convinced himself that his travel to Bethany had the best possible motives, but his bluff honesty wouldn't allow him to dissemble, even to himself.

He longed to see her again.

Truthfully Marcus wanted to marvel at the light in her hair, inhale her perfume, touch her hands.

He spurred Pavor forward.

The aged retainer who answered the gate at Marcus' knock acted addled in his wits as well as deaf. After Marcus hammered loudly on the entry, a quavering voice finally inquired about his business. "A Roman centurion with an important message for Master El'azar," he shouted.

"You'll have to speak up," the servent directed.

Marcus repeated his request twice more, only to be told that the household had all the provisions it needed, as if Marcus were a traveling peddler.

"I'm a centurion!" he roared. "Open this door!" Marcus wondered if he would have to break it in to gain admittance or if vaulting the wall would be faster.

Just then the door swung back and Miryam stood before him.

"Marcus?" she called in a mixture of pleasure and amusement.

The old servant stood nearby, an upraised hoe in his hands to defend against marauders, until Miryam dismissed him.

"Is Rome attacking us?" Miryam asked.

A number of rejoinders occurred to him, but his changed relationship with her made him stop his tongue before any of them popped out.

"I've come to warn you," he said. "You and your brother, that is. Not to go to Passover, to Jerusalem during Passover. It isn't safe. Rebels and . . ." Since his adolescence in Rome he'd never felt shy in the presence of a woman, but in front of Miryam he was absolutely incapable of coherent speech. "Look," he said finally. "Is Yeshua here?"

"No," Miryam replied. "I came south with my family, remember?"

Weighing the fact that he was a Roman officer in uniform against the dread of offending her by questioning her truthfulness, he asked carefully, "Has he been here? Does he have any plans to be here or in Jerusalem soon?"

"What's this about?" Miryam asked. "First Nakdimon ben Gurion and now you?"

Nakdimon?

"Is your brother at home?" Marcus inquired. "Perhaps I'd best explain this all one time."

"Of course," Miryam said, leading the way into the house.

Over the course of the next hour Marcus sat with El'azar, Miryam, and Marta. El'azar welcomed him warmly. Marta was decidedly cool toward him, but not as violently antagonistic as on previous occasions.

Marcus told what had happened to the tower and what he suspected of the rebel plot against Jerusalem. He hinted at the violent response planned by Pilate without actually revealing any details of Vara's operation. Then he concluded by saying, "It's not just Yeshua's safety that concerns me. If he's present in Jerusalem and anything happens there . . . and I'm certain trouble is brewing . . . then he's sure to be blamed. He might be arrested and tried for conspiracy. After what's happened with the Korban funds and the aqueduct, the first person who acclaims Yeshua as king may be driving the nails through his hands."

It was a harsh admonition, the bluntest Marcus had ever delivered. Marta looked shocked; Miryam pale, but calm.

El'azar spoke. "We don't know where he is. But if we hear of his whereabouts, what's to be done?"

"Convince his talmidim to bundle him over Jordan and back north as fast as possible. Barring that, keep him away from Jerusalem . . . here, if you can . . . at least until after Passover."

Marta opened her mouth to speak, then shut it abruptly at a glance from her brother.

Now *there* was a real change, Marcus thought.

"We'll do what we can," El'azar promised.

It was time to go. Marcus would have to hurry to Jerusalem to deliver his official account before Shomron arrived ahead of him.

Miryam accompanied him to the gate. She tossed her head the way she always did when she wanted to say something important. Her message was simple. "Marcus? Be safe."

Did she sense the same imminent danger he felt? "Miryam, promise me . . . promise! That you won't go into Jerusalem this Passover! You must not! No matter who would ask you . . ."

"I promise."

Marcus exhaled loudly, resisting the urge to take her in his arms. Was this good-bye? He searched her eyes and for an instant thought he saw a familiar longing. He swallowed hard. "I'd like to come back, when this is over."

"It's just beginning, Marcus." Miryam touched his wrist. "It's not likely to be over in our lifetime. But . . . yes. Please, there's much I want to say."

"There's no time," he put in regretfully.

"None to waste."

"A dark hour for the world."

"Then we must be a candle," Miryam said softly.

"There's been no flame to warm my heart since you—"

She silenced him with a finger on his lips. "Not now. Not yet."

"Later?"

"Marcus." She glanced away. "So much more I need to explain . . ."

And so they came full circle. He closed his eyes briefly, as if he could shut out every longing. "There's no time. I have to go . . . Jerusalem is . . . I can't stay."

"Then *shalom*, Marcus." She stepped away from him and closed the gate gently.

■ ■ ■ ■

Herod the Great's Jerusalem palace was marvelous to behold: a wondrous place of artificial lakes, manicured gardens, gleaming marble sculptures. It had enough gold leaf on ceiling and trim to finance a centurion's wants for several lifetimes. Only on this visit, Marcus had neither time nor inclination to admire any of it.

Governor Pilate was in his audience chamber, attended by Tribune Felix and consulting with Praetorian Vara. The meeting was already in progress. There was no opportunity to make his report to Felix privately beforehand. To test the waters, so to speak.

Nor was there any chance to draw back. His arrival had been announced, and Pilate had ordered him shown in.

Helmet under his arm and armor buffed as best he was able, Marcus squared his shoulders and marched toward what might be his death sentence.

The governor was seated in the curule chair, the X-shaped seat of judgment used when making proclamations, issuing pronouncements, and passing sentence.

Marcus put no stock in omens, but it seemed a bad sign.

From the elevated platform on which he sat, Pilate peered down on Marcus, making it difficult to judge his expression properly.

Felix kept his gaze turned floorward, not meeting Marcus' eyes.

Vara, bearded as was Marcus and dressed in the robes of a Syrian merchant prince, smirked openly.

Perhaps sentence had already been passed, and Marcus was late for his own execution.

"Come in, Centurion," Pilate remarked.

The words echoed around the emptiness of the hall.

"News has reached me of an attack on the aqueduct project. Is this true?"

The information had indeed traveled to Jerusalem faster than Marcus. Pilate had probably been informed of the disaster within hours of its occurrence. What he could not know and was undoubtedly waiting to hear from Marcus was what had been done about it.

So Marcus told him. Without offering excuses, without embellishing or trying to spread the blame to others, Marcus explained. He recounted the whole sequence of events, including the evidence that pointed toward bar Abba, the arrest of Benjamin and Lev, and their release after the blood covenant ceremony.

Vara scowled and shook his head in apparent disbelief. His visage suggested that Marcus was even more stupid than he'd previously thought.

Marcus ignored him. "There is every indication the rebels are in Jerusalem right now," he concluded. "It is my opinion they will strike here. Who or what will be their targets is not clear."

Pilate coughed and raised an eyebrow. "According to High Priest Caiaphas, it is extremely clear! He and the Sanhedrin are frightened out of their wits. Word has spread on the streets that bar Abba is going to avenge a sacrilege against their God. Caiaphas is certain he is the next target!"

"It seems easy enough to guard the members of the Jewish council until the danger is past," Marcus ventured.

Vara snorted. "Let them fend for themselves. Our only concern is protecting the governor."

"And maintaining the peace," Pilate added. "No riots! There will be no uprising! Vara, you have enough men in disguise to prevent any mob from getting out of control. Isn't that what you promised?"

Vara nodded. "My troopers will be part of every crowd, every gathering, from here to the Temple Mount." Clapping his jewelry-encrusted hand against his leg produced a metallic ring as he struck a concealed sword.

"Keep the bloodshed to a minimum!" Pilate cautioned. "Clubs and whips, not blades, are called for." Turning toward Felix, Pilate asked, "You received a message from Caiaphas moments ago. What does he want now?"

"He's thought of a way to defuse the aqueduct issue, he says," the young officer related. "He wants you to receive a delegation of leading citizens who will spell out their grievance in regard to the Korban funds. These are . . . men who were not consulted before the project was approved."

"Never!" Vara vowed. "They have no right to question His Excellency's orders."

Marcus remained silent, recalling that the aqueduct scheme had been rammed through the Jewish council when more than half of them were absent.

Felix continued, "Caiaphas feels that by giving them a chance to air their complaints, and by giving the governor opportunity to detail the excellent reasons behind the plan, much of the anger will be defused."

"Caiaphas," Pilate commented dryly, "doesn't always say everything he means! By sending the delegation here he expects to shift the focus of the blame from himself to me! But I will oblige him. He'll be more in my debt than ever. Vara, you and your men will of course be here as well."

Vara bowed.

Then Pilate said to Marcus, "Why didn't you crucify the two men involved in the brawl?"

The governor liked to display his political skill at keeping others off balance, Marcus thought. After the conversation had gone well beyond the Tower of Siloam, Pilate abruptly brought it back front and center, trying to catch Marcus off-guard.

It didn't work.

Since Marcus had no intention of making excuses or lying, he had no reason to hesitate. "Because I judged it to be the best way to prevent a bad situation from getting worse," he said. "Two more deaths would only have kept the anger between herdsmen and stoneworkers simmering and led to more bloodshed. The destruction was caused by the rebels. What followed was unfortunate, but not deliberate. If things now remain calm, the damage can be repaired in a matter of weeks at most and the project not further delayed by more trouble."

Vara's expression was maliciously eager, like a vicious dog awaiting the signal to attack.

Pilate rested his chin on the tips of his index fingers and stared at Marcus. After several beats passed in uncomfortable silence the governor observed, "Quite right too. It has always been my custom to release a prisoner at Passover as a sop to the mobs. Let it be announced that the two men at Herodium were freed by my order. Have that proclaimed in the streets so when the pilgrims hear about the attack on my tower, they'll also hear about my mercy in the very next breath. That's enough for the moment. You are dismissed."

Vara appeared disappointed. Clearly he'd expected to arrest Marcus, if not to be ordered to organize an execution.

Eyeing his enemy, Marcus waited for Vara to leave first, then he and Felix saluted and turned to go.

VE-LO

The open scroll of Isaiah was on Nakdimon's desk. Every passage seemed laden with prophecies about the Messiah, Jerusalem, and the future of Israel. The scroll itself appeared to be a jumble of contradictions. By Messiah's wounds the transgressions of Israel would be forgiven? And yet Messiah, as the promised shoot from the family tree of Jesse and David, would rule as King in Jerusalem? Here he was servant of the Lord; there he was given authority over Israel and all the nations! Could the book of Isaiah be speaking of one Messiah and yet two separate events in future history?

Gamaliel believed this was the case. And coupled with the prophecy in Daniel about the Anointed One being cut off, Gamaliel believed the first prophecy concerning Messiah as Redeemer was within a year of being fulfilled.

It was a frightening possibility. All the passages that described the death of the Messiah were followed by further predictions that the nation of Israel would then be broken by its enemies and scattered to the far corners of the earth! The people of the covenant would live in lonely exile until the last days when the Lord, Immanu'el, would shout from heaven to the north, south, east, and west, "Give them up!" At the command from heaven the children of Israel would come home to Jerusalem and once again Israel would become a nation! When that was finally accomplished, Messiah would return to Jerusalem as King to judge the earth and rule over the nations.

Could it be?

The final fulfillment of hope for the Jewish nation would not come to pass until years, possibly centuries, of suffering!

Nakdimon closed his eyes and prayed that none of this would come to pass in his lifetime or the lifetimes of his children. The prospect of judgment on this beloved Eretz-Israel was almost too much to bear.

Only days now before Passover.

Jerusalem resounded with the bawling of sheep and cattle passing through the gates and into the pens of the Temple. The streets smelled of cow dung and hummed with the buzzing of flies.

This year it was expected that the city would be more packed than usual. The buzz everywhere was about the Prophet from Galilee. Would he come to Jerusalem for the Passover? Or would he remain in hiding since the death of the Baptizer? Pilgrims had begun arriving to find a place to stay. Signs suddenly appeared, advertising room rental in private homes for the holiday.

Nakdimon had never much liked the city during this season of the year. This year he dreaded what might happen.

He told his mother, "This year we stay behind these gates. What I mean, Em, is this: lay in all the supplies we'll need, then bar the doors."

At first she stared at him as if he were joking. Then with a harsh glare she said, "You're expecting it to be that bad?"

He nodded. "Almost a certainty."

"What? Over the Korban funds?"

"That. And more." He wouldn't tell her all that he envisioned.

His mother drew herself up. "Then let's go to my house, Nakdimon! The sea air will do the children good! Come! We can be packed by morning and on the road. . . ."

"I can't go, Mother. You know that. As a member of the Sanhedrin, I have to stay. Especially now."

"Stubborn! Like your father! The family times he missed because of this . . . politics! And don't tell me you're doing this for the sake of *HaShem!* The Almighty has nothing to do whatsoever with the inner workings of the Sanhedrin! Caiaphas and his tribe are Roman puppets. You know it, and so does everyone from here to Rome!"

"You're right. That's why I must stay. Gamaliel and I . . . a few others—"

She interrupted him with a dismissive wave. "Please. Spare me your noble causes. You and Gamaliel. Your children grow up, and you're so busy searching the Scriptures for the answers to life that you miss life. Miss it altogether! So! Let me take the children to Joppa. Hannah is trying so hard to fill the empty space left by her mother that she's forgotten how to laugh. And Samuel has never met your sisters. You stay in this sweltering sheep pen if you like. With the flies! The Romans! The *cohanim* and sicarii. But the children could use a lot of fresh air and a whole lot less intrigue. I'm getting old in this dreadful city! My bones ache for a day at the beach. White sand between my toes."

She was right, of course. Nakdimon *was* missing life. Hadassah had always kept him balanced. But no more. Since he had come home from the Galil, he had been obsessed with searching Torah and the *Tanakh* for answers to his questions about Yeshua. He had hardly left his study.

"Yes, Em. You're right. Of course. You're right. I left Yerushalayim hoping to find answers. Instead I've come home with more questions. I . . . fear . . . this is a dangerous time for us all."

She gazed at him with pity. "You've always been a good boy, Nakdimon. But you need . . . a wife . . . a good woman to steer this ship away from the shoals."

"I had Hadassah. I can't let myself love any other." He did not tell her that the only other woman who had sparked his imagination would be unacceptable as a wife. What would his mother say if she knew he had regarded Miryam, sister of El'azar of Bethany, with more than passing interest? Best to say nothing. Best to steer clear of that particular reef altogether.

His mother frowned. "Well then. You'll have to make do with your mother telling you you're wrongheaded."

He smiled sheepishly. "I can't so much as glance away from the affairs set before me now, Mother. Or something terrible may happen here this week. I feel it. I fear it."

"Then should the children be here when it happens?"

"No." He feigned cheerfulness. "All right. Joppa. The sea. Tell them. Get everything ready. I'll hire escorts and porters from the Temple staff to take you to Joppa in the morning."

"Will you come? Have *seder* with us at least?" She placed a hand on his shoulder and squeezed.

"I'll try." He stared at the open scroll on his desk. Words swam before him. He knew well enough he would be in Jerusalem this Passover and nowhere else. "But don't get their hopes up."

■ ■ ■ ■

The mood around the watch fire was mournful.

Emet sat with his head cradled in his hands. He was unable to escape the sense that besides causing the deaths of so many innocent lives, the tragedy had not stopped. It expanded until it included the one innocent life he had cherished most in the world: the lamb Bear.

Zadok had ordered the three apprentice shepherds to stand night watch over the flock bound for the Temple. Then, unexpectedly, the old man accompanied them.

Tomorrow, Zadok said, Emet and the other two boys would return with him to Jerusalem to meet with Rabbi Gamaliel. Rebels who cause wanton destruction and the deaths of civilians, he said, are not soldiers fighting for a cause but criminals. As much as Zadok disapproved of the aqueduct and despised the Roman overlords, he still intended to denounce the rebels who attacked Siloam Tower.

Politics and rebels were of very little interest to Emet. He hurt inside. Yeshua had given him a voice, but when the time appeared to use it to shout a warning, he had failed.

Zadok tramped the rounds of the flock, posted Red Dog in a watchful spot, then returned to the fire. "Don't take more on yourself than y' deserve," he said, sitting next to Emet and rubbing his hands together to warm them. "Your shoulders aren't as yet as broad as a man's, and many men would have failed the test you faced."

Emet sniffed and shook his head. "But it's my fault. If I had told you about Asher right after it happened, then you could have warned someone."

"And that would have been the right thing for y' to do," Zadok acknowledged sternly. "There's a time to keep silent and a time to speak." The chief shepherd's gaze took in a distant horizon, as if examining a scene visible only to him. When he spoke again, his tone was softer. "You were afraid," he said, "and fear makes us forget right and wrong sometimes. But hear me, Emet. You'll never again in your life let that happen. You would give anything to undo yesterday, wouldn't y'?"

Emet wiped his nose on the sleeve of his robe, and big tears welled up in his eyes. "And today."

Zadok continued, "You've learned at age five what many men never grasp: failing to do what is right may have far worse consequences than anything y' fear for yourself . . . and you'll ache inside afterward. There will come a time in your life when this trial will again be yours. On that day you'll remember what happened at Siloam's tower, and you'll not fail."

"But did it have to take Bear too?" Emet said, his voice quavering.

"Yes," Zadok said. "Bear paid a penalty because of you . . . but so it is with every sin offering and trespass offering and Day of Atonement sacrifice. Sin is not imaginary. It piles up on men's backs like loads of heavy stones."

Zadok paused, as if in thought. "Y' saw men crushed, trapped under the timbers of the tower . . . men who could not free themselves, and who needed someone to lift the weights before they died. Sin is exactly like that, except that it cannot be removed any other way than this: some other, some completely innocent other, must remove the burden. And this, the Almighty teaches, requires a death. Do y' understand me, boy?"

"But why the one lamb I loved?"

"For repentance to be effective . . . for anyone to be forgiven and know without doubt that he is forgiven . . . that which is sacrificed must cost something, be precious, even be agonizing in the loss of it." The chief shepherd put his arm around Emet and drew him closer. "You're well and truly forgiven, Emet. It was a blood covenant that was enacted today, but for you it was an act of atonement. And the Almighty sees your heart and forgives you."

Emet and Zadok, Ha-or Tov and Avel sat beside the fire for a long time without speaking. The crickets were awake in the tall grass and frogs croaked in the pond at the far side of the meadow. These and the sighing breeze chorused with the crackle of the burning acacia branches.

Emet sighed. He studied a bright blue-white star overhead and wondered at its name. When a blazing knot of wood popped particularly loudly, Red Dog turned and regarded the humans gathered in the circle.

The boy recognized that something had happened: he was forgiven. It had been a greater struggle, a tougher thing to achieve, than opening his ears, because that miracle of Yeshua's had been so effortless. Forgiveness of sin was harder than making the deaf hear, but it was no less real.

Nor would Emet ever forget the lesson.

Zadok seemed to sense that the time had come to close that chapter and move on, for he said, "Can y' imagine what Father Abraham was feeling on the night before he reached Mount Moriah?"

A threefold refrain of boyish voices urged the old man to explain, which he willingly did. "Our father, Abraham, was a man of enormous faith. When he was well along in years—the same age as I am now—he left his home, family, friends, and all his comfortable surroundings. He journeyed to a far country, this very land on which we sit, because the Almighty had promised it to him and his heirs. You heard me speak of this today, because that was the subject of the blood covenant made by the Most High."

Affirmative replies echoed around the circle. Emet noticed a strengthening of the old shepherd's voice, as if he had recently gained extraordinary power.

"Many years later, the Almighty gave Abraham an heir—his only son, Isaac. And Abraham loved the boy, cherished him, watched him grow, and thanked the Lord God daily for the gift more precious than cattle or land."

Avel waved for Zadok's attention. "Abraham was old when his son was born?"

"Very," the shepherd said. "And his wife, Sarah, was well up in years too. But that's not the story I'm telling now."

Red Dog stood and stared off into the darkness. Zadok stopped speaking and observed for a time. When Red Dog stretched and lay down again, Zadok resumed.

"Many years passed and a time came when the Most High put Abraham to the test. He told our forefather to take his only son to Mount Moriah to sacrifice him."

"No!" Ha-or Tov protested. "He didn't, did he?"

Regarding each child in turn, Zadok explained, "Abraham trusted *Adonai Elohim* more than he feared for his son. He didn't know what the Almighty planned, but he still believed. And so they traveled three days from their home near Hebron toward where Yerushalayim is now. Think of it: in Abraham's mind for all those three days it was as if Isaac was as good as dead. Remember: not only was Isaac Abraham's son, he was his *only* true son *and* the son of the promise. The one means to fulfill the oath sworn by the Most High in the blood covenant. On the second night they reached just about where we are sitting right now."

Avel and Ha-or Tov glanced around.

Emet wondered if that was why Zadok had brought them out here on this night and why he had come with them. In the next breath the shepherd replied to Emet's unspoken queries.

"It was about this same time of year, so the sounds were similar . . . the stars much the same. Isaac slept, not knowing what was in his father's heart. In my younger days I often stood the night watch in this very spot and pondered what Abraham thought about through that long darkness."

Emet wondered too. How could a father who loved his only son still go forward knowingly toward the child's death? What sort of faith could overcome that sort of fear? Did Abraham hold on to the hope that the Almighty would change His mind? Or did he believe that the Most High would bring Isaac back from the dead as Yeshua raised Deborah? But a deliberate killing?

Even though the fire burned brightly, Emet tossed a tangle of dried brambles into the flames, as though the brilliance could drive back his dread of what would happen in the tale.

"The next day Abraham looked ahead and saw the holy mountain, where the Temple stands today. He made his servants stop then, while he and his son went forward together. Abraham even made Isaac tote the wood for the holocaust offering, just as the Romans make condemned prisoners carry their own crosses to the place of execution."

Emet shuddered. He had seen the grisly remains of men crucified by Rome, their bodies left to rot in the sun.

"When they reached Mount Moriah, Isaac realized they had not brought a lamb. He said to his father, 'Here's the wood and the fire, but where is a sheep for the sacrifice?' 'The Lord God himself will provide,' Abraham told him."

The heap of rocks on which Red Dog perched resembled an altar. Emet, peering through the leaping flames, was terrified of what was coming.

"Abraham built an altar where the rock of sacrifice is," Zadok said. "Stone by stone, placed carefully and neatly. And he arranged the wood for the fire. Then he trussed up his son, who did not resist, and put him on top of the wood on the altar. Then Father Abraham reached out and took the knife to slay his son."

The chief shepherd's knife appeared from inside his sleeve. Rays of firelight glinted off the blade, as if the weapon were a tongue of fire in Zadok's hand.

Now Emet pictured what was going through Isaac's mind! "Make him stop!" he shouted.

Zadok smiled. "That is just what the Almighty did. His messenger said to Abraham: 'Do not lay your hand on the boy. Do not do the least thing to him. I know now how devoted y' are, since you did not withhold from me your beloved son."

Avel and Ha-or Tov cheered. Emet shouted also, but his voice squeaked because his throat was tight.

"Abraham used his knife to free his son instead of to kill him! Next he spotted a ram caught by its horns in a thicket of brambles. And so he offered the ram as a sacrifice instead of his son. He named the place, 'the Lord God will provide.'"

The boys applauded, but Zadok was not quite finished. "Another message came to Abraham from heaven: The Lord God said, 'I swear by myself that because y' acted as y' did in not withholding from me your beloved son, I will bless you abundantly and make your descendants as countless as the stars of the sky.'" Zadok waved his hand overhead at the myriad of glowing pinpoints of light. "'And the sands of the seashore; your descendants shall take possession of the gates of their enemies, and in your descendants all the nations of the earth shall find blessing—all this because y' obeyed my command.'"

Emet cheered again, a piping note of joy.

Zadok held up a cautionary finger. "Know this: there was a test, and there was still a sacrifice, even though the Lord God made an escape for Isaac." Zadok's brow furrowed and the creases of his forehead spilled into the vertical scar that crossed his eye and cheek. "A time will come when bulls and goats and lambs won't any longer die as sacrifices. The prophets tell of the Anointed One, the Messiah, and many want him to be king. Isaiah calls him Wonder-Counselor, God-Hero, Father-Forever, Prince of Peace. He's named Son of the Most High."

Emet thought then of Yeshua, of the miracles, and of the cheering crowds. How did that vision tie in with the story they had just heard?

Zadok said, "And Isaiah says his name shall be Immanu'el, God-with-us."

Three tousled heads snapped upright at that utterance.

"But that's what Yeshua . . . ," Ha-or Tov gushed.

"Shh!" Avel hissed.

"The prophet Isaiah also said this about Messiah," Zadok continued, his scowl deepening. "'It was our infirmities he bore, our sufferings he endured. He was pierced for our offenses, crushed for our sins. Upon him was the punishment that makes us whole. By his stripes we are healed.'"

Zadok stopped and stared toward Herodium and the ruined Tower of Siloam. His face was twisted, as if he had eaten something sour; as if his own words were distasteful to him and yet he could not stop himself from uttering them. He gestured toward the lambs. "We had all gone astray like sheep, each following his own way; but the Lord laid on him the guilt of us all. . . . Like a lamb led out to be slaughtered, like a sheep silent before its shearers, he did not open his mouth. . . . He poured out his life unto death, and was numbered with the transgressors. For he bore the sins of many. . . . The death of a completely innocent sacrifice . . . what can it all mean?"

Was the final question something written by Isaiah? Emet wondered. Or had Zadok's own thoughts crept into the open?

Whichever it was, with those words the old man halted abruptly. He stared into the fire while Avel, Emet, and Ha-or Tov exchanged puzzled frowns. The story of Abraham and Isaac was a good one, Emet thought, about trusting the Almighty. Why did Zadok act so morose?

"Get up, then," Zadok ordered at last as he himself stood. Red Dog alertly jumped to his feet, while the boys were slower to unfold their cramped limbs. "Time to make the rounds of the flock."

■ ■ ■ ■

This was a night of too little sleep for Avel, Emet, and Ha-or Tov. Their watch over the flock completed, Zadok led the boys back to the house in Beth-lehem.

Early tomorrow, after chores, they would head to Jerusalem.

But for now, one Passover duty remained before they could go to bed. Special preparations for the Feast of Unleavened Bread had already begun at sunset. Throughout Israel households were searched and cleaned of all traces of leaven as a symbol of clearing away the secret sins of the heart.

"It is," Zadok explained soberly, "like sweeping out from our souls even small fragments of sin. Like a tiny fragment of yeast in flour makes a lump of dough swell up, even a pinch of sin can take over a man's life. And if y' search, you'll find yeast and sin in the most unexpected places. So tonight, with all of Israel, let's clean our house and our hearts. Sweep away blame and anger at others. Remove all self-deceptions so we'll have a new start."

In the home of Zadok, the ritual began after midnight. The old man lit a candle and commanded the threesome to sit in utter silence as he conducted the first search and spoke this blessing: "Blessed are You, our God, King of the Universe, who has sanctified us by your commandments, and commanded us to remove all leaven."

First, he took up the obvious sources of yeast. Two loaves of bread, and a handful of crusts were dropped into a cloth sack. Then he swept the floor and gathered crumbs of bread from the table. With a feather he dusted the ledge of the windowsill and the corners until, at last, a significant pile of crumbs lay heaped on the floor.

He searched the entire house by candlelight three times. At the conclusion he faced Jerusalem and intoned, "All the leaven that is in my possession, that which I have seen and that which I have not seen, be it as null, be it accounted as the dust of the earth."

Avel could hardly keep his eyes open as Zadok finished the ceremony.

"In the morning," Zadok told them, "which is nearer than we wish to think about, we'll carry this leaven to Yerushalayim. There we will deliver the last of the sheep to the Temple and at the signal from the priests we'll burn this leaven. For seven days we'll eat unleavened bread as our fathers did when the Lord brought them out of bondage from Egypt. After the putting away of the old things, lads, we'll be prepared to stand boldly before the council of seventy elders and give account of what we know about what transpired here. Are y' ready?"

The thin reedy snoring of Emet replied. He was fast asleep, resting heavily on Avel's arm.

Zadok softened and scooped up the boy in his arms. "I suppose I'm overly verbose. It's been awhile since I had three little boys under this roof at Passover. There now." Zadok smoothed back a lock of Emet's hair and kissed his brow. "Poor lamb. And who could blame y' for dozing off? What a day. What a terrible long day it's been." Zadok carried Emet to the pallet and summoned the others to come along. It was time, he said. Past time to sleep.

Ha-or Tov was out before Zadok finished his sentence.

Zadok studied Avel. "And one left. You hate to give it up, don't you, boy?"

Avel nodded. "It's just . . . I never spent Passover in a real house before. Never saw a real father search with the candle. I don't want to miss anything."

Zadok smiled gently at this revelation. "A father, you say?"

"What happened to your boys?"

"Ah. A long story, that. Not for telling tonight."

"When?"

Zadok mussed Avel's hair, indicating that the conversation was at an end. "I'll tell you all about it . . . when Messiah comes. How's that? Now, morning will be here soon enough," Zadok warned Avel. "And it'll likely be another long day for us."

"We'll be ready," Avel whispered hoarsely. And then he too promptly drifted off to sleep.

VEKOAH

Morning broke over the Valley of the Sheepfold after the long night of grief, explanation, and cleansing.

Lev did not come to the lambing barn, so it was left to Avel, Emet, and Ha-or Tov to clean the pens and feed and water the ewes. A painful duty. Avel took over the care of Old Girl and her babies so Emet wouldn't have to look at the vacant space left by the death of the one he loved best.

Emet was sent to draw water from the well.

The ewe who had lost her lamb through Zadok's choice had not stopped mourning. Although Zadok had left her with one remaining twin, the ewe paced and bleated pitifully and would not be comforted.

Old Girl stood calmly as the triplet babies nursed. Bear's fleece cap lay discarded in the straw. The ewe nudged it with her nose as if to inquire where the black sheep had gotten off to.

Avel scooped it up and thrust it into the pocket of his tunic.

He loaded the barrow with old straw and wheeled it out toward the light. Emerging, he saw that Emet stood stock-still beside the well. Avel shielded his eyes and stared off across the pastures.

Lev was coming back. Dirty and disheveled, with his usual cocky swagger reduced to the trudge of a man who walked with the weight of sorrow on his back.

Avel dumped the straw and joined Emet at the well. He withdrew the lamb's cap and pressed it into Emet's hand. The child gazed at it a moment, then pressed it to his cheek. His eyes moistened and he murmured, "Poor Lev."

"Yes," Avel agreed. Even in pardon the load would be heavy on his soul. How could it not be?

At that instant Lev raised his eyes to Emet. The head bowed again and the pace did not alter. On and on he came up the hill to where the boys waited for him.

As he came near it was evident that he had been weeping. Eyes were red and swollen. His thick lips trembled. He raised his arm in greeting and let it fall again. And then he came to Emet. His shadow covered the boy. He shook his head, trying to speak. Again his head wagged from side to side. He groaned and fell to his knees before Emet. He reached out to touch Bear's cap with his finger. He began to weep openly.

"Sorry! So sorry! So . . ."

"Ah, Lev!" Emet cried, embracing him. "Lev!"

There followed a time when man and boy hugged and sobbed together as Avel stood apart and watched an incomprehensible change in the two.

At last Lev sat back on his heels. He wiped Emet's tears away with the scrap of fleece and then his own. "Stump," Lev whispered. "I know what he meant to y'."

"Yes," Emet concurred.

"Today is the day of preparation for the Passover. I'd like to wear his covering as a sign of redemption. The blood of the lamb upon the doorpost of my heart. As it was that first Passover in Egypt. I've been thinking on it all night, y' see? They would've crucified me, and rightly so, for I'm guilty of shedding another man's blood. But would y' tie this fleece round my neck then as reminder to all who see it that the lamb was killed and the life of old Zadok stands as a payment if any more blood is spilled? And will y' forgive me, boy, for the unkindness I lavished on y'? For y' didn't deserve my spite!"

"Gladly." Emet placed his hand on Lev's brow in a wordless benediction, a bond of forgiveness and peace between them. And then, knowing well enough how to tie, he tied the leather laces which had held the fleece on Bear and slipped the collar over Lev's bowed head.

There was one thing more to do.

Lev sniffed and wiped his red nose with the back of his hand. "Blue Eye's still down there. A fine, wise dog, he was. Come now, boys. We've a duty. Fetch me a spade. Call Ha-or Tov. We'll go together to the field where he lies. I'll bury him."

■ ■ ■ ■

Zadok covered Avel, Emet, and Ha-or Tov with his tallith and faced in the direction of Jerusalem. He began to recite the words of Isaiah:

"In the last days the mountain of the Lord's Temple will be established as chief among the mountains; it will be raised above the hills, and all the na-

tions will stream to it. Many peoples will come and say, 'Come let us go up to the mountain of the Lord, to the house of the God of Jacob. He will teach us his ways, so that we may walk in his paths.' The law will go out from Zion, the word of the Lord from Jerusalem. He will judge between the nations and will settle disputes for many peoples. They will beat their swords into plowshares and their spears into pruning hooks. Nation will not take up sword against nation, nor will they train for war anymore. Come, O house of Jacob, let us walk in the light of the Lord."

Zadok recited these hopeful words on every occasion before he set out to travel to Jerusalem. But, Avel thought, as he observed Zadok's somber demeanor, the chief herdsman didn't sound too hopeful that he would see this promise fulfilled.

Something had changed in Zadok's thinking between yesterday and today. He determined he would not stay in the Holy City overnight for the Paschal feast.

What troubled him?

The question rippled through Beth-lehem. Had the old shepherd ever before spent the first night of the Holy Week outside Jerusalem?

Perhaps in the distant past, but not in the living memory of anyone at Migdal Eder. For thirty years Zadok and his wife had driven the last of the lambs through the Sheep Gate and then remained in the city until the conclusion of the feast.

Perhaps this year, since the old woman's passing, Zadok wanted to change the routine?

Whatever the reason, Avel was glad for it. The boy thought about bar Abba, Asher, Kittim, and the curved blade of Dan's knife. The rebels were surely in the city of the Temple of the Most High, preparing to make their own sacrifice of human blood today. Avel did not want to be on hand if and when things broke loose!

Zadok left orders that he and the boys would return to Beth-lehem for their Passover *seder*. No other shepherd in the company was invited to the meal. Everything, he declared, must be properly prepared, the table set with five places and ready for them.

Zadok and his three young apprentices drove the last seventy-two lambs toward King David's capital. These sheep were the finest of the flock, reserved and hand-fattened for the feasts of Israel's ruling council and the family of the high priest.

With Jehu dead and Lev stained in the blood of another, some said it was natural Zadok had chosen the boys to go with him. Others eyed them enviously as they departed.

Red Dog managed the herd easily, circling and bumping the heels of any stragglers. It was an effortless journey up the highway toward the Holy City. The distant buildings of the Temple, high atop Mount Moriah, glistening in the sun like a snowcapped peak.

They marched in grim silence, listening to the hissing of revolution on the lips of the travelers around them.

Concern for what lay ahead clouded the face of Zadok and spilled over into the minds of the boys.

At last Emet clasped Zadok's sleeve and gave a tug. "Why is the whole world coming to Yerushalayim, sir?"

"To remember the Passover, as the Lord commanded us to remember for all generations."

"Remember what?"

There was irony in Zadok's reply. "That we are the children of the Lord's covenant with Abraham and Isra'el. We are the children of Abraham, Isaac, and Jacob. We are free men."

Free? Avel wondered. Ha-or Tov nudged Avel hard in the ribs as a troop of Roman cavalry rode ahead of them toward the gates of the city. What did their presence say about freedom?

Zadok scooped up Emet protectively and placed him on his shoulders. The old man cleared his throat. "Remember what I've told y', boys?"

Avel did not reply that Zadok had taught them so many things it was difficult to know which lesson he was referring to.

Zadok continued on without breaking stride. "Every word in Torah means something about our future, as well as our past. All the Law and the Prophets proclaim to us the truth about Yerushalayim's Hope . . . the coming Messiah. You recall what God promised Abraham? That all the world would be blessed through Abraham and the line of Isaac? That blessing will come with our Messiah, the Lamb of God who will take away the sin of the world?"

Emet tapped the giant man's head. "When will he come?"

Zadok did not reply at first. But his pace quickened, as if the herdsman found strength in the retelling of the story.

"Everything means something. Every word, every story in Torah points us toward the coming of the Messiah. Like the stars of a constellation shine against the black night sky and make the outline of a bear or a lion, so do the points of light within Torah all connect up until we see clearly who our Messiah will be and why he must come to us."

Avel encouraged Zadok with a word, though the aged shepherd scarcely needed coaxing to connect these gleaming stars of Torah's constellations.

"Long before the first Passover, our fathers were shepherds. Jacob, son of Isaac, son of Abraham, was renamed Isra'el by the Angel of the Lord. Jacob had twelve sons and from them came the twelve tribes of Israel. These twelve sons were also shepherds. They had flocks and a peaceful life here in Eretz-Israel. But they were jealous of their younger brother, Joseph, because he was old Jacob's most beloved son. They wanted to be rid of him. One day Jacob sent Joseph out to deliver food to his brothers. The brothers tied Joseph up, stripped off his coat, threw him in a pit, and sold him to passing traders. The traders carried Joseph away to Egypt, where he was a slave. The brothers told old Jacob that a wild beast had killed his beloved son.

"But the Lord had a plan for good to come from this evil deed. After many trials, Joseph was made to be right-hand advisor of the king of Egypt. Very famous and powerful.

"His brothers, meanwhile, were starving because there was a disastrous drought in Eretz-Israel. With permission of their old father, Jacob, they traveled to Egypt in hopes of buying grain to make bread. They were brought before their brother Joseph, but did not recognize him because he was wearing the clothes of a prince of Egypt. Joseph could have had them killed for what they did to him. Eh? Instead Joseph turned away and wept to see them because he loved them. He had mercy on them in spite of what they had done to him. They embraced and wept, and all was forgiven. Joseph, though cast out and rejected by his brothers, became the savior and redeemer of his family. The household of Jacob, numbering seventy people, was brought to Egypt. There Joseph gave them a land where they could live in peace."

Zadok paused, as if to let the boys consider the happy ending of this tale. Then the old man resumed. "This is a picture of our Messiah. He, the most beloved son of the Father, will be hated and rejected by his brothers. Yet he will become our Savior. He will offer to Israel the bread of life and forgive their transgressions against him."

"How?" Emet demanded as they began the ascent into Jerusalem.

Zadok welcomed the child's curiosity. "Back to the story for the answer. Many years passed. The children of Israel became prosperous and grew to a nation of many hundreds of thousands in Egypt. The Egyptians, who feared them, made them slaves. They oppressed them cruelly. The Hebrews were put to work building the cities of Egypt, which stand even to this day. Torah says there arose a king in Egypt who did not remember Joseph. He hated the Hebrews and issued an edict that all male babies two years old and younger must be slaughtered." Here the face of Zadok clouded. Sadness weighted his words. "And so they were killed. The babies. Killed by the evil king. All Hebrew baby boys were slaughtered. All, that is, but one."

"How did he get away?" Emet asked.

"His mother made a basket for him and lined it with pitch. And she placed her baby boy inside and put the little boat on the waters of the Nile to drift. The baby's sister, Miryam, followed along the shore to see where the boat would go. From the pools beside the palace the daughter of Pharaoh heard the baby crying. She fetched the basket from the water, declared the gods had sent him to her, and made the baby her own son. Then Pharaoh's daughter saw Miryam hiding in the reeds. She sent Miryam to find a woman from among the Hebrew slaves who could nurse the baby. In this way the child was nursed and loved by his real mother and grew up to be a mighty prince in Egypt."

"What was his name?"

"Moses. This mighty name in the Hebrew language contains the same letters as Messiah. Its meaning is 'of the Lamb.'"

"More lambs again."

"Moshe spelled backwards in Hebrew spells the word *HaShem*, meaning 'The Name.' *HaShem* is what we call the Almighty when we cannot speak aloud his most holy name. Every detail in Torah has a deeper meaning, as I said. So we see Moses' purpose in life was to declare The Name and the Law of the Almighty to the descendants of Abraham. And to lead us out of bondage."

"Did he?"

"Yes. And the life of Moses also points us to God's plan for our salvation. Moses gave up his position as a mighty prince, just as our Messiah will give up his place in heaven to come and live among men. Moses went off to a far land and lived there as a stranger. The Messiah will come down from heaven to live among us as a stranger, a sojourner on this earth. Moses became a shepherd. Messiah will be a descendant of David and will be called the Good Shepherd of Israel. Like Moses led our fathers out of slavery from Egypt, so our Messiah will lead his flock out of bondage much more terrible. And we will see his Kingdom in Yerushalayim. Our Deliverer is coming. That is the true meaning of Passover."

Ha-or Tov jogged to keep up. "But when?"

The chief shepherd was silent for a long time as they walked. At last he replied, "When. Yes. Every day I have asked, when? When, Lord, is the Deliverer of Israel coming? But there is no answer. Tonight in Bethlehem we will share the supper of unleavened bread and we will ask the question once again." He touched Emet's foot. "Perhaps Emet will hear something I have not heard before." He reached out to tap Ha-or Tov's head. "And Ha-or Tov will see what I have missed." And then he pulled Avel closer to his side. "And you, Avel? Your heart will understand a secret that has long escaped me. Yes. Maybe tonight."

"And what about Passover?"

Zadok returned to the narrative. "Well, Moses the prince ran away from Egypt, like I said. And he was happy as a shepherd. But the cries of the Hebrew slaves went up before the Almighty's throne. So one day Moses was out with the sheep when he looked up and saw a burning bush on the hillside! It was a bush like our wadi sage, which resembles the seven-branched candlestick in the Temple. So there was a fire in this bush, but the bush didn't burn. When Moses approached this wonder, the voice of the Almighty spoke to him and told him that he must return to Egypt and free the Hebrew slaves from bondage."

"And what happened then?"

"Could Moses refuse such a command? He went back to Egypt to his people. He told them he had been sent from the Almighty to deliver them. They didn't believe him, of course. Grumbled against him. Threatened to kill him. Nearly did too." The old man thought for a time before he picked up the story again. "So . . . nine times Moses and his brother, Aaron, brought plagues from the Almighty down on Egypt. But Pharaoh still wouldn't let the people go. Dreadful plagues."

Avel chimed in, "And finally the night of Passover came, right?"

Zadok continued, "Yes. At last! Finally the last plague was pronounced upon the wicked ruler and the land that had oppressed God's beloved children. The Lord declared through Moses that he would send the Angel of Death over the land of Egypt to kill all the firstborn. Pharaoh didn't believe it. Foolish, proud Pharaoh. So the sentence of death on the whole land was fixed. This judgment was fast approaching."

"All the firstborn were to die?" Emet asked. "But what about the firstborn children of the Hebrews?"

Zadok held up a finger. "Ah-ha! It could be a problem! How was the angel to know which was which? The firstborn of Egypt or Israel? The Lord had it worked out. He gave Moses a way to save those who believed God's word! God commanded Moses to tell the people that if they wanted to save themselves and their children, they must kill a lamb and sprinkle the blood of the lamb on the doorposts of their houses as a sign. Then the Angel of Death would see the mark and pass over any household with the blood of an innocent lamb on the lintels of the door."

Emet glanced skyward at this, as if expecting to see the fierce visage of the angel soaring above them.

Zadok's voice became hushed as he went on with the narrative. "It was on this very night, those many years ago, that the families of Hebrew slaves sacrificed the first Passover lamb and marked their doors with its blood as a sign they believed God. And when the sun went down, the full moon came up. The Angel of Death came as promised. With his breath, he swept away all the firstborn of Egypt. There was crushing grief throughout the land. Except among the Hebrews. None who believed God and sprinkled the blood of the lamb on the doorposts perished."

"But why?" Emet wondered.

"Because they had faith and acted upon God's word. God provided a way of salvation for those who believed and obeyed! Then the wicked king told them to get out. Which they did."

"And so," Emet concluded triumphantly, "is that why we are commanded to have Passover?"

Zadok patted the boy's hand. "Well done. We remember, but in remembering we are also given a powerful look into tomorrow! Each Passover the death of the Paschal lamb is also a mighty prophecy that points to a future event! On a Passover yet to come, the Almighty will send the beloved Messiah, his only Son, to Yerushalayim as the final Lamb of sacrifice. Like all perfect lambs, Messiah will take our inquity upon himself. Our hearts will be marked with the blood of his sacrifice. We will be covered in his righteousness . . . the way the orphan lambs were covered in the fleece of another lamb. When God looks at us he will see that Messiah loved us enough to die in our place. That we are precious to him. And we will be given eternal life. It is a mystery. But it is truth. This is Jerusalem's Hope. It's our hope for final redemption and freedom from death."

Zadok raised his arms as if to embrace the city.

"Now, here's the rest of the story. Bearing the bones of Joseph, Moses led the Hebrew people out of slavery, through the wilderness, and finally to this land, our homeland. Eretz-Israel. In the same way, Messiah will lead our hearts out from the bondage of fear and death into the joy of hope and a new life. We will be forgiven and saved by

God's own provision. And then the law of the Lord will be carved into our hearts forevermore. In this way the Lord's promise to Abraham to bless all the earth through his descendants will be fulfilled. Remember how Abraham offered his son to the Lord right there upon Mount Moriah where the Temple now stands? Children! Lift your eyes to Yerushalayim! See it! Know the truth that Abraham and Isaac were really there making a covenant with the Almighty! *Elohim! Adonai! Yahweh! El Shaddai! Immanu'el!* The covenant is forever!

"Know this, for in this lesson is the one true meaning of Passover. As God promised in holy Scripture, the Messiah will be a descendant of Abraham, Isaac, and Jacob! He will be from the tribe of Judah. From the line of David. Born in Beth-lehem, within the circle of Migdal Eder, he will be as a lamb destined for sacrifice. He will come out of Egypt. Be called a Nazarene. Perfect in wisdom and mercy, he will make the blind see. The lame to walk. The deaf will hear. He will be rejected and despised by his brothers. And then, as it was prophesied in exact detail by King David in the twenty-second psalm, this Lamb of God, God's only Son, will carry the wood of his holocaust to a place where he will die as atonement for the sins of the whole world. But he will rise from death to life and rule as King in Yerushalayim. And all who call on him for forgiveness will be truly forgiven for what we have done to this world and to ourselves and to others."

The Messiah as the final Lamb of sacrifice? It was a grim scenario, Avel thought, as they trudged nearer to the looming city walls. This was not what everyone in Israel wanted or expected. The people longed for something else. A political kingdom here on this earth where enemies were crushed by a powerful king with an army. And yet the glimpses Zadok had offered from the Torah confirmed the truth of what was coming.

Avel was certain in his heart Yeshua was the Messiah. Could Zadok mean that Yeshua would suffer and die? And this when Avel had only just found him? Couldn't he skip over that part and simply live as King in Jerusalem?

No! Not Yeshua! Avel's heart cried out with every step. And yet, Yeshua had sent the boys into Zadok's care to be taught the lesson of the sheepfold, had he not? So this was what Yeshua meant when he said Moses and the prophets had written about him. Yes. It was a harsh reality indeed to think that man's need for redemption would cost so dear a price.

VI KIM

The closer he got to Jerusalem, the more Avel struggled with his feelings. It was true he was proud to be counted amongst the shepherds of Migdal Eder, bringing perfect lambs to the Temple. Jewish law permitted work to be done on the Day of Preparation only until noon, so it was essential to see the lambs disposed in their pens before that hour.

Part of what Avel experienced was the tumult of the huge crowds. At Migdal Eder sheep outnumbered humans, and quiet could be counted on most hours of the day. Here, in Jerusalem, throngs of pilgrims jammed the roads. To be thrust into the teeming warren of the Holy City at Passover was to be overwhelmed by chaos and confusion.

Though Avel had grown up in the middle of it and had experienced the sights, sounds, and smells of Passover every year of his young life, this year he found the turmoil unnerving.

Humans were a lot more unruly than sheep!

Jewish pilgrims from distant parts of the Roman world stopped mid-street to gawk at the sights, to gossip, or to haggle over fruit in the stalls. Self-important Pharisees, unmistakable with their broad phylacteries on foreheads and arms, paraded ostentatiously about. Rich merchants were trailed by retinues of servants; harried mothers fretted over losing their children in the mobs; Torah teachers loudly vented their opinions on obscure doctrines.

It was a carnival atmosphere.

Then why did Avel also have such a sense of dread?

More than revulsion at the noise and confusion, Avel had a nagging premonition of danger, an anxiety that a serious threat loomed nearby.

He told himself it was because of the death of his friend Hayyim in such a crowd scene. Arriving in Jerusalem brought it back: the awareness of threat that had also been present that day. Avel had been a horrified witness as Hayyim was trampled by a Roman's horse.

Hayyim had been killed during the bread riots at the Feast of Purim a little more than a month earlier. It felt like no time ago . . . and yet a lifetime since.

How could both be true?

Avel could not sort it out. Did the recollection of Hayyim's death account for all his present fear, or was there something more?

At the end of his musing he knew only that he'd be relieved to get away from the noisy hordes and back to the relative peace of Migdal Eder. He had lived as a Jerusalem Sparrow out of necessity and as a small rebel out of hatred of the Romans. Now Avel recognized what he truly wanted: to be a shepherd at home in Beth-lehem.

There was contentment at having recognized and named the desire of his heart. Avel had a sense of place, of belonging, as never before in his life.

That satisfying realization temporarily shut out the dread, closing a door on fear . . . until the band of apprentice shepherds neared the Sheep Gate.

Even after the trek up from Beth-lehem, the journey of the herdsmen was not complete upon reaching Jerusalem. At this holiday season it was impossible to drive a flock through the city streets. A detour was required, all the way around the city walls to the Sheep Gate at the northern end of the Temple Mount.

There, despite being under the watchful eye of the Roman fortress of the Antonia, a tightly packed, excited mob had gathered.

With Zadok leading, using timely nudges of his staff to part the multitude, they advanced toward the gate until Avel was near enough to see what the excitement was about.

Graffiti was scrawled on the walls of the passage: *Death to the Korban traitors! The fall of Siloam's tower is the punishment of the Almighty! Be ready to strike!*

In reeking letters that dripped onto the paving stones, the messages appeared to be written in blood.

Animal, or human? Avel wondered.

The tension in the archway and in the surrounding passages was not the convivial enthusiasm of Passover! The air, rank with anger, smoldered with talk of rebellion.

"The tower proves the anger of the Most High against traitors and blasphemers," Avel heard a man announce.

"The tower's collapse was caused by rebels," retorted another.

"Then the rebels are doing the work of the Almighty" was the reply.

These were not the wealthy of Jerusalem doing the talking. Avel was not hearing the sentiments of the ruling class. The agitated sounds of hostility came from the working men of Jerusalem, augmented by the country twang of villagers from the Galil.

"They killed the prophet and some of us," proclaimed a cobbler, referring, Avel surmised, to the death of Yochanan the Baptizer and the violence at Purim. "And they think we've forgotten already."

"Come along, boys," Zadok ordered, jabbing left and right with his shepherd's crook. "Make way there!"

They were able to make better progress then, but only as far as the Sheep's Gate Inn.

A solid wall of pilgrims blocked further motion while leaving a space in front of the hostelry's entry.

"What's this, then?" Zadok demanded. "We have a delivery to make."

"Hold on, old man," snapped a burly Galilean. "They're bringing out a dead body."

That explained why everyone kept back. There would be no Passover celebration for anyone defiled by contact with the dead.

Avel scrambled up on a balcony. He got a glimpse over the crowd as the corpse was brought out. At that instant Avel recognized two faces below him. He saw the features of Zacharias, the Ethiopian servant of Nakdimon ben Gurion, frozen in shock and horror.

The boy also identified the body: it was the hawker from whom Nakdimon had rented the donkey. His throat was slashed from ear to ear.

■ ■ ■ ■

Outside the Sheep Gate was a pool of water for the flocks and herds coming to the Temple. Beside this pond was Marcus. The centurion was in disguise and had the hood of his cloak flipped up over his head. He leaned against a broken column left over from some ancient ruined structure. The looming height of the Temple Mount bathed both the pool and Marcus in shadow.

A decade of legionaries led by Guard Sergeant Quintus doubletimed up from the Kidron Valley. Shouting, "Get out of the way!" Quintus led his men toward the scene of the hawker's death.

As the troopers passed, Marcus called out to Quintus, then stepped back into deeper shadow.

With the stump of the pillar between them, Marcus carried on a conversation with Quintus while remaining unseen by passersby. "You're too late to do him any good," Marcus informed him. "The man murdered in Sheep's Gate Inn."

"Who was he?"

"A traveling hawker. Nobody seems to know his name."

"Killed in a brawl?" Quintus said hopefully.

"Assassinated," Marcus corrected. "Murdered in his sleep and the room smeared with his blood. They're here. Keep your eyes peeled for bar Abba and others. And keep marching up and down. The more your men are seen in the streets, the better."

Quintus swore, "There's precious few of us for it. Praetorian Vara has more'n half my men out of uniform and wandering about in the crowds. And Vara's own soldiers are playing at provoking trouble, shouting traitorous slogans and the like, to see who agrees. Can't tell who anybody is! Had two men from different cohorts denounce each other as rebels! What about you, sir?"

"Right now I'm following a servant of Nakdimon ben Gurion. The man was near the Inn when the murder was discovered."

"Are you thinking he's a rebel?" Quintus asked. "Or his master? What's the connection?"

"Right now I'm just watching," Marcus retorted sharply. "And trying not to jump to conclusions. Will your squadron be at Pilate's audience this afternoon?"

"We've been ordered to keep away so as not to antagonize the delegation of Jews," Quintus replied scornfully.

"That's dead wrong," Marcus concluded. "But too late to change it now. Do your best."

"And you, sir," Quintus returned. Then he added, "And watch your back too, sir. A rebel'd just love to put a blade between your ribs . . . or Vara, who could blame the rebels after. But here, I almost forgot a message. Governor wants to see you . . . right away."

■ ■ ■ ■

A faithful servant was better than a well-paid informant. Zacharias the Ethiopian was Nakdimon's eyes and ears on the street.

"And, sir." Zacharias trembled as he described the scene at the Inn of the Sheep Gate to Nakdimon. "The hawker's throat was cut from ear to ear! The words *death to all apostates* and *traitor* were scrawled on the walls in his own blood. The innkeeper showed me the bloody bedchamber himself. And there was more written boldly beneath the arch of Sheep Gate!"

Nakdimon pressed his fingers together in thought. "What word of this man's murder on the streets?"

"That the hawker, like the dead stonemasons crushed by the Tower of Siloam, has received a just punishment from the Almighty!"

"The people are against the Sanhedrin then?"

"Oh sir! All! All of them! And those who aren't are afraid to speak! There's not a word of support for our rulers that anyone dares to whisper!" Zacharias mopped sweat from his brow, "They're all saying death should come to any who spent the Korban funds for Rome's projects! Every mouth contains a curse against Caiaphas and the Sanhedrin. Some openly proclaim that the time is right to restore a righteous king to Yerushalayim. That any who gives information to the Sanhedrin has become apostate! And by the blood that flows from the hawker's throat, they vow that this is the fate of all who oppose righteousness."

Had the hawker been a member of the rebel band, after all? Otherwise how had his assassins known that the hawker had offered information to Nakdimon and thus to the Sanhedrin?

"Who do they say will overthrow the council?"

The old servant shook his grizzled head from side to side. "Many say by the sword of bar Abba."

"And?"

"Others proclaim Yeshua of Nazareth will come to Jerusalem and call down fire on the council chamber and the Temple Mount! He'll destroy the Temple, they say, the same as he drove out the money changers last year!"

"Do they say he's in league with bar Abba?"

"Some say there's a secret alliance between the two. I've heard that bar Abba's rebels are all Galileans. Like the talmidim of Yeshua. Violent, uneducated men."

"Yeshua is neither violent nor uneducated," Nakdimon countered.

"Still the people remember how Yeshua drove out the money changers from the Temple in his rage. There's speculation that he'll avenge the murder of his cousin, Yochanan the Baptizer, this week! Slaughter Herod Antipas and restore the throne of David!" Zacharias declared. "They twitter about it. They look for it! Hope that blood will run!"

So already the mob had perverted the message of Yeshua. *Blessed are the peacemakers.*

"Yeshua has nothing to do with bar Abba," Nakdimon claimed.

"The people aren't convinced of that, sir! They'll acclaim him if he comes! With one voice they'll shout the hosanna! They'll gladly stand by and cheer when he brings judgment and vengeance upon the rulers of Rome and Israel together!" The servant glanced nervously toward the barred gate of the house. "Your name is among the seventy."

"I'm not afraid of the mob."

"The mob didn't slit the hawker's throat. But an assassin through the window of the inn at night."

"The walls of this house are high."

"Be glad the children are away with your mother, sir. As for me, I'll be sleeping light."

"I'll sleep with a clear conscience and a sword by my side. So I'll sleep soundly no matter what happens."

"You should have Temple bodyguards here at the house, sir. And so should every *cohen* and member of the Sanhedrin until the holy days are over. I tell you! The people are praying for revolution! Hundreds of thousands have come expecting it! Rome can't kill them all. They've not been so stirred up since the days when the Maccabees stormed the gates and recaptured Yerushalayim from the Greeks!"

■ ■ ■ ■

The domed hall of the Sanhedrin council chamber was a bigger vault than any Emet had seen, apart from the arch of the sky. Many of the elders displayed sternly critical faces. They represented more wealth and more learning assembled in one place than Emet knew existed.

The boy had seen death up close in the face of the murdered hawker. He sensed the nearby existence of Kittim. The memory of Asher's knife at his throat lingered.

He was afraid, and even in this room his foreboding had substance.

When the disapproval he sensed from the elders was added to his apprehension, it was almost more than the five-year-old could bear.

It all made him feel very small and frightened. It was good to have Zadok's hands resting on his shoulders. He appreciated the friendly presence of Nakdimon ben Gurion. Otherwise Emet would have bolted and run out of the hall.

"What's this?" demanded Caiaphas. "Nakdimon ben Gurion, is there a reason to bring these street rats into our meeting?"

Nakdimon, flanked by his uncle Gamaliel, nodded toward Zadok. "I'm certain the chief shepherd of Migdal Eder appreciates the warmth of your greeting," he commented with sarcasm.

Grudgingly, the high priest started over. "Zadok of Migdal Eder is welcome."

Emet's eyes widened and his heart beat faster. He'd known that Zadok was someone extraordinary. To be chief shepherd of the Temple flock made Zadok important, but the high priest of Israel recognized him and called him by name!

Nakdimon continued smoothly, "These apprentice shepherds are the important witnesses I mentioned. They know bar Abba's band and can tell about the destruction of Siloam's tower."

Peering down over his long nose like a bird of prey, Caiaphas fixed his gaze on the boys. "Which of them will talk first?"

At the same moment that Emet was gently pushed forward by Zadok's hands, he felt warmth flow into him. "This boy, whose name is Truth," Zadok replied.

"He's scarcely bigger than a lamb," Caiaphas remarked scornfully.

"I can tell what I know!" Emet asserted, remembering Zadok's words: *there is a time to speak.* "I saw rebels doing things to the Tower of Siloam. I saw Asher of bar Abba's band."

"How do you know him?" another of the council inquired.

"Because we were with them for a while," Emet said. "We lived in their camp."

At this a few of the Sanhedrin twitched aside the hems of their robes, as if Emet were indeed a rat. Others looked nervous; among these was the *cohen hagadol* himself.

"And where are they now?" Caiaphas inquired. His voice was not altogether steady as he spoke.

"I don't know," Emet said truthfully, "but I think they're here in Yerushalayim. I feel it."

"What's their intent?"

"They want to kill you," Avel added helpfully.

"First the tower and then us!" another of the council stressed. "The killing has already started . . . at Sheep's Gate Inn! Where will they strike next?"

The orderliness of the proceedings dissolved into a babble of worried voices.

Evidently the story of the murdered hawker had already reached into the council chamber. Emet examined the costly drapery and polished furnishing. He observed the faces of grown men contorted with anxiety.

So wealth and learning did not eliminate fear.

Much of Emet's sense of unworthiness evaporated.

"It's worse than you think," Nakdimon commented. "The dead man was another who was coming to give testimony about bar Abba."

The hubbub in the chamber increased. Many of the members shouted that the contingent of Temple police delegated to protect the council must be increased. Some suggested that the Roman governor should provide extra legionaries to assist the Temple guards.

"That move would certainly send a message to the *am ha aretz*," Gamaliel observed wryly. "The common people already believe that this body and the Romans speak with a single voice."

"At the urging of Nakdimon ben Gurion and Reb Gamaliel I've brought my apprentices from Migdal Eder," Zadok said loudly, but with dignity. "Do y', or do y' not, have any more questions for them? It is the eve of Passover."

"Yes," Caiaphas said, controlling himself with difficulty. "We know bar Abba was seen in the Galil . . . near the charlatan Yeshua of Nazareth. Do these boys know anything about that?"

By common consent Emet spoke first for the group. "Yeshua fixed my ears. And I can speak."

"And I see," Ha-or Tov said.

"Bar Abba wanted to make Yeshua king," Avel added.

"Ha!" exclaimed Caiaphas, pouncing on the words. A murmur of satisfaction buzzed in the chamber.

"But so did everyone!" Avel explained, shouting over the din. "Yeshua wouldn't! He left them all!"

"How can this testimony be trusted?" one of Caiaphas' cronies retorted. "The boys admit they were with the rebels. They might still be secret spies for bar Abba!"

Nakdimon declared forcefully, "I myself was in a Galil. I saw the occasion of which the boy speaks. I verify his story completely. Yeshua absolutely refused any suggestion that he would lend his name to rebellion!"

"So now Nakdimon is also Galilean?" the high priest noted scornfully. "Have you become one of his talmidim?" And then, "Is Yeshua here in Yerushalayim?" He pinned Emet in his glare. A crafty note had entered the high priest's tone.

"We left him in the Galil," Avel spoke up. "Walking across the sea."

Scoffing and harsh laughter greeted these words.

"The great Nakdimon vouches for the testimony of children?" jeered another of Caiaphas' associates.

Nakdimon swelled up at the mocking. Emet saw Gamaliel lay a restraining hand on his arm. The boy understood that most of these men had already made up their minds about Yeshua. Nothing anyone said could convince them otherwise.

"Enough," the high priest concluded. "Master Zadok, you and your charges may go. We still have to discuss the delegation to Governor Pilate."

A chorus of "Not me" and "Let someone else" echoed in the room. The prevailing sentiment was that no one wanted to be connected with the aqueduct and the anger it generated.

Not when rebels with daggers roamed the streets of Jerusalem!

Caiaphas didn't suggest he would personally head the mission to Pilate. However, he still managed to sound peeved at the reluctance of others. "Come, gentlemen," he demanded. "Governor Pilate must be reassured. It's merely the rabble of the *am ha aretz* who object to the aqueduct. The issue has been used by traitors to harm the peace of our land. We must convince the governor we're not rebels, while our protest to the governor will show the common people that we share their concerns. Now," Caiaphas continued, "who'll take on this important task?"

None of the elders was convinced.

Emet heard the protests: none of the Sanhedrin wanted to go anywhere except with a great many guards. No one was eager to go clear across Jerusalem where sicarii in the Passover crowds could attack them.

"My nephew and I will," volunteered Gamaliel, "even though we tried to warn you against the scheme."

While the debate continued as to which other members should be part of the deputation, Zadok ushered his young charges out of the chamber.

Suddenly Avel appeared to be struck by an idea. He tugged at Zadok's sleeve. "I've thought of something else."

"Then speak up," Zadok encouraged. "A moment more, Lord Caiaphas. This boy has one thing to add."

"The rebels attacked a caravan." Avel stepped forward. "We didn't see it. But afterward someone brought a leather pouch into the rebel camp. He said it must have come from one of the travelers. They found a note telling about a conspiracy among the rulers. Defiling the Temple. Stealing the Koban money. Giving it to Pilate."

"This isn't news," Caiaphas said.

Emet thought the high priest sounded nervous, despite his indifferent words.

"It's on all the lying lips in Yerushalayim," someone scoffed.

"But bar Abba also said it gave the names of two key conspirators on the Sanhedrin," Avel added. "He didn't mention names, but I thought you should know."

Silence fell over the council. Faces, ashen and fearful, reflected uncertainty as to what should be done.

Zadok and his apprentices closed the doors to the Sanhedrin chamber. Even the solid oak panels didn't entirely shut out a rising flood of babbling apprehension and mutual recrimination, led by the high priest himself.

■ ■ ■ ■

Gamaliel drew Nakdimon aside into a space between two pillars of the Sanhedrin meeting hall. "Did it cross your mind we might know the identity of the two council members chosen as rebel targets?" he inquired in a hushed voice.

"What do you mean?"

"The message I sent you on the eve of your departure for the Galil."

"I read it and tucked it safely . . ." Nikdimon clapped his hand to his side where his purse hung.

Gamaliel correctly interpreted the response. "And you lost it when you were attacked on the road."

"Yes," Nakdimon concurred. "Yes! That pouch didn't contain money, only your message. What with the blow on my head, I didn't think about it, but . . ."

"But it was addressed to you, signed by me, and suggested that you and I keep secret what we knew about the use of Korban for the aqueduct. I think I said the use of the money could not be *prevented*, but to a rebel eagerly seeking a mark for assassination, it's ambiguous enough to be misconstrued."

A light of comprehension flooded Nakdimon's face. His eyebrows shot up. "So the rebels think *you and I* are key figures in the sacrilege?"

Gamaliel nodded without speaking, then continued, "Still game to go with me to Pilate?"

"Of course," Nakdimon said stoutly. Then he added, "But I'm more glad than ever I sent my family out of the city."

Turning back to the council, Gamaliel suggested to Caiaphas, "Can the learned council select eight more members to join the delegation with Nakdimon and me?"

"Only ten?" Caiaphas responded questioningly.

"If we are at risk, then why expose more lives to danger?" Gamaliel retorted, "and if the words of ten men are not enough to appeal to Governor Pilate, then more may seem a mob instead of a delegation." He added thoughtfully, "And we know how the governor feels about Jewish mobs."

BE-RUHI

Outside the Great Hall of the Sanhedrin, at the foot of the Temple Mount steps where he could in no way defile or interfere with the religious ceremonies, Red Dog was waiting. Avel watched worshippers heading up toward the sanctuary detour around the animal, though Red Dog never snarled, barked, or showed his teeth.

There was something in the alertness of the dog's keen eyes, Avel thought. He appeared to scrutinize each passerby . . . and it was unnerving.

The bubble of clear space where Red Dog sat was a welcome respite for Zadok and the boys to regroup and organize themselves for taking leave of Jerusalem.

The crowds coming toward the Temple were growing ever thicker. Avel, who had begun the day wishing he could stay in Beth-lehem, was more eager than before to get back there again.

On the Day of Preparation for the Passover the time of the evening sacrifice was moved up and performed earlier in the afternoon. This was to accommodate the slaughter of a hundred thousand Passover lambs, which had to be carried out well before sunset.

A representative of each family—or group of ten, which the Law prescribed could share a single lamb—made his way to the holy precincts. Previously selected lambs had to be identified, claimed, and readied for slaughter. A hundred thousand lambs meant a hundred thousand worshippers . . . minimum, not including all the priests and Levites who assisted, or the onlookers from faraway who had no intention of missing the ceremony.

Passover was the one observance of the year where each head of a household performed the sacrifice himself, unless he were traveling, unwell, or ritually unclean and unable to do so.

More even than the Day of Atonement, Passover brought every

family directly into contact with the commandments, provisions, and decrees of the Most High. It linked the history of Israel with its present-day inhabitants and their longing to be free. It connected God's divine intercession in the life of the nation with His particular involvement in the lives of individual believers.

It was a reminder that God's promises were forever and His memory also. Sworn judgments might be postponed . . . but never escaped.

Passover was the counterbalance to the year, the twin of the set of hinges on which Jewish life pivoted. Just as the Day of Atonement occurred in the first month of the civil year and the seventh month of the religious cycle, Passover took place in the first month of sacred time and the seventh of the secular calendar.

But the stipulation that each family must slaughter its own lamb was a significant one: every household in Jerusalem on Passover would see its representative come home with innocent blood on his hands, spilled by his own hands.

It reminded the Jews that back in Egypt no firstborn escaped the Angel of Death by proxy or good intentions. Every household had to be marked by the blood of the lamb.

Despite the importance of the day, Avel was glad to be leaving. There had been enough of blood and slaughter, he thought. And in their small circle a lamb had already been sacrificed.

It seemed more than enough for one Passover.

Recrossing the Temple Mount platform to exit by way of either the Sheep Gate or the Golden Gate was out of the question. It would take hours to fight through the crowds in that direction.

Zadok aimed their course toward the nearest exit. "Keep close together, boys," he urged. "Don't get separated. But if y' do get lost, go to the sheep pens in the Temple Court. I'll find you there."

Even though Passover was a time of celebration the atmosphere among the pilgrims remained full of political discussion and unpleasant speculation.

"It's the truth!" Avel overheard a Galilean swear to his fellow traveler. "Some of the Sanhedrin are going to apologize to Pilate for making trouble about the Korban. I tell you, this bar Abba fellow has it right! There *is* a conspiracy between the council and the empire."

So word of the meeting between the governor and the council members was already out on the street. But somehow it had been twisted. The elders were somehow in a plot with Pilate against the *am ha aretz*.

But was the speaker really so stupid as to shoot his mouth off in public? Or was he an agent sent out by Caiaphas as a spy?

Red Dog barked sharply, and Avel looked up.

The animal seldom made noise except to warn of danger. What . . . or who . . . was he reacting to?

Who could tell? Avel was surrounded by a solid wall of humanity. He might be no more than one layer of pilgrims away from bar Abba himself and never see the man.

Parting the multitudes was like swimming upstream. In all Jerusalem it seemed only Zadok and his companions were going away from the sanctuary.

Avel scanned the nearby faces but didn't recognize any in the mob. Of course there were so many that they all blended together.

Zadok held Ha-or Tov's hand, who held Emet's hand, who held Avel's hand. In this way they snaked through the jostling swarm.

Red Dog did his best to herd them, running forward and back, circling around his little flock of humans. But his appearance no longer seemed to intimidate the determined pilgrims. Nor was Zadok able to clear a path with his staff. The mood in the populace was turning more hostile as frustrations mounted. "Watch who you're poking, old man," someone complained.

"I hear there are soldiers in disguise ready to catch the rebels," another Galilean ventured.

"Watch what you say," his companion noted. "They'll arrest anyone they *think* is a rebel."

"Have you looked around you?" suggested the first. "We are millions! If only Yeshua of Nazareth had come south with us. He would have been crowned king before the day was out!"

At the name of the Rabbi of Nazareth, Avel turned to study the speaker. The man appeared vaguely familiar. Had he been in the crowd when Yeshua fed the thousands with his barley loaves? Had he come to Ya'ir's house to see the miraculously raised Deborah, or in the Capernaum synagogue to hear Yeshua preach?

The horde was too thick, the glimpse too fleeting.

A ponderous fat man waddled between Avel and Emet, forcing Avel to let go of the smaller boy's hand. It was no matter; Avel would link up again as soon as the fellow moved out of the way. Avel heard Emet calling, "Wait! I've lost Avel!"

"It's all right," Avel shouted back. "I'll catch up."

The heavyset traveler stopped to wipe his brow, then turned in place as if unsure of his direction. All he had to do was let the multitude sweep him along, Avel thought. How could he have mistaken the path?

Avel squeezed around the roadblock by fitting behind a brace of jars outside a shopfront.

Congratulating himself, the boy emerged on the other side, expecting to see Zadok's white hair shining like a beacon above the rest.

But the chief shepherd was nowhere in sight.

Where had they gone so fast?

Avel darted out into the stream, dodged a pair of villagers in matching saffron-colored robes, was screeched at when he stepped on a matron's toe . . . and still couldn't spot Zadok.

Had Avel missed a turn somewhere? How had the others disappeared so quickly?

He wasn't overly concerned. Avel was confident he could find the Valley Gate on his own; he'd catch up to them once out of the crush.

Scurrying through every opening that presented itself, Avel found himself in a narrow lane that curled around toward the northeast.

This couldn't be right; it was taking him back the wrong direction.

He turned about, intending to retrace his steps.

As he passed an alleyway, an arm shot out from behind him. A sweaty palm clasped itself across his face. When another arm grabbed his midsection, Avel was rudely and silently jerked back into an alcove.

He couldn't breathe! The hand was pressed so tightly on his nose and mouth that he was suffocating. Thrust farther into the dark recess, he felt a brick's sharp corner stick him in the side.

Then he felt the tip of a dagger on the back of his neck. "If you cry out, you're dead!" Asher's voice hissed. "Will you keep quiet?"

Avel nodded frantically and the pressure on his mouth and nose eased. The boy gasped for air as his death was discussed.

Kittim flanked Asher! "Just kill him now," Kittim urged. "He's already been more trouble than he's worth."

"Listen, boy," Asher said. "You're lucky it's me as caught you or you'd have a hole in your windpipe already. Don't give me any trouble or I won't have a choice, see?"

Avel agreed.

"What do you want him for?" Kittim demanded. "We know he's already been to the council and talked about us. Kill him!"

"Not so fast," Asher retorted. "He can be useful, can't you, boy? You were a Sparrow here, eh? You can show us around, yes? Take us by the shortest way?"

Avel nodded again. Anything to keep alive until Zadok came looking for him.

"That's good, then," Asher said. "No tricks!"

■ ■ ■ ■

The moment Nakdimon and Gamaliel left the Sanhedrin chambers they were surrounded by the crowds going up to the Temple. Gamaliel, accompanied by nine other elders of obvious dignity and rank, was instantly recognized by Jerusalemites. Since the delegation moved counter to everyone else, the question of their destination was instantly raised.

Though they walked purposefully and without speaking, it was not long before speculation surrounded them.

Rumors of a meeting involving Pilate and some of the council were already on the streets. Making the connection between that report and these men was a simple matter.

Many in the throngs were curious, but others were openly hostile.

"Selling us out?"

"Sacrilege, that's what it is!"

"Walk on," Nakdimon urged the more timid of the group, who wanted to scurry back to safety. "Walk on. We have nothing to be ashamed of."

"Defilers of the Temple!"

"Going to bow and scrape to the Romans?" one bystander jeered, planting himself across their path. "It's bad enough for Rome to have its hands in our pockets, but you have to help it dip into the Korban too! Blasphemers!"

Before the file of men had crossed the elevated viaduct connecting the Temple Mount to the city near the Gennath Gate, the process of tale-bearing threatened to overwhelm the truth.

Around the core of ten elders an accompanying mass formed.

Like repeatedly dipping a candlewick in hot wax, the column grew, adding more and more numbers of followers until the flow down the causeway was entirely reversed.

Pilgrims, anxious to see the confrontation between Gamaliel and Pilate, were swept along toward the palace.

This too was enhanced and embellished by rumor and conjecture. *"Pilate has ordered all who oppose the aqueduct scheme to surrender!"*

"These honorable men are going to be arrested and put in prison for speaking out against the aqueduct," another added.

The indignation that bubbled in the populace increased in fervor; only now it was directed at Pilate and not at the elders.

"*No rebellion,*" someone urged. "*No violence! Don't give them any excuse to shed blood. Remember what day it is.*"

"*Gamaliel says he's afraid Pilate plans to spill his blood!*" a Galilean shouted.

"*Not if we all go with them,*" his companion retorted.

By the time the deputation reached the outer courtyards built by the butcher king and now occupied by the Imperial governors, it had grown a thousandfold.

At the rear of the throng were hundreds who had no idea what the procession meant. From across the Holy City residents and pilgrims joined the assembly. Some were excited holidaymakers. Some were eager to protest against Rome. Some had heard there was going to be another distribution of coins and bread, as Herod Antipas had provided in the city merely a little over a month earlier.

And mingled with the rest were two groups of tense men, who clasped cudgels and daggers under their robes: Vara's men and bar Abba's.

■ ■ ■ ■

Frantically scanning the faces in the multitudes, Avel hoped to spot someone to whom he could appeal for rescue.

He saw no one he recognized.

Perhaps it was for the best. Kittim had replaced Asher as Avel's guard. Not only would Kittim be quick to strike if Avel cried out, but such an appeal might cause the death of another as well.

Avel could only try to stay alive until a chance for escape presented itself. Remembering what Zadok said about meeting at the sheep pens, Avel believed he would be safe if he could get back there.

Kittim dragged Avel into a squalid house in the Valley of the Cheesemakers, below the southwest corner of the Temple Mount.

Inside were bar Abba and others of his band.

"So one of our runaways has turned up," bar Abba said, staring at Avel. "I hear you've been talking about me to the Sanhedrin."

"Let me kill him," Kittim suggested. "I'll use his blood to paint more slogans. The fat, pious council members are already quaking."

"Not now," bar Abba corrected. "He couldn't tell the Sanhedrin anything they didn't already know. And I hear he came south with Nakdimon ben Gurion. Perhaps we can sell the boy's life to him for a ransom."

"But I thought we planned—" Kittim began.

"Enough!" bar Abba said, raising a cautioning hand. "I know what I said."

It was at that instant Avel realized Nakdimon was one of the rebels' intended victims. Bar Abba planned to use Avel as a ruse to get close enough to kill Nakdimon!

"The crowds on the Temple Mount are perfect for what we have in mind," bar Abba added. "Pilate thinks we'll fall into his trap since he marched a cohort of legionaries out of the city. The Romans are pretending the city is undefended! All right, here's the plan: I've already sent others to join the pilgrims outside the Temple and rile up the crowds about the Korban money. They'll encourage the mob to go and protest at Pilate's palace. When the authorities hear how angry the people are, Pilate's disguised soldiers will have to go along too. Only we won't be there! We'll be on the Temple Mount. Wait for the last of the ceremony, when it's closest to sundown. Then when the council members attend to their sacrifices, that's when we'll strike!"

AMAR

Nakdimon, bullnecked and powerful, shuddered as the delegation approached the triple towers of the city wall. How many thousands trailed along behind them?

As he and the noisy, wrangling mob passed under the arch of the first parapet, he suddenly remembered its title: the Mariamme Tower, named after Herod's favorite wife . . . the one the butcher king murdered in a fit of jealousy and suspicion.

Yet Nakdimon's sense of danger was not fear for his own safety so much as a premonition, a dread of something yet unknown.

Imperial Rome and her servants, like Herod, were also jealous and suspicious. The Romans had the will and the disposition to be as vengeful as a woman scorned.

Governor Pilate, in the matter of the military standards bearing the face of Tiberius, had first shown incredible insensitivity to Jewish beliefs and values. He had then backed down in front of the mob, but afterward used every excuse to hunt down and execute those who had embarrassed him.

It was said that even bar Abba had not started as a bloodthirsty assassin, but had been hounded to it by the legions of Rome.

Nakdimon and his compatriots were again approaching Pilate with an explanation of how and why Siloam Tower had fallen. Not by the consent of the Sanhedrin. Not by the hand of the shepherds. But by the will and design of revolutionaries. This was something no Roman official suffered easily from a conquered people. Pilate feared only one thing: that a bad report of his ability to maintain order would be conveyed to the emperor.

If a Roman prefect failed miserably enough, he would be branded "no friend of Caesar."

At that point a graceful exit by way of suicide was the best outcome for which the ruined politician could hope.

The aqueduct scheme had been a joint undertaking of the high priest and Pilate. Caiaphas had assured the governor that his actions in bringing fresh water to the Holy City would meet with widespread *approval* in Judea and *improve* his standing with the Jews.

With the sabotage of Siloam Tower, would Pilate react with suspicion and anger at what he might regard as betrayal?

How could he not?

And now Nakdimon was approaching at the head of an army. The thousands on his heels were not followers of the Sanhedrin. This rowdy demonstration was not of Nakdimon's doing, but would Pilate stop to think of that?

Or would his natural wariness lead him to feel threatened?

Rome, when pushed, always pushed back . . . harder and fiercer than they were challenged.

Nakdimon glanced up again at the looming height of Mariamme Tower.

If Rome was stung with indignation, the empire was ruthless enough to reply with the destruction of Jerusalem and the Jews. Then the conquerors would name a building to commemorate the Holy City's vanished glory.

Here lies Jerusalem, killed in a fit of jealous rage.

Requiescat in pace . . . rest in peace.

O Elohim, Nakdimon prayed. *Don't let that happen here today.*

■ ■ ■ ■

Marcus responded quickly to Pilate's summons. Arriving at Herod the Great's palace, he discovered that the governor had left word for him to be sent in at once.

The centurion wondered what was afoot now. Had Vara succeeded in convincing Pilate the Siloam Tower destruction could be blamed on Marcus?

Was Marcus walking into a prison cell . . . or worse?

But why not arrest him and return him in chains?

Marcus entered the courtyard of the palace as a squad of servants draped a platform in purple bunting. The curule chair, Pilate's judgment seat, was ceremoniously carried outside and installed on the dais.

Pilate's own valet met Marcus at the entry to the state apartments and conducted the centurion farther.

It was the first time Marcus had ever been this far inside the Jerusalem palace. In all Marcus' years of service to Rome in Judea, he'd never once been invited or expected in these innermost halls. It was ironic that such a summons would come now.

The valet bowed Marcus into Pilate's private study, then bowed again as he left Marcus there. The room was richly paneled in oak. The light surface was inlaid with strips of almond and olive, the varying shades of wood forming a crisscross pattern.

In one corner of the room was a marble altar, carved as a miniature of the Temple of Augustus in Caesarea. In front of this stood Governor Pilate. His back was to the entry, nor did he turn when Marcus entered.

As Marcus kept silent and observed, Pilate took a pinch of incense from an alabaster box and sprinkled it over a glowing coal. The aroma of frankincense spiraled up with the smoke.

On a shelf formed by the roof of the temple model stood a pair of idols. One was a black onyx Apollo, recognizable by his handsome, youthful face, the laurel wreath around his temples, and the harp he carried. Apollo was regarded as the god of light, music, and prophecy.

The companion figure was bronze, unless it was actually gold, which was the way it glinted in the lamplight. It was a reduced version of Augustus himself, god made manifest, *pontifex maximus*, the bridge between the gods and men.

Pilate stood for a time, as if in contemplation, then with a slight turn of his head acknowledged Marcus. "The rebels have begun their murders?" he queried.

Marcus acknowledged the report about the hawker. Then he added that the sentiments he'd overheard in the city were strongly against the aqueduct. "It might be wise to postpone today's meeting until after the Passover," he suggested.

"No," Pilate said flatly. "I'll show no such weakness. Not this time. Besides, it's the Jewish council who must fear the rebels. If they are frightened enough of bar Abba to come to me on their holy day, so much the better."

"Then," Marcus said, seeing that Pilate's mind was made up, "at least increase the number of uniformed soldiers on the streets. It's not too late for such a display to quell any more violence."

"That is precisely the opposite of Praetorian Vara's excellent plan," Pilate scolded. "I've sent Tribune Felix and the uniformed cohorts out of Jerusalem. We'll lull the rebels into thinking we're unconcerned about them. When they make any move at all, we'll crush them."

"Excellency, I don't think—" Marcus began doubtfully.

"Correct," Pilate concluded harshly. "And you're not to, either. I summoned you here to keep you from trying to dissuade Tribune Felix from doing his duty."

Marcus guessed then that Felix had also tried to talk Pilate out of Vara's foolish scheme. Pilate's pigheaded stubbornness gave Marcus a premonition of disaster.

"You'll stay here until after this audience," Pilate concluded. "Station yourself in the courtyard."

"Excellency," Marcus said, saluting. There was nothing else to do but obey and hope for the best.

■ ■ ■ ■

The preparations for Pilate's audience were finalized. The brass fittings and bright red tunics of the governor's personal guard were striking in the midday sun. The curule chair on the dais, vacant for the moment, faced the gate of the courtyard with the awful dignity of Imperial Rome.

On the battlements trumpeters stood ready to announce Pilate's entry as the personal representative of Emperor Tiberius, near kin to the gods.

Rome grants this meeting as a special favor, out of its might and benevolence.

Marcus was inside the courtyard of Herod's palace. He heard the tramp of feet and the murmur of the crowd coming from the direction of the Temple Mount. It was not the sound of Passover pilgrims going by outside. The noise increased, rolling up and over the parapets. Tumult catapulted over the walls in a siege of sound.

"Don't open the gate!" Marcus called in a sudden premonition.

A trumpet blast from the ramparts overwhelmed his words. Six legionaries in ceremonial dress uniforms threw back the bolts to the entry.

The gates crashed open, and the guards were flung aside by the incoming tide of humans. Overwhelmed and pushed out of the way, they made no move either to reclose the portal or to draw their weapons.

In minutes the courtyard overflowed with a thousand Jews. Several thousand more pressed in on the scene from the streets outside.

Another blare of the trumpets shattered the day, momentarily stilling the throng. What was about to happen?

Governor Pilate appeared on the balcony above the central square. His chin upright, his purple-bordered robe gleaming white, he was the embodiment of Roman dignity.

But Marcus saw him hesitate. Clearly Pilate's first glimpse of the quadrangle was not what he expected. An instant of fear, of uncertainty, crossed his face.

Marcus also realized that Pilate knew he could not retreat, could not allow any Jews to say they saw Pilate afraid.

Marcus understood what Pilate remembered. This courtyard, packed with hostile Jews angry about sacrilege, was a twin to what had taken place in Caesarea in front of the governor's house there. That had been the site of Pilate's greatest defeat, of his humiliation.

Pilate had to go forward. This time he had to prove he was the master.

The governor advanced down the steps and approached the Imperial seat of judgment.

It was not a throne, but when seated on that X-shaped stool, Pilate spoke for Rome.

Life and death were in his hands.

He stood in front of the curule chair.

The multitude remained hushed, waiting.

It took several minutes for Nakdimon and Gamaliel to push their way to the front.

Gamaliel spoke. "Honored Governor, we have come to speak with you about the aqueduct."

A low rumble emerged from the throng. Anger, controlled but simmering, bubbled beneath the surface.

In that instant Marcus knew that the mob had seen the same vision as Pilate. Righteous indignation had put Rome to shame once before. Today it would do so again.

In a louder voice Gamaliel continued, "But first we want you to know that though we who come from the Sanhedrin are against the use of Korban for the water project, nevertheless . . ."

At the first use of the word *Korban* the growl increased again.

"Nevertheless," Gamaliel repeated forcefully, "we do not support revolution. Those who attacked the Tower of Siloam are criminals. Do not hold either the council or the people responsible for the actions of rebels."

"*What?*" demanded voices from the horde.

"*What about the sacrilege?*"

Pulling back the sleeve of his robe, Pilate extended his right arm.

An aide thrust a scroll bound with scarlet strings into his hand.

What was about to happen? Some in the crowd hushed the more outspokenly hostile. "*We want to hear him,*" they urged.

"I know about what happened at Siloam's tower." Pilate's words rang across the square. "I know that death and destruction were caused by rebels who are the enemies of Rome. But they are also the enemies of peace. They use terror to spark rebellion, and innocent lives were lost."

How was Pilate managing to remain calm? Marcus wondered. The man had never acted this courageous before.

Marcus scanned the crowd, now divided between hostile muttering and words of approval.

There was the answer! Drawn up in a knot in the center of the throng was Praetorian Vara and several of his men. Marcus followed Vara's eyes. Time and again Marcus saw Vara deliver an intense stare to another and receive an answering nod in response.

The swarm of people was full of clusters of disguised legionaries.

What shout of warning could Marcus make? To whom could he make it? Could Pilate's air of calm prevail?

"I have decided to be lenient," Pilate said, "and continue my usual custom of granting special clemency at your holy season." He flourished the scroll aloft. "Here is the official pardon for Lev, the shepherd of Migdal Eder, and for Benjamin, son of Oren the master mason. Look! I here set the Imperial seal to it."

Pilate seated himself in the chair of judgment. The aide unrolled the scroll. Another produced a wax taper. Pilate readied his signet ring to press into the decree.

There was a fraction of a second when it appeared that calm and reason would triumph.

Then from somewhere in the center of the mob a voice called out, "*What about the Korban?*"

"*What about sacrilege?*"

"*Stealing from the Almighty!*"

Pilate waved his hand to the walls. There was another blare of trumpets, drowning out the sounds of protest.

■ ■ ■ ■

Emet heard yet another ringing flight of trumpet calls resound across the city of David. Like the other two, this third also came from the direction of Herod's palace. The host of pilgrims gathered at the sanctuary were waiting for trumpets to issue a signal. But it wasn't a Roman signal, not the shrill note of the foreigners occupying the land of Israel.

Among those packed into the course of the Temple there was much speculation about what the signals meant.

No one knew.

Emet paid them scarcely any heed. His whole attention, his ultra-sensitive hearing, his every nerve, were tuned to any sign of Avel.

Where could Avel be? Emet's fears grew with each passing second. With Zadok plunging headlong through the crush, they had searched every bit of the return journey to the Temple Mount without finding the boy. He was not on the steps leading to the Sanhedrin chambers. He was not near the pens holding the lambs. He was not in the gallery watching the preparations for the Passover sacrifices.

Because of the vast number of lambs to be killed in the space of a few short hours, every last detail was prepared in advance.

A hundred thousand lambs.

Three courses of worshippers would bring their lambs to the altar. Since each head of a household would perform the sacrifice himself, the Court of the Priests was already packed with the first division of the worshippers. The doors to the court were already shut behind them.

A double file of priests were stationed at arm's length up to the altar of sacrifice. Every priest held either a golden or a silver bowl.

When the signal was given, the blood of the first sacrifices would be caught in the bowls and the containers passed by hand up toward the altar.

Empty vessels traveled down the other file.

A continuous fountain of blood would pour out at the base of the altar, until every lamb in the first course had been slain.

The worshippers readied themselves to sing hymns of deliverance and praise.

The time was fast approaching when the first of the three courses of slaughters would begin.

Emet could not keep dread from his mind and heart. At every turn he visualized the dead hawker, his throat slit. It was the fate awaiting every lamb presented here today . . . as it had been Bear's fate.

He prayed it would not be Avel's!

On the parapets of the sanctuary a column of priests appeared, carrying silver trumpets.

The crowd hushed expectantly.

All eyes turned upward to watch.

All except those of Zadok, Ha-or Tov, and Emet, who continued to search everywhere for Avel.

The moment had arrived.

The first blast of the trumpets was a short, sharp sound, demanding attention. *Take notice, the commands of the Almighty are before you!*

"*Thekiah*," Emet heard Zadok murmur. "The prophesied Messiah is coming."

The next skirl of notes was a warbling cry of alarm.

"*Theruah*," Zadok remarked. "God's special providence. A nation of priests before the Most High."

Another curt, emphatic blare of the horns.

"*Thekiah*," Zadok repeated. "Our king will soon appear. Judgment comes with him!"

■ ■ ■ ■

In Nakdimon's ears the din was deafening. The Roman trumpets on the ramparts of the governor's palace continued to resound. Call after call rang out: not of alarm, but in recognition of the special favor offered by Governor Pilate to his ungrateful and undeserving subjects.

The crowd around Nakdimon surged forward, up to the very edge of the podium on which Pilate sat.

The front rank of the horde had witnessed Pilate's words of pardon for Lev and Benjamin. They had seen the imprint of the Imperial signet into the smoking wax.

But all they could hear were the blaring trumpets competing with the jeers of the hecklers coming from behind them.

"*Sacrilege!*"

"*Blasphemy!*"

"*Idolators!*"

Were these inflammatory words shouted by rebels, intent on rousing the mob to insurrection?

Were they the deliberate incitements of agent provocateurs, planted in the horde to give Pilate an excuse to fall on them and arrest them?

Or were they the sentiments of roused members of the *am ha aretz*, the people of the land, determined to show Pilate they had no fear of either him or Rome? Were they relying on Pilate's forbearance, his regard for the emperor's displeasure?

As for the governor himself, he sat stiffly in the judgment seat. His expression was frozen on his face, halfway between the self-congratulatory smile of a minute earlier and a frown of severe displeasure.

Like the danger of the moment, it could go either way.

Life or death was in his hands.

From the right side of the multitude a handful of men sprinted forward and gained the stage. A squad of obviously frightened young troopers crossed their pilums to block the access toward Pilate.

The gesture was more ritual than real.

The javelins in their hands looked puny compared to the seething force in the thousands of onlookers.

Nor were the more zealous of the new assault frightened of the legionaries.

In the faces of the armed guards they shook their fists at Pilate. They harangued him. They called him *blasphemer, defiler of the Temple.*

Another swarm of hecklers rushed on the dais from the opposite side.

Pilate rose from his chair, genuine alarm in his eyes, though his face remained a mask of icy, emotionless bravado.

He despised them . . . and feared them.

A deadly combination.

The Roman horns stopped playing in confusion. Their bright, cheery chorus died in a futile cacophony of squawks and groans.

The Roman trumpet calls were replaced by warbling notes that struck the ear like a battle cry heard from far off. The first echoes of the Temple Mount services reached all the way to the palace of the butcher king, to the ears of the crowd in front of Pilate.

Thekiah! Theruah! Thekiah!

Kingdom! Providence! Judgment!

The impassioned ranting grew louder and more heated.

Spittle flew from the lips of the foremost in the rabble. A fleck landed on the hem of Pilate's robe.

Nakdimon saw Pilate take a step back, as if he would withdraw from the scene.

Perhaps it was not too late. Perhaps all could still end peacefully.

Then Nakdimon saw Pilate raise his hands from his sides. With deliberation he grasped the lapels of his toga. It was a Jewish gesture, as if the Roman would tear a strip from his garment in token of mourning.

But the governor did not tear the cloth.

Nor did he withdraw into his private chambers.

With his left palm still planted on his chest, he made a slashing motion through the air with the other hand.

The cutting stroke of a Roman blade.

Cries of alarm erupted from the crowd as clubs, knives, and short swords flashed into view from under hundreds of robes.

ADONAY

All around Marcus Longinus the terrified assembly tossed and rolled like the ocean.

In the first flash of panic, when swords and cudgels appeared, the mob surged backwards and forwards, with no clear direction in mind and no clear desire except escape.

What had they expected, these momentary heroes?

Their numbers had given them false courage that evaporated at the first display of Roman force.

It was too late for them now.

Marcus watched, helpless.

Protestors, jammed together, trampled one another to get out of reach of Vara's men. The rank smell of fear rose up from the mass of frantic pilgrims in a choking torrent. With it was the hot odor of spilled blood . . . and the stench of death.

Troopers indiscriminately slashed with swords and crushed heads with clubs.

Pilate may have ordered the guards to act solely for his defense. He may truly have desired to limit the bloodshed. But even that was now out of his hands.

A Samaritan legionary caught a wild-eyed Galilean on the point of his dagger. He thrust it upward into the man's midsection, twisting the blade as he drew it back. The wounded man howled, clutched his stomach with his hands, and fell lifeless to the pavement.

Gangs of Vara's soldiers gathered around defenseless men, chosen seemingly at random. After clubbing them into unconsciousness, they surrounded the others and repeated the brutality.

Any show of resistance guaranteed carnage.

But surrender conferred no safety, no escape.

Marcus drew his own sword from under his tunic.

But who to strike? How to defend anyone in this wild melee?

Upon seeing another Roman display a gladius, those nearby clawed one another in a futile attempt to escape from him.

None of the protestors seemed to have any weapons. The only blades Marcus observed were in the hands of legionaries. Could it be there were no rebels in the throng?

The trumpets blared again from the battlements. It was now a true call to arms. From side corridors leading off the courtyard, still more legionaries emerged. These made no attempt to hide their enjoyment as they waded into the clash. Short swords whistled overhead as they split skulls and hacked faces.

Marcus caught a glimpse of Pilate, his cadre of bodyguards wrapped around him like living armor. The governor scampered away from the carnage he had unleashed.

The frenzied crowd broke for the gate, crushing scores against the beams on either side, trampling others in the turmoil. No one gave ground for anyone else. More were killed by panic than by the legionaries.

The thousands outside the gate who had been pressing inward turned and sprinted back the way they had come: east, toward the Temple.

A knot of struggling people jammed the gate. Pressure from others climbing over their backs bore them to the ground. They were crushed to death.

The mob burst from the courtyard.

Vara whirled his sword around his head. The Praetorian shouted, urging his men to pursue the Jews.

Across this sea of chaos Marcus caught sight of Nakdimon ben Gurion. The huge man shielded Gamaliel with his own body as panic broke against him like waves against a rock.

Nakdimon spotted Marcus. His expression deepened with revulsion and shock as he took in the sword in Marcus' hand.

No time to explain.

Pulling back the cloak and revealing his features, Marcus ran toward the gate. As he went he snarled orders at the legionaries, batting down their weapons. He threatened them with crucifixion if they did not put away their weapons and return to their barracks at once.

Only a few obeyed.

Vara and two cohorts of the most murderous were among the

throng. The trail of blood and dead bodies at Pilate's door stretched toward the Temple Mount and the altar of sacrifice.

■ ■ ■ ■

Nakdimon couldn't believe his eyes. Marcus Longinus was one of the disguised Roman soldiers carrying out the assault on unarmed Jews! As he watched, the centurion bolted in pursuit of more victims.

Bellowing, Nakdimon shouted for Pilate to call off his troops.

But the governor had already retreated into his palace.

Left behind was a carpet of bodies: some writhing in pain, others lying ominously still.

Nakdimon let Gamaliel out of his protective embrace. Together the two men stared at the carnage, even as the horns on the walls continued to blare.

The scene near the platform was horrifying. It was still worse closer to the exit. The cobbles of the butcher king's courtyard were slippery with blood.

Hundreds of wounded, dozens of dead.

Kneeling, Nakdimon offered assistance to a man with a sword wound on his head and a fractured collarbone.

Many victims had been stabbed or clubbed, but many more bore the unmistakable imprints of having been crushed in the mass terror.

How could this have happened? It was the very tragedy that he and his uncle had tried to prevent. It was the worst disaster in Nakdimon's memory. Much worse than the Purim bread riots.

The disguised soldiers had been there all along, expecting and eager for trouble. The fervor of their attack underscored their fanatical hatred of the Jews.

And the governor had unleashed them with a gesture.

Pilate had known what the result would be. He must have known.

There would never be another Passover as grim as this one. No future disaster could ever eclipse the horrors of this day.

Shouts of fear continued to rain down on Jerusalem as the butchery continued outside the gates.

"Rouse yourself, man," Gamaliel urged, grabbing Nakdimon's shoulder. "Go see if you can stop this! Go! I'll organize help for the wounded."

Shaking off his stunned dismay, Nakdimon charged out of the courtyard.

■ ■ ■ ■

Beside the sheep pens, Emet deciphered the sounds of the day. To his hearing, something was off. There was a discordant note in the plaintive symphony of the Passover sacrifices. What was it?

To be sure, the trumpets of the priests continued to proclaim their calls to remembrance, participation, and expectation. Past, present, and future were all extolled in the music of the day. The notes jangled, breaking and rebreaking over the sanctuary.

But that wasn't the error reaching Emet's ears.

Nor was the problem with the singing of those participating in the first division of the sacrifices.

> *Hallelu Jah!* the Levites sang.
> *Hallelu Jah!* the worshippers responded.
> *Praise the Lord, you servants of the Lord!*
> *Praise to the name of the Lord!*

Some of the singers had no musical ability. That much was evident even to Emet's untutored hearing. Particularly guilty of murdering the pitch were the throngs of Galileans with their twang. Of course they made up in fervor what they lacked in ability, and their passion only made matters worse.

But no, that still wasn't what was wrong.

Perhaps it was Emet's nervous search for Avel? The boy never stopped seeking and worrying about his friend. Could that anxiety explain why the harmony of the day felt off?

Then there came a moment when the first division completed their sacrifices. There was a lull in the hymns. Trumpeters fell silent.

Then Emet heard it: the strident notes of Roman horns, blowing the alarm. It was a signal for battle. *War, bloody war,* the heralds of the empire announced!

Growing louder, approaching nearer, were human voices crying in alarm. A wail swelled up from the city to crash against the Temple Mount, drowning the bugle calls of Rome.

Like the bleating of thousands of sheep being ravaged by wolves, the clamor of panic overwhelmed all other noises.

Nor was Emet the only one to take note of the disturbance.

The uproar of distraught thousands stunned those participating in the Passover ceremonies. *What's happening? Do you hear it? What is that?* Babbling inquiries posed many questions, gave no answers.

Like a stone thrown into a placid pond, the ripples of destruction rapidly neared the Temple gates.

■ ■ ■

It resembled a flock of sheep herded by dogs, Marcus thought.

The difference was every time a straggler fell behind, the dogs pounced on him and beat him into the pavement.

At the corner of the old Hasmonaean Palace a brave group of Galilean pilgrims clustered. With their bare hands they tore apart a discarded barrel to use the broken staves for defense.

Opposing swords with splintered lengths of timber was heroic.

Heroic, but futile.

Their resistance infuriated the legionaries and they hurtled into the group. One of the Jews went down at once, stabbed and beaten. Three of the protestors managed to knock one of the troopers off his feet.

Another Galilean was struck down.

Then another.

The Roman troopers advanced relentlessly. The Jews' courageous stand couldn't last much longer.

The confrontation blocked the street, momentarily keeping the bloodthirsty pursuers from more victims. Woman and children darted into houses and down alleyways.

Marcus pounced on the first trooper he reached. Seizing him by the neck, Marcus heaved him against a wall.

The Samaritan turned with his club raised, ready to shatter a Jewish skull. Instead he met the fiery gaze of the infuriated centurion.

At his throat was the point of Marcus' sword. "Drop it!" Marcus demanded. "Who are these others? Their names?" He gave him a shake. "Call out their names!"

Sullenly the legionary did as ordered.

A fraction of a lull presented itself. Marcus thrust himself into the middle of the fight. He beat down the weapons of the assailants.

Without regard for his personal safety, he planted himself facing the troopers. He hoped the Jews would not hammer him in the back with the barrel staves.

"Get to the barracks!" Marcus commanded the soldiers.

"We're following Praetorian Vara's orders," a surly Idumean growled.

"Now you're taking orders from me," Marcus corrected. "I have your names. I'll flog the hide off any who disobey. Go!"

Marcus watched their retreat to see that they complied.

The Passover pilgrims offered their thanks, but Marcus only shook his head. "Help where you can, but stay away from the Temple," he warned. "This isn't over!"

Ignoring his own advice, he sprinted onto the elevated causeway, following the trail of wounded left in Vara's wake.

The upheaval reached into the courts of the sanctuary as the whole city convulsed.

■ ■ ■ ■

Emet heard another trumpet blast add its shrill racket to the chaos. On top of the Antonia fortress, just outside the sanctuary, signal flags fluttered in the breeze.

A cauldron of tumult poured out across the Temple Mount from the west. Knots of fleeing pilgrims appeared in the midst of the sacrifices. Close after these were others waving clubs and brandishing blades.

The shrieking became general. Consternation was replaced with panic. The Passover ceremonies exploded in mayhem.

Thousands of lambs bolted, adding to the confusion.

"Hang on to me!" Zadok ordered "Keep close." Until now the area inside the sheep pens felt like a refuge, a place of security from which to search for Avel.

Not any longer.

The overpowering peril Emet sensed had arrived.

Running from the attackers, bands of worshippers fled toward the Temple, crying out for protection.

The stricken pilgrims reached the greater mass of worshippers, trampling the older and weaker of their number underfoot.

A panicked surge carried hundreds toward the altar, where they slipped and fell in the puddles of gore.

Onrushing troopers clubbed them where they lay, mingling their blood with the blood of the sacrifices.

A man with a dagger flashed toward Zadok.

Emet and Ha-or Tov huddled behind the shepherd.

As the attacker neared, Red Dog flung himself forward, leaping into the man's face with snapping jaws.

Distracted, the assailant thrust out his hands to protect himself.

With a whistle that cut through the surrounding clamor, Zadok's staff whipped toward the man's head, connecting with a crack.

In the midst of all the confusion Emet spotted Avel.

Across the square, being dragged by his arms, was the missing apprentice shepherd. Kittim yanked him forward. Asher was close behind.

Yelling, Emet pointed this out to the old shepherd.

Grimly Zadok shouted back, "Don't let go!"

Then they plunged into the combat to rescue Avel.

■ ■ ■ ■

Avel's heart pounded.

One of Kittim's hands gripped his hair. The other held a dagger in readiness to stroke. No one would intervene to save his life when Kittim decided he was too much trouble to drag along.

And that end could come at any time.

Whatever assassinations the rebels had planned for this Passover, the wholesale slaughter happening in the Temple courts threw even them into consternation. Armed men stabbed and beat all those around them.

It was utter madness.

Now was the moment, Avel thought, as two Galileans collided directly in front of them. Another knot of confusion separated him from Asher, a few paces behind.

As Kittim lunged in one direction, Avel wrenched himself free.

He didn't know which way to run. It didn't matter so long as he could lose himself in the turmoil.

Amazingly he heard someone call his name.

A corridor through the mob opened for the space of a breath.

Zadok strode toward him, knocking aside all in his path.

Then Avel's head was yanked backward.

Kittim's fingers dug into Avel's hair again. A knife flashed in the afternoon sun.

■ ■ ■ ■

Marcus reached the Temple Mount and emerged from the porticoed gate at the top of the causeway.

What met his eyes was a nightmare beyond his wildest fears, a massacre of incredible proportions. Demons had flocked to Jerusalem to inhabit the bodies of ferocious Roman troopers.

Marcus saved countless lives, but the ripples of carnage spreading out in front of him seemed unstoppable.

Then the centurion caught sight of Praetorian Vara.

The man's brutish features were streaked with blood. His sword arm rose and fell relentlessly.

The chief of the demons, without doubt.

Stop him and stop the butchery?

Marcus fought his way toward Vara, but it was like wading through quicksand.

■ ■ ■ ■

Emet screamed. But his high voice had no strength amid the din. He couldn't hear his own words of alarm. It was as if he'd been struck mute again in the second he saw the knife poised over Avel.

Zadok's arm shot out. The crook on the end of the shepherd's staff plucked Kittim's elbow in mid-swing, tugging the rebel off balance.

The dagger flew end over end through the air.

Avel ducked around Zadok. Emet clutched him tight.

Every time Kittim tried to loose himself from the crook of Zadok's staff the old shepherd yanked him sideways again.

A fresh wave of rioting swirled toward them. Avel, Emet, and Ha-or Tov sheltered behind Zadok.

There was no such refuge for Kittim.

With a final heave on the staff, Zadok lifted Kittim completely off his feet.

The rebel fell amid the stampeding throng.

For an instant his fingers reached up. Then his anguished cry was abruptly cut off as he was trampled.

The cause of the heightened terror was revealed. A frightening figure loomed up close to Kittim's pulverized body. Gore-spattered bald head and vicious eyes were matched by ferocious swings of a short sword. The shadow of a bulky, coarse-featured man fell across Zadok.

Emit heard the voice of Marcus yell the name *Vara!*

Vara's blade hacked up and down, wounding and then batting out of the way.

Zadok's white-haired head rose over the other worshippers like a bastion of resistance. With an animal-like noise, Vara locked his attention on the shepherd as his next target.

The first blow of Vara's sword was caught on Zadok's staff. The tough acacia wood rod bounced with the strike, but did not shatter.

Zadok jabbed at Vara's face, just as he would have repelled an attacking wolf.

The blade was the superior weapon, the longer reach of the staff Zadok's sole margin of safety.

Red Dog, who protected the boys against attacks coming from other directions, responded to Zadok's command. Barking and snarling, Red Dog raced toward Vara, biting him on the leg.

Vara struck downward at the dog, who twisted sideways, out of reach.

Sparks erupted as the tip of Vara's sword scraped the paving stones. He raised his blade for another swing, only to miss again as Zadok's staff snatched Red Dog out of the way.

But in protecting the dog, the shepherd had used up his last bit of luck.

Vara's next blow came from Zadok's blind side, catching the shepherd's crook just above where Zadok gripped it.

The staff was knocked to the ground. Vara shouted in victory as he raised his weapon high to finish the old man.

■ ■ ■ ■

Across the battlefield of the Temple Mount Marcus rushed to intervene in just one fight—Vara's assault on Zadok. Pure evil and lifelong righteousness confronted each other in human forms . . . and evil was poised to win.

Marcus was too far away! The shepherd was already disarmed, the fatal blow already descending.

The centurion screamed—a cry of outrage!

Between Zadok and Vara something moved. A boy—it was Avel—lifted the shepherd's staff. Jabbing it upward, he struck Vara in the throat.

From a stooped position, in the hands of a child, it could not have carried much force. But it threw off Vara's killing stroke.

It delayed Zadok's death for half a second.

Long enough for Marcus to barrel into Vara from behind.

Vara and Marcus, tangled together, rolled heavily onto the pavement. First to regain his feet, Vara had not lost his weapon.

From his knees, Marcus raised his sword in time to block a thrust sweeping toward his head. Parried, Vara's blow rebounded in his hand, and Marcus recovered his stance.

Rushing on him, Vara used his compact bulk. Anticipating such a move of brute force, Marcus deliberately gave up a pace of ground. Their swords rang together.

Again the two blades met.

Again Vara charged.

Marcus once more stepped back . . . and tripped over Kittim's body.

The centurion stumbled, his guard flinging wide, opening his neck to a killing stroke.

Vara stormed in.

Unable to counter, Marcus flung his sword at Vara's face, then rolled to the side as the thrust descended.

Disarmed! There were no options left.

Marcus tackled Vara around the knees, bringing the Praetorian crashing down.

The two fought for possession of Vara's sword. Marcus closed his hands around the grip, while the fingers of Vara's other hand clawed at Marcus' face.

Driving his elbow into Vara's jaw, Marcus gained control of the weapon.

The gouging at his eyes stopped.

Marcus heard Avel shout, "He's got a dagger!"

A glimpse of the new threat gave Marcus no time to think. He spun away from the thrust, at the same instant tugging sharply upward on Vara's wrist.

The dagger tip struck Vara's sword, glanced off, and sliced into Vara's own arm.

The Praetorian howled and his grip loosened.

Marcus wrenched the sword free and jumped up while Vara was still prone.

Putting the tip of Vara's blade at the man's throat, Marcus commanded, "Drop the dagger! Call off your men! Now! Or you're dead!"

More trumpet calls echoed from the Antonia. The rhythmic tramp of marching feet accompanied by the pounding of drums reverberated across the Temple Mount.

"You better kill me," Vara said through gritted teeth. "Either way you'll be crucified for this."

"Legionaries!" Tribune Felix shouted from the head of a column of uniformed soldiers. "Put down your weapons! By order of the governor, you are to cease fighting at once!"

Stepping back, Marcus gratefully lowered the sword.

The Passover massacre was finally at an end.

ZEVAOT

And so that day the blood of the multitudes was mingled with the blood of their sacrifices on the Holy Mountain of Zion.

Zadok, chief shepherd of the flocks of Israel, wept.

The Messiah had not come. Had there ever been such a day of mourning?

Emet, gathered in Zadok's arms, was carried from that place out through the Sheep Gate and beyond the walls of the city. Avel and Ha-or Tov walked beside the Roman centurion who had saved them.

The three boys were lifted onto the back of Marcus' great black horse and led away from Jerusalem along the deserted highway south toward Beth-lehem.

In the west, the sun was setting. A single shaft of light shot up like a pillar and pierced the clouds. Zadok watched it for a long time and then, at last, he spoke. "In the day when our fathers left slavery we came to the sea and could go no farther. The chariots of Egypt and all her armies were at our backs. God set a pillar of fire between us as the waters parted and we crossed over. So we were saved."

The sun pillar hovered above the earth like a beacon for a time and then began to fade as the world darkened.

"See how the Shekinah glory stands far away," Zadok said sadly. "The Lord did not come again to the great city. We are forsaken." Tears clung to his white beard. His staff was stained with blood. "Immanu'el, they told me! I was a young man then with sons of my own to hope for! Rachel and I had much to hope for. What was it about? What did such sacrifice mean? Immanu'el, they told me! And . . . I thought this year he would come to Yerushalayim! But it was not to be."

By this, Emet knew the old man's hope had died today. There was no remedy for his grief. They passed the miles in silence, each remembering the day.

■ ■ ■ ■

Where was the Messiah the Jews longed for? Marcus pondered. Where was the Deliverer? Savior? King of the Jews who would set Israel free from its array of enemies?

Bar Abba had fled to the wilderness in defeat. He was no Messiah.

But what about Yeshua of Nazareth? Where was the one from Galilee who could heal the sick and feed the multitudes by a word and raise the dead back to life? What about him? Why was he not here in Jerusalem on such a day, wading in the blood of his broken kinsmen, restoring them to mothers, sons, fathers, brothers, who wept for their loss?

Wisely, Marcus thought, Yeshua had stayed away. Had the Master known what calamity was to come on a city impatient to be free? It was fortuitous that Yeshua had chosen to remain in the north on such a wretched Passover as this. The events of this day would long be remembered and recited by those who witnessed them. Some would blame Pilate. Others, bar Abba. Some would curse the Sanhedrin. Many would declare that this was the hand of Yahweh, passing judgment for the violation of Korban. Yes. Perhaps they would comfort themselves that this was the fault of a transgression of the laws of Moses.

Marcus was certain that if Yeshua had been here, somehow he would have been blamed with bar Abba and the rebels for inciting the mob.

The boys dozed while the two men, oppressed by visions of slaughter, reached Beth-lehem at last. Watch fires of the shepherds winked on the hillsides. Flocks and herds slept. The place seemed peaceful, unchanged, though everything had changed.

Hope for the promised Kingdom had perished on the bloodstained cobbles of Jerusalem.

Outside the low garden wall of Zadok's house, Marcus halted Pavor and lifted the weary boys to the ground. A lamp burned in the window. The fragment aroma of the old man's garden mingled with the scent of roasted lamb. Surely at such a late hour the *seder* supper had been eaten by everyone in Israel except Zadok and the boys.

The shepherd asked Marcus, "Our people are enemies, yours and mine. But you . . . you . . . proved yourself to be . . . not what I thought you were. Will you, then, join us for the meal of remembrance?"

The full moon was high, lighting the Valley of the Sheepfold like a torch.

Marcus considered the invitation. Then he raised his eyes toward the brooding outline of Herodium. What would the people say after the Jerusalem massacre if the chief shepherd of Israel's flocks broke bread with a centurion of Rome? "It would not be proper, sir," Marcus replied. "But I thank you for the invitation."

"Perhaps one day it will be put right, all of this. Peace on earth, they told me. Peace, they promised. But it was so long ago. Maybe I didn't understand," Zadok whispered. "I had hoped. *Hoped!* That maybe this year the hour would come when it would be as our prophet Isaiah saw in his vision. That swords would be beaten into plowshares and . . . and . . . redemption . . ." The old man seemed to shrivel as the words and the hope died in his throat.

Marcus extended his hand. "Perhaps one day Jews and Gentiles will break bread as brothers, sir. Until then, I will watch and wait with you. I will hope with you that the vision of your prophets is coming and that we will live to see it."

He waited at the wall as the boys and the dog followed Zadok into the house. The door closed solidly behind them.

Marcus hesitated, wishing that the old man would emerge again, compel him to come in and break bread with them.

But the bolt slid into place with a loud and final thud.

Marcus did not belong here. He knew that. Still, he longed for a nation, a homeland, a woman . . . Miryam . . . to love him. His heart yearned for the child they might have had. And perhaps other children. He could be content in a one-room house clinging to the hillside of this troubled backwater called *Israel* . . . if only! If only!

He inhaled the fragrant scent of the garden. And there was something else on the breeze. *What? Perfume? Not here. Not here.*

He remembered the night in Galilee when Miryam had bravely entered the house of Simon the Pharisee and anointed the feet of Yeshua. The night had been filled with an aroma like this . . .

He closed his eyes and breathed in again. And then it was gone. Just a memory made more intense by loneliness.

As he mounted Pavor and spurred the black horse on toward Herod's fortress, Marcus knew he could never have what his heart desired most.

■ ■ ■ ■

It seemed to Emet that Zadok was breaking apart before their eyes.

For a few minutes after they entered the house Emet thought perhaps everything would be all right. They were home. Safe. So many others would never go home again. But here they were, alive and well. It was reason to rejoice, wasn't it? They would eat the meal of remembrance and go on with their lives. That was best, wasn't it?

Zadok and the boys washed hands and feet in the basin by the entrance.

At the snap of Zadok's fingers Red Dog lay obediently in the corner.

In a subdued tone Zadok thanked *Adonai* for watching over their going out and coming in. He took the clay lamp from the window ledge and held it up to examine the room.

Everything for the *seder* was ready for their return—just as Zadok had commanded.

The Paschal meal was complete. Every morsel meant something. First was *matzah*, three cakes of unleavened bread, the bread of affliction. There was a bowl of *Haroseth*, the mixture of nuts and dates meant to symbolize the mortar with which the slaves had built their oppressors' cities. And there was a heap of boiled eggs, symbolizing the eyes of Hebrew slaves searching for a deliverer. A bowl of salt water represented inconsolable tears. Besides that the plate of bitter herbs memorialized the bitterness of bondage. A pitcher of wine was near the head of the table. And finally there was the fire-roasted shank of lamb, remembering the lamb of God's covenant with Israel whose blood, when sprinkled on the doorposts of the Hebrews, was a signal that the Angel of Death should pass over this house.

By this sign the firstborn of Israel were spared.

It was as fine a banquet as Emet had ever seen! It was to be his first real Passover meal partaken among those who loved him. Almost as if he was part of a real family! The table was set with plates, cups, and seating cushions for five guests.

Why five, Emet wondered, since there were only four of them?

They stood silently gazing down at the feast. Zadok seemed to consider it as though it was meant for someone else.

What were they waiting for? What thoughts passed through the shepherd's mind? Why did they not sit and begin? It was late, after all.

Was Zadok expecting another guest? The centurion had gone away. Why five?

Zadok stooped and placed the lamp beside the bread, like a mourner puts a pebble on a tomb. Then he straightened, clasped his hands before him as if he would pray again. He murmured, "Yes. Yes. It's fine. Wonderful. Yes. A lovely supper, Rachel." His face clouded with grief as he stared down at the feast.

Suddenly startled, Zadok stared into the faces of the boys. "Where is Rachel?" he asked.

They did not dare reply. He might as well have asked, *Where is hope? Where joy?*

With a gasp, remembering, the old man covered his face with his hands.

"Oh Rachel! Rachel," he moaned softly. "My children! My sons!" A single plaintive cry escaped his throat as Emet, Avel, and Ha-or Tov rushed to embrace him. "My sons! My boys!" He sank to his knees and sat for a long time like a man sitting *shiva.* Tears streamed down his face. He did not move or speak.

Red Dog whined and stood, worrying. Emet lay his cheek on the old man's head. Ha-or Tov gazed sadly into the light and said nothing.

Avel patted Zadok's back, as if he were comforting a child.

What a day it had been. Tragic. Shattering. So many fallen. Beyond comprehension. It was not playing out the way Emet had expected.

Zadok checked his emotions and commanded them at last. "Please. Sit. It's late and there's much to explain. Everything means something. . . ."

They obeyed, leaving the one place at the head empty.

Emet asked, "What makes this night different from all the rest?"

"*Avadim hayinu.* We were slaves to Pharaoh in Egypt. Tonight," the old man explained haltingly, "all Jews, sons of the Covenant, remember our years of slavery in Egypt and how the Lord commanded us to believe his promise of salvation and put the blood of the lamb upon the doorposts of our houses. The Egyptians, who did not believe, lost firstborn of their children, flocks, and herds in all the land. We were spared from death on that horrifying night. By that sacrifice and sign the Lord brought our fathers out of bondage." Zadok's voice caught. "And yet we must . . . grieve . . . how can we not . . . for the death of other . . . sons. Children. And . . . and . . ." Tears welled up again. Chin sank to chest. In a barely audible whisper he spoke again to someone not there. "Rachel. I'm sorry. . . ."

Perhaps Avel and Ha-or Tov did not hear him. There was an uneasy silence. Could Zadok go on?

Emet shuddered as he exchanged a look with Avel. What should they do? There were songs to sing! Prayers to be prayed! The stories of passing through the sea and dozens of other wondrous miracles to tell! The table was set. The meal ready. Bread to be broken. The cup to be filled and passed and shared. But Zadok could not speak, and none of the three boys knew what came next.

"How can we help?" Avel asked.

"What should we do?" Ha-or Tov queried the shepherd.

Zadok raised his head, slowly examining the trio. "Immanu'el, y' said. You came to Beth-lehem to tell me. As . . . others once came. And I dared to hope again. I had hoped before. Long ago. You see? I've looked for him every year since the first. But now . . . how can I go on hoping for one who promised to come but never comes?"

Avel repeated Yeshua's message. "Maybe soon . . ."

Zadok shook his head. "I've become an old man waiting for his arrival. I had hoped to share this *seder* with him."

Emet asked boldly, "But how do you know him? Were you in Galilee?"

Zadok's lips turned up in an enigmatic smile. "Perhaps one day I can speak of it." With that Zadok exhaled loudly and seemed to remember his place in the ceremony. Aged hands trembled as he reached out for the middle piece of *matzah* and held it up before the flickering flame. Light shone though its fragile, pockmarked surface. He intoned, "The *lehem oni,* the bread of affliction, is pierced and scarred. By its marred visage we remember the lash of our oppressors. But when it is broken and part is put away till the end of the meal, it becomes for us the hope that our Messiah will come to each of us in the future . . . to truly set our hearts free. He is the Hidden One who will come as our Redeemer. . . ."

"Soon." Emet focused on the tiny pinpoints of light that emanated from the surface. Yeshua had called himself the bread of life. Yes. Was this what he meant?

Zadok blessed the bread and broke it. A portion he hid in a napkin and the other he distributed to the boys. He placed a morsel on the plate before the empty seat.

"Whose place is this?" Ha-or Tov asked. "Who was meant to sit there?"

Zadok held the answer close for a moment. Then he said slowly, "One who has decided to wait awhile longer before he comes." He hesitated. "But tradition says that on this night Elijah or the Messiah himself in the disguise of a sojourner may be standing outside at the door waiting to be invited in. We are commanded to remember that we were also sojourners and to treat such a one kindly. And so we set an extra place. Just in case." He cupped Ha-or Tov's chin in his hand. "You, boy. Since y' asked. Go on now. Open the door."

Emet's breath caught with expectation. Would *he* be there?

With a self-conscious shrug Ha-or Tov climbed to his feet. He smoothed his tunic. "What do I do?"

"Open the door and ask him to come in." Zadok handed him the lamp.

Ha-or Tov's red locks shone in the light. His gaze was intent. Lips were pressed tightly together. Jaw was set.

Avel clasped Emet's hand as Ha-or Tov threw back the bolt.

What if . . .

Red Dog, expecting to be let out, got up and padded over to escape. He waited at Ha-or Tov's heel as the boy slowly cracked the door and extended the lamp through the opening. He peered into the night. Red Dog whined.

What if . . .

Emet strained to see. But there was only darkness, an empty space beyond the threshold.

Ha-or Tov grinned sheepishly and said to the air, "*Shalom.* Welcome. The table is set for you. Come in and break bread with us."

Red Dog pushed past him, escaping. And then . . .

Beyond the reach of the circle of light came a familiar call. "*Shalom! Shalom!* Good Light! Are your brothers inside? And Zadok as well?"

Ha-or Tov's mouth fell open. His eyes widened. So he had come!

"It's . . . it's . . . *you!*"

Emet and Avel hugged each other and shouted for joy as they charged to greet Yeshua! *Baruch HaShem! Blessed is He who comes this terrible night to Beth-lehem to share the Passover lehem oni with us!*

Yeshua had come for them!

The door swung back, revealing the Master as he strode up the path through the garden. Red Dog danced before him, as if greeting a familiar and well-loved shepherd. Yeshua smiled broadly, patted the canine, and embraced Emet, Avel, and Ha-or Tov. Then he took the lamp and entered the dwelling as if he had been here before. Ducking his head, he crossed the threshold.

In confusion Zadok tried to get up and knocked over the bowl of bitter herbs. He clambered to his feet and gawked at the tall, swarthy stranger.

Yeshua pronounced a blessing on Zadok, the house, Migdal Eder, and all who lived in Beth-lehem.

Zadok stammered, "Who . . . who are you?"

Mischievous light glinted in Yeshua's warm brown eyes as he asked, "Don't you know me, Zadok? Old Zadok, shepherd of the flock? Don't you remember me?" And then Yeshua approached the old man and enfolded him in his arms as one coming home after a long journey. And Yeshua said, "*Ha lahma anya*. . . . This year we are slaves, next year we will be free. This year we are here. Next year in Jerusalem!"

All time seemed to stop. Zadok, like a blind man who had just received his sight, raised his fingers to touch the cheek of Yeshua. Hands shook with emotion. He kissed the Master on one cheek and then the other. "So," he said. And then again, "So . . . it is true!" He dropped to his knees, bowed his head, and cried loudly, "Blessed is the Lamb of God who has come to take away the sins of the world! Lord, I am not worthy to receive you! I am a man of unclean lips and a doubting heart!"

Yeshua placed both hands on Zadok's grizzled head. "Get up. Stand up, friend." Another touch on the old man's shoulder. "You are released from your vow."

"All these years? Released?" Zadok struggled to rise. He led Yeshua to the table and showed him the place where he could sit. But Zadok could not speak. Emotion stopped his voice. Each time he opened his mouth to say a word, tears of happiness broke loose.

Emet, giddy with relief at Yeshua's arrival, crowded into the space between Ha-or Tov and Avel.

Then Yeshua began to explain the story of Zadok. "For nearly thirty-two years you haven't spoken of it, Zadok. Now should I tell these three what a friend you are?"

Zadok nodded, blinked in wonder at the pierced bread on Yeshua's plate, and wiped his eyes with his hand.

Yeshua gazed only at Zadok as he told the story. "You were a young shepherd of the Temple flock in Beth-lehem, in the year of the census of Rome. Crowds flooded in, packing every room and inn. There came late a young woman from Nazareth and her betrothed. No place to stay. No room. She was great with child and there was no place for her to deliver. So you cleaned a stall in the lambing barn and gave her fresh straw. You hung curtains for her privacy and your wife sent soup. You knew what was coming . . . a lamb.

"You, with others who are now gone, were standing watch over the sheep that night. Suddenly a blinding light surrounded you as you looked at the stars. Then you heard singing . . . and saw the angels of heaven! To you the glory of heaven was revealed! With rejoicing you believed what was announced to you! Peace on earth to men of goodwill, they sang. For unto you a child is born . . . *HaShem* was revealed to you, the shepherds of the Temple flock. Immanu'el. God-with-us. Then you came running to the stable to see for yourself! And you were first to welcome him in the hour of his coming. You fed his family from your own table. It was you who carried news of all the wonders that had happened here in Beth-lehem to the Temple courts when you brought the lambs for sacrifice. You sought out old Simeon and told him that the One he had been waiting for had finally come. And when the baby was brought into the Temple for dedication you stood nearby. You and your dear wife, Rachel, brought the baby and his mother and Joseph into this very house to live for a time with your three small boys." Yeshua swept his hand around the room. "This house. And here they stayed on in joy and safety until the warning came . . . the terrible warning. And on the night they fled away from Beth-lehem you made a blood covenant that you would not tell where they had taken the baby. Or what message you heard from the angels until Messiah came to you." At this, Yeshua turned his eyes on Emet, Avel, and Ha-or Tov. "This is what a true and faithful heart beats within this shepherd! He gave everything he loved so that the Redeemer might live and someday give his life as a ransom for the world. Remember what price one shepherd paid for remaining steadfast!"

"What price?" Emet asked, seeing the pain on Zadok's old face.

"Tell them, friend," Yeshua urged Zadok.

After a long moment Zadok began. "Kings and princes from far-off lands followed the baby's star here to Israel. We all had seen the star and wondered about it. Sure. But when we heard the angels and knew . . . what rejoicing! Then old Herod inquired of the priests where Messiah should be born. Beth-lehem, they said, was the city declared by the prophet Micah. And we all knew that too. After all, Messiah is the son of David. Where else would it be? And so that jackal Herod sent his soldiers here among our flock. Here. To Beth-lehem. Among those of us who wanted nothing more than to raise our children in peace. But old Herod, he wanted to be unchallenged as king. He didn't know the meaning of the Scriptures. . . . So he gave the order to his butcher soldiers. . . . The command was to kill all baby boys two years old and younger who had been born here within the circle of Migdal Eder. This, then, was the price evil exacted from the families of Beth-lehem. . . . Our sons were slaughtered like lambs." Zadok added hoarsely, "Only one . . . little lamb escaped."

Just as Moses had escaped the sword of Pharaoh, Emet mused.

Zadok touched the leather patch over his eye. He rubbed his thumb across the scar. "I fought them. But there were so many, y' see. She, Rachel, I mean, tried to hide the boys. But my littlest son cried, poor thing, and so the boys were all found and murdered."

Stunned silence. The empty house echoed with the grief of that night.

"And what happened," Avel asked, "to the one who got away?"

Yeshua smiled and held them with a look, as though he knew some great secret yet to be revealed. Retrieving the pierced fragment *matzah* from the napkin, he held it up before the light. "Blessed are you, *Adonai*, who from the beginning has declared your provision, love, and mercy to all the world!" And then to Zadok he added this benediction, "Blessed are you who mourn, for you shall be comforted!"

In that moment the fleece of God's love so covered the three boys—Avel, Ha-or Tov, and Emet—that Zadok saw them as his own.

And so the Passover was eaten. At the last, Yeshua raised the cup to his lips and proclaimed, "Now we are here. . . . Next year in Jerusalem!"

EPILOGUE

...A nd so we, the smallest of his flock, shared that Passover with Yeshua, who is both Shepherd of Israel and firstborn lamb. There are a thousand wondrous events recorded concerning Israel and Messiah that occurred long before my lifetime.

Are these not revealed in the writings of Moses and the prophets, and in the scrolls we call the Antiquities of Israel? Yeshua often spoke of what the prophet Isaiah wrote about him: "The Spirit of the Sovereign Lord is upon me because the Lord has anointed me to preach good news to the poor, to proclaim the year of the Lord's favor. . . ."

I am an eyewitness to that year.

And what of all the momentous events that transpired in the life of Yeshua and his talmidim in the months and years following? Events that forever changed the world as we knew it?

What of Zadok, chief shepherd of the flock? Marcus Longinus? Carta? Miryam? El'azar? Nakdimon? Ha-or Tov, Avel, myself, and all the hundreds of those whom Yeshua healed? We were children, men, women; slave and free; rich and poor of all nations. All of us, in our own time and by separate paths, came to believe and are convinced that Yeshua is the Holy One of Israel.

Our stories are recorded in the scrolls of the Anno Domini Chronicles and preserved beneath the Temple Mount in Jerusalem until the end of days. We proclaim to all the world the year of the Lord's favor.

Read on then, friend, that you may find hope and joy in Yeshua in this darkest hour of our history. Our ink is the blood of ten thousand martyrs. Yet they and we will live because God will raise us up when Messiah returns to Jerusalem as he promised. I myself give testimony that I heard his promise to return.

The Holy Scriptures give proof about who Yeshua is and why he came. The testimony concerning Yeshua's love and mercy bears witness that he came not only to redeem Israel but to heal every wounded heart. This is Jerusalem's Hope.

This is Eternal Truth.

Peace unto you, my friend. I am Emet, son of Zadok, chief shepherd of the flock at Beth-lehem.

I declare to you, Anno Domini . . .

With a whisper Moshe completed the reading and raised his head to meet Alfie's intense gaze.

It was quiet in the great hall, yet for an instant Moshe thought he heard the stirring of the flocks of Migdal Eder. Was that a wisp of smoke from the watch fires?

At last Alfie asked, "What did he mean, *Anno Domini*?"

"A.D. It's Latin. Unusual he would use it here. A.D. is a common marker for time . . . for the centuries that followed the birth of Christ. *Anno Domini.* It means 'the year of the Lord' . . . and yet Emet did not record the exact year he was writing. I don't understand."

Moshe scanned Grandfather's list of books. There, beneath the entry for Emet's scroll, were these instructions written in the rabbi's trembling hand:

Moshe, here are the sections you must next study:
A.D. CHRONICLES

Did the A.D. *Chronicles* compose a separate shelf in the library? Perhaps a chamber that contained personal accounts documenting the events of Yeshua's time on earth and after?

"Emet gives us no date," Moshe mused aloud. "No year. No time frame. But why?"

Alfie rubbed the stubble on his chin and answered slowly, "I think, you know . . . because here, in the heart of Jerusalem, there aren't years. Only . . . what's it called? *Anno Domini?* One year. His year. The year of the Lord's favor. Not time as we know it. Not as on a clock. See? No time at all. Backwards. Forwards. Jesus in the middle of all time. See? Already written. Written before it happened."

Moshe nodded, remembering what the old rabbi had said when he first revealed the hidden chamber to Moshe: *"You'll have to learn to tell time. . . ."*

Was this what the old man had meant? That all of history was centered on the coming of Messiah to redeem the human heart? A.D.! *The year of the Lord's favor!*

Moses, King David, and the ancient prophets of Israel had all looked forward to the year when Israel's Redeemer would come. Since that moment mankind had looked back to the hour, day, and year when Yeshua stretched out his arms and cried in triumph, *"IT IS FINISHED!"*

Alfie held up his fingers to form a cross. "The old ones looked for him to come. We look back. And there in the middle is the Lamb of God. Jerusalem's Hope. Here. Here he is. Jesus! Here in Jerusalem! Jesus . . . coming again. A king this time. Just when everyone thought God had forgotten about Jerusalem."

■ ■ ■ ■

Ki lo ya'aseh Adonay Elohim davar ki im galah sodo el avadav ha-nevi'im.

Amos 3:7

Zeh devar Adonay el Zerubavel lemor lo ve-hayil ve-lo vekoah ki im be-ruhi amar Adonay zevaot.

Zechariah 4:6

FOR THE BEST IN PAPERBACKS, LOOK FOR THE

In every corner of the world, on every subject under the sun, Penguin represents quality and variety—the very best in publishing today.

For complete information about books available from Penguin—including Penguin Classics, Penguin Compass, and Puffins—and how to order them, write to us at the appropriate address below. Please note that for copyright reasons the selection of books varies from country to country.

In the United States: Please write to *Penguin Group (USA), P.O. Box 12289 Dept. B, Newark, New Jersey 07101-5289* or call 1-800-788-6262.

In the United Kingdom: Please write to *Dept. EP, Penguin Books Ltd, Bath Road, Harmondsworth, West Drayton, Middlesex UB7 0DA.*

In Canada: Please write to *Penguin Books Canada Ltd, 10 Alcorn Avenue, Suite 300, Toronto, Ontario M4V 3B2.*

In Australia: Please write to *Penguin Books Australia Ltd, P.O. Box 257, Ringwood, Victoria 3134.*

In New Zealand: Please write to *Penguin Books (NZ) Ltd, Private Bag 102902, North Shore Mail Centre, Auckland 10.*

In India: Please write to *Penguin Books India Pvt Ltd, 11 Panchsheel Shopping Centre, Panchsheel Park, New Delhi 110 017.*

In the Netherlands: Please write to *Penguin Books Netherlands bv, Postbus 3507, NL-1001 AH Amsterdam.*

In Germany: Please write to *Penguin Books Deutschland GmbH, Metzlerstrasse 26, 60594 Frankfurt am Main.*

In Spain: Please write to *Penguin Books S. A., Bravo Murillo 19, 1° B, 28015 Madrid.*

In Italy: Please write to *Penguin Italia s.r.l., Via Benedetto Croce 2, 20094 Corsico, Milano.*

In France: Please write to *Penguin France, Le Carré Wilson, 62 rue Benjamin Baillaud, 31500 Toulouse.*

In Japan: Please write to *Penguin Books Japan Ltd, Kaneko Building, 2-3-25 Koraku, Bunkyo-Ku, Tokyo 112.*

In South Africa: Please write to *Penguin Books South Africa (Pty) Ltd, Private Bag X14, Parkview, 2122 Johannesburg.*